MW00929174

The Sun and the Shrub

The Quest for Faith

The Sun and the Shrub

A Trilogy

Book I of III

The Quest for Faith

By

Loretta M. McKee

Copyright © 2016 by Loretta M. McKee

All rights reserved. This book or any portion thereof may not be reproduced or used in any manner whatsoever without the express written permission of the publisher except for the use of brief quotations in a book review or scholarly journal.

All images presented in this novel are provided by Pixabay.com, where all images are released free of copyrights, can be used royalty-free, and individual attribution is not required under Creative Commons CC0.

This novel has been copyrighted under the service of Copyrighted.com:

<a target="_blank" href="http://www.copyrighted.com/copyrights/view/qo9l-lu0b-ezu2-li5c"><img border="0" alt="Copyrighted.com Registered & Protected

QO9L-LU0B-EZU2-LI5C" title="Copyrighted.com Registered & Protected

QO9L-LU0B-EZU2-LI5C" width="150" height="40" src="http://static.copyrighted.com/images/seal.gif" /></a>

First Printing: 2016

ISBN 978-1-329-79888-5

Loretta M. McKee
the.sun.and.the.shrub@gmail.com
https://www.facebook.com/loretta.mckee.54

Ordering Information:
For details, visit the publisher's Facebook page or contact the email listed above. Also, visit

This book is dedicated to all the girls in the world who never had a father like mine.

Love,
Loretta M. McKee

Faith means believing the unbelievable.
–Gilbert K. Chesterton

Table of Contents

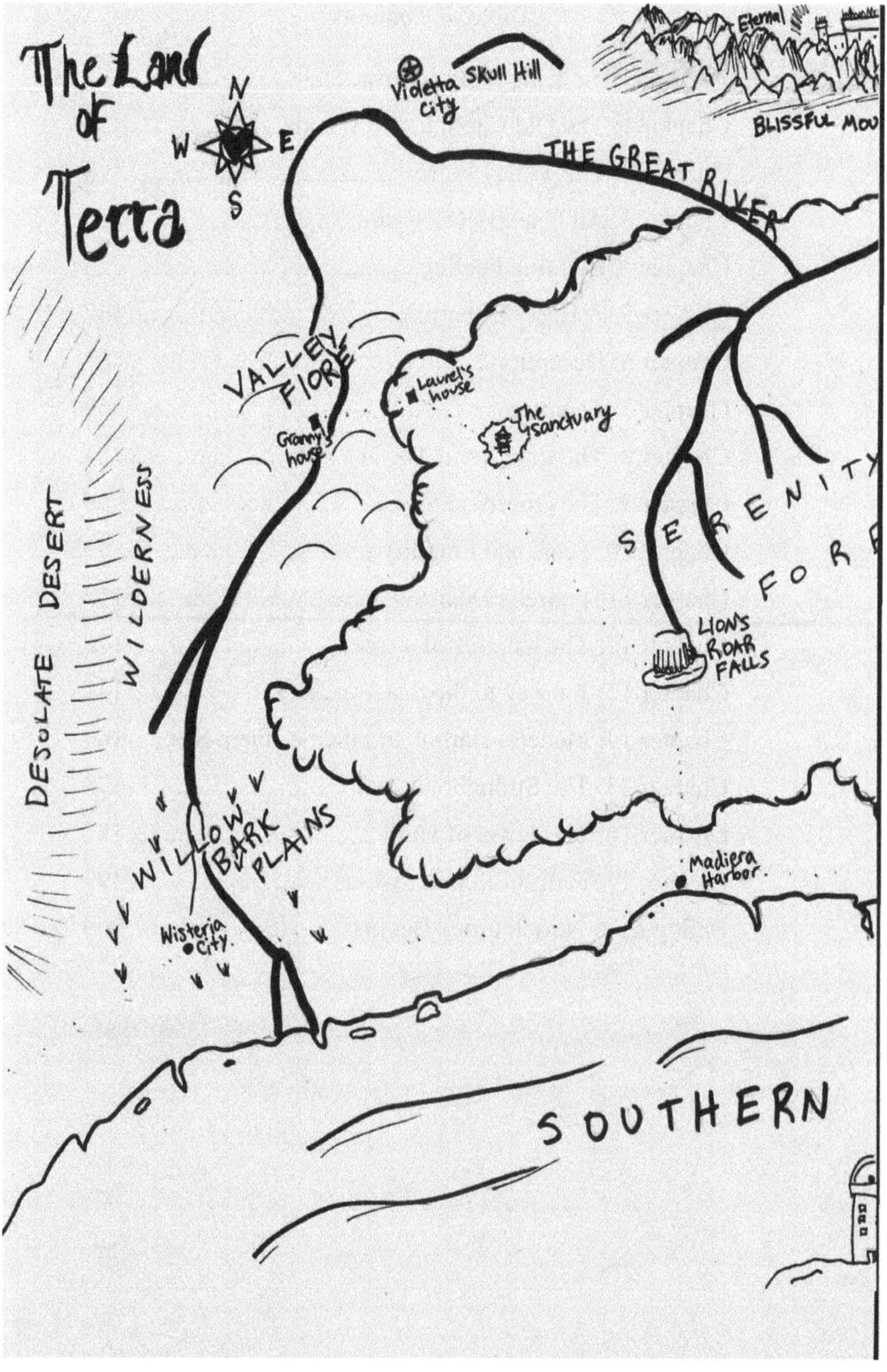

The Land of Terra
N
W
E
S
Violetta City
Skull Hill
Eternal
BLISSFUL MOU
THE GREAT RIVER
VALLEY FIOR
Laurel's house
The Sanctuary
Granny's house
DESOLATE DESERT
WILDERNESS
SERENITY
FOR
LION'S ROAR FALLS
WILLOW BARK PLAINS
Wisteria City
Madiera Harbor
SOUTHERN

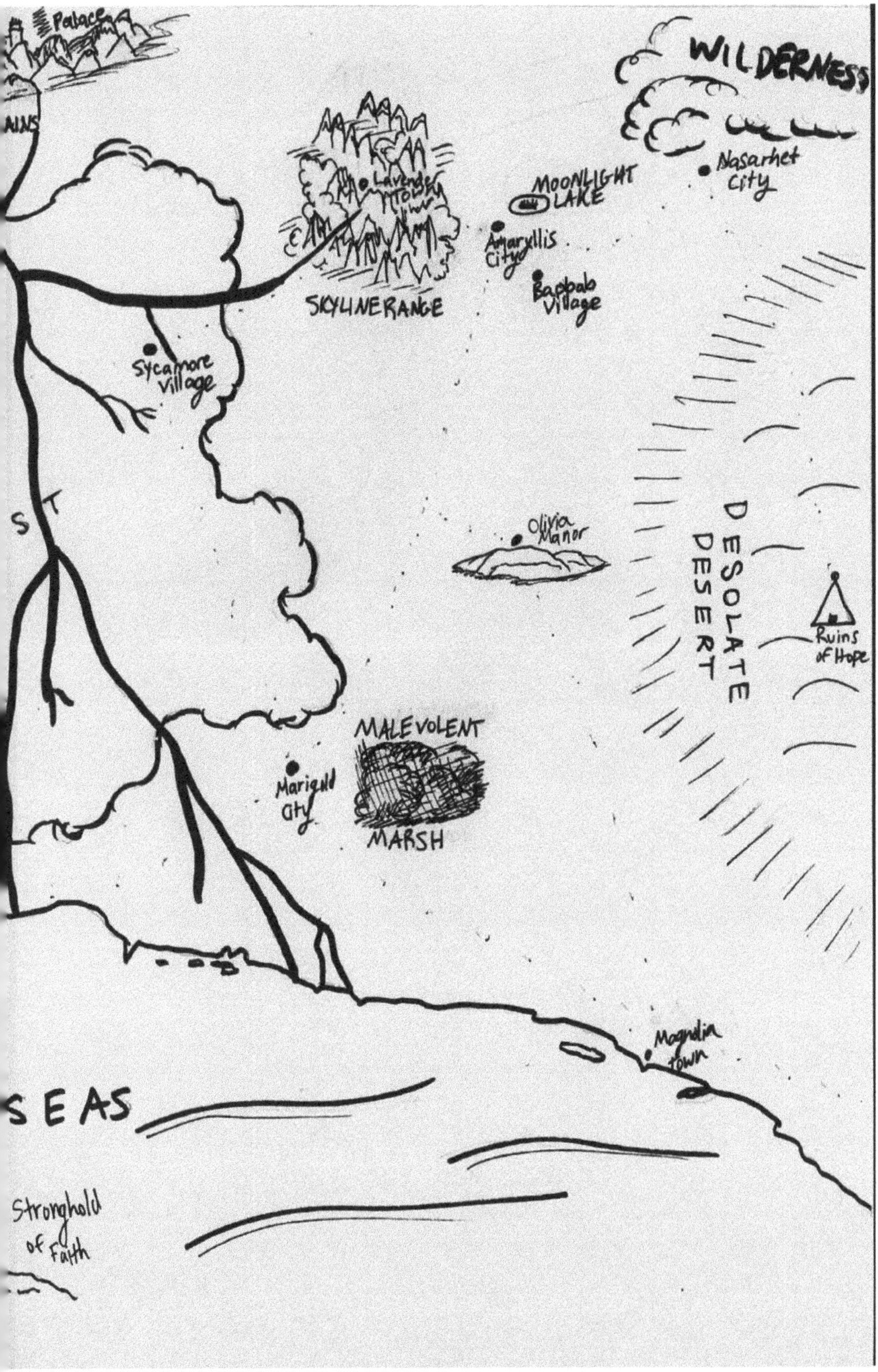
Palace
AINS
Lavender
SKYLINE RANGE
Sycamore Village
S T
MOONLIGHT LAKE
Amaryllis City
Baobab Village
WILDERNESS
Nasarhet City
Olivia Manor
DESOLATE DESERT
Ruins of Hope
MALEVOLENT
MARSH
Marigold City
Magnolia town
SEAS
Stronghold of Faith

Prologue
The Kingdom of Terra

Once upon a time, there was a mystical Kingdom[1] called Terra. Terra was a world of rich and vibrant colors, aromas, sights, and sounds. The land was fertile with an abundance of floral life and thriving ecosystems, and many animals of all sizes and shapes inhabited the Kingdom. The Kingdom stretched from the northern Blissful Mountains to the great Southern Sea and from the Desolate Desert in the East to the Valley Fioré in the West. In the center of this vast Kingdom laid the thriving woodland of peace known as Serenity Forest, an alpine range called the Skyline Range, a land of bluffs and ridges known as the Willow Bark Plains, and a cluster of shady swampland known as the Malevolent Marsh. Many cities and villages were spread across the Kingdom, but none of them was more precious than the majestic capital city of Violetta.

Emperor Abba[2], the ever-compassionate Sovereign of the land, governed Terra with a deep, endearing love for His citizens, and His people, in return, cherished Him. Ruling mercifully from the Eternal Palace in the Blissful Mountains, the Emperor instilled a vibrant state of peace and prosperity throughout the land. However, a time came to pass when a great evil lurked in the mighty Kingdom, and from this evil, a terrible sickness spread over the whole Realm of Terra. This sickness dreadfully affected all the subjects of the Kingdom as a grievous darkness enveloped the hearts of both the old and the young.

As a result, the people of Terra became accessible to the most evil desires of the heart, the likes of which they had never known before, for the people of Terra had always lived joyfully and honorably. As the sickness spread, the citizens' hearts succumbed to deep prides, angers, avarices, gluttonies, lusts, envies, and sloths, and Emperor Abba greatly distressed over the fall of His people. However, the great Emperor was determined not to abandon His beloved citizens to the darkness of their sins. War was thence declared on the horrendous evil that had sought to destroy the Kingdom, and countless battles ensued over many years across the lands of Terra.

The Emperor assembled heroic armies of loyal warriors, all of whom wanted the destruction of the vicious evil that threatened to turn them away from the good graces of their Sovereign. The Emperor also sent many messengers across the land to unite the citizens against the evil that had entered Terra. Though the evil was defeated many times in battle and the messengers' words spoke with truth and justice, many of Terra's citizens continued to enslave themselves willfully to the vile pleasure of their sins. Consequently, numerous citizens joined the armies of the evil that had

---

[1] When referring to the Monarchy of Terra, all nouns (such as Kingdom, Realm, etc.) will be capitalized.

[2] When referring to the Emperor of Terra, all nouns (such as Sire, Liege, etc.) and pronouns (such as Him, He, etc.) will be capitalized.

entered the Kingdom; they viciously attacked the Emperor's faithful subjects in battle as kinsmen were divided between those who fought for freedom from evil and those who willingly succumbed to the evil's enslavement.

As time passed, the darkness of the people's hearts grew stronger and stronger, and those citizens who fought for their freedom from sin found that struggling against their weaknesses was becoming more and more difficult. With each passing day, the people began to lose the very virtues that would keep them from falling completely into sin: faith in their Monarch, hope for peace, and true love to endure all hardships. Seeing this, Emperor Abba hid away these virtues from the destruction of the darkness and decided that in time they would be restored to the people of Terra by His own lineage sent from the Eternal Palace. In doing so, the Emperor intended to awaken the citizens from the dark slumber of their hearts and save them from their sins.

Chapter 1
The Old Cabin in the Woods

"No, get away! Momma!"

Laurel sat up in her straw mattress gasping for air. She was sweating profusely, as her heart pounded in her chest. Looking around, Laurel found herself in the small log cabin she had always known as her home. The cabin had only one room, but there were obvious signs of great care taken into its making.

The cabin was made from strong pine trees that grew deep in Serenity Forest, where Laurel lived. The pines had been sawed into many logs, which were skillfully laid on solid foundation to build up the sturdy cabin. The floor was made of a hard, gray rock that had been hand-sculpted into oval stones, which were held together by a thick mortar. A single door stood at the western wall of the cabin, and four square windows inhabited the northern and southern walls. Despite the skillful artisanship that showed from the cabin's impressive design, the aging lodge displayed many signs of decay, for some of the walls were infested with termites and other annoying insects, while the roof of the cabin frequently leaked during rainstorms.

Aside from Laurel's straw mattress, the small lodge contained very few pieces of furniture. A round cedar table with three matching chairs stood across from the young maiden's bed. In one corner of the cabin, a small fireplace would be used ineffectively to provide heat during the cold winter months. In another corner, an old wooden cabinet stood holding a cracked basin and a chipped pitcher that served as a sink. The only place to sit comfortably in the entire room was in the worn seat of a rocking chair that silently creaked in the breeze of an open window. All of this Laurel observed as she calmed herself after her terrible nightmare.

Rubbing her fair-skinned face, she picked up her tired, lanky body and looked into the small mirror that resided on the wall beside her bed. She gave a little groan at the sight of her weary expression and matted hair. The young maiden's bright hazel eyes were also filled with fatigue from her restless night. With a quick combing from a small brush that hung on a rusty nail by the mirror, Laurel's dirty-blond hair relaxed to its normal length at her shoulders. And like any sixteen-year-old, the young maiden complained about her lack of a good night's sleep.

"The same thing seems to happen to me every night," she said to herself. "I go to bed *tired*, a nightmare keeps me awake *all* night, and I wake up *tired*!" Laurel's pale blue nightgown swayed at her knees as she rubbed her eyes again. "Well..." she yawned, "maybe something good will happen today."

After replacing the brush, Laurel stooped down to a little brown chest below the mirror. From inside the chest, she pulled out a plain yellow dress with a short white collar and a pair of brown sandals. In the corner beside her chest, she dressed behind a large, oak dressing screen that was carved with the images of some woodland creatures found in Serenity Forest. Coming out, she gingerly smoothed the creases of the dress' skirt, which came down just below her knees, and donned her sandals, before draping her nightgown on the dressing screen and closing the chest that held her few belongings.

Yawning, the maiden walked over to her makeshift sink, where she freshened up and dried her mouth and face with a frayed cloth. Taking the basin in her hands, she carefully poured out the old water through the open window and replaced the basin atop the small cabinet. Afterward, she stooped down in front of the cabinet and opened its rickety doors, and from inside, she took out a small basket containing fresh apple slices and a loaf of bread. After examining the food, Laurel gobbled down two of the apple slices and placed some in her dress pocket.

"At least there were no worms today!" she chuckled to herself, licking the fruit's sweet taste from her lips.

Laurel replaced the basket of food and closed the cabinet. Then, she got up from her stoop and ran to the cabin door. Opening the door, Laurel's eyes squinted as they met the glow of the early morning sun. Serenity Forest was truly a beautiful sight in the morning as the leaves of the forest canopy glistened in the sun's rays and the long dark trunks of the oaks, pines, and other green trees gave the forest a mystical ambience. Standing in the open doorway, Laurel inhaled a sweet-smelling breeze that whistled through her hair. All her life, Laurel had lived in the woods of Serenity Forest, and she had always found the quiet stillness of the trees intriguing in a mysterious way. It was as if the curious paths of the forest would one day lead her…somewhere. But to where, Laurel did not know. Still, this little vision always played around in her mind.

Laurel mused for a moment or two on her imaginative insights before picking up an old, wooden bucket next to the cabin door. She took a small brown key that hung near the doorway in the cabin, and routinely locked the door before placing the key carefully in the pocket of her dress. Then, she set off down a small woodland path toward the West.

I shall be in need of water soon, Laurel thought. *I ought to head down to The Great River, then… Maybe, I shall pick a few berries near the river's edge for a mid-morning snack!*

Laurel giggled to herself as the thought of gobbling down some delicious berries tickled her appetite, and she continued down the forest path with a cheerful step, as she engaged her mind with this scrumptious thought. It may come to the attention of a few questioning observers of the loneliness that possessed Laurel's life. "Where are the girl's parents?" one may ask. Laurel could not even answer this question herself, if asked, for she had not seen her parents since she was very young.

Laurel knew only a few details about her parents, besides one or two tender memories from her childhood. She remembered that her father was a skilled lumberjack who had built the cabin she now lives in, and her mother had long dark hair. She also knew that the name "Kei" had related in some way to her father, possibly as a surname. At one time, Laurel had once known the happiness of family life as she lived in the small cabin with her parents. However, for some reason, a reason not even Laurel knew herself, they left her one day, leaving her to live all alone in the woods.

Because she was so young when her parents had disappeared, Laurel could not remember all of the events of that day. In spite of this, Laurel believed that her parents were coming back to get her from wherever it was that they had traveled. She believed that, even after all of these years alone in Serenity Forest, her parents still loved her and were trying everything to return to the life that they all had once known before. All she had to do was wait and wish with all her heart that everything she desired would come true.

By this point, most people in Laurel's position would have left the forest long ago, but Laurel was a girl of great fragility and ignorance. She would not know how to go about finding her parents, even if she could ever make her way out of the forest all by herself. Knowing this, she firmly held to the desires of her heart, which believed that the best way to find her parents was to let them come for her. With her innocent disposition, Laurel would try her best to remain cheerful no matter how badly it seemed, with each passing day, that something terrible may have happened to her parents.

All of this steeped in Laurel's thoughts, which was not uncommon, as she continued on the forest path due west. After a while, the tall, thick-trunked trees began to thin out and shrink in size, as Laurel, quickening her pace and pushing past the lush, green bushes, was nearing the edge of the forest. In a flash, Laurel found herself amidst an open field of the greenest grass in all of Terra. Just beyond the field was an array of sloping hills, where a few scattered flowering trees flowed in the gentle breezes of the land. When these soothing winds waved over the grassy hills and brushed against Laurel's cheek, the sweet child could not resist breathing in their refreshing breath.

"Ah," Laurel sighed in a blissful daze, "the Valley Fioré!"

Chapter 2
The Valley Fioré

Laurel began climbing the gentle, sloping hills of the Valley Fioré. The verdant grass caressed her legs as she swung the old wooden bucket at her side. Coming to the top of one small hill, the considerate girl paused in order to appreciate the scene before her. The Great River, the source of all the creeks and streams found in Terra, lay just ahead of a lone blossoming tree. The slow moving river glistened in the early morning sun, and the babbling of the water beating against the river's smooth rocks reached the ears of Laurel atop the hill. With childlike glee, the maiden raced down the hill at full speed towards the river, as the bucket knocked against her knee. Without good judgment, Laurel jumped into the shallow water that flowed up to her shins.

"Ha! That is *so* cold!" Laurel shrieked, and she laughed in spite of herself.

Laurel gingerly stepped over a few nearby stones towards the other side of the river, where she filled her bucket with the cool water and, finding a large berry bush, gobbled down those delicious berries that had occupied her earlier day-dreaming. Turning around, Laurel observed the battered, log hut she had visited so many times on her daily journeys to the Valley Fioré. The hut stood, misplaced it seemed, in a grassy field that stretched far beyond the horizon and to the outer boundaries of the Valley Fioré. Behind this rustic lodging, there stood another weather-beaten hut, though smaller in size, that served as a dwelling place for a small herd of goat, sheep, and a brood of chickens, all of which could be heard bleating and clucking in the early morning air. The humble abode, which the young maiden now approached from the river, was the home of her only companion, Grandma Arliana. Grandma Arliana, or "Granny" as she liked to be called, was an elderly woman who had lived alone in the Valley Fioré for longer than Laurel could ever remember.

Grandma Arliana was short and chubby with a hunchback that caused her great pain whenever she got up to walk around. She had long, wrinkly fingers that had the softest touch, but when her soft hands firmly wrapped themselves around her long, black cane, anyone within a few feet of the old woman was in danger of getting a knock on the head. This, however, happened only whenever Grandma Arliana was in a cranky, frustrated mood, which was almost all the time. As a result, Laurel would frequently walk back to her log cabin a little sore in the head as a result of her daily attempts to care for the troubled old woman. In spite of this, Laurel enjoyed her daily visits to Grandma Arliana's hut, for she knew that the old woman was really an innocent dove deep down.

She is just frustrated, Laurel thought one day after Grandma Arliana had given her a firm whack on the head for spilling a water pitcher all over the floor of the hut. *She cannot do much by herself because of her aching back. That is why she is so cranky, most of the time.*

This unlikely pair of a grouchy, old woman and an uncertain girl was not always in a state of frustration and tested patience. The two knew only each other for company in their little corner of Terra. Despite their differences, they found in each other someone to talk to, someone to help, and someone to share in a friendship. Today, Laurel made her way to the small hut to visit her old friend once again. Walking to the faded purple curtain that served as the door of the hut, Laurel placed her water bucket in the shade of the grass roof and entered.

Inside, Grandma Arliana's hut was much smaller than Laurel's log cabin. A cauldron of soup was kept warm by a few embers that burned in the fireplace that stood to the left of the door. A table, waterlogged from the hut's leaky roof, with four rickety chairs stood in the center of the room. At the hut's back wall was a wooden bed where Grandma Arliana laid in her frayed, green nightgown. Her long gray hair lay in a tangle against the pillow, and the threadbare covers had been drawn up to her chin. When Laurel had entered the hut, Grandma Arliana's eyes had fluttered open, and, taking hold of the cane that rested beside her bed, she sat up with an effort.

"Good morning, sunshine!" Grandma Arliana greeted wearily as she waved her cane in greeting to Laurel.

"Good morning, Granny!" said Laurel as she made her way to the old woman and sat beside her on the bed. "Why are you not out of bed? Do you not feel well?"

"Oh, I did not feel like getting up today," Grandma Arliana grumbled suddenly, fingering her cane. She did not meet Laurel's questioning eyes.

"Well...come on! Here, let me help you up," Laurel cheerfully began pulling at Grandma Arliana's arm.

"No! Do not!" she grimaced, flashing her cane between herself and Laurel.

Laurel frowned. "What is wrong Granny? Why do you do this every morning?"

Grandma Arliana gave a long, frustrated sigh as her wrinkly fingers tightened around her cane. Laurel braced herself for a smack on the head and maybe an insult or two, but Grandma Arliana only rested her cane at the side of her bed and rubbed her forehead.

"Look, Laurel. I am not feeling so good today," the old woman's hard voice seemed weaker than usual to the young maiden. "Just...just leave me alone for a while."

Laurel looked down at her friend with great concern. "Are you sure? I mean I could —"

Grandma Arliana interrupted Laurel as she turned in bed to face the bare wall. "Just leave. For now...I just want to sleep," she mumbled tiredly.

Laurel sighed and stood beside the bed for a moment, unsure of what to do. Then, she bent over Grandma Arliana, planted a sweet kiss on her cheek, and exited the hut.

Laurel stood outside the hut, feeling the winds of the Valley Fioré as they wisped around her hair. She silently thought aloud to herself, "Granny... She seems so frustrated... I wish I knew what to do for her."

This was not the first time Laurel sensed a weakness in Grandma Arliana. During many of Laurel's visits to the old woman, she noticed the physical and mental strength of her friend deteriorating, and this pierced Laurel's heart. However, there was something more; Laurel sensed a weakness in Grandma Arliana that seemed to penetrate her very being, like a wound. Even in her own heart, Laurel sensed this same weakness, which caused her to be uncertain with herself. The maiden also believed that this same weakness, whatever it may be, was the cause of her depressing nightmares. Laurel had these awful dreams almost every night, and they were always the same.

In her dreams, Laurel would find herself alone in the forest during the darkest part of night, trying to find her way to a place that she could never remember. A choking mist would roll around the trees and grassy brush as an icy wind howled eerily in her ear. The forest path would be covered with long, rigid roots, which constantly tripped and faltered Laurel, keeping her from following the path she pursued. Suddenly, a terribly cruel monster would begin trailing Laurel from behind the darkened trees. This was the most frightening part of Laurel's nightmare, for the gentle child truly despised the creature that haunted her steps.

She never saw its face, but she would hear its long, ragged cloak scruff against the sullen forest path as it shadowed her. No matter how fast she would run, she could never escape the monster, as it always seemed to be right at her heels. Finally, after a long and frightful chase, Laurel would fall to the ground from exhaustion, and the creature would try to strangle her with its black claws...

Laurel shook her head as she tried to forget the memory of the terrible nightmare. She had been leaning against Grandma Arliana's hut as her thoughts drifted to this dreadful recollection. *All right*, she told herself sternly, *go away bad thoughts!*

She stretched her arms out and gave a little yawn as she wondered what to do. Suddenly, hearing the bleating of the goats, the young maiden decided to visit her animal friends in the shed behind the hut and give them a good-morning's greeting. The goats, sheep, and chickens all resided together under the roof of the same shed, which was only a single, circular room with thin walls and a thatched roof. The animals were organized with the goats living on the left side of the shed, the sheep on the right, and the chickens fenced in the back. The animals greatly benefited Grandma Arliana in that she always had an ample supply of goat's milk, wool, and eggs for enduring the many hardships of living in isolation. However, Grandma Arliana's animals were not the best or most prized in quality at times.

"Gudrun! Did you kick out the fence again?" Laurel exclaimed, on entering the shed and finding the door to the goats' fence wide open. Quickly, Laurel gathered the mischievous perpetrator, who had escaped from the goats' pen, and placed her with the other bleating kids, before closing and hitching the rickety door.

"And you, Mable," Laurel began again turning to the chickens, who began clucking loudly at one another, "stop picking on your brothers and sisters! Just because you hatched first does not mean that you get to be the boss!"

Lastly, Laurel examined the sheepfold from across the fence and took note of one large sheep that laid along the straw flooring, surrounded by the others of the flock.

"How are you holding up, Ginger?" the maiden spoke with a soft and tender voice, and the sheep gave a tired bleat in response. "Hmm, do not worry! Your little baby will be coming soon, so just stay strong for a couple more weeks. You know, I am sure your baby will turn out as smart and as clever as you!"

After giving all her animal friends their morning breakfast and checking their fencing, the young maiden left the shed and returned to her place at the entrance of Grandma Arliana's hut, where she began again to wonder what to do next. Laurel looked down at her water bucket that sat in the shade of the hut's grass roof by her feet, and then out into the Valley Fioré as she studied the little yellow and purple flowers that danced in the breezes. Her thoughts then returned to those of her dear friend, Grandma Arliana, and the old woman's well-being, for Laurel suspected that there was no change in her friend's sour morning disposition ever since performing her morning chores.

"Hmm…" Laurel mused to herself. "Maybe…just maybe Granny would feel better if I did something for her."

She began considering some ways on cheering up the grumpy woman and, after a while, decided to pick a bouquet of flowers. With any blessing, the surprise could recover a merrier spirit in her closest and only friend. Leaving the bucket behind, Laurel skipped over the rocks of The Great River towards the ample waves of colorful flowers, where she constructed a most beautiful bouquet. The gentle breeze that continually wisped through the valley tickled Laurel's fair face as she bent to pick even the little flowers hidden in the tall grass. Laurel began to hum a little tune and wonder about her little life.

There was not much excitement in living one's days without family or friends, except for the amity of a stubborn, old woman, whose frustration could not vouch for her at times as the best of companions in a secluded valley. In fact, the only real pleasure Laurel derived from her stays with Grandma Arliana was of their conversations about the old woman's book collection, which she kept stored away in an ancient trunk underneath her bed. From these stories of adventure, excitement, and companionship, Laurel developed much of her understanding of the world, which was overall very much in need of a truer education. She never knew what life was like beyond the Valley Fioré or her little scope of Serenity Forest; many times, though, she fancied herself determined to pursue the curiosity and wonderment that pressed her little spirit into leaving her aged cabin in the woods for a grand adventure.

However, her concern for Grandma Arliana suppressed these childlike fantasies and dreaming, for she felt obligated, as the old woman's only companion, to stay by her side in good times and bad and to assist her as long as she was able. Still, the simple girl longed for a life that was much more than the one she now possessed, but her whimsical daydreaming was enough to satisfy her bold desires…at least for now.

I wonder what would happen if today was different from all of the other days. Laurel thought as she picked a small, budding yellow flower and inhaled its sweet fragrance. *What would today be like if I went on a fantastic journey? Where would I go…across the land and to the sea? What sort of people would I meet? What would I do there? I wonder…*

Suddenly, Laurel heard an unusual noise that distracted her from her reveries: the neigh of a horse, which could be heard a little ways away beyond a small hill. By now, Laurel was south of Grandma Arliana's small hut on the east side of the river, and the neighing sounded northward. To get a better view of her surroundings, the young maiden climbed a nearby knoll, determined to seek out the mysterious sound.

I know I heard something, Laurel thought as she surveyed the valley below.

Unexpectedly, Laurel spotted, in the shade of a lone flower-filled tree, a beautiful white horse. The tall mount wore a dark brown saddle over a richly purple blanket. His long, blond mane wisped in the valley winds, and his hooves shined with a gleaming gray tone. Laurel was amazed to see the magnificent creature as she had never seen a horse in all her life, for horses were not native to the Valley Fioré. She had only seen pictures of horses in the Grandma Arliana's adventure novels.

Presently, Laurel slowly crept down the hill towards the horse, which was munching grass under the shade of the tree. She tightly held her bouquet of flowers to her chest as her heart beat rapidly with delight at her mysterious finding. As Laurel came closer, the horse noticed her between his eating but remained calm, despite her presence. Once she was a few feet away, Laurel tried talking to the horse to see if she could befriend him.

"Hello, Mr. Horse!" she whispered as she inched forward.

Mr. Horse watched her inquisitively for a moment but then turned away from Laurel, busily eating away at a nearby shrub.

"Aw! Come on, Mr. Horse! Look here," Laurel called again, circling the horse so that she could face him.

She made a few kissing sounds, trying to get the horse's attention, but they came to no avail, as the horse quickly dismissed her presence for attention of his hungering stomach. As she drew evermore closer, Laurel suddenly spotted the horse's reins that hung loosely at his right shoulder, and she contrived the notion to sneak forward and grab the reins.

Maybe, if I can catch the horse, I can make him my friend! Laurel thought humorously.

Just as she came within arm's reach of the reins, an interesting image sewn on the horse's blanket caught her eye. Stitched on each side of the blanket was a large yellow sun with eight-pointed rays; a big red heart sat in the sun's center as a crown of green, leafy branches circled the heart. Laurel studied the image for a moment, trying to remember if she could recognize the unusual icon. However, she had no time to recall anything as a shout from behind surprised her.

"Wait! My horse...!"

Laurel turned quickly to see who was calling, when she noticed a young man from the top of a nearby hill coming towards her. Greatly confused, Laurel began stepping away from the horse. Suddenly, she lost her balance by tripping over a large tree root, and her bouquet spewed into the air as she fell to the ground. The horse became deeply frightened by this and stomped wildly at the earth. It reared up right by Laurel's head.

Chapter 3
An Unexpected Visitor

The frightened maiden stared up in bewilderment as the horse snorted and reared at her head. Suddenly, she found the horse's owner standing before her as he tried to calm his horse. The tall and slender man looked to be only a few years older than Laurel. He had a muscular build with a lightly tanned complexion. His long golden-brown hair curled at the ends and hung just above his shoulders. Laurel marveled at the man's distinguished attire as he wore a white, long-sleeved shirt, which flowed loosely around his extended arms, and long black pants that came down to his black riding boots. Coupled around his neck, a purple-red cloak flowed down to his ankles.

Keeping his stance in front of Laurel, the man's gentle voice talked sweet words of tranquility and assurance, which soothed his startled horse. Finally, the steed calmed down from his rambunctious attitude to a temperate nature, and the man caressed the horse's muzzle with care. Sighing with relief, the young man turned to Laurel who sat looking up into his face. Laurel caught sight of his bright sunlit eyes and his gentle expression, which gave him an elegant appearance. He held out his hand for Laurel, while holding onto his horse's reins.

"Are you all right, Miss?" The man's voice carried a serene tone.

At first, Laurel did not know what to do in her embarrassment and surprise, but she quickly took the man's hand and allowed him to help her up anyway.

"Oh...yes. I—I am all right," stuttered Laurel as she quickly removed her hand. Unthinkingly, she began smoothing out her dress, never taking her eyes off the man.

He smiled, "I am glad. Please, I apologize for my horse. I am truly sorry that he caused you so much trouble and frightened you."

"Oh, well..." Laurel replied shyly, "I am the one to blame for startling him in the first place. I mean...I overreacted to your calling and..."

"Do not worry," the man assured her. "I am afraid my horse is a terrible troublemaker. You see, he wandered off from my sight while we were journeying in the valley, and I have been looking for him for some time now. Thank you for finding him."

"Oh! You are welcome."

For a moment, the two were silent. Laurel was uncertain of what to say, and the man was busy reassuring his horse more considerately by stroking his mane and securing his horse's saddling. Then, the man knelt down by Laurel and began picking up her scattered flowers.

"These are yours, correct?" He asked handing the small bouquet up to Laurel.

She took them timidly in her hands. "Thank you...um?"

"Sol," the man replied getting up. "My name is Sol, like the sun," and he made a courteous bow to Laurel.

She gave a small curtsy in recognition. "I... My name is Laurel," she said almost inaudibly.

"Laurel?" Sol inquired. "Like the small tree."

This made Laurel giggle, "I always thought of laurels as only small shrubs."

Sol gave a hearty chuckle, which surprisingly pleased Laurel. The horse nuzzled against Sol with his soft nose as if wanting attention. Sol wrapped his arm around the horse's neck and gently scratched his long ears.

"And this is Philippe, the one who causes *all* the trouble."

Laurel laughed warmly at this but watched the gentle horse, awed by the fact that only moments ago Philippe was inches away from greatly hurting her.

Sol must have noticed this for he continued, "He really is a sweet horse, and I know he did not mean to frighten you. Right, Philippe?"

Philippe gave a soft neigh as if in agreement. Laurel giggled again and began to stroke the steed's nose. Soon, Philippe was warming up to Laurel, for he allowed her to scratch behind his ears. Suddenly, Philippe began sniffing and snorting around Laurel's dress pocket.

"Oh!" Laurel exclaimed knowingly, and she took out her apple slices from this morning.

"Are you looking for these?" Laurel held the squishy slices out for Philippe, and his fat lips tickled against Laurel's hands as he ate every slice.

"He is really hungry," Laurel said looking up at Sol.

Sol smiled, patting Philippe's neck. "I know. We have not yet eaten breakfast, so we had better continue our journeying and find a place to rest."

Laurel thought a moment. Though she had only just met Sol, she was very curious about who he was, and she was anxious to know more about this unexpected visitor. She looked towards Grandma Arliana's hut and wondered if she was not being too daring in wanting Sol to stay.

"Well... Would you like to stay *here* for breakfast?" Laurel asked.

Sol seemed to ponder this question in surprise for a moment. Even though she did not know anything about him, Laurel had the feeling that Sol did not want to be intrusive.

"Maybe you should ask someone you know first. I mean, it would only be proper," replied Sol as He looked to Philippe who was playing with His cloak.

"Oh, well..." Laurel started.

Gee, now I feel dumb, she thought awkwardly.

Laurel knew she was in a predicament, for her parents were not home. On top of that, she had not seen them in years, so she thought fast of what to say next. Laurel pointed towards Grandma Arliana's house.

"My friend lives just past The Great River. Would you like to meet her?" she invited.

Sol looked over at the hut in the distance. "Certainly, if you wish so, Laurel."

Laurel started ahead as she called back, "Come on! You shall really like her." Sol smiled pleasingly and followed the happy girl with Philippe trotting behind him. Sol and his horse trailed Laurel over the river and up to Grandma Arliana's hut.

"Wait here," Laurel said, motioning to Sol. "Allow me a few moments to inform my friend of your presence, first. Then, you may knock to enter."

Sol nodded and began securing Philippe to an old post nearby. Laurel walked through the curtain to find Grandma Arliana sitting up in bed as she read from one of her picture books, which she had gathered from the trunk under her bed. She was still wearing her green nightgown, and her long gray hair was still matted together from sleeping; however, it looked as though she had freshened up by herself sometime after Laurel had left. Still, the old woman sat quietly on her bed, and her face showed great interest as she flipped through the pages of her book. Laurel rushed over to Grandma Arliana with her bouquet waving in her hand.

"Granny! Granny! You shall never believe what just happened to me!" Laurel cried excitedly.

Grandma Arliana started at hearing Laurel's voice in the quiet of her home, and she set her book down with a look of surprise.

"Good gracious, what is going on?" Grandma Arliana exclaimed. "Laurel, you know not to sneak up on me like that!"

"But Granny–Ouch!" Before Laurel could explain herself, Grandma Arliana had whipped out her cane and given Laurel a light knock on the head.

Grandma Arliana sighed, closing her book with a little annoyance. "All right, Laurel. Now, tell me what was *so* important that you just *had* to burst in here so loudly." Rubbing the sore spot on her head, Laurel's face lightened at the thought of telling her tale.

"Well, I was outside picking flowers for you — oh, here!" The maiden handed the small bouquet of flowers to Grandma Arliana, who took them with a little astonishment, and a small smile appeared on her wrinkled face.

"Anyway," Laurel continued, "I saw this horse and —"

"A horse?" Grandma Arliana interposed between smelling her bouquet. "You mean like the ones in my books?"

"Yes! Exactly!" Laurel exclaimed excitedly as she noted Grandma Arliana's interest. She sat down on the bed next to the old woman, who seemed to ponder Laurel's words.

"Interesting..." she murmured, "Why would a horse wander into this part of Terra? Are you certain you saw a horse? Maybe you were just dreaming again, Laurel."

Laurel shook her head, "I promise you, I was not dreaming. I really saw a horse, and I even fed him some apple slices! Oh, I also met his owner, who seems to be quite an interesting person, and—"

Grandma Arliana held up her hand for Laurel to stop. "What do you mean by the horse's 'owner'? There has not been a single passerby in the Valley Fioré for years... Oh, you must be joking, Laurel!"

Taking the old woman's hand, Laurel's face showed with great earnestness, "No, Granny. I am serious! I met an actual person, and... and...he is waiting outside."

Suddenly, there was a gentle knock on the old wood of the hut. Laurel and Grandma Arliana looked towards the faded purple curtain that covered the hut's opening. Looking back at Grandma Arliana, Laurel noted an expression of revelation and wonderment flood the wrinkled face of her friend.

"Just a moment!" Grandma Arliana's voice rang calmly.

She motioned for Laurel to hand her a dark blue robe that hung over the bedpost and she feebly wrapped the warm robe around herself. Carefully and with Laurel's help, she made her way to the oak table and sat in the nearest chair. Laying her bouquet of flowers gently before her and smoothing her hair into place, she gave Laurel permission to allow her acquaintance into the hut. Laurel walked to the entrance of the hut and pushed back the curtain. Sol stood on the other side, having waited patiently.

Laurel, smiling sweetly at her guest, greeted him, "Will you please come in?"

Sol nodded with a polite smile and entered. He stood in front of the old, waterlogged table, while Laurel took her place at Grandma Arliana's side.

"How do you do, madam?" Sol greeted to Grandma Arliana as he gave a small bow in her direction.

"Fine, thank you," Grandma Arliana replied. She seemed a little surprised by Sol's politeness and respectful tone, and most especially by his presence, but she gave him a cheerful smile in return for His bow.

"Granny," Laurel spoke up, "this is Sol, the one I was telling you about." Then she turned to her guest, "Sol, this is my friend, Grandma Arliana."

"I am very pleased to meet you," said Sol. He stood tall with an air of elegance about him, and he folded his hands in front of him contentedly.

"As am I," Grandma Arliana replied. She paused for a moment as if going over something in her head. "Sol... like the sun, I suppose?"

Sol nodded, "Yes, madam."

"Sol... Yes...very good name," Grandma Arliana mused as if she tried to remember whether she had heard the name before. She held her black cane in her hand beside her chair and instinctively twirled it as she thought to herself.

"Well, young man," she continued, "Laurel and I are very surprised to see an unknown face in the Valley Fioré, for not many people have journeyed to the valley in years. I was wondering what brought you out to this region of Terra."

"Well," Sol began, "I have been traveling around Terra for some time now. Earlier this morning, I journeyed into the valley on my horse, and I stopped to rest for a while afterwards. When I was ready to continue my traveling, I found that my horse had wandered off without me. Because of Laurel, my horse has been safely returned to me." He then turned to Laurel saying, "Thank you again, Laurel."

"Oh, you are welcome," she replied, and she gave a shy smile to Grandma Arliana.

"Well, I am glad to hear that my little Laurel could help you," Grandma Arliana chuckled. "At any rate, what business, if you do not mind my asking, do you have in the Valley Fioré?"

Sol gave a light chuckle, "O, I do not mind at all, madam! For now, I am only passing through, for I am heading northwards towards the mountains. There, I am going to meet up with a friend of mine, and we shall continue the remainder of travelling together."

"So, I suppose you are an avid traveler, young man? And what is your purpose for these travels?"

"Mostly, I am doing just that: journeying from one place to the next, but my intention is to become more informed and experienced with the different people and customs of Terra."

"Indeed, that sounds like an adventurous employment of your youth!" Grandma Arliana stated, satisfied with the polite man's words.

"Thank you, madam. Now, if you would give me your blessing, I would like to join you both for breakfast, as your kind friend, Laurel, has asked of me."

With this, the old woman turned towards the young maiden, who blushed with coyness as an unassuming smile spread across her face.

"Is it all right with you, Granny?" Laurel inquired, with a hint of pleading in her small voice.

"Though I would not want to intrude," Sol spoke up resolutely, "for I understand the improper circumstance of my unexpected arrival."

Grandma Arliana smiled at this sense of well-mannered respect, and she replied, "It would be no trouble at all, young man! Besides, Laurel and I would be delighted to have another seat filled at the table, and I believe we could provide you with a little work in return for your food."

Sol nodded smilingly. "I would not want it any other way."

With the agreements made, Grandma Arliana gave Sol instructions for his work in the animal shed, while Laurel contentedly began the meal preparations.

When Laurel went to summon Sol for breakfast, she noticed his work on the fencing of the pens. Sol had fitted the entire goat pen in place, which Gudrun had broken earlier that morning, with careful workmanship. The young maiden was also surprised to notice that Sol had laid a fresh bale of straw and grasses into each animal pen, which normally would have taken Laurel more than half an hour to complete.

"What a very good girl you are!" Sol's voice then came from the sheep's pen, and Laurel turned to find the gentle man kneeling before Ginger and the other sheep.

Sol chuckled cheerfully as the sheep jumped and hugged around him as he petted their soft wool; some of the baby sheep even licked and kissed at his face, to which he returned sweetly by rubbing his nose against their faces. Laurel took this moment to observe Sol and wonder more about his character, as she leaned against the doorway of the shed.

He seems so kind, she thought admiringly, *and he is so sweet and gentle to Ginger and her kids. Never have I met anyone from outside of the Valley Fioré...but if the rest of the world is anything like Sol, then I want to see it all...*

That was when Sol noted the presence of the watching maid, as one of the sheep began bleating at her from the pen. When he saw her, Sol's eyes lighted with cheer, while Laurel stared with a little shyness.

"Hello again, Laurel," Sol began.

"Oh, hello. I—uh—" Laurel stammered; she was almost speechless at the revelation of her studying Sol. "I—I just came to tell you that, um, breakfast is ready."

"Thank you," he replied getting up from the pile of sheep, who bleated with sadness at his leaving.

"I, uh, noticed your work on the goat pen," Laurel ventured.

"Oh, yes. I straightened the fencing and remade the lock so that the goats cannot kick it open so easily."

"Oh, that is perfect!" Laurel exclaimed happily, as she examined the improved door. "You do not know how many times Gudrun has gotten out of her pen! She is a very naughty goat."

Sol laughed, bending over the goat pen to stroke Gudrun's head. "Well, I am certain that you shall have no trouble now if she tries to kick down the door."

"Hmm, thank you again, Sol," the young maiden replied, leading the way out of the shed.

"You know," Sol started as the two walked back to Grandma Arliana's hut, "if you really do have a lot of trouble with your goat trying to escape from the shed, then maybe it would be better if she and the others had a larger pen built for them."

"You might be right," Laurel considered. "I suppose it must be dreary for her to live in such small living quarters, and I have thought about trying to build the goats and sheep a larger enclosure. Then again, I am not very good with my hands, so it might take a while, if I ever get around to it."

"I see," Sol replied as he looked off into the field behind Grandma Arliana's hut, and Laurel wondered what his thoughts might be considering.

At breakfast, the three enjoyed a simple meal together as they ate toast with jam and drank cups of warm tea. Grandma Arliana delighted in discussing and asking Sol questions about everything related to his travels around Terra, while Laurel was content with listening to the two. While she ate quietly, the inquisitive maid began pondering a strange notion that had wiggled its way into her thoughts. She had noticed that since Sol entered the hut Grandma Arliana's cranky and sluggish disposition had changed into that of a cheerful, serene nature.

Maybe a change in presence has done well for Granny's heart, Laurel thought to herself. *It is as if Sol's company has somehow softened her heart a little.*

That was when she caught Sol's eye as he passed her a bowl of blueberries. He gave his sweet smile to Laurel, and she returned it shyly, before Sol returned his attention back to Granny who began asking about his horse.

And maybe… He has softened mine as well… Laurel thought suddenly with a blush, but she then decided to push the idea from her mind.

After the meal, Sol decided that it was time for him to take his leave, not wanting to stay longer than was proper. He thanked Grandma Arliana and Laurel for their hospitality, stating how delicious and filling the breakfast was for him.

"You are welcome, Sol," Grandma Arliana replied as she petted Philippe, for Sol had invited her to meet his horse, while he packed away some leftover toast that Laurel had provided for him. "Oh, what a pretty horse you are," the old woman whispered into the horse's ear, and Philippe nickered with delight at the attention.

"Sol, where did you say that you were heading to now?" Laurel asked as Sol climbed into his saddle, once he had refastened Philippe's saddling.

"Northward to the mountains. If I leave now, I should meet my friend within a day or two, though I may have to travel during the night."

"And what is this?" Grandma Arliana cried in surprise, seeing what little belongings Sol carried with him. "No tent? No blankets or pillows or extra foodstuff and equipment? And how shall you shelter yourself tonight?"

Sol chuckled, "O, as I always do, madam! I enjoy sleeping under the stars, whether I rest in the tall grasses or high in a tree. And as for my little supplies, I am more of what you would call a 'free-bird' when it comes to traveling; I simply go where the wind takes me with my focus on the present."

Grandma Arliana shook her head unsatisfactorily at this explanation. "Ah, the freedom of youth! I suppose I shall never understand!"

Sol laughed heartily and seemed to enjoy the informality with which Grandma Arliana spoke towards him. "I thank you again for your hospitality, and though I shall not be journeying this way for a long time, I hope you shall grant me the permission of returning here again in order to repay you further for your kindness."

"Of course, young man, whenever you are in the valley, you have my consent to call on us as often as you desire."

"Thank you, madam," Sol nodded towards the old woman, and he smiled down sweetly at Laurel as he expressed his gratitude once more for her help in finding Philippe.

"You are welcome again, and I wish you safety," she replied amiably.

Sol nodded contentedly and said in return, "And, Laurel, may I have *your* permission to call on you whence I return?"

Laurel started in surprise at this but gladly stammered, "Oh... Why...yes, of course!"

Sol nodded peacefully, "I appreciate that."

Laurel hid her reddening face with a smile as she and Grandma Arliana backed away from Philippe. Sol then gave a command to the horse, and Philippe began to trot past the river heading northward. After a few yards, Sol looked back to wave at his two new acquaintances, and the young maiden and old woman returned his gesture. They watched the young man and his horse until the slopping hills finally obscured their view.

"What an interesting morning we have had today, true, Laurel?" Grandma Arliana chuckled as she made her way back into her old hut.

As the maiden continued to look on where she had last observed Sol, Laurel suddenly remembered a thought she had contemplated early that morning: *I wonder what would happen if today was different from all of the other days*. She chuckled at herself as she considered the events of the unbelievable morning.

Be careful of what you wish for, Laurel, she thought with a wide grin as she followed Grandma Arliana into the hut. *You might just get it!*

Chapter 4
Budding Feelings

Many days had passed since Sol's departure from the Valley Fioré, and Grandma Arliana and Laurel continued with their normal, isolated lives as though Sol had never come to their little part of Terra. However, their daily thoughts drifted, ever so often, to that mysterious man who had peaked their wonderment and brought a joyful sense of new companionship into their lives. And yet, the two friends never talked amongst themselves about Sol, for the idea of his promised return seemed unlikely. Sol was the first person in many, many years to have travelled so far into the western lands of Terra, so Grandma Arliana and Laurel saw no reason why he or anyone else would ever consider journeying into the valley at all. With hopeless uncertainty, the two friends looked to one another for further companionship as they always had. However, their friendship soon faltered as Grandma Arliana's irritating health problems caused great tension between the two friends.

One day, as Grandma Arliana and Laurel were preparing lunch, their thoughts were occupied with memories of Sol, who seemed so distant from them, as they set up the wooden table with delicious eggs, berries, bread, and other scrumptious foods. That morning was unnaturally silent for the two friends, for their quiet considerations seemed to possess all of their attention, and even Laurel seemed as though she were walking in a daze. Her reveries were shattered, however, by the sound of a clattering bowl and of a frustrated groan from Grandma Arliana. Laurel looked up from the table, where she had been arranging the food, to see the old woman bent over, and holding her trembling fist as she stared down at the bowl of soup that she had dropped.

"Ack!" Grandma Arliana mumbled with disdain, "My bones are killing me, I know it..."

"It is all right, Granny," Laurel began, coming over to her friend. "I shall clean up the mess. Why not just sit down for now and — "

"No! No! I can do it, Laurel!" the old woman cried out irately as she waved Laurel away from her.

"But your hand... You look a little tired now, so please sit down, while I prepare the lunch."

"Now, Laurel, I said I can do it! So just get away and let me clean up the mess myself!"

"But, Granny — !"

Despite Laurel's attempts at stopping her, Grandma Arliana swiftly looked around for a towel and, spotting one on a nearby stool, she hobbled towards it with great difficulty. Laurel, however, reached the stool before her friend and quickly took the towel out of reach from the old woman.

"What are you doing?" the old woman cried angrily. "Now, hand me that towel!"

"But, Granny, I think that you should take a rest. You have not been looking well for a while now. It is all right; I can prepare the lunch!" Laurel spoke with her sweetest voice as she tried to persuade her friend, but her kindness seemed only to annoy Grandma Arliana even more. Irritably, the old woman took the towel from the young maiden's hands and gave her a swift knock on the head with her cane.

"I told you! I *can* do it! You think I am just some feeble biddy who cannot do anything on her own! Well, I *can*, I tell you. I can clean up this mess by myself, I can fix lunch by myself, and I can do everything by myself! I do not need you hovering over me like I am some invalid who is on her deathbed!" Laurel, at first, took Grandma Arliana's words in silence as she rubbed the sore spot on her head, but soon the effect of her dear friend's angry tone began to hurt more than her head.

"Fine, you old biddy!" Laurel exclaimed furiously without thinking as she held back a stream of hot tears. "If that is how you feel, then go ahead! Do everything all by yourself! I am tired of taking care of you and your nasty attitude!" Hastily, the young maiden rushed past the old woman and headed towards the doorway.

"Where do you think you are going?" Grandma Arliana called, her voice still denoting anger.

"I do not care!" Laurel cried back, "I just hope it is far enough away from you!"

With that, the girl flew out of the hut and ran as fast as she could into the hills of the Valley Fioré. Huffing, more with anger than exhaustion, she stopped to catch her breath at the lone flowering tree that stood across from the river; her heart beat rapidly with a torrent of enraging emotion. Without thinking, Laurel took off again northward, just wanting to get as far away from Grandma Arliana's hut as possible. The fury and annoyance that she felt towards the old woman fueled her legs with power to keep running and to never look back. Her pink dress blew in the wind of her strides as her long hair wisped about her face. She never even stopped to brush away the tears of resentment and sorrow that flooded down her cheeks with hot, fiery passion.

For how long or far Laurel ran, she could not remember, but after a long while, her body soon gave into fatigue, and she collapsed in the tall grasses, panting and huffing mightily. She sobbed with all her might and wailed with sadness at the anger she felt towards Grandma Arliana.

Why? Why is she so mean to me? Laurel thought in despair. *All that I have ever done for her was to be her friend and to help care for her! Fine, I do not care! My life will be all the better without her...*

With her tears still flowing like an endless stream, Laurel rolled over on her back and stared up at the bright, white clouds of the blue sky. *I should just leave her as I said...but where would I go? O, what am I to do?*

Laurel sighed with frustration as she wiped her tears and closed her eyes, and tried to clear her thoughts. The wind from the valley whistled in her ears and the chirping of birds flying overhead filled the maiden with a peaceful silence. As she listened to these pleasing sounds and found herself drifting into a serene sleep, Laurel suddenly heard a huffy, snorting sound close to her head, and she felt fat, tickling lips brush across her forehead, which caused her eyes to flash open swiftly.

To Laurel's surprise, Philippe was busy sniffing and snorting away at her long hair from behind. Laurel sat up quickly and turned around to the horse, which seemed happy to find her.

"What are you doing here, Philippe?" Laurel asked in amazement as she petted and caressed the horse's muzzle. "Did you run away from Sol again?" The maiden giggled as the horse nuzzled at her face guiltily. "Well, I suppose us runaways should stick together, huh? Nevertheless, I am sure that Sol is wondering where you ran off to, so we better find him." Just as Laurel took up Philippe's reins, she heard someone calling from a nearby hill and she turned quickly to see if it was Sol.

"Hey, there! Hold on!" came a determined voice, but Laurel immediately realized that the voice was not Sol's as she saw a twelve-year-old boy, whose countenance made him seem much older, running down from the hill towards her. "Hold on a minute!" cried the boy again.

The boy was short in stature but very athletically built. He had short brown hair that swayed just below his ears. He wore a cream-colored tunic and green, loose-fitting pants, which came down to his ankles, with a golden sash tied around his waist. The young boy's bright green cloak was fastened around his shoulders, and he wore dark sandals at his feet. When he came to Laurel and the horse, the watchful maiden was able to observe his facial features, which were handsome and wise for his age as his bright green eyes danced in the light of the sun.

"Thank you for waiting," were his first words. "I did not mean to startle you if I did, but I am in a hurry to retrieve this horse you have here. I have been searching for him since early this morning, you see, and I thank you most kindly for finding him."

"This is not *your* horse, is it?" Laurel asked confusedly.

"Oh, no! Actually, he belongs to my master, but we decided to split up in order to search for him. My name is Peterel, by the way," and the young boy stuck out his hand cheerfully, which Laurel shook kindly.

His master? I wonder what he means by that. Laurel wondered.

"My name is Laurel," she began, but before she could inquire the name of the young boy's master, Peterel gasped with delight.

"Oh, so *you* must be Laurel from the Valley Fioré! My master has told me so much about you and your friend Grandma Arliana."

"O, yes? Then, you must know Sol?"

The boy laughed with joy at the name. "Why yes! He is my master! I follow him on his travels around Terra."

"Ah, yes, I believe Sol mentioned something about that the last time I saw him," Laurel replied, delighting at this connection. "By the way, can you tell me where Sol has gone off to, for I would very much like to speak with him again?"

Before Peterel could reply, the two heard a familiar voice calling for their attention from the nearby hill. They turned and lightened with joy to see Sol strolling towards them.

"Master! Master!" Peterel cried as he ran towards Sol. "I found your friend, Laurel, and she found Philippe, too!"

Sol gave a whistle to Philippe, who obediently returned to his owner. Sol shook his head at the mischievous horse. "You naughty horse!" Sol said teasingly. "Who gave you permission to run off again?"

Philippe nuzzled his nose close to Sol's face as if trying to make amends, and Sol laughingly accepted the penitence of his horse and looked up to greet Laurel. "Laurel, I am glad to see that I can count on you to find my horse for me!"

"O, well, this time it seems he found me," Laurel replied cheerily, coming up to the young man.

"So, Laurel, what brings you out this far into the Valley?" Sol asked.

"Oh, well, I just thought I needed some fresh air!" she laughed uneasily as her heart remembered Grandma Arliana.

"Laurel?" Peterel began as he merrily took hold of her hand, "Sol and I were wondering earlier this morning if you would allow us to visit at your friend's home."

"That is, if you do not mind," Sol added considerately.

Laurel's heart was torn at this request, for though she delighted in the thought of receiving her new acquaintances for lunch, her thoughts anxiously returned to her previous argument with Grandma Arliana. Despite her uncertainty towards how the old woman would receive her, Laurel gave the affirmative to Sol and Peterel, also inviting them to stay for lunch. With this approval, Sol and Peterel followed Laurel southward to Grandma Arliana's hut. They walked along together, with Philippe striding ahead of them with a restless spirit, and Sol related his previous journey in the northern region of Terra. He and Peterel had met just as they had planned and, travelling across the region from many weeks, had greeted many people and seen many interesting sights.

"And how has everything been in the valley, Laurel?" Sol inquired after a while.

"Hmm… The weather has been wonderfully lovely as always. The flowers grow more and more with each passing day, and the cool breezes have brought a pleasantness to the sun's warm rays. However, there has not been much rain lately, but I think it is just a simple dry spell."

"And how have you and Grandma Arliana faired since I last saw you?"

Laurel gave another uneasy laugh as she replied simply, "Oh…just well…"

Before Sol could inquire further, Philippe drew his attention as he impatiently tried again at striding ahead of the group. "Here, Peterel," Sol said to his friend, releasing the horse's reins, "keep an eye on Philippe and let him gallop ahead of us, since he seems eager to stretch his legs. Only, be sure he does not get away again or go too far."

"Yes, sir!" Peterel replied as he climbed into the saddle and rode off into the hills ahead.

Laurel could not help laughing as she witnessed this. "What a lively horse he is!"

"I know! Sometimes I wonder what will become of him, having such a wild spirit!" Sol chuckled. "Anyway, how did you say that you and Grandma Arliana were fairing, again?"

"Um, fine…" Laurel replied, though this time much less enthusiastic than the last.

"You seem a little troubled, if you do not mind my saying so. Is something amiss?"

"Ah, well, it is somewhat complicated and personal," Laurel continued, hoping to throw off the conversation, and for a while, Sol seemed to perceive this.

However, after the two had continued on their walk for a few moments longer, Sol casually began again, "I know that we have only just met, Laurel, but if there is anything troubling you and Grandma Arliana, then I would be more than happy to assist you both in any way that I can."

Though Laurel could not perceive any unwanted advances from Sol's declaration, she still felt discomfort at the thought of telling him of the frivolous and ridiculous argument that had ensued between herself and Grandma Arliana. On the other hand, Laurel knew that sooner rather than later, as they were briefly to arrive at the old woman's hut, Sol would become aware of her stiff relations to Grandma Arliana, whether by the old woman's disposition or her own.

Noting Laurel's pause, as she quietly regarded all of these things, Sol made the comment, "If now is an unwelcomed time for visitors, then I would not object to your wishes for Peterel and I to visit you all at a more appropriate time."

"Oh, no! I would not dream of that!" Laurel assured him. "Besides," she continued somewhat reluctantly, "it does not seem my situation will improve any time soon."

"Why? What trouble are you in?"

At length, Laurel related her concerns of the changed temperament of Grandma Arliana. "I do not know why, but lately it seems that she has been grouchier than usually. I mean, I understood before, if in the morning, she did not want to get out of bed or talk to me for a while until she had overcome her morning moodiness, but now her temper seems to be set off at any time and over any circumstance! For instance, she becomes furious if I even help with the chores or prepare the meals, as if she is determined to do everything on her own, as if she does not need my help anymore. And…anyway, we were arguing again this morning, but this time, I was so frustrated that I ran off and that is why I was out so far from the hut when you found me."

"I see," Sol said, considering all that Laurel had said. "I can imagine with what concern you endure these difficulties, but when it comes to someone like Grandma Arliana, who is not as young as she used to be and realizes this every day, you have to remember that there are many years of struggles that weigh on her heart."

"What do you mean?"

"Well, someone as old as Grandma Arliana, who has lived in such a far out region of Terra, which is no easy task, wants to feel and know that she can still do the things that she could many years ago."

"But…she cannot do the things that she could many years ago! I mean, with her back pains and the aching in her bones…"

"Yes, I know, and that is something that she needs to realize. However, in the end, all that she wants is to know that she is useful, despite her age and weakness."

"But she is useful! I know that! I mean, I do not know what I would be doing now, if I did not have her as my friend."

Sol smiled at this saying, "And how often have you told her that?"

Laurel stopped in her tracks suddenly as she considered the shrewd man's words. "Gee… You know, I cannot remember the last time when I told Granny how happy I am to be her friend…or how glad I am to see her each day…and… But I do so much for her," she continued, looking up to Sol. "She must know that I appreciate her company."

"It is true as they say, 'Actions speak louder than words.' However, sometimes we all need someone to *tell* us just how important and cherished we are to them. I mean, just think of her living out so far away from the rest of the world…when was the last time she heard someone say, 'I love you!'?"

Laurel looked guilty saying, "Not very recently…"

The girl looked up, then, when Sol took her hand kindly. "You know," he said, "the past is not as important as the present, for it is in the present that we can change everything."

"I guess this means that I should not run away, then, huh?" Laurel asked teasingly.

"Come on, then!" Sol replied smilingly as he pulled her along towards Grandma Arliana's hut.

"Still, I do not think that *I* should be the one to say sorry *first*, since *she* started the trouble," Laurel murmured with displeasure.

"That is all the more reason for you to start, then!" Sol replied smilingly.

Once the two arrived at the hut, they could perceive Peterel and Philippe continuing down the river, as the horse's new sense of freedom seemed to be running away with him. Sol gave a small chuckle to this as he motioned for Laurel to carry on without him.

"I shall be right back as soon as I recapture the fugitive!"

Laurel laughed as Sol parted from her, and taking a deep breath to muster all of her strength, she reentered the hut with anxious steps. When the maiden entered, her eyes instantly met with those of Grandma Arliana, who sat quietly on her bed with her hands folded in front of her.

"Laurel, you came back!" the old woman cried with relief at seeing her friend, but suddenly checked herself as she continued indifferently, "I—I thought you decided you had enough with me."

"Granny," Laurel began coming towards her. Peering penitently towards her true friend, her eyes turned downward as she replied, "I am sorry. I am sorry...for my impatience this morning and for the things I said and for...running off like I did. It was not very...kind of me."

"I agree!" Grandma Arliana replied, her voice brimming with irritating pleasure.

"Granny—!" The young maiden's voice rang with annoyance, before she quickly caught herself and began again with a sigh. "Granny...I am especially sorry for...for not telling you very often how...how happy I am to be your friend."

At this, the pleasure-filled smirk of the old woman that had just begun to spread across her wrinkled face suddenly vanished with astonishment. "Wh—what did you say...Laurel?"

Laurel looked up with an apologetic smile as she replied, "I love you, Grandma Arliana."

The old woman stared at the young maiden in disbelief for a long moment, as if not expecting such a statement. Unexpectedly to Laurel, Grandma Arliana grabbed her cane that leaned next to her against the bed and struggled to her feet. Hobbling slowly towards Laurel, her eyes never turning from those of the young maiden, the old woman smiled apologetically and embraced her dearest friend with sincerity and love.

"I am sorry, too," she spoke up in her frail voice, "very sorry! Laurel, I do not know what I would be doing if I did not have you as my friend!"

"Me, too!" Laurel returned as the two parted and, realizing the happy tears streaming on each other's cheeks, they laughed warmly at their reconciliation.

"Look at us!" Grandma Arliana sniffled. "Arguing over such nonsense and then sniffling like a couple of ninnies!"

"Well, I guess there is no one else that I would rather spend such a morning with!" Laurel laughed with good humor.

"Same here! Now, let us forget such nonsense and return to our lunch."

"Oh, and I better go get the others!" Laurel cried as she started for the entrance to the hut, when Grandma Arliana pulled her back.

"Wait, what do you mean? Get who?"

"O, goodness! I almost forgot to tell you! Well…when I left you this morning, I ran pretty far north and found such a surprise. You see, I met Sol in the valley and—Ow!" Laurel stopped suddenly in the middle of her explanation as Grandma Arliana knocked her gently in the head with her cane.

"Sol!" the old woman cried astonishingly. "Why did you not tell me that you met Sol again? Where is he?"

Laurel groaned as she rubbed her sore head, but replied, "He is still out in the valley. He told me to carry on without him because he was looking for his friend and his horse, and—Ow!" The gentle maid stopped again as Grandma Arliana struck with her cane once more.

"He left! Well, why did you not ask him to stay for lunch?"

"I did! He said that he would be waiting outside and—" Laurel broke off as she quickly ducked her head in time before Grandma Arliana's cane could deliver a third smack to her sore head.

"Well, why did not say so in the first place?" Grandma Arliana hastily replied after administering her cane. "Now, go on and invite him in!"

Laurel could only sigh with exasperation, rubbing her aching head as she turned to leave. *Some things will never change, I suppose!* She told herself.

"And…Laurel?" the old woman called once again.

"Yes, Granny?" the young maiden returned tiresomely.

"I love you, too," Grandma Arliana smiled lovingly. A tender smile spread across Laurel's face as she received the sympathetic words of her fondest friend.

"I shall be right back," she said, leaving the room with happiness in her heart.

After a most delicious and friendly lunch, the four sat in the shade of a tall apple tree that stood behind the old hut, enjoying the fondest of each other's company. Grandma Arliana rocked softly in an aged rocking chair, which Peterel brought outside for her. Laurel, Sol, and Peterel sat together in the grass, while Philippe munched noisily on the fresh green a few feet away. They talked amongst themselves of Sol's previous travels with Peterel, whom Sol had introduced to Grandma Arliana during lunch. Peterel also mentioned his work for Sol as his personal assistant: guiding his way on his travels, helping him through dangers, and keeping records of each journey.

"All this responsibility for one boy! And so young, too!" Grandma Arliana exclaimed in amazement.

"Oh, it is not much," replied Peterel. "I have been journeying from one place to the next for all my life, so I enjoy a ramble through the country side or around the seaside now and then. Oh! By the way, Laurel, the lunch that you made was simply delicious! I truly delighted in those bread cakes with strawberry jam!"

"Yes, Laurel!" Grandma Arliana chimed in, "Your baking is getting exceptionally better!"

"Indeed, thank you again, Laurel, for such a wonderful meal!" Sol spoke up.

Laurel blushed happily from the praise of her companions. "O! You are all welcome!"

Everyone then sat back, Grandma Arliana in her rocking chair and the three acquaintances against the tree, as they all let out a deep sigh of contentment.

"So, Sol," Laurel began after a moment, "what brings you back into the Valley Fioré this time?"

"Actually, I have been meaning to discuss that with you," Sol replied, turning to Grandma Arliana. "If you would permit me to repay you for your kindness, then I would be glad to build a larger pen for your animals."

"Would you really do that?" Laurel asked in astonishment as Grandma Arliana sat speechlessly in her rocking chair.

"Oh, thank you! Of course, you may!" the old woman finally cried happily. "Thank you, and help yourself to any tools that we may have in the shed, as well."

"Well, since that is settled," Sol began as he rose to his feet, "then I shall get started on the pen right away."

Grandma Arliana happily continued to thank Sol for this kind gesture of helpfulness as Peterel looked to his master with a supporting disposition saying, "I could go with you, too, if you would like any help."

"Thank you, my friend, but I have another idea." Sol replied as he suddenly turned to Laurel asking, "Laurel? I was wondering, if you choose to, would you like to ride Philippe around the valley for a while."

Laurel caught his eye with great surprise at his asking. "Could I, really?" she inquired eagerly.

"O, yes!" Peterel exclaimed cheerily. "And I can go with you, then."

"Is this all right with you," Sol asked, looking to Grandma Arliana, who listened curiously.

"Please, Granny, may I go?" Laurel asked anxiously; both her voice and her eyes pleaded earnestly with the old woman.

"You may," Grandma Arliana replied with a chuckle, "but remember to watch the time and not to get lost."

Laurel rushed up to her and embraced her graciously. "Thank you, Granny!"

"Well, I would do anything to have some peace for a good nap right now!" the old woman cried jokingly as she patted Laurel's head.

Peterel then stood and gave a small bow to the old woman. "Thank you, madam. I promise to look after her while we are gone."

Grandma Arliana reached her hand out to him and he took it smilingly. "I know, my dear," she said with a wink. "And remember, my name is 'Granny' to you."

Peterel chuckled, "Of course, Granny."

Sol then gave a whistle to Philippe who quickly came to his side. He checked the saddle and reins to be sure that they were secure and reminded Peterel not to ride Philippe too fast. Once everything was all set, both Sol and Peterel turned to Laurel, who stood looking up at Philippe's saddle.

"You know," Laurel began slowly, "I actually never rode a horse before, so…"

Sol took her hand in his and smiled reassuringly. "Do not worry. Peterel will look after you. Just remember to hold on tightly."

Laurel smiled and allowed him to help her into the saddle behind Peterel, who had cheerily jumped in ahead. Once Peterel firmly took the reins in his hands, he circled Philippe around to Grandma Arliana and Sol.

"Well, we will see you in a little while, Granny," Laurel said to her dear friend as Peterel tipped his head towards the old woman and his master. Then, he commanded the horse into a slow walk.

"Have fun and stay together!" Grandma Arliana called, waving her wrinkly hand.

Laurel looked back and waved. "Do not worry and have a good nap!"

"Be a good horse, Philippe!" Sol called out as he waved to the two on horseback. "And do not give Laurel any trouble!"

Laurel and Peterel laughed at this as they turned their attention to the Valley Fioré stretched out before them. Then, the young boy commanded Philippe into a fast trot.

"Hold on now, Laurel," he said as he gave a loud shout to the horse, "Philippe, fly!"

Philippe neighed energetically and suddenly took off at great speed past Grandma Arliana's hut and over The Great River. Laurel felt the horse's powerful hooves beating beneath her against the soft grass of the Valley Fioré. Her hair wisped fiercely in the wind of Philippe's gallop. Peterel raced Philippe up the rolling hills, around the numerous blossoming trees, and through the sloping plains of the valley. The horse bellowed with delight at his speed, and his nostrils flared with each snort and puff that he grunted as he increased the length of his strides. True to Peterel's command, riding the mighty steed felt like taking flight across the great blue sky.

As she clung closely to Peterel from behind, Laurel's mind raced with thoughts of excitement and utter freedom. *I feel as though I am flying! This is so amazing! It is like being one of the birds in the sky…*

She laughed to herself in wondrous enjoyment as Peterel brought Philippe atop a large hill. He slowed the horse to a stop, and the two viewed the large expanse of the valley below them. The gentle breeze of the Valley Fioré blew into their faces, and they inhaled together the wind's fresh breath with tranquil enjoyment. Below them, the thin branches of scattered trees waved freely in the open air, tails of grass blades curled together in the bright sun, and a myriad of little flowers dotted the vastness of the valley. After a moment, Peterel looked back at Laurel as a large grin appeared across his face.

"How do you like riding Philippe?" he asked enthusiastically.

"O! I think that it is the most wonderful thing in the world!" Laurel sighed ineffably, "I have never experienced anything like it in my entire life."

Peterel laughed heartily, "I was hoping that you would say that!"

He then nudged Philippe into a slow trot down the hill to continue their traverse around the Valley Fioré. For a while, Laurel and Peterel were silent as they enjoyed the scenery of the rolling hills before them. As Laurel listened to the crunching of Philippe's hooves in the grass and the breeze of the wind in the leaves of a nearby tree, she felt the soft fabric of Philippe's horse blanket brushing against her legs.

"Peterel?" Laurel asked, suddenly.

"Yes?"

"I was wondering about that image on Philippe's blanket… What is it for?"

"Oh, so you noticed!" Peterel began, taking a quick look at the horse blanket. "It is a coat of arms."

"A coat of arms? What is that?"

"A coat of arms is a symbol that represent a family. In this case, the family represented is my master's family."

"So, what is the significance of the symbols in the seal? I mean, there is a sun, a heart, and the wreath."

"The sun has eight rays representing eight virtues: humility, gentleness, compassion, righteousness, mercifulness, purity, peacefulness, and strength in suffering. These are the virtues which my master's family vows to rule their lives. The wreath represents victory and loyalty. Now, the heart in the center represents the kindness and clemency in the love of my master's family. You know, love is the greatest of all the other virtues, for one cannot truly live life without compassion and sincerity. That is what Sol has taught me in his words and deeds."

As Laurel listened intently to Peterel, she was amazed of the goodness that he spoke about Sol and his family.

"Hmm..." she mused. "That is really marvelous."

Laurel's thoughts then drifted to Sol as she realized how much she wanted to know of him. However, her coyness prevented her from asking Peterel anymore about his master as they continued on their ride, talking of many different subjects, through the Valley Fioré.

Peterel and Laurel returned to the hut after spending most of the afternoon riding around the Valley Fioré. Grandma Arliana had finished her nap by then and had removed herself to her dining table inside to read from the many books from her trunk. Sol, on the other hand, was still outside in the little field behind the animal shed, planning the dimensions and position of the new pen. While Peterel took care that Philippe was brushed and groomed, Laurel visited the animals in the shed to feed them for the afternoon.

"Here you are, little ones!" Laurel called to the chickens as she scattered breadcrumbs and seeds around the clucking birds for their meal.

As for the sheep and goats, Laurel supplied each with a heap of fresh, green herbs and grasses. While she attended to this chore, the young maiden's mind filled with ponderings of her two new companions. She felt very happy that Peterel and Sol had arrived that day, especially since Sol's advice towards Grandma Arliana had helped to renew Laurel's friendship with the old woman. In addition, the happy girl was overwhelmed with the joy of having had the chance to ride Philippe. Now, she considered her surprise when Sol had asked to build a fence for the animals, since such a request was most beneficial to the lifestyle of the goats and sheep, who longed to have more room to stretch their legs. This idea must have been playing in the minds of Gudrun and her sisters at that moment, for as Laurel was leaving their pen, thoughtless of her present chores, the three mischievous kids stealthily stole out through the gate right past the young maiden.

"What in the world?" Laurel began as she realized the escapees running out of the shed. "Hey, wait! Come back here, you goats! Come back!"

The maiden's crying was to no avail, for the speedy kids paid no heed to her calls and continued their escape. Seeing this, Laurel raced out of the shed and looked around in search of Gudrun and her sisters, who were now on their way past The Great River and out into the hills of the Valley Fioré.

"Gudrun! Gudrun, come back here!" Laurel called again with frustration.

"Laurel, what is wrong?" Sol cried as he came from the field behind the shed.

"It is Gudrun! She and two of her sisters have escaped. Please, you have to help me find them!"

"Of course, where have they run off to?"

That was when Peterel came running up to them calling, "Laurel! Laurel! I saw your goats running off into the valley; though, they hurried off before I could stop them."

"We better hurry, then! Come on!" Sol started as the three rushed towards The Great River.

Suddenly, Laurel heard Grandma Arliana calling from inside the hut. "Laurel? Laurel? What is going on out there? Laurel?"

"Oh! That is Granny!" Laurel sighed anxiously, stopping in her tracks. "Peterel, do me a favor and keep Granny company. If she finds out that I accidently let the goats escape, then she will be furious! Please, just keep her busy?"

"All right, I shall see what I can do, but you both should hurry along then," the young boy replied as he hastened back to the hut.

"Thanks!" Laurel called after him as she followed Sol, who unhitched Philippe from the post, in case they needed his help to retrieve the goats.

The two and the horse swiftly made their way to the highest hill in the valley and looked out among the tall grasses and the colorful flowers for the missing goats.

"Look, there are two of them heading north!" cried Sol after quickly spotting the fugitives.

"And there is Gudrun!" Laurel pointed eastward. "She is headed towards Serenity Forest. You can go after the other two! I shall take care of Gudrun!" Laurel shouted as she hurried down the hill after the kid, while Sol galloped away atop Philippe.

"Gudrun, wait!" Laurel shouted following the naughty goat.

As the chase continued into the forest, Laurel was amazed at how fast and nimble little Gudrun ran, for the goat kept a good distance away from

Laurel, though the young maiden was running at full speed. Despite this, Laurel persevered through the brush, past tree after tree, and over countless tree roots. Laurel, though, soon began to despair as her legs began to throb with fatigue. Suddenly, Laurel came to a small clearing where crisp, green grasses and bright, sweet-scented herbs danced in the breeze of the forest winds. There, she spotted Gudrun, who happily munched on the delicious flora that was laid out like a feast before her.

Now, if I can just reach her without making a noise… Laurel planned as she tiptoed ever so carefully and slowly behind Gudrun.

Inch by inch, she made her way to the hungry kid, whose scrumptious endeavor stole all of her attention. Despite her attempts at stealth, misfortune befell Laurel as a dry stick gave way to her sandal and created the loudest crackling sound that Laurel could ever imagine hearing. The tips of Gudrun's ears drew back at this sound, and when she discovered Laurel's presence, she took off again through the clearing.

"I shall not let you escape!" Laurel cried as she mustered the last of her energy into a single leap towards the goat. Gudrun bleated and cried with distress as she realized her defeat, for the maiden fortunately caught the troublesome goat by her back legs.

"Ha-ha! Got you, Gudrun, you naughty goat!" Laurel laughed triumphantly as she pulled the guilty goat towards her. "Now, you listen here, Gudrun!" she said, holding the squirming goat tightly as she got to her knees, "I shall not have you running off whenever you please! So, be a good goat and stay in your pen next time!"

At this, the goat finally surrendered, seeing her efforts futile. She bleated apologetically and began licking at the young maiden's face, as if hoping to seek her forgiveness.

"Now, now!" Laurel giggle, trying to resist the affection. "Oh, all right, Gudrun! I forgive you! Now, let us get you home; it has been a long chase, and I am done with your silly games."

Gudrun bleated with agreement as she snuggled into the sweet maiden's arms. Laurel chuckled to herself as she rose from the grassy clearing, ready to turn back to Grandma Arliana's hut. Suddenly, Laurel heard a strange noise sound from behind: *Snort! Snort! Gruff!*

Turning curiously, Laurel was both amazed and frightened to behold the red eyes of a large, brown boar staring curtly at her from across the clearing. Without warning, the boar gave a loud, gruff cry as he charged towards Laurel. The girl cried out in fear and ran with all her might towards the first low-branched tree she spotted. Quickly, she jumped up and into the tree, climbing with Gudrun in her arms as high as she could. There was a deafening *thunk!* as the boar slammed into the tree at full speed. Shaking away the results of the impact, the boar looked up towards Laurel and ragingly slammed into the tree repeatedly. The tree shivered and trembled with each body slam of the boar, frightening Laurel with the thought of accidently falling out of the tree by such force.

"Stop that!" Laurel tried to reason with the boar. "Stop, you mean pig!"

The boar would not be reasoned with; in fact, he seemed to crash even harder into the tree at the sound of Laurel's voice. Not knowing what to do, Laurel broke off a short branch beside her and hurled it at the boar, hitting him right on his large snout. The boar shook this off for a moment, but soon he angrily commenced his attack on the tree. Displeased at the current situation, Gudrun began squirming and wriggling out of Laurel's hold.

"Quit fidgeting, Gudrun — Wait!" the fearful maiden shouted as the irritated goat leaped out of her arms and down towards the boar.

Gudrun landed squarely on the boar's back, as he finished a final charge on the tree, and jumped behind him into the grass. With his attention fixed on the little kid, the boar ran after Gudrun at full speed in anger.

"No, wait!" Laurel cried, when to her amazement, Sol appeared in the clearing, riding atop Philippe. He cut off the boar from its path, as Gudrun hid away behind a flowering bush.

The angered boar was startled at first, but swiftly he managed enough courage to advance towards Philippe, ready to mow down the noble steed. Facing the wild pig, Philippe reared up his front legs mightily, neighing and snorting in protest. The mad pig was frightened beyond his wits, and he quickly drew back from the horse, cowering in fear. Then, Sol dismounted from Philippe, and Laurel wondered what he meant to do to the pitiful boar, which squealed with fright at the young man's approach.

All of a sudden, Sol began speaking with the pig saying, "Now, now, calm yourself, little pig! I mean you no harm."

The boar obeyed Sol's request, and formerly, sat down at the young man's command. This scene perplexed Laurel, who leaned over the high branches in order to get a clearer view, wondering how and why Sol could speak to the wild boar.

"Listen here, little pig," Sol continued, "you have placed yourself in very grave trouble, what with chasing after a young maiden and her little goat out of unfounded rage! What do you mean by behaving so maliciously and shaming your own kind?"

The boar, sadden it seemed by Sol's reprimands, turned its nose to the ground and gave a mournful, shame-filled snort.

"Now, now, having a pity-party will do you no good," Sol soothed, kneeling down before the penitent pig. "Just, please, in the future, do not get so heated when someone wanders into your territory, especially young maidens. Besides, this forest belongs to everyone and every animal! Are we agreed, little pig?"

Sol chuckled as, when he petted and scratched the boar's hairy ears, the repentant pig friendly nosed the genlte man's hand. "Very good," Sol replied to this kind gesture. "Now, run along and try not to get yourself into any more trouble." With that, the wild boar scampered away, happy to have received such genuine forgiveness.

"Sol!" Laurel cried suddenly, when she saw the pig's departure.

"Are you hurt, Laurel?" Sol asked, hurrying to the tree.

"Oh, no," she called back, "but… Where is Gudrun? Is she all right?" Despite the curious child's longing to know of how Sol spoke to the pig, she was still much too perplexed to believe that the scene she had just witnessed was real.

"She is safe hiding in the brush. You can come down, now; the boar is gone and will not harm you anymore."

"Oh…right, um…" Laurel began, looking down the tree as she wondered how to make her descent. "Uh…Sol?" she continued anxiously. "I—I think I need help."

"Do not worry. I shall be right there," the young man called as he jumped up to one of the branches and began climbing towards Laurel.

"Sorry, this is my first time climbing a tree!"

"O, it is all right! I am just glad you are safe. It seems you have had many 'firsts' this day, what with meeting Peterel, riding Philippe, climbing this tree, and having a run in with that boar, no doubt!"

"Yeah…" Laurel chuckled as she watched Sol climbing up the tree. "Uh, so about that boar…um, was it me or were you, um—"

"—talking to him?" Sol interjected.

"Yes! I mean, how did you know that he would listen to you and…just how did you do it?"

Sol laughed at this as he reached the branch where Laurel awaited him. "It was something that I have found to be useful on my journeys throughout Terra. You would never know it, unless you ever tried yourself, but all living creatures are quite reasonable if you know how to speak with them. Anyway, this should come as no surprise to you, for I speak with Philippe all the time, which has never concerned you before!"

Laurel shook her head with hilarity, not knowing what to make of Sol's peculiar behavior, though she struggled to hide a small smile. "All right, Mr. Animal-Talker, how about getting me down from this tree, now?"

"Okay, for getting down this tree: just take your time and move cautiously, and face the tree as you climb down because it can be a lot easier going that way. So, first place your foot here and…" Sol then related to Laurel with each step the best course for climbing down the tree, assisting and guiding her way; the maiden was very grateful to Sol, especially once they reached the ground. As Laurel made an awkwardly graceful jump from the low branch of the tree, Sol caught her quickly to cushion her fall to the ground.

"Are you all right?" he asked, helping the young maiden to steady herself.

"Oh, yes, thank you. I—" Laurel said looking up at Sol, and she unexpectedly met his eyes.

For some reason, Laurel found that she could not speak as she stood so close to Sol with her hands resting at his chest. Looking into Sol's eyes, Laurel felt like she was melting in a warm sun, and her face blushed bright red with her heart thumping in her chest. Her thoughts began swirling with many questions: *What is wrong with me? Why do I feel... so strange? It is just...when I look at him, now, I see something mysterious, almost majestic...in his eyes...*

Despite Laurel's sudden speechlessness, Sol only gave a gentle smile as he parted from her saying, "Well, I am glad to see that you are unhurt! Come; let us return to Grandma Arliana."

"R-right..." Laurel agreed timidly as she followed Sol, who took up Philippe's reins, to the brush where Gudrun hid.

Much to their amusement, the two found little Gudrun asleep amongst the green shrubs, tired from the endeavors of her grand escape. Laurel gently took up the kid into her arms, lest the naughty goat wake up from her valued-quietness, and Sol and the modest maiden quietly made their way through the forest. Evening was drawing near as the sky was turning a dark purple, and a few cotton-balled clouds began circling overhead, which could be seen through some of the leafy canopies of the trees. Crickets and other noisy creatures were heard chirping all around. A light wind blew around the trees, causing Laurel to brush her hair from her face almost continuously.

Carrying Gudrun carefully in her arms, Laurel looked up to Sol who led the way with Philippe at his side. "Sol? Thank you again for saving Gudrun and me. I mean, I do not know what I would have done if you had not come!"

"You are welcome, Laurel, but the thanks *should* go to Philippe, for he was the one who put the boar in his place!" Sol replied, scratching behind the ear of his horse, which neighed delightfully of the praise.

Laurel laughed at this good humor saying, "No, really! Thank you! I mean, just think what would have happened if you had not come..."

"Do not dwell on it anymore," Sol said, looking back at her with a sweet smile. "I mean, you did not mean to have a wild pig chase after you, and besides, the important thing is that you are safe. You know...I would be terribly hurt if something bad had happened to you."

"Really?" she asked suddenly.

"Of course, Laurel," He replied softly, turning away to Philippe. "I...
I really care about you."

Laurel's heart pounded in her chest at Sol's reply. "Oh... I—I am so
glad," she whispered silently.

They walked on through the rest of the forest in silence again. The
loud chirping of the cicadas rubbing their legs in the high evergreens could
be heard in the trees. Tiny fireflies danced in the dim forest and the fresh
northern winds continued to blow through the trees.

Something about Sol...fills me with wonder, Laurel pondered as her head
rushed with kindhearted thoughts of the mystifying man who walked beside
her. *Since the day I met him, he has reminded me of a prince from a fairytale. He is
very amiable, intelligent, and sincere. He seems courageous and strong and...he is
handsome... Then, to top it all off, he has a way with animals, just like a fairytale
prince! I wonder if all of this is real, or am I dreaming again? Can such a fairytale
dream be true?*

Soon, as the two youths continued their walk silently through
Serenity Forest, Laurel found herself in the familiar area where her cabin
resided. The cabin, shaded by the low-growing trees, creaked and groaned
eerily in the forest winds.

"What a charming cottage!" Sol admired as he walked past the home.
"Is this where you live?"

"Well, yes..." Laurel replied anxiously, and a bit embarrassed at the
state of her dwelling, for she was uncertain if Sol would inquire further about
her parents and of where they were.

However, Sol made no other comment of the cabin, other than how
alluring it appeared to him. Laurel was relieved by this; however, for some
reason, she felt disappointed that he had not asked of her parents at all.

Suddenly, the young maiden found herself saying, "Sol, there is
something I must confess about my parents: they are not—"

"—I know," Sol spoke up quickly.

"You do?" Laurel asked surprised, wondering if he knew at all of
what she was referring.

Sol nodded. "Yes, Granny told me about them when you and Peterel
were out in the valley with Philippe. I did not mean to discover this without
your knowing, but she alluded to their departure all of a sudden, and then,
felt the need to clarify."

Laurel looked down with a vengeful glare as she muttered to herself,
"Granny! That *old* woman...!"

"Please, I never meant to upset you by discovering what happened
to your parents," Sol began, gazing sincerely at the charming girl. "In fact, I
would rather drop the subject, if my discussing it brings offence to you."

"Oh, no, not at all!" Laurel replied, amazed by Sol's propriety. "Actually, I feel a lot better now that I know that you have been acquainted with the subject. I mean, if we are to be friends, then I would very much like to discuss my family and even yours now and then…"

"Friends," Sol mused as he looked up to the stars, which now could be seen twinkling through the lush canopy. "The word is endearing to me. Whenever I hear it, songs come to mind that I have heard here and there. For two friends are very much like a song, in that they complete each other, with one being the words and the other being the music. Without the two together, they are only a verse with no melody or a tune with no voice. You know, though a person could have everything in the world from money to power, from fame to talent, from health to fortune, if they had not even one friend in the whole world to share their life with, then they would really be the poorest man alive. Laurel," Sol continued, taking the girl's hand into his, as he looked back at her, "if we are to be friends, then there is one thing that I want you to know: if you are ever in need of anything, anything at all, then you can always come to me, for I promise to always help you whenever you are in need."

"Sol… You… You know, I am a very clumsy fool," Laurel replied shyly, looking down. "I mean, I am always getting into trouble, whether it is with Grandma Arliana or…or wild boars — but if you would really like to be my friend…as I would like us to be, then you must know that I shall probably be needing your help more often than you could ever imagine!"

"If what you say is true, then, as your friend I would not want it any other way," he declared smilingly. "Besides, I believe that you are wrong to call yourself a 'clumsy fool'. I do not think that at all, Laurel; I think that you are darling! I think that you are…lovely."

Laurel started at her new friend's words as she felt her hand holding tightly onto his. *He said that he thinks I am…darling and lovely…! O, what is wrong with me? Why does my heart tremble at these words?* Laurel thought these things curiously as she and Sol continued their walk together with little Gudrun and Philippe, returning to Grandma Arliana's hut.

Since Sol had already returned the other two goats, Gudrun was the last to be replaced into the shed, when Sol and Laurel had finally returned to Grandma Arliana's hut. After, they found the old woman and Peterel sitting at the dining table with a large pile of books strewn in front of them. Grandma Arliana's face was buried deeply in a thick book, as she related in a mumbled voice the contents of its pages to Peterel, who eagerly listened to the old woman's words. Because Grandma Arliana was so mesmerized with her reading, she had not noticed that Laurel and Sol entered the hut, but she was quickly called to their presence as Peterel rose to greet his master and Laurel.

"Master! Laurel!" the young boy called cheerily from the table.

"Well, it took you long enough to find Gudrun, Laurel!" inquired Grandma Arliana.

"What!" Laurel cried in astonishment, approaching her old friend. "How did you—! Peterel, you did not—?" Suddenly, Grandma Arliana whipped out her cane and knocked Laurel squarely in the head.

"Ow!" Laurel cried, cradling her head in her hands.

"Do not think that you can hide your doings from me, Laurel. I have my ways," replied the old woman triumphantly and mysteriously. "Besides, I could hear you calling "Gudrun, wait!" from miles away!"

"Uhh! Granny!" Laurel exclaimed as she rubbed her sore head, "You did not have to smack me like that!"

"Hmm!" Grandma Arliana huffed with annoyance. "Well, that will teach you not to cover your mistakes, next time." Then, she turned to Sol, who had stood quietly during the spectacle. "Hello again, my dear!" she cried happily. "I thank you very much for helping Laurel. She is always getting into some kind of trouble here, so it is good to see someone else looking after her for a change!"

Sol cleared his throat and replied, "Well, it was the least I could do, madam."

Grandma Arliana then turned to Laurel, who was now trying to compose herself, and smiled teasingly. "So, Laurel, how far did Gudrun get this—? Goodness! What happened to your dress?"

Laurel looked down at her pale pink dress that was now blemished with several large grass stains and a small rip or two at the hem. Looking up at the old woman's surprised face, Laurel shrugged knowingly.

"Oh... I—uh, well... After I found Gudrun, I was chased by a wild pig," she sighed with a chuckle.

Suddenly, Grandma Arliana burst into laughter. She laughed so hard that her side ached with pleasure.

"You—you were chased—Ha!—by a pig!" she bellowed.

Laurel gave a halfhearted chuckle and looked from Peterel to Sol, who both seemed to be amused by the laughter of the old woman. Looking back at Grandma Arliana, who continued her laughter, Laurel began feeling a little perturbed.

"I cannot believe," Grandma Arliana laughed again, "that you were *chased* by a *pig*! Ha!"

Laurel glared down at the old woman. "Okay," she huffed, "it was not that funny! You do not have to keep laughing..."

The old woman leaned on the table with glee, but soon her laughter began to subside. She looked up at Laurel who stood with her arms folded as a mighty pout spread across her face. Grandma Arliana patted the young girl's arm gently.

"I am sorry, Laurel," she said after a moment. "It was just the thought of you getting chased —" a small squeak of laughter tried to escape from her wrinkly lips, but she quickly caught herself. "Sorry, dear! It is just that that must have been the funniest thing you have ever gotten into! Anyway, you are all right?"

Laurel sighed resignedly, "Yes, I am just fine."

"Good!" Grandma Arliana said smilingly. Then, she gave a little yawn and stretched her arms out in front of her. "Well," she continued, "I suppose that, seeing how late it is getting, we should have ourselves a good supper before it is time to retire."

Accordingly, dinner was swiftly prepared, and the four new friends enjoyed their present meal together, delighting in their companionship. As they conversed, it was discovered that Sol and Peterel, who had been given permission previously to stay in the valley in order to complete their work on the animal fence, had planned to set up camp somewhere out in the field. However, Grandma Arliana decided that the two could use the animal shed as their present shelter. Both seemed content with the thought of a roof over their heads, despite having to share that roof with the smelly animals, and they sincerely thanked the old woman for her kind contribution. Once Sol and Peterel had bid their farewells for the night, Laurel began the final chore of the day: preparing Grandma Arliana for bed. As she did so, her mind swirled with the joyful thoughts of her new friendship with Sol.

"So, Laurel..." the old woman began secretively, seeing the dreamy composure of her friend, "Sol sure is a sweetheart, is he not?"

"Yes..." Laurel sighed amiably. "He is the kindest boy I have ever met, though he and Peterel are the only ones I *have* ever encountered."

Grandma Arliana nodded as she continued, "And he seems very sincere and caring, true?"

"Yes," Laurel agreed again as she lofted a blanket onto the bed; her mind was still dreamy and dazed with thoughts of her charming friend.

"And he is your Knight in shining armor?"

"Well—Hey, wait a minute!" the maiden exclaimed, suddenly coming to her senses.

"What was that, Laurel?" The old woman asked with a teasing grin. "What was your answer, my dear?"

"Nothing! I mean... Oh, you!" Laurel cried, turning away in embarrassment; her bright face burned as red as a tomato, while Grandma Arliana gave a wheezy laugh at the sight of her friend.

"Come on," the young maiden began with an uneasy but stern voice, "let us get you ready for bed."

Chapter 5
A Hasty Departure

As promised, Sol, with Peterel's assistance, worked vigorously to construct the new fence for Grandma Arliana's animals. During the time of the build, the four companions grew more and more in their friendship with a lively and cheerful sense of fondness for one another, and perhaps as a result, Laurel found Grandma Arliana feeling more merry and sympathetic than ever before. Thus, she began to wonder if Sol really did have the ability to warm hearts as she had once thought.

Well, she reasoned to herself one day as she watched her three friends talking happily together, *Granny has shown greater patience and mercy towards my clumsiness since Sol and Peterel arrived, and she has not been her grouchy old self in a while, too!*

As the days went by, Laurel also enjoyed spending time with Sol and Peterel as the three grew in an especially tender friendship. Whenever Grandma Arliana gave her consent, which was very often if not always, the three friends planned little adventures around the Valley Fioré, practically every day. Sometimes, they would make up games to play or make-believe scenes from one of Grandma Arliana's adventure novels, occupying themselves like long-lost childhood friends. Other times, the three would find a quiet place under a tree or amidst the flowering valley grasses, where they would discuss many different subjects. During this pleasant growth of mirth and companionship, Laurel was amazed to find herself admiring Sol as her dearest friend.

After many weeks of hard labor, the new fence was finally completed, much to the happiness of Gudrun, who was eager to stretch her legs in a full sprint across this spacious play area. The new enclosure also came as a great joy to Grandma Arliana, for she appreciated the beneficial gift for her dear animals provided by the excellent workmanship of the two youths. Laurel, too, expressed her gratitude of her friend's work; however, a sudden, saddening thought arose in the maiden's mind as she wondered, now that their repayment for Grandma Arliana's hospitality had been carried out, if Sol and Peterel would soon decide to leave the Valley Fioré once more to continue their journeys. With this consideration in mind, Laurel wondered anxiously, if her two friends did agree to leave again, how long would she have to wait for their next return?

"So, Laurel, the big day is almost here, right?" Grandma Arliana chuckled cheerfully. Wearing her simple blue dress and green slippers, Grandma Arliana sat in the seat of her dining table looking up at the young maiden as she waited for her answer.

The four friends had come together again to enjoy another delicious lunch made by Laurel in Grandma Arliana's hut. The accomplished girl had made a flavorful blueberry pie with sweet glasses of apple cider, which provided a sweet fragrance of aroma that filled the hut. Once everyone had been seated for the scrumptious meal, Laurel had begun handing out the plates and utensils across the table. As she gave Sol a plate of blueberry pie, Laurel paused for a moment to ponder the old woman's question, and swaying considerably on her feet, her plain yellow dress twirled about her ankles.

"What day would that be?" Sol asked, sitting across from Grandma Arliana, as he began pulling up the sleeves of his long white shirt to eat.

"Gee, Granny," Laurel said after a moment, "I cannot remember…"

Grandma Arliana gave a playful chuckle. "Why, Laurel! I have never known a person who ever forgot their *birthday* before!"

"My… my birthday!" Laurel exclaimed, sliding down in her chair.

"Your birthday is coming up?" Peterel inquired with excitement. "When?"

"My birthday! I cannot believe that I forgot," Laurel murmured astonishingly to herself.

Grandma Arliana chuckled again, in disbelief and pleasure, while Sol even laughed heartily in joyfulness.

"When is your birthday, Laurel?" he inquired the question again.

"Oh, it is…" Laurel blushed as she tried to remember, "Oh, about four weeks! Goodness, it came so quickly this year!"

"How old are you going to be?"

"Seventeen."

Grandma Arliana sighed dreamily, "How time flies! I remember you when you were only this tall," she held her hand up a few feet above the ground, "but now… You are really growing up, Laurel."

Her eyes began to shine as if they would leak with tears at any moment. Laurel smiled bashfully, and she patted the old woman's hand with love.

"Do you have any ideas of what you want to do to celebrate?" Peterel asked as the young maiden continued handing around the scrumptious pie.

"Oh, I do not know… Nothing too big, just —"

"*Nothing too big!*" Grandma Arliana exclaimed in astonishment, wiping at her eyes. "It is your birthday, Laurel. Of course, we should do something big. I mean, you deserve it."

"Well, I —" Laurel began quietly, but Grandma Arliana quickly interposed.

"We will have a grand party, just the four of us! Oh, you shall be here, right, Sol? And you, too, Peterel?" When the two nodded, the old woman continued, "I shall make the cake…of course, you *may* have to help me with the recipe, Laurel. Then, we could find a way to decorate the hut for you. You know, one of my books may have just the perfect ideas for preparing your party. Oh! I just know that this birthday party will top all of the others for you, Laurel," And the old woman quickly got up from her seat and began rummaging through the books that she kept in the trunk under her bed.

"Yeah," Laurel began halfheartedly, as she struggled to keep a smile on her face, "that would be…wonderful…"

After lunch, Grandma Arliana wanted to stay inside to begin preparing for Laurel's birthday, for once her mind was set on an idea then there was no stopping her work in progress. So the three youthful friends decided to ride Philippe out into the Valley Fioré for the time being. After a few hours of journeying up and down the numerous sloping hills, they came across an apple tree near The Great River, where they could find rest under its peaceful shade. Laurel stretched her arms high in the air as she reposed against the trunk of the magnificent tree. Sol sat down next to her, after loosening Philippe's saddle and reins as the horse nibbled on nearby shrubbery. Peterel decided to spend his time climbing the tall apple tree, where he could view from above the large expanse of the valley. From their relaxing position beneath the apple tree's shade, Laurel and Sol delighted in breathing the fresh scent of the gentle breezes as they blew across the flora of the Valley Fioré.

Together, Sol and Laurel continued their many talks about the great wonders of this little region of Terra. Both had an interest in botanical and faunal life, and they shared their thoughts on the variety of flora and fauna that they had seen on their many walks throughout the region together.

"I think my favorite creature will always be the butterfly," Laurel continued the conversation. "Granny has some books about butterflies in her trunk, and I have always liked looking at the pictures of them. I never knew that butterflies, as well as other animals, came in so many shapes, sizes, and colors."

"What is your favorite flower?" Sol asked, examining a small wildflower in his hand.

"Oh… I really like roses. I think they smell so sweet and are so beautiful to look at, though they are very rare to find in the valley and in Serenity Forest."

"Do you have a favorite color rose?"

"Hmm… I think I like the yellow ones the best. I mean the red, pink, and white ones *are* so pretty, but I never really see many yellow roses when they bloom. I think their rarity makes them even more precious in my sight." Laurel giggled as she listened to herself talking so dreamily. She turned to Sol then and asked, "Sol, what about you? Do you have any favorites as well?"

"Well," Sol began, "I do not have a particularly favorite animal. I enjoy everything about each creature because no two species are alike. I mean, they are all special in their own way, so I cannot really say that I favor one more than another." Hearing this, Philippe looked up from a half-eaten shrub and gave an anxious neigh to his master. Sol laughed saying, "Of course, Philippe will *always* be one of my dearest companions, despite the fact that he causes me trouble from time to time."

"Yes!" Laurel said laughingly, "Especially like on the day that we first met!"

"Yes, especially then!"

"I do not think that I shall ever forget the moment when I first saw Philippe. I thought that he was the most magnificent creature in the whole world. I remember trying everything to get his attention, but all he cared for was his stomach!"

"Ha! That is Philippe for you," Sol said.

Laurel chuckled to herself as she recollected. "I remember one time when I tried calling to him by a name that I made up for him."

"Really?"

"Yes, I called him 'Mr. Horse'."

Sol chuckled warmly at this, but Laurel looked down a little awkwardly. "I know that it sounds silly," she began, "but I thought that I could get Philippe's attention. Though, it did not work at all."

"I do not think it is silly but very sweet," Sol said, taking the innocent maiden's hand, which rested on the smooth, green grass beside him. He gave Laurel a warm smile, and she smiled graciously back.

It is funny, Laurel thought. *For some reason, I do not feel so shy when I am with Sol now. Instead, I feel at peace...*

"Oh, Sol?" Laurel began again, with sudden interest. "I almost forgot to ask — what is your favorite flower?"

Sol gave a small chuckle as he answered, "Again, I enjoy them all: from daffodils to carnations and tulips to violets, from azaleas to camellias, and from geraniums to roses! For me, I think, 'Why pick one when they are all so beautiful?'"

"Oh," Laurel murmured, thinking this over. "Well, I shall always be partial to yellow roses!"

Sol chuckled again. "Good. I am glad, Laurel, because this is for you." Sol held his empty hand out before the curious child and slowly turned his palm face down. Then, he swiftly turned his hand up again revealing a beautiful yellow rose, which had instantly appeared in his hand.

Laurel gasped in disbelief, "How did you do that?"

Sol's only answer was a small wink as he placed the delicate flower into Laurel's hand. The young maiden carefully brought the yellow rose up to her face and melted in its sweet ambience.

"O, it is so beautiful, Sol! Thank you."

"I am glad that you like it, for I meant it for you and you alone. Think of it as an early birthday present," Sol said, as his eyes glistened in the rays of the afternoon sun that shined through the leafy branches of the apple tree. Laurel's heart seemed ready to leap out of her chest at this sight of Sol.

Oh no, she thought to herself, *I think that I may have been a little wrong when I thought that I could face Sol without being so...so... Oh!* Laurel held her yellow rose close to her face to hide her blushing, while Philippe, who sauntered over to his master's side, suddenly demanded Sol's playful attention. *For a long time, I have been feeling so differently with Sol, but what I am exactly feeling... I just do not know, nor do I understand. Is it only a feeling or... Oh, I do not know...but is any of this possible with Sol, even though we have only just met? Still, we have known each other for a few weeks and −*

Turning back to Laurel once Philippe's hungering for the lush valley grasses diverted his concentration yet again, Sol suddenly asked, "Laurel, I was wondering if I could ask you a question."

"Absolutely," Laurel replied, straightening herself. "What is it?"

"During lunch, when Grandma Arliana was talking about your birthday, I thought you seemed a little...reserved. I mean, you did not appear very eager to talk about preparing for your party. Is this true?"

"Well, yes. I guess so."

Sol nodded. "Would this have anything to do with your parents?"

Laurel looked away from him for a moment, for his deduction was true. Ever since the day her parents had journeyed away, Laurel had never enjoyed her birthdays very much; her mind would always swirl with thoughts of doubt against her parent's love for her, as her heart ached when the renewal of her birthday drew near each year. After realizing Sol's concern, Laurel's thoughts anxiously returned to all the memories of her parentless birthdays.

"Well... I..." she began, but she soon found her voice choking in her throat, breaking off her explanation. Despite this, the troubled maiden felt her heart pleading desperately for her to reveal all that ached her spirit, so she continued, "It is just... I really miss my parents, and my birthdays just keep reminding me that I have gone another year without seeing them or knowing where they may be. I mean... I know that Granny means well in preparing me a party, but it is sometimes too hard to go through with them each year since my parents are not here to celebrate." She chuckled uneasily as she continued, "You know, they have been gone for so long that sometimes I wonder if..."

Laurel broke off then and looked back at Sol, who sat quietly listening. "I am sorry," she began again. "This is probably something that you are not interested in hearing."

"Not so," he said, taking hold of Laurel's hand again. "You know that if there is anything you need, whether it is someone to talk to or someone to give you advice or someone to build you a pen for your goats, then you can always rely on me. No matter what, Laurel, if you need someone to talk to, then I shall be here to listen." Sol's bright smile, which shined like a thousand warm suns, seemed to melt away the turbulence of Laurel's heart as the shy maiden returned the gesture, looking down at her hand within Sol's own.

"You know what, Sol?" Laurel began with a shy, amused voice as she twirled her yellow rose between her fingers.

"What is that, Laurel?"

"If had known any better, then I would think that you were a prince."

"A prince?" Sol asked, entertained.

"Or a king, whichever you prefer!" the maiden giggled.

"And why would you think of me as someone as imperial as a king?" the young man laughed cheerily.

"Well... I do not know. I mean, there is something about you that seems more than you disclose, but in a good way. Something about you seems...royal!"

Sol laughed again with good humor, and Laurel delighted that her little fantasies had interested Sol's amusement. "A king..." Sol pondered after a short moment of reflection. Suddenly, the mystifying man turned to Laurel with a serious countenance as he relayed, "I confess, Laurel, that what you have discerned is true. I, in fact, am Sol, king of the *ants*!"

The humored maiden giggled at this saying, "Now, that is too silly! Besides, I think king of the *pigs* would suit you better, if I remember correctly that you *reason* with boars!"

"Indeed, I believe you are right, Laurel!" Sol chuckled.

The two laughed at this hilarity, humored by their childlike bantering, as a wave of breezes billowed across the valley and past their faces.

"Sol?" Laurel started, after a moment of silence, "I really do appreciate what you said before about being there for me. I mean, with my parents...gone and all, and having no other companion than Grandma Arliana, with all her fluctuating moods, it is...wonderful...to know that there is someone like you in my life right now. You know, as I said about my parents, sometimes I wonder a lot about...what they think about me, if they think of me at all and..."

"You know, Laurel," her gentle friend interposed carefully, "sometimes it is difficult to discern between reality and that which is uncertain, but still we must try to believe and have faith in order to understand the truth."

The girl pondered with interest Sol's words, and she asked with great curiosity, "Sol, what is faith?"

"Faith? Faith is the confident belief in the truth. It means that, despite whether or not we have a material 'proof', we believe in the absolute truth no matter our uncertainty, our fears, or our despair in what lies ahead. We have faith in all that is good."

"Well, I guess I do not have much faith in anything, then!" Laurel replied resignedly. "I have never been one to pass a day without uncertainty about...well, everything, especially towards myself. I mean, I—I always get so anxious about my clumsy disposition and my habit for either making a mess of something or getting into trouble, as you must be *well* aware of by now! I know that it is a bad habit to be scrupulous, but I just really do not like to make mistakes, even though I usually make a lot of them. And for some reason, I cannot help worrying about everything I do and—"

"Laurel?" Sol spoke up again with a soft, sincere voice. Laurel, who realized her rambling stopped to look up and meet Sol's eyes, the two watched each other tenderly for a long moment before Sol continued, "Laurel, I think you are truly a wonderful girl. I can see how deeply is your compassion in the way that you tend to Grandma Arliana, even though you both become frustrated with each other from time to time. I see that you are always trying to do your very best and being as loving and kind as you can. I admire that in you, Laurel. However, I wish that you were not so hard on yourself. It is one thing to be aware of our faults in order to mend our transgressions, but it is another to weigh scruples on oneself over innocent misgivings. Laurel, my dear, you *are* a very good person, and that is the truth!"

"Truth..." Laurel murmured bashfully as she pondered Sol's words. His eyes, as they watched her, were bright from the sun's dancing rays. *What is truth...?* Laurel questioned herself as her thoughts trailed away with ponderings and wonderments of Sol.

Looking away smilingly, Sol abruptly rose to his feet saying, "I think it is getting late, Laurel. We should be heading back to Grandma Arliana's hut, now. Do you agree?"

"Oh...yes. Of course!" Laurel's consciousness returned to the present.

"Now, where has Peterel wondered off? I hope not too high into the branches!" Sol chuckled to himself as he helped the young maiden to her feet. "Peterel!" he called loudly, looking up into the tree from which the two had sat under. "It is time to go, Peterel! Where have you gone to this time?"

"Up here, Master!" Peterel called, sounding as if in the very sky.

Sol and the maiden looked up towards the canopy of the flowering tree but could not detect the boy from where they stood.

"Do you think he is all right?" Laurel asked concernedly, following Sol as he backed away from the tree, searching concernedly for his friend.

"Look, there he is!" Sol said, pointing up to the highest branch, where Peterel sat, as he looked northward and into the horizon.

"Peterel, what are you doing up so high? You should come down before you fall!" Laurel cried anxiously.

"No, he is fine, Laurel," Sol chuckled with amusement. Then, he cupped his hands over his mouth, shouting, "So, Peterel! Tell us, what do you see...?"

Sol stopped abruptly as he observed the far-off expression on Peterel's face, and for a long time he and the young boy were silent, as if pondering some deep intuition, as they looked from one to the other and towards the northern horizon. Later, Laurel did not question Sol or Peterel of their strange behavior, and they too were silent on the subject, during the return journey to Grandma Arliana's hut. However, the questioning girl could not help wondering about the cause for the serious and reflective air that seemed to grow tensely between the two friends.

That evening, when dinner had been prepared, Laurel went to retrieve Sol and Peterel from the animal shed, where they had departed to after finishing the chores of the day. Just before she ventured to knock on the weathered wood of the shed, the young maiden heard the soft murmuring of her two friends from inside, and due to her inquisitive nature but against her better judgment, she listened attentively to their conversation from outside.

"What do you propose that we do?" she heard Peterel ask earnestly. "You know that sooner or later the others will be more involved than ever."

"They are involved anyway, as we all are," Sol replied meditatively.

"Yes...but *they* are coming to the valley, and I observed one of their scouts from atop the tree today. Master, they could be here any day now."

They...who is they? Laurel wondered as she strained to hear, her curiosity growing with every second that passed. *And involved in what? What does Peterel mean...?*

Sol sighed considerately, and there was a long pause, which agonized Laurel. Finally, Sol spoke up, "Then, there is only one thing we can do..."

There was another pause before Peterel continued, "When are we going to tell them?"

"Tonight. After dinner. Agreed?"

What does Sol mean...? What is going on? Laurel pondered confusedly. Suddenly, she realized the injustice of her eavesdropping and quickly knocked on the shed, lest she hear any more of the conversation.

Sol swiftly opened the door, "Oh, Laurel, is dinner ready?"

"Uh—yes. Granny is waiting for us, now," the discomforted maiden replied, ashamed of her wrongful curiosity. "I, uh, cooked some fish and prepared a little fruit."

"Did you hear that, Peterel?" Sol happily asked the boy as the three walked back to the hut. "Laurel has prepared a feast for us!"

"Yum! Sounds delicious!" Peterel licked his lips with hunger.

The maiden laughed at this jovial chatter, and she continued through dinner in the liveliest of spirits with her companions. She decided to disregard the private discussion that she had heard between Sol and Peterel, as she was too perplexed by its indefinite meaning to consider it further. However, throughout dinner, she kept a close eye on Sol, who retained his charismatic, spirited personality as if nothing was amiss, and Laurel reflected intently on how the young man mentioned that he had something to reveal after dinner.

I wonder what he means to tell us. That was a strange conversation... Laurel thought as she finished off the last morsels of her fish.

"Excuse me," Sol began, rising from his chair, once everyone had completed their meal. "There is something important that I must tell you."

"Yes, my dear?" Grandma Arliana asked energetically, having enjoyed the delightful evening. Laurel, however, became instantly concerned, for she was uncertain of what Sol had in mind to say.

"First, I wish to thank you both for your hospitality, which you have given to Peterel and me during our stay with you. We are both truly grateful for your kindness and sincerity in caring for us."

"Hmm, you are welcome!" Grandma Arliana interjected admiringly. "Still, Laurel and I should also be thanking you both, as well, for if you had not returned to us, Sol, then we never would have had the lovely pen which you have built for our animals. Indeed, we are most grateful for your help in all that you have done for us!"

Sol smiled gratifyingly. "Thank you. I made you both the promise that I would return to repay you for your kindness towards me, and I have returned and accomplish this. Now...now, I believe that it is time for Peterel and I to leave."

Grandma Arliana's smiling expression instantly dropped from her face in utter disbelief, and Laurel's heart was caught up in a whirlpool of despair as her worst fears were realized.

"Leave?" Grandma Arliana exclaimed sadly, "What do you mean leave?"

"It is time for us to continue on our journey as we had planned," Peterel spoke up, after having quietly observing the scene from his seat. "We only meant to stay with you all for as long as it took to build the fence."

"We never intended to stay longer than was necessary," Sol continued, "and now it is imperative that we renew our journey in the South as soon as possible."

The old woman and Laurel were silent for a long moment as they tried to accept all that Sol and Peterel had revealed to them.

"When are you planning to leave?" Laurel asked as she looked up into Sol's eyes, hoping that she did not already know the answer.

"Tonight," he replied solemnly, watching her face for the slightest change in expression.

"Tonight!" Grandma Arliana sighed with grave expression. She sighed again despairingly, as if trying to make sense of her own feelings and reality. "I know that if you both are serious with your decision, then there is nothing that I can say to make you both reconsider, but... Is your decision final?"

"Yes," Sol replied. "I know it is sudden...but it would be for the best if Peterel and I were on our way tonight."

The young man seemed to want to say more, but no words formed from his mouth. The four friends were again silent, lost in thought, and going over every emotion that invaded their hearts.

"I guess...we should get to our packing, right, master?" Peterel asked, slowly getting up from his seat.

When Sol nodded, Grandma Arliana also rose from her seat. "Laurel and I shall prepare you something for your breakfast tomorrow."

"Thank you," their friend replied. He made a final look towards Laurel, who dazedly followed the old woman's quick movements, and suddenly caught her eye for a few seconds. Then, Sol and Peterel exited the hut, and all was quiet that night as the four prepared for their cheerless farewell.

Every heart was weighed with the thought of the departure, even Philippe seemed sad during this solemn occasion, whose head hung low with a sense of sorrow. Still, all gave their very warmest smiles, embraces, and words of future health and happiness. Grandma Arliana made sure to give Sol and Peterel each a small kiss on the head and reminded them repeatedly to watch over one another. Laurel, on the other hand, was a little distant, for her head was still in a daze, as she realized more and more that her friends' departure was not a dream. Sadly, she felt deep within her heart that Sol and Peterel would not return, if they ever will, for a very long time it seemed. However, when the time for departure drew near, the girl finally found the courage to ask Grandma Arliana of a very special desire.

"Granny," Laurel began timidly, "may I see Sol and Peterel off into the valley?"

The old woman smiled softly, her tearing eyes shining from the risen evening moon. "Certainly, Laurel, but do not go out too far from the sight of the hut," Grandma Arliana replied, pointing out into the sloping valley. "Sol, Peterel, you take care of yourselves, now. Understand?"

"Yes, madam, we will," Peterel answered as he took hold of Philippe's reins for his master.

"Thank you," Sol replied, smilingly to the old woman. "Since you shall see us off," he turned to Laurel, "we will walk with Philippe until we part."

Laurel nodded, and she followed her two friends and the horse over The Great River as they waved back to Grandma Arliana.

"Be safe!" the old woman called tearfully after them as she leaned back on her cane and watched the three make their way through the Valley Fioré.

The three friends and Philippe waded through the tall, swaying grasses, climbing over the many sloping hills and enjoying the beauty of the Valley Fioré in the twilight. The nearby trees swayed in the northern breezes, and small, nocturnal birds could be heard calling from their nests in the leafy branches. Scurrying mice ran to their nests in the dark grasses, and small moths flitted around the cool, nightly air. The dark shrubbery around the hills shook and quivered as small herds of rabbits and coveys of quail hurried to their homes. Soon, the three stood at the top of one hill for a long moment as a gentle breeze blew into their faces. They breathed in the winds pleasant aroma, which refreshed and enlivened their spirits. Laurel looked behind her to see where Grandma Arliana's hut stood.

"I think this is as far as I should go," she related sadly, as she turned to Peterel and Sol, who watched her with solemn expressions.

Before Laurel could continue, wanting to relate her sadness at the thought of their leaving, Peterel quickly ran up to her side and embraced her longingly. Though they did not say a word, it took every ounce of strength in the innocent child's heart to prevent her tears from overflowing. "I shall miss you, Peterel!" she whispered tenderly, holding him sorrowfully in her embrace.

When they released each other, Peterel wiped his nose gently and looked up into the young maiden's face. His wise eyes sparkled in the twilight as he gave a parting smile, filled with hope and wisdom, to his dear friend. Then, Laurel caught Sol's warm, shining eyes, and the two watched each other for a long moment, as if words would only ruin the great bond that they now felt between them.

Still, Laurel spoke up cheerlessly, "Well...I guess this is goodbye." She held out her hand for Sol, which was all she could think of to do.

Suddenly, Sol took both of her hands into his and held them close to his heart. "Laurel," he said softly, his eyes meeting hers with tenderness. "I tell you, this is not goodbye. One day, we shall see each other again. I promise."

Laurel's face reddened, and her whole body stiffened with bashfulness at these words and even more so when Sol brought her hands up to his lips and innocently kissed them. He looked into her eyes again with a loving smile.

"I guess...we better be off now," he said after a moment, and he released Laurel's hands, which slowly dropped to her side.

The sad maiden watched, as if dreaming, as Sol and Peterel climbed onto Philippe, and Sol took up the reins, ready to depart.

"I wish you safety," she said amiably, trying to restrain her sadness. "And...I hope we really do...see each other again."

"Be assured," Peterel started, "we will come for your birthday, just as we said."

Laurel smiled happily at this, and the weight of her heart seemed to ease at that moment.

"Laurel?" Sol asked earnestly. "Do you still have the rose that I gave you today?"

"Oh? I, uh..." Laurel looked down at her dress for a moment as she pondered in silent distress, *Where did I put his rose? Have I lost it?*

"Here," Sol said, holding out the lost, yellow rose, which had mysteriously appeared in his hand.

Laurel stared at the precious rose bewilderingly, before gently grasping it in her hand.

"I gave it for you, Laurel, so please promise me that you shall keep it always."

"Yes...I shall," Laurel replied, looking up into Sol's bright eyes.

Sol sighed peacefully, "Good."

Laurel hid her sullen face as she backed away from Philippe, for the time was too late to continue any more farewells. After saying goodnight, Sol gave a strong command to the horse, and Philippe began to trot down the hill southward. Peterel and his master looked back to wave, and Laurel returned the gesture, her heart swelling with sweet sorrow. She watched her two dearest friends, until they were nearing the far horizon of the valley and the darkness of the night had swallowed all that the girl could perceive of their existence. As Laurel lowered her hand, her heart too fell into deep misery as copious tears streamed from her moonlit eyes.

What is this heaviness in me? Laurel questioned as she turned back for Grandma Arliana's hut. *It is as if my heart is drowning.* She suddenly found herself rubbing her hands where Sol had kissed them. *What is this aching that torments me…when I think of Sol?*

Chapter 6
Deception

The next morning was filled with silence and sorrow for Grandma Arliana and Laurel, as their hearts regretted the departure of Sol and Peterel from the Valley Fioré. Breakfast felt dreary and monotonous as the two prepared their meal with little warmth or care. When they sat down to eat, Grandma Arliana and Laurel were not at all surprised to find themselves without hunger, so the two sat gloomily for a long moment looking into their cheerless meal.

"Oh! This will just not do!" Grandma Arliana suddenly cried as she knocked her hand against the table. "Laurel, we cannot go on with this miserable business of moping all day! We are going to have to get on with our lives just as we did the last time Sol left."

"Yes, but then he had not stayed with us for as long as he did this time, and Peterel was not with him, too," Laurel moped depressingly.

"Looks like you really made some friends, huh, Laurel?" Grandma Arliana asked as she studied the sad expression of her friend.

Laurel sighed sadly. Her mind seemed to be drifting between thoughts as she replied, "Yeah...I guess so..."

"Well, I am happy for you, Laurel, but remember what you told me! Sol said that he would come to see us again, so until then, let us go on with our lives."

"Yeah...well," Laurel sighed again, "I wonder if he really meant it."

"Laurel! You said that Sol was your friend, and friends believe in each other, just like you believe in me!"

"So?"

"*So* do you believe in Sol?"

Before the young maiden could answer, the two heard a strange rumbling that sounded almost like thunder. They instantly stood up and listened attentively as the rumbling sounded closer and closer near the hut.

"Do you think a storm is coming?" Laurel asked concernedly.

"No...no, I do not think it is that," Grandma Arliana murmured as she listened to the strange rumbling. Then, without a word, the old woman quickly grabbed her cane and hastened to the door of the hut.

"Granny?" Laurel called as she followed the old woman outside.

To their astonishment, they saw in the midst of the valley a large dust cloud stirred up from the galloping of five gray steeds carrying five burly equestrians. They wore thick, black armor that shined in the sunlight and large, black boots and gloves. Their gleaming helmets covered most of their head, except for their faces, which were shady, solemn, and foreboding. They must have noticed Grandma Arliana's hut, for the five turned their steeds towards The Great River, where Grandma Arliana and Laurel stood.

"Laurel," the old woman began gravely, "get inside the hut."

"Why? — what is going on?"

"Do not ask questions. Do as I tell you!" Grandma Arliana spoke severely, and Laurel, a little started by her friend's threatening tone, quickly returned to the hut. However, she stayed close to the entrance where she could peer through the curtain for a clear view of all that would happen.

Swiftly, the band of equestrians arrived at the hut, their muscular horses snorting with energy. "Good day, ma'am!" greeted one of the men from atop his steed.

"What is it you want?" Grandma Arliana replied seriously.

"This is a quaint dwelling you have here," continued the man, ignoring the old woman as he scanned the little field where her hut stood. "A little out of place in such a remote part of Terra, do you agree?"

"What do you want?" Grandma Arliana repeated, her cane tightening in her wrinkly hand.

"All right then, I shall not beat around the bush," the man replied flatly, shifting within his saddle. "We are rangers, skip tracers, bounty hunters, whichever you prefer. At any rate, we are searching for a criminal who has escaped our sight since a few weeks ago."

"A criminal? If that is what you are after, then be on your way! This is a respectable home where the likes of criminals are not welcomed, nor the likes of you bounty hunters. So be off!"

"Ah! We cannot be too sure of that!" the man said as he pulled a folded parchment from his pocket. "Have you seen this man before?" he asked, unfolding a wanted poster.

From the entrance of the hut, Laurel watched in astonishment as she stared into the bright eyes of Sol, whose face was drawn in charcoal on the parchment. *Sol? That face is Sol!* her mind cried with distress.

Grandma Arliana only looked at the poster for a few seconds before turning her gaze to the dark eyes of the hunter. "No," she said expressionlessly. "No, I have not."

"Take a longer look, grandma. This man is wanted on multiple accounts for identity fraud, espionage, sedition, treason, and disturbing the peace. He is wanted dead or alive and is not to be trusted. *Have you seen him?*" the hunter stressed these last words, as if trying in some way to pressure an answer out of the old woman.

Furiously, Grandma Arliana stared up at the man saying, "No, I have not! Now, that you have your answer, be on your way!"

"Come on, commander!" started one of the men. "This old hag is too senile to know anything."

"You are right," the commander replied with a harsh laugh. "Besides, who would want to hide away with this witch?" Suddenly, the hunter noticed Laurel standing in the doorway of the hut. "Hey, girl? Have you seen this man?" he asked, holding up Sol's wanted poster.

Before the astonished maiden could answer, Grandma Arliana spoke up, "She cannot answer you. She is deaf and mute."

The commander laughed spitefully, "What a funhouse this place is! Come on, boys, we have a criminal to catch and hang!" The man tipped his head towards Grandma Arliana and Laurel with a final piece of advice, "Well, keep your eyes open, ugly crows!"

As swiftly as they came, the five equestrians galloped away past The Great River and headed south into the Valley Fioré. Grandma Arliana watched them until their little dust cloud had disappeared into the horizon. Then, she quickly passed Laurel, entering the hut. The maiden watched her bewilderingly, as the old woman wearily sat down with a sigh.

"Granny?" Laurel began after a moment, her mind hazed with confusion. "What...what..." Her voice trailed off suddenly, not knowing what to say.

"Do not believe a word they say, Laurel," the old woman spoke up gravely. "Nothing they say is true. I know it... It just cannot be true."

"But, Granny!" Laurel cried in anguish. "They...said that Sol —"

"I know what they said!" Grandma Arliana spoke up furiously, "But I do not believe it."

"How can you not! Those men...they said that they were looking for a criminal, and the man on the wanted poster was Sol! Sol!"

"I know..." the old woman replied, her voice quieting to a whisper.

Laurel paced the floor in distress as the reality of this knowledge pierced her heart.

"There must be an explanation for this," Grandma Arliana began after a while. "Maybe, there is more to this than —"

"O, come on, Granny!" Laurel cried painfully. "Admit it. Sol has lied to us! He used us to find a place where he could hide from those men!"

"We do not know that for certain, Laurel!" the old woman cried alarmingly.

"No! It is true! I know it is..." Laurel sighed as she fell sorrowfully into a nearby chair. "I...I heard them before they left..." She stopped as tears flowed down her cheeks and her throat seemed brunt with fire.

"Heard what?" Grandma Arliana asked, turning towards Laurel. "From whom?"

"Sol and Peterel," the distressed girl sniffled. "Before they left last night, before they made know to us of their departure, I heard them talking about a 'they' who were coming to the valley, and that 'they' would be coming soon. Sol said that he and Peterel had to get away in case we got involved. *Involved*!" Laurel turned her face downward and cried into her hands.

"This…this must be a misunderstanding, Laurel." Grandma Arliana said, coming closer to her friend.

"No! It is true!" Laurel cried again, before looking up at the old woman. "And you…you lied to those men! Why? When you saw Sol's face on that poster?"

The old woman's expression turned grave again and her voice was stern as she replied, "Even if you had told me all of this sooner, I still would have lied. I do not know why, but something in me, deep in my bones, wants to believe in Sol."

"Well, I do not believe," Laurel grimly declared as she rose from her seat. "I do not believe in him…and I never will!"

Abruptly, the young maiden fled with all her might from Grandma Arliana's sight and out of the hut. However, she did not get very far at all, for she stopped at The Great River outside the field of the hut and looked out into the Valley Fioré. All around the weeping child there were grasses and hills and flowers and sky, but no one to turn to, no one to seek, no one to find. For once in a long while, Laurel felt totally alone, and this knowledge burdened her heart with a torment of grief. Not knowing where to go, Laurel found herself following the flow of the river past Grandma Arliana's hut.

O, how could he have lied to us, she thought despairingly. *How could both of them…even little Peterel. What is going on? Why are these things happening?*

Then, Laurel placed her hand against her side and felt the soft petals of her rose peeking from her dress pocket. She had placed the rose there for safe keeping early that morning, not wanting to lose sight of it. Now, she gently took it from her pocket and for a moment admired its mysterious fragrance and unwrinkled appearance. Suddenly, her heart was filled again with despondency as her mind wandered to her many memories and joy-filled days with Sol.

He spoke of faith…and truth. I gave out my heart to him whenever I needed someone to listen to me. I… I thought that I had found a friend in him…someone who would understand me. I really…liked him, too…

As warm, frustrated tears streamed down from Laurel's eyes, she wiped them away in anger, as she voiced aloud, "No! There will be none of that! Whatever is the truth and whatever is false, this is all too much for me."

The young maiden peered into the splashing river that flowed beside her and observed the dejected eyes and sorrowful face that reflected back at her. Then, she gave a hesitant look at her rose before tossing it into The Great River, and she watched as it slowly flowed with the crystal, blue waters away and down through the Valley Fioré.

What kind of life do I have? Laurel questioned bitterly as she walked back to the hut. *Where am I going? What am I doing? Where do I belong?*

That day she would wander through the valley and the forest, trying with all her might and heart to forget those happy times of joy when Sol and

Peterel had delighted in her companionship. Despite her endeavors, when she would return home, Laurel would step into her dark cabin and close the door behind her, locking away the memories of Sol. She would turn the knob of the oil lamp that hung by the door, and a dim wave of light would shine throughout the cabin, revealing the emptiness of her life. The air would be still and silent, except for the creaking of the cabin as the wind blew against the roof. Laurel would lean back against the door and sigh deeply, her mind in torment from this day's misgivings. After a final effort to forget all of her troubling memories, one word would unwittingly rest on her tired lips.

"Sol…"

Chapter 7
Tempters

Shivering under a tattered quilt, Laurel stirred the embers of her cabin's stone hearth, trying desperately to warm herself. The icy winds of Serenity Forest thrashed against the cabin's roof, and Laurel wondered if her home would outlast the harshness of Terra's deadly winters. She sighed with frustration as the small twigs that cooked slowly in the fireplace refused to keep the flames alive.

"Laurel," came a soft voice behind her, "do not trouble yourself over that fire. There is nothing that we can do now except wait until Poppa comes home with the logs."

"But, mother!" Laurel whined, looking over at the short woman who sat reading a book in a nearby rocking chair. "Poppa is taking forever, and I am *cold!*"

"Now, now!" her mother exclaimed, looking up from her book with great disapproval. The woman's brown eyes shimmered in the light of a small candle that sat beside her on the wooden dining table. She wore a long purple dress and a dark shawl with black moccasins. Her long brown hair was tied back in a bun, revealing her tanned, middle-aged face. "Laurel, come here and sit with me as we wait for Poppa. I do not want to see you moping by that fireplace any longer! Besides, it would do you good to learn some patience."

"Oh… Fine!" Laurel exclaimed resignedly. She replaced the black stoker on a large metal rack that hung by the hearth and, as she wrapped her quilt tightly around her long green nightgown, shuffled across the room in her white slippers to sit at the dining table beside her mother. Laurel's mother contentedly resumed her reading, while the young maiden listened to the wind's ghostly howling.

Gee… I hope Poppa is all right, Laurel thought anxiously. *That wind is so nasty… I hope Poppa makes it home safely.*

Laurel started suddenly as the large cabin door was thrown open, slamming against the cabin wall. An icy wind blew in a cloud of flurrying snow as a large man carrying a load of newly chopped logs stood in the door. He was very tall and burly, for his stature seemed built for hard labor. He wore a long brown cloak around his dark blue coat, as well as black working pants and snow boots. The man's face was covered with a thick salt-and-pepper beard that curled around his chin, and his blue eyes glistened on his weather-beaten expression.

"Poppa!" Laurel called in surprise as she quickly rushed to help her father into the cabin, while her mother struggled to close the door against the unforgiving winds.

Together, the three pushed the door back with all of their strength and locked it securely. Then, the family brought the load of firewood to the hearth where it was placed in a wooden box. From a holster strapped against his back, Laurel's father removed a heavy ax and placed it against the wall of the cabin.

"Whew!" the man sighed heavily as he removed his worn winter gloves. "What a tempest! You do not know how *good* it feels to be back in such a warm cabin."

"Say that a little louder," Laurel's mother began teasingly. "I do not know if *Laurel* heard you!"

"Aw, mother!" Laurel cried embarrassingly as she began tossing a few logs into the fire. "Do not bring that up... I did not mean to be so impatient. I was just really cold and—"

Laurel's father laughed in his deep, booming voice, "Well, Laurel, now you have your fire, so you shall not have to complain any longer about the winter."

"At least until we run out of logs again," the child's mother muttered to herself, and the two chuckled to themselves, despite Laurel's huffy pout glaring at them.

"Ah, come now, Laurel!" Her father replied, seeing the annoyed maiden's expression. "We were only teasing... Now, come give your Poppa a big hug!" He then rushed to the young girl in an attempt to catch her in his mighty embrace.

"No, Poppa!" Laurel playfully cried as she ducked under the large man's bulky arms and dashed around the room. Though the girl was swift in her speedy escape, the jolly man quickly caught her in his arms and cradled her like an infant. The two laughed joyfully together as Laurel's mother looked on merrily. Being held there in her father's warm embrace, Laurel felt an odd object poking out from his coat.

"Poppa, what is this?" Laurel asked feeling the object that rested at his chest.

"Oh! I almost forgot!" He said as he released Laurel from his hold and retrieved the questioning object. Laurel's father produced then a long golden chain of a series of bright, crystal beads that shined in a spectral of colors when exposed to the firelight. The chain had two sets of beads and two gold pendants. The first set of beads was the smallest in length and was attached to the first pendant, which was in the shape of a sun. The second set of beads was a larger series and was connected at both of ends to the second pendant, making a necklace-like appearance. The second pendant was round in shape and showed one engraving of a man's portrait on one side and an engraving of a woman's portrait on the other.

Laurel's father held the beaded chain in front of the young girl's face. "I found this while I was getting the logs. 'What a very peculiar object,' I had thought, when I found it lying in the snow. I was wondering who could have lost such a precious chain, but when I looked around, there was no one in sight nor were there any footprints indicating anyone but myself in the woods. I wonder what it was doing there…"

Laurel stared astonishingly at the chain as she noted the first pendant, which was an eight-pointed sun with a large, red heart wreathed with laurels engraved at its center. Her mother then came up behind the two to observe the mysterious ornament. "Oh, yes, it is very peculiar but also very stunning. What a strange find this is! Do you suppose that — ?"

"I have seen this image before," Laurel interrupted as she took hold of the striking ornament, staring at the first pendant.

Her mother chuckled in amusement, "What do you mean by that, Laurel? How could you have seen this before?"

"Believe me. The image of this chain is very familiar to me! I am certain…"

"Well, where have you seen it before, my dear?" her father asked with interest.

Laurel paused thoughtfully for a moment, but she found, to her dismay, that she could not remember. "I…I do not know."

"Hmm… Are you sure this chain is familiar to you? Maybe you just imagined it."

"Oh, yes!" Laurel's mother exclaimed with a small chuckle. "Yes! That is it. Laurel must have imagined it. Oh, you know how creative your imagination is, Laurel. You probably thought that you saw it before from some dream or from an image in a cloud formation or — "

"No! I am telling you the truth. I have seen this symbol before! It is just… I cannot remember from where." Laurel then sat down in a nearby chair in deep despair as she clutched the chain to her chest. She knew that this symbol was very important to her, but neither her mind nor her heart could explain why. Noticing her eyes beginning to shimmer with tears, Laurel's father sat in a chair next to the girl and placed a gentle hand on her shoulder.

"Now, now! No need for tears, Laurel! If what you say is true and if you have seen this chain before, then I am sure that you have not completely forgotten where it came from. Now, let us see if we can bring back your memory, so start by relating to me anything you can recollect."

"Well," Laurel sniffled as she looked down at the golden chain in her hands, "these symbols… they represent something, and they belong to…to…a family — "

"What family is that? We are the only people who live in this part of Serenity Forest, so it cannot belong to our family."

"Well… it was not any ordinary family. It was…a…" Laurel fingered the engraved symbol of the glorious pendant as she tried to remember. "I… I think that it belonged to a prince's family."

"Ha!" Laurel's mother chuckled to herself. "A royal family! What an imagination."

Laurel looked up indignantly at the laughing woman. "I am serious, mother! He...seemed...almost like a prince..."

"All right, Laurel," her father assured her. "I believe you. Now, do you know why someone would be roaming Serenity Forest in the dead of winter?"

"Well," Laurel paused again to think, and soon she could recall small details related to the mysterious pendant. "There was...um... He... He was looking for his horse, and..."

"Who was looking for a horse?"

"Um...The prince who can talk to animals."

Suddenly, Laurel heard her mother's voice ring with shrill laughter. "Ha! A prince who talks to animals? What will be next?"

"Mother! Stop laughing! I am serious! Anyway... I said that he *seemed* to be a prince, or at least that was what I thought... He came looking for his horse at a tree in the Valley Fioré, and I found the horse for him...and...his friend told me about this image on the horse blanket."

Laurel's mother did not hear the pleading maiden, for her laughter chimed loudly in her ears as she held her stomach with hilarity. Laurel turned to her father whose face expressed a look of disbelief. "Poppa, please believe me! I am really telling the truth. Look, I remember that this symbol represents the qualities of the family. Like the sun represent eight virtues and the heart shows compassion and mercy and —"

"What is his name?" Laurel's father asked suddenly.

The young maiden looked up slowly with surprise. "What do you mean?"

"The prince," her father replied. "Can you remember his name?"

"His name..." Laurel sat in a daze as she tried to recollect her memories. "His name... His name..." Her thoughts were interrupted, as her mother's boisterous laughter seemed to flood her mind. Tears then began to roll down the maiden's cheeks.

"I... I cannot remember his name!" Laurel cried, squeezing the chain closely to her chest as she reviewed the scattered memories of her mind. However, all seemed hopeless as the young man's name could not be recalled.

"Laurel? I am sure it is all right," her father began as he wiped the maiden's tears from her face.

"No! It is not! I must remember his name. I must! O, why can I not remember?" The despair-filled maiden cried. She suddenly turned towards her mother, who continued her shrill laughter, and the noisy mirth began to ring distastefully in Laurel's ears. "Will you be...quiet!" Laurel shouted at the top of her lungs with great fury and irritation.

She stood up quickly to face her mother, and the wooden chair was knocked down in her anger. "Stop laughing at me! I told you I am telling the truth, and I shall not have you making fun of me!" Laurel's mother stopped her cackling abruptly, and she watched the girl in astonishment. Laurel's father was also silent, surprised by the offensive tone in Laurel's voice.

Suddenly, a concerned expression appeared on her mother's face, and she approached Laurel slowly. "Laurel... Do you feel all right? I mean, you look a little pale."

"Yes, I see what you mean," Laurel's father spoke up. "Laurel, you do look a little sick."

"What are you talking about? Of course, I am fine. Now, let me try to remember the name—"

"Laurel, maybe you need to lie down," her mother began again as she placed a hand to Laurel's cheek. "You look as though you have a fever."

Laurel suddenly felt hot, all of a sudden, and a trickle of sweat began flowing down from her forehead. Despite this, she held her ground, "I am not sick! Really, you must trust me. I—"

"Maybe, that is what this is all about!" interrupted her mother, "Maybe, your fever has caused all of this nonsense about that chain and that image?"

"No! No, forget the fever! I must remember his name," Laurel said as she turned away from her parents' concerned faces. Suddenly, a strange feeling overcame Laurel. Her head began to hurt terribly with a painful headache, and she started to sweat profusely. Her skin felt hot, like it was scorching and baking in the air, and her breath felt chokingly short. Feeling dizzy and weak, the maiden fell abruptly, but she quickly caught herself by holding onto the wooden table nearby.

"Laurel! Laurel, are you all right?" the maiden heard her parent's fear-filled voices.

Turning around, Laurel saw the concerned faces of her parents as their lips moved with pleading earnest, but she did not hear anything except the ringing of her ears. The faces of her parents became murky and distorted as the cabin suddenly began spinning around her. Losing all sense of herself and everything in view, Laurel began falling forward before her parents.

What is his name? Laurel's thoughts repeated as she fell into a sweltering darkness. *What is his name? His name... name... His name is...*

"Sol!" Laurel cried, awakening from her dream as she jolted up in bed. Although a feeling of relief swarmed through the maiden's heart at finding herself in the familiar straw mattress, terror seized her thoughts as she realized the cause of her body's hot and sweaty sensation.

Fire.

Hot, sweltering flames roared loudly and flashed in brilliant reds and oranges as they consumed every piece of furniture, every article of fabric, and every inch of Laurel's cabin. A dark smoke curled in the air, and Laurel felt her lungs burning as she choked on the thick smoke. Quickly, Laurel tore her blanket away with fright and leaped out of bed. She rushed past a wall of flame that incinerated her dining table and sprinted to the cabin door. Barefoot and wearing only her green nightgown, Laurel ripped open the door and found, to her horror, Serenity Forest in flames.

The once beautifully green oaks, pines, and cider trees were now roasting amid large bright flames. Leaves, now ablaze and hot, rained down from the forest canopy like small, scorching fireballs. The earth became arid and ashy. The air smoldered in dark, suffocating smoke. For a moment, Laurel took in the terrifying sight of the burning forest. All of a sudden, Laurel heard a loud cracking sound from the trees around her cabin.

Looking upward, Laurel beheld a large fiery evergreen swaying amid a sea of flaming trees. The tree's strength began to weaken as its trunk suddenly split apart and fell into the trees burning before it. Laurel screamed as the domino of trees began to fall directly over her home. She sprinted with all her might away from the falling, burning mass as it crushed the cabin, sending a cloud of smoke and flames into the air. Laurel fell into the ashy earth, sweating and crying. She looked back at her only home in all of Terra, now in flames and destroyed.

Grandma Arliana... I must get to Grandma Arliana, Laurel thought swiftly as she tried to keep despair and fear from taking over.

Laurel hastily picked herself up and ran though the burning forest westward. Her bare feet ached as she trampled and tripped over large roots and burning leaves. Her whole body moved in one painful throb as she sweated and sweltered in the heat of the flames around her. Tears of anguish rolled down Laurel's eyes as she wondered if this dreadful night would be her last. Laurel pushed through the ashy shrubs and debris of the fiery trees and soon found herself coming to the outskirts of Serenity Forest.

Leaping over a small burning shrub, Laurel tumbled through a mass of hot bushes and into the tall grasses of the Valley Fioré. Laurel got up wearily and swiftly fled over a small hill and looked out across the valley. She dismayingly found the lush grasses of the valley bursting into flames as the fire in Serenity Forest spread with great speed. Laurel then bounded down the hill and across the sloping plains of the Valley Fioré to The Great River.

Oh! Thank goodness, the fire has not spread to Granny's hut! Laurel thought to herself at seeing the worn hut still intact across the river. Laurel hopped over the cool, wet stones of The Great River and winced as the cold water splashed against her burned feet. Puffing and panting heavily, Laurel ran to the hut's entrance and pushed past the purple curtain.

Inside, all was quiet, as if the fiery scene outside the hut was all a dream and nothing more. Laurel searched in the dim light for Grandma Arliana, and seeing movement under the covers of the old bed, Laurel suspected the old woman to be fast asleep. Laurel hobbled languidly on her hurting feet across the hut and up to the bed where Grandma Arliana slept peacefully.

"Granny!" Laurel choked hoarsely, for her throat was burned from the forest's hot smoke. "Granny, wake up!" Laurel could not see the old woman, for her back was turned to the young maiden. The bed covers wrapped around the old woman from head to toe.

"Please," Laurel began again, swiftly pulling back the covers, "we must—"

As the covers were pulled away, Laurel stood in silent horrification. Though the light was dim, she knew that the body lying in the bed was not Grandma Arliana, nor was it human. Slowly, the creature sat up with its back facing Laurel, and the maiden slowly took a few steps backwards. The creature's long cloak hid its body, but Laurel saw one arm extended over the covers, which revealed a scaly, dark hand with sharp, black claws. Then, the creature slowly turned in the bed to face Laurel. The dark, ragged cloak hid the creature's face, but Laurel's heart beat with terror as she beheld two piercing, red eyes staring back at her.

Suddenly, the creature let out a loud, bloodcurdling screech. Laurel screamed in horror as she covered her ears and tried to escape the vile creature, but in the dim light, Laurel knocked into a chair by the dining table and fell to the floor. Before the terrified girl could get to her feet, a blast of fire flew over her head and destroyed the chair in front of her. Looking back with terror, Laurel saw the creature standing before her with its scaly, clawed hand extended and smoking. The creature's red eyes seemed to fix themselves on Laurel as a sinister grin could be seen through the shadow of its dark cloak.

This — this thing! I have seen it before, Laurel reasoned, looking up at the terrifying creature. *It is the creature from my nightmares! It — it is real!*

Menacingly, the creature's hand began to glow bright red, and Laurel, paralyzed with fear, looked on as an ominous flame sparked between the creature's claws.

What do I do? Laurel's thoughts repeated in her head. *What do I do?*

Just as the creature took another step towards the maiden, it let out a sharp cry of pain as a golden arrow shot from out of the darkness and into its chest.

"Halt!" came a voice behind Laurel.

"Surrender now, you vile beast, or die!" came another.

Looking back towards the entrance, Laurel was amazed to see Sol, wielding a magnificent sword in his hand, with a strange figure standing beside him. The figure resembled that of a handsome youth with two long wings of bright, white feathers. He was tall with short brown hair, and he wore a pair of dark sandals with straps that wrapped up to his knees. A cream-colored tunic that draped down to his knees was tied around his waist by a golden sash. A long green cloak wisped around this figure in the wind of his wings, and he brandished a bright, silver bow in hand. As he quickly mounted another golden arrow from a large quiver that was strapped to his back, Laurel suddenly recognized the winged figure from the mysterious wisdom in his deep, emerald eyes.

Peterel? Laurel questioned dazedly, wondering whether she was still dreaming.

Seeing Sol and Peterel, the dark creature before Laurel grimaced aloud, pulling Peterel's arrow out of its chest, and a dark, putrid fluid leaked from its wound.

"Peterel, cover me!" Sol cried as he rushed towards the creature.

"Yes, master!" Peterel affirmed, shooting another arrow, but the creature quickly ducked from its path and launched a fireball at Sol.

Sol jumped on top of the table before him and parried the fireball with his sword. Suddenly, Sol's sword glowed with a brilliant, white light, and the blast of fire was swiftly extinguished. Sol rushed again at the creature as Peterel shot another arrow, which pierced the creature in its side. The dark beast screeched in terror as Sol jumped from the table and brought his sword down onto its head. Then, its headless figure fell to the ground in a pool of black goo draining from its wounds, while the head rolled across the floor at Laurel's feet. The maiden jumped in surprise as Sol appeared at her side.

"Laurel, are you all right?" he asked quickly, wrapping his arm around her.

"Sol! Sol, what is going on here? Where is Grandma Arliana? And what is that—that *thing*? The forest is on fire!" Laurel cried, her body trembling with fearful relief. "And... Peterel?" she marveled at the winged man.

"Please, Laurel, there is no time to explain, right now. We must get you out of here," Sol replied, starting to his feet, but Laurel took a hold of Sol's arm and kept him at her side.

"But—but Grandma Arliana. She—"

"—is safe. I promise you, Laurel, but you must trust me. Please, come with me," Sol pleaded with both the measured sound of his voice and the soft gaze of his eyes.

Laurel sighed uneasily as the knowledge of the equestrians and the wanted poster swirled through her head, but as her circumstances gave her no choice to question further, she nodded in agreement and started to her feet. However, the maiden quickly slid back to the floor, for her feet, wounded from her fiery sprint in the forest, pained her from moving.

"My feet..." Laurel winced. In an instant, Sol gently took the young maiden's hand into his, and Laurel felt a strange wave of peace swell within her heart.

"It is all right, Laurel," Sol's voice rang softly. Suddenly, Laurel felt a power growing in her as the young man helped her up, and her feet, too, no longer ached. "Now, there is no time to waste. We must be swift."

"Master!" Peterel shouted from behind the two. The winged companion stood near the entrance and, as he looked back towards Sol and Laurel, an expression of deep apprehension appeared across his face.

"What is it, Peterel?" Sol asked as he and Laurel approached.

"We have company."

Peterel pulled back the curtain as the three stepped outside. Almost all of the Valley Fioré was engulfed in flames, and black smoke circled high into the air all around. Peterel pointed up towards the sky, and Laurel saw a strange formation of dark ominous clouds appearing overhead. The clouds hid the starry night sky, and they roared with an angry thunder like the cry of multitudes of beasts.

"They are coming, master," Peterel continued as his wings fluttered restlessly behind him.

"Who?" Laurel asked timidly.

"Tempters[3]," was Sol's reply, his voice sounding with an air of disgust and contempt. "Come! We must leave, quickly!" he ordered, pulling Laurel around the hut, where Philippe awaited them.

"I shall cover you from behind, master, to give you time for your escape," Peterel said, after helping the two onto the horse. Then, he loaded another golden arrow into his bow.

Sol nodded, taking up the reins. "Laurel," he whispered into the young maiden's ear from behind, "hold on tightly to Philippe. I promise you everything will be all right."

With a discomforting nod, Laurel clutched onto the horn of Philippe's saddle as Sol commanded the horse forward; Philippe galloped ahead with Peterel flying closely behind. Rushing towards The Great River, Philippe leaped easily over the dark water and onto the other side, and then Sol steered the charging horse through the burning and smoking grasses of the Valley Fioré. Suddenly, the sound of fearsome howls rumbled from

---

[3] When referring to this race of creatures, this term will be capitalized. There is also a plural and singular form of the term with *Tempters* being more than one of the creatures and *Tempter* being one of the creatures.

within the dark clouds above. Laurel looked skyward and beheld a swarm of demonic creatures with bat-like wings emerging from the ominous billows.

"Th — they can fly?" she gasped frightfully, noting resemblance of these terrifying creatures to the one from Grandma Arliana's hut. Sol and Peterel eyed the shadowy creatures who perceived the threesome, as they navigated through the blazing valley towards Serenity Forest.

"Peterel, distract the Tempters until I can get Laurel to safety, then draw them northward to the rendezvous point where the others can assist you."

"I shall not fail, Master!" Peterel flew up towards the swarm of Tempters. Wielding his silver weapon, Peterel shot one of his golden arrows at the mass of Tempters above him. The golden arrow suddenly glowed with a golden shimmer as it approached its mark. Just as the shimmering arrow pierced one Tempter in its chest, a bright, blinding light blasted from the arrow and blinded the whole swarm of Tempters. Laurel heard the creatures' agonizing cries as they quivered with pain and collided into each other in mass hysteria.

"Sol, what is going on here?" Laurel asked anxiously, her mind whirling with confusion and astonishment at everything she saw and heard.

"I cannot explain right now, Laurel," Sol replied as he instructed Philippe down a tall hill; they were quickly approaching the forest. "The circumstances are too dangerous," Sol continued almost to himself. He took a quick glance back at Peterel, who began shooting more hopeful arrows at the Tempters, before exclaiming, "Now, hold on!"

Sol gave Philippe a firm kick to pressure the horse into a faster gallop into Serenity Forest. The forest continued to burst with flames, as the bright burning fires scalded every tree and shrub into smoldering ashes. Sol steered Philippe around burning bushes and past hot fallen branches. As smoke from the burning flames circled overhead, Laurel could feel her lungs burning once again, and she started to cough and choke in the fiery smoke.

Sol held up one end of his cloak to the maiden saying, "Here, breath through this," and Laurel complied.

As the two pushed through Serenity Forest, which was now an inferno, they soon came upon a small crossroad of woodland paths leading in different directions. Sol pulled on the reins to stop Philippe, and he looked towards each path, discerning which one to take.

"The fire is spreading from the east to the north and west," he reasoned aloud. "If we want to escape this holocaust, then our best path of travel is south. Still, we must travel east, after a while, in order to reach The Sanctuary."

"The Sanctuary?"

"Yes, it is a safe haven deep in the forest, where I am taking you," Sol said, as he directed Philippe on the southward path. "My mother is waiting for me there."

His mother... Laurel's thoughts began, when the crackling of hot bark sounded in her ears.

Turning around, the two saw the trunk of a large oak tree split apart and fall speedily towards them. Sol pulled Philippe's reins sharply to the right and kicked the horse's sides, and Philippe hastily sprinted away from the falling tree. The burning oak fell just a few feet behind them, blocking the paths back towards the Valley Fioré, and a cloud of ashes and flames rose up towards the forest canopy. A loud shriek sounded with such bloodcurdling ferocity, and the two looked down the woodland path before them. There, a small band of Tempters appeared from behind the shadows of the burning trees. The Tempters smiled wickedly as their red eyes locked onto those of Sol and Laurel, and their bat-like wings showed themselves from the backs of their ragged cloaks.

"Wha—what should we do?" Laurel asked with fright, as the Tempters slowly advanced towards them.

"Stay here!" Sol commanded. He quickly dismounted from Philippe and charged at the Tempters.

"Wait! Sol!" Laurel cried, but Sol did not listen.

Seeing this, the Tempters flapped their wings and flew towards Sol, and their sharp, black claws blazed with fiery flames. Unsheathing the sword from his side, Sol cut down the first Tempter at his right and then parried the slashing claws of another. He pushed back the Tempter and brought his sword down against it, slicing off its head. Two more Tempters on either side of Sol launched a series of raging fireballs. Sol quickly jumped high into the air and flipped back over one of the Tempters, and both creatures screamed in pain as their own fireballs wounded each other, destroying both of them. Sol landed on his feet behind three Tempters, and catching them off-guard, he swiftly rushed at them and attacked them with a series of slashes and whacks from his sword.

As Laurel, in astonishment, watched Sol defeating every Tempter that he came across, she noticed one Tempter still hiding behind the shadows of a burning tree. As Sol drew closer to where the Tempter was hiding, the creature's claws began glowing bright red, as if it was planning to attack Sol from behind. Suddenly, Laurel felt a boiling rage within her at realizing this, and without thinking, she took up Philippe's reins and kicked the horse into a gallop straight for the Tempter. Seeing this, the Tempter tried to open its attacks on Laurel, but Philippe dodged the fireballs and plowed into the vile beast. The force of the impact was too great for Laurel to overcome, and she suddenly fell off the horse and onto the ashy ground.

Laurel slowly got to her knees but found herself in such a daze that she could not stand. She heard a scraping sound before her, but when she looked up, the maiden found the world spinning and whizzing around her. Then, she perceived a dark shadow crouched on the ground a few feet in front her. Laurel gathered her composure, and suddenly recognized the dark shadow as the Tempter that Philippe ran over. As the creature stood up quickly with its head resting unnaturally against its shoulder, a disgusting crackling sound came from the creature's neck as it cracked its head back into place. With a wide grin peering from beneath its cloak, the dark beast stared down menacingly into the young maiden's eyes.

Then, the Tempter screeched in anger at Laurel, and its wings flapped threateningly as it flew towards her. The young maiden screamed frightfully and covered her face with her arms. Instantly, the creature dropped before Laurel and wailed in pain as Sol pierced the Tempter with his sword. Laurel looked up to see the point of the sword sticking out of the monster's chest. Sol withdrew his sword back and the Tempter collapsed to the ground and expired.

"Sol!" the young maiden cried, embracing him with thankfulness. Once she released Sol, Laurel saw that all of the other Tempters laid sprawled and dead on the woodland path. In the distance, the two heard the screeches of more Tempters advancing.

Sol looked up toward the sky through the burning, billowing canopies. "Laurel," he began, looking back at the anxious maiden, "I want you to leave now with Philippe."

"Oh no!" Laurel cried in astonishment.

"He will lead you to the Sanctuary. I shall stay here to drive off the attention of the Tempters."

"But I— Sol, I do not—"

"Please, Laurel! Go!"

"But what is—!" Laurel started again, but Sol quieted her as he put a finger to her lips. The wailing of the Tempters grew louder and louder with each passing second.

"Laurel, I know you do not understand what is happening here, but you must listen to me! You shall be in greater danger, if you stay here any longer. Believe me when I tell you that everything will be all right. Now, I want you to take Philippe and go southeast from here to the Sanctuary. Do not worry about getting lost, for Philippe knows the way, and remember, no matter what happens and no matter what you see, do *not* turn back and do *not* stop. Keep going until you find the Sanctuary, hidden deep in the forest, and I promise that you shall come to safety. Do you understand?"

Looking up into Sol's earnest eyes, Laurel nodded reluctantly, "Yes, I understand."

Sol then removed his cloak and fastened it around Laurel's shoulders, and looking into his eyes, Laurel saw the hidden expression of sorrow overcome the young man's face. Afterward, Sol called for his horse, who immediately trotted back to his master's side, and Sol helped Laurel mount onto Philippe's saddle. When Laurel started for the horse's reins, Sol quickly took her hand into his, and he took out a shining, gold ring from his shirt pocket. Two small hearts ending with a single leaf formed upon the ring around a small, beautifully white diamond that sparkled in an array of different colors.

"Laurel, take this ring and never remove it from your hand," Sol began, placing the ring on her finger, "for it will protect you always." Laurel looked down with emerging uncertainty into the eyes of her friend. "Now… Go!" Sol parted as he released Laurel's hand.

With one spank from his master's hand, Philippe galloped swiftly down the road. Laurel thought it was all a nightmare, unsure if she was still asleep in her bed. At that moment, the wailings and gnashing of the Tempters came ever closer above the forest canopy, and suddenly from behind, a swarm of Tempters descended from the sky. Sol, his sword readily in hand, charged at the beasts and began taking them down one by one. Some of the Tempters caught sight of Laurel and Philippe escaping, and they cried out with boiling rage as they flew after the young maiden and the horse.

"Fly, Philippe! Fly!" Laurel commanded the horse, and Philippe ran with all his might through the embers that engulfed the forest. A frightening chase underwent between the Tempters and Philippe as the vile creatures launched a series huge fireballs in every direction, hoping to block Philippe's path and vaporize the horse. With Sol's cloak swaying in the wind of Philippe's speed, Laurel searched through the forest's flames for escape routes and winding paths, while Philippe dodged the Tempters' dastardly attacks.

The fire that blazed through Serenity Forest seemed to have no end, as Laurel encouraged Philippe to stride faster in their escape. Two of the Tempters swiftly flapped their wings to the point where they flew right up to Philippe's sides. The Tempters gave Laurel wicked grins as their claws began to blaze with a bright, red glow. Laurel kicked Philippe to run faster, and the horse jumped through a narrow space between two tall oaks. The Tempters had no time to think as they instantly crashed into the two trees and fell to the ground.

"Good going, Philippe!" Laurel applauded with relief as she patted the horse's neck. Philippe neighed in response as he jumped over a crisp tree branch and charged deeper into the blazing forest. Suddenly, a large, raging fireball exploded in front of Philippe, and Laurel quickly pulled at the horse's reins to stop him from hurtling into the blaze of fire. As Philippe halted, another blast of fire erupted from the shadows of the forest, creating a small circling flame around the startled horse.

Laurel turned Philippe all around, searching for an exit, but the blazing flames raged high in the air, making it impossible for Philippe to jump over them. A warlike cry sounded across the wall of fire, and Laurel observed a small band of Tempters gathering together. They snickered and sneered tauntingly from behind their ragged cloaks, and their red eyes seemed to scorch with the flames that burned around Laurel. Then, the Tempters approached their trapped prey, their claws flaming with a bright, hot fire, and Laurel screamed for Sol as the vile creatures aimed a fiery blast of infernos straight at her.

Laurel covered her face, and Philippe neighed boldly in the few seconds before the flames would burn them to a crisp. However, Laurel found herself still sitting unharmed on Philippe's saddle, though the sound of burning flames exploded in her ears. The young maiden looked up slowly, and in bewilderment, she found a golden, transparent force field glowing brilliantly around her and Philippe. The Tempters' fire blast still raged from their long, black claws, but the flames could not penetrate the strange aura that shielded her. Looking down at her left hand, Laurel saw the ring that Sol had given her glowing brilliantly with a golden light.

Sol's ring! Laurel thought in bewilderment. *It – it is really protecting me! How can this be? Oh my!*

The befuddled Tempters fomented their rage, and their claws burned even brighter as they tried to penetrate the ring's protective aura. As Laurel's heart suddenly troubled in fright, she saw the force field flicker faintly. With the flames growing stronger, this alarmed Laurel, since she did not know how long the ring's power would last under the Tempters' raging flames.

What do I do? I cannot stay like this forever! I have to find a way to get out of here… But how?

Laurel's thoughts were interrupted suddenly, as a series of golden arrows shot through the air and exploded in a bright, dazzling light around the Tempters. The dark creatures screeched in agony as the light blinded them, and they fell back into the shadows. Once the blaze of the blast ceased and the protective aura of Laurel's ring slowly diminished, the frightful maiden looked up to the burning canopy to see Peterel in the midst of a small band of winged soldiers.

Each soldier wore white robes tied at the chest by different colored sashes, and a pair of sandals was worn on their feet as cloaks of all colors were fastened around their shoulders. They also wielded magnificent weapons in their hands, including bows, swords, and spears. Their brilliant wings fluttered in the air as they stared down at the Tempters, who hissed wildly from the darkness. One of the winged soldiers, who seemed to be the group's leader, hovered in the air between the two armies, and the Tempters seemed to bow their heads reluctantly as he addressed them.

The winged soldier was tall and held the form of a young man, whose age looked older than that of Peterel. A golden sash tied his long, white tunic, and her wore a long, red cloak over his tunic. He carried a spear in one hand with a double-edged sword belted at his side. He was very handsome with curly, dark brown hair, fiery brown eyes, and a muscular figure; his countenance was princely.

"Vile Tempters!" he spoke in a strong, booming voice. "Your defeat is certain! Surrender now or face the Emperor's Wrath!"

Again, Laurel covered her ears as the Tempters squawked furiously at the winged man's words, and they flapped their bat-like wings with fury as they charged at the small army of winged soldiers. With their swords unsheathed and their bows taut, the winged soldiers flew at the Tempters. A chaotic rage of slashing swords, fiery claws, and exploding arrows erupted as the two armed forces clashed. As this ferocious battle waged on, the noble soldier who led the army of winged warriors threw his spear into the belly of one terrifying Tempter. Then, he unsheathed his mighty double-edged sword and unleashed a fury of slashes against every Tempter that dared to challenge him.

The Tempters fought with all their might as the flaming fire swirled around them in Serenity Forest, but they were no match for the virtuous courage of the winged soldiers. Quickly, the Tempters' forces vanquished. Seeing their horrific defeat, a few cowardly Tempters tried to escape into the forest's flames, but Peterel shot them down with his bright, golden arrows in a series of fantastic explosions.

"Peterel!" Laurel cried from the circle of fire that still surrounded her and Philippe.

Peterel flew down to the distressed maiden, calling to her from outside the circled flames. "Do not worry, Laurel! I shall get you out of there." Then, he took in a deep breath.

Cupping his hands like a trumpet around his mouth, Peterel let out a bellowing gust of wind and blew out the fire like a birthday candle. Without thinking, Laurel quickly dismounted from Philippe and ran up to Peterel, as if to hug him, but she stopped shortly in front of him as his new and strange appearance troubled the weary maiden.

"P-Peterel?" she inquired suspiciously, looking up into his bright green eyes.

"Do not be afraid," Peterel smiled gently. "It is I."

"Peterel...what — what happened to you? I mean...what are you?"

"I am a Wingel[4], Laurel" he revealed.

"A Wingel?"

"Yes, a Wingel!" began a booming voice. Turning, Laurel saw the great Wingel, who had led the small battle against the Tempters, approach her. His eyes showed brightly on his face after exerting much strength to overcome the Tempters, and his large white wings fluttered in the breeze of his walk. As Laurel looked up at the looming Wingel before her, she felt as though she was facing a valiant hero or a mighty prince.

"We are the Wingel," he explained, "a race of flying beings with the great power of shape shifting. We can transform into various disguises but always retain the wings on our backs, which we secure to hide our identity, hence the name *Wingel*. Since the beginning of our existence, we have sworn to protect, honor, and fight for the Royal Family of Terra." Then, the Wingel, as a sweet smile appeared across his face, gave a small bow towards Laurel saying, "As for myself, I am the general of the Emperor's Wingel Army, and because of my fighting spirit and my devout loyalty to His Majesty, many know me as "The Emperor's Wrath". However, you may call me Mikhail."

---

[4] When referring to this race of creatures, this term will be capitalized, and is the singular and plural form of the creature. This word is pronounced *Wing-el.*

Chapter 8
The Enchanted Tower

With placid but swift urgency, General Mikhail revealed to Laurel of his troops previous maneuvers to rescue her dearest friend, Grandma Arliana, from the attack of the Tempters. After, they had withdrawn her with an escort of Wingel from the Valley Fioré to safety. Now that Laurel was in the protective guard of the Wingel Army, the general decided that their next objective was to escort her safely to the Sanctuary, where they assured that Grandma Arliana would be waiting for her. Seeing that she was in no condition to object, due to her own ignorance of the situation and the weariness received from this nightmarish reality, the young maiden agreed. Though she was somewhat hesitant, Laurel hoped that, in following the Wingel to the Sanctuary, she would comprehend the mysteries behind this bewildering, unpleasant night. After short deliberations with his convoy, General Mikhail order for a few of the Wingel to stay behind in order to blow out the roaring flames that continued to blaze within Serenity Forest and to assist any animals injured by the fire. The others set off with Laurel in the direction of the Sanctuary.

Despite the young maiden's uncertainty and misgivings towards all that had happened this night, Laurel was at least grateful and relieved to have Peterel by her side, whom she realized was still the same lighthearted and clement friend that she had known previously. After a while, as the Wingel Army made its way through the forest, Laurel found the courage to proclaim her confusing and troubling questions in the hopes of reasoning through her nightly adventure.

"P-Peterel? So…back there…those things you fought were called…Tempters?"

"Yes, the Tempters," Peterel replied, flying beside Laurel as she rode Philippe. "They are wicked, nasty creatures and are not to be trusted. They are able to appear nice and friendly at times, but they live to deceit and destroy. They will try the most dastardly deeds in order to bring about the heinous ruin of others. That is why they are called the Tempters because of their successful plotting and scheming to entice evil in others."

"So…they were the ones who started the fire… Why?"

The Wingel paused a moment in reflection before he continued in a somber tone, "They were after you, Laurel…and Grandma Arliana."

The maiden looked on in bewilderment as she replied, "Why were they after *me*? Why did they attack my home? What is going on?"

"The Tempters found out that Sol had been coming to see you and Grandma Arliana," General Mikhail spoke up, as he led the group deeper into the forest, "so they planned the attack on both of your homes, as they do to all whom they discover to be in contact with Sol."

"When some of the Wingel helped Grandma Arliana escape from the Tempters," Peterel continued, "they said that she mentioned something

about these mysterious riders who had entered the Valley Fioré the day after
Sol and I left. Do you remember?"

"Why…yes… Yes, they said that they were looking for Sol. They
said…" Laurel's voice trailed off suddenly as she remembered Sol's wanted
poster.

"They said that he was a criminal," Peterel sustained for the young
maiden. When the uneasy girl nodded, the Wingel rejoined, "Laurel, that day,
when Sol and I left the valley, it was because of those riders. I saw one of them
scouting the area, and I realized that the rest of their kind would quickly
follow. We, Sol and I, had to leave because those riders…*they* were
Tempters."

When Laurel gave a distressful look towards the Wingel, General
Mikhail stressed, "Do not be fooled by their outward appearance, for just as
the Wingel have the power to disguise their identity, so do the Tempters."

"Grandma Arliana told us that they were looking for Sol," Peterel
said, "and though you both did not reveal anything to them, it seems that
they were too suspicious, so they went forth with their plan to attack your
home."

"But, wait," Laurel began confusedly, "what does Sol have to do with
the Tempters, and why are they after him? And about —?"

"I am sorry, dear maiden," The general interrupted with a deep sigh,
"but we are not the ones who must reveal to you all that you ask. The one you
seek is awaiting our arrival at the Sanctuary."

"You…you mean, Sol's mother?" Laurel asked, thinking back to the
young man's words in the forest.

The general nodded. "Yes, she will answer all of your questions, in
time. For now, I believe that it is best to ride in silence and to focus our
attention on the matter of escorting you safely through the forest. The sooner
we arrive there, the sooner all of your questions will be answered. Until then,
it is best to contemplate on all that has passed."

With that, the army of Wingel fell silent. Even their many, fluttering
wings seemed to flap more quietly as they followed beside Laurel and
proceeded deeper into Serenity Forest. Reluctantly, Laurel fell silent with the
others, but she was still troubled by her many questions and concerns of this
horrific night. As she rode silently on Philippe, the anxious maiden wondered
if perhaps this whole adventure was simply a very long nightmare that would
surely end in only a few moments. However, no matter how hard Laurel tried
to convince herself of this, her heart knew that everything was real.

Despite the aching, apprehensive feeling that welled up within her,
Laurel's heart told her that everything would be just fine, as Sol had said.
Though his mysterious ways and doings confused her, she tried her best to
believe in him, though her doubts troubled her with each passing minute. She

was also still uncertain about the Wingel, but since they had saved her life only a few moments ago, she felt the need to trust them. Moreover, they were leading her to Grandma Arliana, which Laurel hoped was a sure promise.

Suddenly, the young maiden's thoughts returned to her terrible ordeal in the woods, making Laurel quiver with dread, and Philippe's reins trembled in her clenched hands. Her body began to ache again, this time with a sick, frightful feeling, as she thought about the Tempters. Of course, she remembered those vile creatures from her nightmares, but she had never thought that they existed or had plans to harm her. The dark, shadowy figures of these evil monsters appeared in her mind's eye, and her heart began to relive her horrible nightmares of being lost in the woods as the Tempters haunted her.

Those things..., Laurel agonized in thought, *how could they have been real? And... since they are real...then all those nightmares that I have had... Were my nightmares the workings of those devilish creatures? Were they taunting me or...were they really trying to hurt me in my dreams...? And then, those...riders...those horsemen...*

Such thoughts froze Laurel's heart with a stabbing fear. She tried to push them from her mind, but they had already leaked into the deepest parts of her soul. Laurel's thoughts then returned to the words of Mikhail and of how he was taking her to see Sol's mother in the Sanctuary, just as Sol had commanded of Laurel before she had left him.

Oh, Sol, Laurel thought anxiously as she fingered the mystical, gold ring that rested on her finger, *who are you...?*

As the night slowly crept along and the whispering of the wind and the chirping of the nocturnal insects hummed in the air, Laurel and the small convoy of the Wingel Army continued their journey silently through Serenity Forest. Soon, they came upon a tall hedge of shrubbery, found amongst the thickest trees of the forest paths. All stopped before this great obstacle, expect for General Mikhail. While most people would have ventured onto another path in order to continue their journeying, the great Wingel approached the enormous shrubbery with one hand outstretched before him. When he stopped just a few feet before the hedge, Laurel watched the great Wingel astonishingly as he spoke in a loud voice:

"In the name of the Emperor, Lord and Ruler of Terra, I, His humble servant, pledge my allegiance and command for our entry!"

Without warning, the hedge seemed to sway at the authority of the general's voice and obey his words. Suddenly, the leaves and vines of the hedge pulled back and retreated from the path that was once a dead end, revealing a small clearing through the thicket. As the convoy of Wingel continued into the open, Laurel became even more amazed by the peculiar sight she observed. Amidst this breezy clearing, there stood a magnificent tower that stretched high above the tall forest canopies. Each story of the tower was adorned with long, wooden balconies and large oval windows.

The tower stood in the center of a large moat that had been dug deep into the earth and was filled with crystal-clear, blue water. The tower itself, which looked to be many years old, was made of a hard, red brick, and long, flowering vines grew about the tower's sides. The tower's spire was made of a dark stone and was completely bare of openings, except for one window on its northern side. As the convoy advanced towards the tower, Laurel was awe-struck, for she had never seen such a magnificent structure.

"Is this...?" the young maiden began slowly, but her astonishment caught the question in her throat.

Peterel nodded. "Yes, Laurel, this is the Sanctuary, the fortress of the Emperor's Army."

At hearing this, Laurel questioned suspiciously, "This is...a fortress?" For the tower seemed both too aged and unsupportable for a protective dwelling of any kind.

Some of the Wingel smiled at Laurel's concern as if they knew something that was still hidden to her. Then, Mikhail looked back towards Laurel and replied, "Things are not always what they seem, dear maiden. You shall come to understand this once we enter the Sanctuary."

With that, the convoy came upon the small moat that surrounded the tower. One of the Wingel put his fingers to his lips and let out a loud, harmonious whistle. Suddenly, at the front of the tower, a wooden drawbridge, which was connected to the tower by a dark chain, began to creak and groan. Then, the door started to open downward over the moat, and a loud bang sounded as the large door contacted the edge of the moat. Peering inside the Sanctuary, Laurel saw that the tower was dark, making it difficult to see anyone or anything, and she had an ominous feeling that the tower seemed abandoned.

"Come, Laurel," Mikhail said coming up to Philippe's side. The general then held out his hand for Laurel so that he could help her off Philippe. Laurel hesitated for a moment but took the Wingel's hand as her heart assured her to trust him, for Grandma Arliana's sake at least.

"Take Philippe to the stall and have him cared for," Mikhail said to one Wingel, and the Wingel led Philippe around the tower towards the rear side.

"After you, my dear," Mikhail began again to Laurel, motioning for her to lead the convoy into the Sanctuary. The maiden stared up at the mighty tower, unsure if she even wanted to continue forward.

Well, I have made it this far… she reasoned with uncertainty as she and the convoy of Wingel entered the dark tower. All of a sudden, Laurel was bathed in a flash of dazzling light, and she flinched as her eyes adjusted to this startling brightness. Once the light fell comfortably on her eyes, the awe-filled maiden looked around her in wonder.

Laurel found herself standing in a large rectangular room, which contradicted the tower's external, circular shape. The walls of the room were a light, cream color with golden leaves and flowers painted up their sides and around the windows. Light poured into the room from these large windows and from strange candlesticks, which burned with no flame but glowed with an intense, spherical light, that hung along the walls. The floor was made of a smooth marble that was designed with different patterns of flowers, vines, and colored circles. A short staircase with golden rails and red, marble steps stood in front of Laurel. Atop the stairs was a balcony where a large, wooden double-door stood, and below the balcony, on either side of the staircase, were two doors that led to other rooms of the tower. Large marble columns stood in the four corners of the room. Placed elegantly around the stairs and doors were vases of flowers of all sizes and colors.

This tower… It must be mystical in some way, Laurel thought, *for how could all of this fit in such a narrow tower?*

"Are you amazed by what you see?" Peterel asked as he came from behind Laurel.

"This is an enchanted tower!" Laurel marveled, as all of her previous anxiety seemed to fade from her mind.

"Yes," General Mikhail replied, coming up to the young maiden. "You see, my dear, this tower—this fortress—was designed and constructed by the Emperor Himself. He wanted not only His Army, but also His people to have a safe haven to come to in times of distress. This Sanctuary," Mikhail continued, blissfully observing the room, "is a sign of our earnest desires."

As Laurel listened to the words of the Wingel, pondering about the Emperor and who He was, she noticed that the high ceiling of the room was painted to resemble a blue sky filled with large, feathery clouds. In the center of the sky was an eight-pointed sun with a large, red heart wreathed with laurels in the center of the sun.

"The Emperor's Seal…" came a soft, melodious voice.

Surprised, Laurel looked towards the staircase, where this sweetness originated, and found a shrouded woman standing atop the balcony. She was in the company of two very tall Wingel maidens, who wore long white dresses with sashes of weaved flowers.

"The symbol of His magnificence in Terra," the woman continued again, her arms folded peacefully behind her, as she gazed up at the ceiling.

Laurel had never seen a woman as enchanting as the one now standing before her, and her instant thought was of how everything about the woman was perfect in every way. The woman was very tall and slender with a fair-skinned face of youthful beauty. Her eyes were earthen in color, yet exhibited a tint of blue like the sea. Her lips were red as roses, and her cheeks naturally blushed with the color of a pink sunset. The woman's long, golden hair ran down her shoulders and was covered by a flowing, white veil that was draped down her back and across her shoulders. She wore a long cream gown, which was fastened by a golden sash and ran to the length of her sandaled feet, and a light blue cloak flowed down the front of her dress. Modestly, all that could be seen of the woman was her pure face, hands, and feet.

Her adorable charm was unlike anything that Laurel had ever experienced. The woman's beauty, which seemed to make even the purest rose appear tainted in some way, gave to her being a glow as if from a radiant, inner light, whose source was love, gentleness, compassion, modesty, and a host of other glorifying virtues. As Laurel suddenly found herself in the presence of this radiant and regal-looking woman, she realized that all of her anxieties and fear seemed to vanish into thin air, and a wave of peace washed over her heart.

"The sun has eight rays," the woman continued, still looking up at the seal, "and each ray represents a virtue, which my Emperor rules and lives by. The wreath of laurels represents the loyalty which He validly rules over Terra, and the heart represents His eternal promise to always rule Terra with love." The woman turned to Laurel then and smiled down at the maiden saying, "But you are familiar with this already, Laurel of Serenity Forest, for my son has been in possession of this same image, true?"

"Your son...?" Laurel began slowly, still mystified by the woman's beauty.

The woman chuckled warmly at this, and her laughter sounded pleasantly in Laurel's ears, like soft, flowing music. "Yes, my dear. I am Mariah, Mother of Sol who is King of Terra and the only Son of Emperor Abba. I am the Queen of Terra."[5]

At hearing this, Laurel's heart felt as though it would leap out of her chest. *The Queen of Terra!* she marveled, *And – wait, Sol! Did She say that Sol is – The King of Terra!*

Laurel glanced around unthinkingly at the Wingel convoy beside her and found them all kneeling on the ground as they bowed to the Queen. Overcome with astonishment, Laurel followed their example, quickly kneeling to the ground with her head bowing practically in her lap. At that moment, the Queen made Her way down the stairs with graceful, measured steps; the two Wingel, who accompanied Her, followed close behind. She

---

[5] When referring to Queen Mariah and King Sol, hereafter, in text as well as in dialogue, all nouns and pronouns related to these characters will be capitalized.

stopped right in front of Laurel, but a sudden fear prevented Laurel from looking up at Her.

"Do not be afraid, Laurel of Serenity Forest. I know why you are here, and I understand what you have been through this night. I also understand that it is with regard to your friend that you are concerned, true?"

Laurel turned her head upward hesitantly, and meeting the Queen's caring eyes, she nodded slowly. "How — how do you know my name?"

Queen Mariah smiled gently. "My Son has told Me much about you, my dear."

Suddenly, the Queen knelt down before Laurel to meet the breathless girl's eyes. The maiden looked on in surprise as the Queen took her hands into Her own saying, "Come, Laurel. There is nothing here to fear," She smiled so brightly that Laurel felt as though her heart would instantly melt.

As the young maiden allowed the Queen to raise her to her feet, she thought in a daze, *This Queen…She is just like Her Son…*

"General Mikhail," Queen Mariah began, turning to the Wingel general, who still knelt before Her, "I thank you sincerely for bringing Laurel safely to the Sanctuary. You have once again shown your loyalty to the Crown."

Mikhail rose at the sound of his name, but the rest of the convoy remained on their knees in honor of the Queen. "Thank you, Your Majesty."

"And you, too, Peterel," the Queen said turning to the Wingel. "Thank you for assisting Laurel this night."

Peterel, who was kneeling beside Laurel, started at the Queen's words. Looking up at Queen Mariah, he replied, "O my Queen, I assure You that what I did was nothing that any other Wingel would have done, as is our duty. Therefore, there is no need to thank me for my actions; only I give the praise ever to our Emperor."

Queen Mariah gave a nod in acceptance of these praising words and then returned her gaze to the young maiden. "Laurel," She began softly, and the girl watched her wonderingly, "I know that this must have been a long night for you, and seeing your exhaustion, you must be in need of rest."

Laurel looked down then at her dress under Sol's cloak, which she still wore tightly at her shoulders. Her once green nightgown was now covered in soot and dirt from her forest escape, but Sol's cloak showed no sign of the forest fire as it was mysteriously clean of both soot and ashes. Laurel's hair was also stringy and tangled around her face, and her eyes were red with fatigue. All in all, Laurel was in need of a restful slumber.

"My dear, I know that you must have many questions about everything you have experienced this night and more, and I have been awaiting this moment to answer them all. However, you may decide to discuss these things once you have rested. In the end, the choice is yours."

Laurel hesitated a moment as she thought of the tired aching of her body that wished to fall comfortably into a warm bed, but at that moment, all of the questions that she wanted and needed to ask came to mind, and she struggled with her conflicting needs of comfort and understanding. In the end, one vital question tugged at her heart with utter importance. "Please... Your — Your Majesty... Um... Sol...the — the King said that I would find my friend here."

"Mmm," the Queen's voice hummed knowingly, Her head bowing at the name of Her Son. "You speak of Miss Arliana."

"She — she is here! Grandma Arliana!" Laurel exclaimed with eagerness and relief.

"Yes, my dear," Queen Mariah said as She turned towards the balcony, still holding onto Laurel's hand. "Allow me to take you to her?"

As her heart fluttered excitedly, Laurel nodded in agreement. Queen Mariah smiled sweetly at this, and Her hand gently tightened around Laurel's.

"General Mikhail, please dismiss the convoy," the Queen softly requested, and She turned to the band of Wingel saying, "Thank you all for everything."

All of the Wingel seemed to sigh joyfully at the Queen's words, and Mikhail gave the command to dismiss them, all except Peterel. He lingered by Laurel's side for a moment before lightly patting her shoulder. "Once again, I am glad that you are safe, Laurel," Peterel started softly. "I shall be seeing you soon."

"Thank you...," Laurel smiled hesitantly but nevertheless gratefully, for she still did not know what to think of her friend's strange identity. After the Wingel followed General Mikhail and the others into another room. Laurel followed the precious steps of the Queen and Her Wingel servants up the red marble stairs to the balcony.

Grandma Arliana, she thought anxiously, *I am coming for you...then we, together, can find out what is going on here...* Her thoughts then drifted to Sol as she climbed to the top of the stairs, *Sol... Please come back soon. No matter what is going on... No matter what...I want to see you again... I want to know...who you really are...* The Wingel then opened the door that stood at the top of the balcony where the parlor room was located.

"Laurel!" gasped Grandma Arliana as Laurel stepped inside. Laurel gaped in wonderment to find the old woman wearing a purple, silk nightgown that flowed down to her ankles, a dark blue robe around her shoulders, and soft, white slippers on her feet.

Grandma Arliana was seated at a round, glass table, where evidence of late night tea and chocolate chip cookies had been served, and three chairs stood around the glass table, one of which Grandma Arliana was seated in. The chairs were made of a soft cushion colored a light shade of blue. The floor of the parlor was made of elegant tiles painted with an orange and yellow diamond pattern. The walls were golden in color with tinted stencils of flowers and leaves painted across them. The ceiling was adorned with a bright chandelier that used the strange candles that lighted the room with no flame. A stone fireplace stood on the right wall as a strange, wooden door panel stood on the left wall. A large, round window, that stood opposite of Laurel, looked out into Serenity Forest, enchantingly as if the tower was rectangular in shape and not round.

"Granny..." Laurel sighed as if in a daze. With happiness overflowing her heart at seeing her friend once again, Laurel rushed to Grandma Arliana and embraced her warmly, and the old woman tightly wrapped her arms around the joyful child. Happy tears streamed from both of their faces as they enjoyed their jubilant reunion.

"Granny! I am so glad that you are all right!" Laurel cried in the old woman's arms, "I was really worried..."

"I know you were, my dear!" Grandma Arliana replied. "I was worried, too, but everything is going to be all right, now. I promise you. Everything is going to be all right."

As the two parted to look at each other, Queen Mariah came towards them saying, "Laurel, the time has come for you to understand all that has happened this night, and if we wait any longer, the seeds of doubt and mistrust will surely fall upon us all. Please, Laurel, will you allow me to tell you everything?"

After looking for a long time into the eyes of the Queen, Laurel finally nodded in agreement. "Yes," was her simple answer.

"Very well," Queen Mariah replied. She then turned to Her Wingel servants, "Bring slippers for the young maiden's feet and more food for her to eat."

Then, the Queen motioned for Laurel to sit in the chair beside Grandma Arliana. The Queen finally sat across from the two friends once the Wingel had given Laurel a pair of white slippers and a delicious drink of tea with sandwiches for her nourishment. Despite the food's scrumptious appearance, Laurel was too anxious, for the moment, to take more than a small sip from the floral, china teacup.

"Now," the Queen began again, "where would you like Me to start, in telling you everything?"

As Laurel thought of all her restless questions, she let out a deep sigh as she could not choose from any of them. "Well... I—I want to know why those monsters—those Tempters—why did they burn down the forest? Why did they try to attack us, and what is all this about the Emperor and...and Your Son...the King? I mean...I have never heard of anything about this *Kingdom* before, and I...I just want to know what is going on here... I guess…just start at the beginning, I suppose," she said this last part more as a thought to herself than as an answer to the Queen's question.

"'At the beginning' you say? Hmm… Yes, I believe that I have the right story to answer all that you ask… This story was indeed the story that started it all, anyway. 'At the beginning'…" Queen Mariah paused a moment as if thinking over the tale that she was about to relate. "Well… In the beginning…"

And this was the story she told…

Chapter 9
The Queen's Story

"Long ago, the land of Terra began with the arrival of the great Emperor Abba, in a time of growth known as the Age of Emergence. He came from a faraway Realm with the desire of creating a peaceful world filled with love and joy, for He planned to establish a Kingdom for His people to populate. The Emperor, being of wise and mysterious faculties, used His mystifying powers to grow the flowers and shape the mountains and fill the seas of Terra for the delight of His coming people. The Wingel, the flying, shape-shifting servants of the Crown, also labored for the Emperor's desires. They, too, had journeyed from the Emperor's faraway Realm, where they had come into existence. The Wingel were born from the Emperor, Who had shaped them from pure and radiant light, creating their nature as shape-shifting beings by the mystical properties of light. The Emperor has always been their Master, whom they loyally serve, and so, with the Wingel's help, Terra was formed as a beautiful, prosperous land for the Emperor's people.

"However, the joy that filled the Emperor's heart at the commencing of His preparations was soon overshadowed by a great sorrow. As mentioned before, the Wingel are beings made from essences of light, and this is shown in the goodness and loving beauty of their hearts. Nevertheless, the Emperor did not create them to love and obey Him without control, for He wanted His servants to choose to serve Him with all of their hearts. Now, among the most loved of the Wingel was Lumen, a Wingel who was also most favored by the Emperor. At the beginning of his servitude, Lumen pleased the Emperor through his submissive service towards his Master, Who loved His servant as His dear friend.

"As time passed, however, Lumen became prideful of his high standings with the Emperor, and he came to regard himself as even greater than his own Master. Because of this, he began to despise his servitude to the Emperor who loved him. Shortly after, his whole existence succumbed to his pride as he sought the power and riches and rule of Emperor Abba. With a deep and raging abhorrence for his Master, Lumen gathered the Wingel servants together to rally them in a coupe d'état against the Emperor. Lumen accused the Emperor of oppressing his servants and deceiving them when He professed His love for them. Despite Lumen's plotting, one Wingel boldly opposed these outrageous accusations and spoke justly on the Emperor's behalf. This Wingel was none other than General Mikhail himself, and he condemned Lumen for his evil intentions and warned the other Wingel against this unjust plotting.

"Having been given the will to choose, the entire Wingel race was divided between those who remained loyal to the Emperor, under the command of Mikhail, and those who, under Lumen's command, despised their now-former Master with all of their heart. With this great divide, Emperor Abba was outraged with Lumen and his followers and sentenced them to banishment from the Eternal Palace in the Blissful Mountains, the place of the Wingel's and the Crown's inhabitance. In addition, He stripped the traitorous Wingel of their beauteous, glittering forms into ugly, monstrous forms, which they continue to retain to this day, as their permanent and primary appearance. Now, their hideous forms serve as a reminder to all of the despicable contents of their spirits.

"Consequently, a great and terrible war began among the Wingel, which was later called The Great Wingel War. In this war, Lumen sought to continue his plot to overthrow Emperor Abba, despite the Emperor's demand for his banishment. In response to this, Emperor Abba gave to His loyal Wingel weapons of amazing beauty and power to fight Lumen's forces. To Mikhail, now the general of the entire Wingel Army, He gave a magnificently powerful sword called Triumphus, which was named for its promise of victory to any swordsman who possessed it. And so, General Mikhail led the faithful Wingel Army into battle against Lumen and his dastardly followers. It was a long, ferocious battle as Lumen's forces heatedly tried to overtake the Eternal Palace, but Mikhail's army fought valiantly to protect the Eternal Palace and was able to repel Lumen's forces from the Blissful Mountains. They escaped into the far reaches of Terra and hid deep in the world's shadows, licking their wounds in their own hate and disgust for the Monarchy.

"With the banishment of the fallen Wingel, the Emperor and the faithful Wingel resumed the preparations for the coming people of Terra, though their hearts were still disturbed and embittered by Lumen's treachery. To Emperor Abba's great joy, the time of His people's coming to Terra finally came, and He rejoiced in their pleasure and happiness at His preparations for them. All was at peace during this time, as the new Age of Harmony commenced in Terra. This was the time when the people loved the Emperor, and He was in love with them all as His children, His family.

"Lumen despised and loathed the glorious reign of the Emperor and the peace that thrived throughout the land of Terra. As a result of his changed appearance, he was now called Malum, meaning 'Evil One' as he became the 'Enemy of the Emperor'. Likewise, the fallen Wingel were now called Tempters, for they are the ones who tempt the Emperor's people to love evil. Fueling with an evil rage in his prideful being, Malum gathered the Tempters and set about their plan to destroy this great happiness that blossomed in the hearts of Emperor Abba's people.

"Malum cast a diabolical Curse[6] over the whole land of Terra, which came as a great and terrible sickness that enveloped the people's hearts with a thick, evil darkness. This sickness is the source of all death and disease,

---

[6] When referring to the sickness that Malum placed onto the people of Terra, this word will be capitalized.

anger and bitterness, pain and vice that everyone feels in their hearts and their passions. Because of this, Malum and the Tempters were able to weaken the people's hearts to the vilest sins and tempt them to disobey their honorable Emperor by luring the people into following their false declarations. The Emperor tried everything in His power to thwart Malum's evil plans, as war was waged once again on the evil one and his followers. This, my friends, is the very same War[7] that we are fighting today."

---

[7] When referring to the conflict of the Kingdom against Malum and the Tempters, this word will be capitalized.

Chapter 10
Fears and Fragility

When Queen Mariah had finished Her story, She sat back in Her chair and watched the expression of Laurel's face as the young maiden considered everything she had heard. Laurel gave an exhausted sigh as she also sat back in her chair. Her heart seemed to throb and whirl as she replayed the Queen's story in her mind. After a few moments, the young maiden finally spoke with an anxious, but soft voice.

"So what You are saying…" Laurel began, shifting uneasily in her chair, "…is that Terra…is in a state of war? With those Tempters?" When Queen Mariah nodded, Laurel continued, "And that fallen Wingel, Lumen—err—Malum, put a curse on the people of Terra…a—a sickness?"

Queen Mariah nodded again, still watching Laurel's face. "Yes, my dear, a sickness that weakens the heart."

Laurel shook her head slowly in disbelief, whispering to herself, "How can this be? This is not the Terra that I know…" She looked up with concern into the face of the Queen. "And Sol… He is…?"

"The King of Terra and the first born and only Son of Emperor Abba."

The young maiden turned away again. Her heart trembled at these words. Suddenly, Grandma Arliana placed a hand onto Laurel's, and the girl looked up into the old woman's face. "Laurel, I know that this is all difficult to understand now, but in time, I promise everything will make sense."

"You… Did you know about this all along?" Laurel asked slowly, gazing into her dear friend's eyes.

The old woman looked down resignedly with a sigh, at this question. "Yes, Laurel. I did know…about everything," she replied finally. "Except about…Sol, that is. Sol—being the King of Terra…that is new to me—"

"But why have you never told me of the rest of this before?" Laurel interrupted fretfully.

When Grandma Arliana sighed again and did not meet the uneasy girl's eyes, Laurel gently gripped at the old woman's wrinkly hand. "What is it, Granny?"

"I am sorry, my Queen," Grandma Arliana began, turning to Queen Mariah. "It is true that I have never spoken of these things to Laurel, and I was wrong for leaving her in the dark like this."

"Well then, should you not explain yourself now, Miss Arliana?" Queen Mariah asked, Her eyes watching Grandma Arliana with sincerity.

When Grandma Arliana turned to the young maiden, she sighed nervously as she began, "Well, Laurel… I had two reasons for not telling you about…Malum and the Tempters and…everything else. The first reason is because… I—I was…trying to forget about…what this war has done to me, to my family."

"What do you mean?" Laurel asked, straightening in her seat.

"Well, you have always known me as the only inhabitant of the Valley Fioré, and for many years, I have wanted to keep things that way, besides having your company, of course. However, before I came to live in the valley, I lived far away from here in a grand village near a small mountain range. When I lived there, the village was in great distress over this War with the Tempters. The whole land was in distress, of course, but my home was receiving heavy attacks from Malum's forces.

"Well, the stress of the War, with all the people dividing between the Emperor and the fallen Wingel Malum, was too much for my family, and we all...eventually...broke apart..." Here, Grandma Arliana paused a moment, as if renewing old memories of this time, but when she sighed again, she continued her story, "And so...to cut a long story short, I decided that I had enough with this War and what it did to the people. So, I just...left and hoped that I would never have to deal with any of this ever again...but I guess I was wrong," and the old woman gave a small smile as she related this last part.

"I see..." Laurel said, considering what Grandma Arliana had told her.

Then, the old woman took both of Laurel's hands into hers and held them softly but with a firm grip. "Laurel, I know that this is a lot to consider in one night, but do not make the same mistake that I made. I tried to run away from all of this, and I ended up losing sight of what is important in life. And now...I have decided not to run away again," and Grandma Arliana's gaze fell on the Queen with an assuring smile. "I want to stay, if You shall have me."

"Of course," the Queen began motherly, "you may stay...both of you." Her eyes softened onto Laurel's and with a loving smile She asked, "*Will* you stay?"

Suddenly, Laurel felt at war with herself as she watched the Queen's pleading eyes. Despite her uncertainty of the War and of her role in the whole affair, she felt attracted to the idea of such an adventure. She had been dreaming her whole life of being a part of something as dramatic and grand as this, and she wanted to know more about this new world that had opened up to her and especially of Sol, who was the *King* of Terra. However, deep in her heart, something troubled the maiden about staying with the Queen and Her subjects and being a part of the War. For some reason, though, she could not understand what that troubling thing was at the moment. Laurel looked down as she considered her answer to the Queen's question.

"Well," she started timidly, "I—" However, before Laurel could finish her sentence, a loud knock came at the door.

"Yes, come in," Queen Mariah called.

When the door opened slightly, a Wingel in a long flowing gown appeared saying, "Your Majesty, forgive me for interrupting, but Your Son has arrived."

"Yes, thank you," Queen Mariah said, rising from Her chair.

As the Wingel held the door open, she announced in a melodious voice with her head bowing low, "Presenting His Majesty, King Sol!"

"Sol!" Laurel gasped with relief as the King entered the room. Despite having previously clashed with the Tempters in the ashy, burning woods of Serenity Forest, Sol was pristine. His clothing appeared unsoiled, but His face showed signs of exhaustion. When He saw the three at table, Sol bowed to the Queen, who in turn curtsied His way, before coming towards Laurel and Grandma Arliana.

"Sol, You are unhurt!" Grandma Arliana exclaimed, rising to greet her Friend.

"Yes..." Sol sighed as He took the old woman's hand into His own. "I am glad that you are both safe, too!"

Meanwhile Laurel, who watched Sol questioningly and unsurely, for a moment, only wanted to gaze at Him as she contemplated all that she had learned of His Kingship from the Queen.

The King of Terra... she mused in her head, when Sol turned to her.

"Laurel...you are now aware of the War."

"Y—yes, Your Mother—the Queen told me..." Laurel stammered, feeling uneasy as the subject was quickly changed back to their awful circumstance, and she suddenly wished that she was invisible, even from Sol.

"My Son," Queen Mariah called suddenly, and everyone turned to the Queen. "We have been talking for far too long at such a late hour, and I believe that it would be for the best if Miss Arliana and Laurel retired for the night."

"Yes, Mother," Sol agreed, bowing to His Queen, "and I shall see to Your request Myself." Then, motioning for Laurel and Grandma Arliana, He asked them to follow. The old woman, and the young maiden in imitation, curtsied to Queen Mariah and bid Her a good night. Queen Mariah, in return, gracefully offered them a good night's rest.

"Good night and peaceful dreams," She said to them both, but Laurel caught the Queen's glance. She watched Laurel softly with Her motherly eyes, and Laurel remembered how they had pleaded for her to stay at the Sanctuary.

I feel as though even now She is still pleading with me to stay, Laurel thought, lost in the Queen's benevolent gaze.

"Laurel?" Sol called to her from across the room, "Are you coming?" He stood by the wooden door panel with Grandma Arliana, who had come to the King's side while Laurel was deep in thought.

"Oh! Uh, right!" Laurel started, quickly following.

"Now," Sol began, turning to the young maiden, "do you see that small button there?" He pointed to a metal slab next to the door panel where a small triangle-shaped button was found.

"Uh, yes?"

"Push it and see what happens."

Looking curiously at the strange button, Laurel gave it a gentle push with her finger, and to her astonishment, the wooden door panel suddenly opened, revealing a small room furnished with red carpeting, oak walls, and golden hand railing.

"After you," Sol motioned to His friends, making way for them to enter the tiny room.

Timidly, Laurel followed Grandma Arliana, and their faces showed with an expression of curiosity as they entered the room. "What is this room for?" Laurel asked as Sol entered after her.

"It is called an elevator. We use it to travel to different floors of the Sanctuary, since it is a lot faster than taking the stairs. Here, Laurel, press this button now," Sol pointed to a round button with a white number 7 in its center. When Laurel pressed this button, the elevator door quickly closed, and she felt the small room lurch upward abruptly. Without a second thought, Laurel swiftly took hold of Sol's arm before she lost her balance.

"Do not worry! You shall get used to it after a while," Sol laughed, looking down at the perplexed maiden. Laurel smiled shyly at Him, but when she spied Grandma Arliana's wide grin out of the corner of her eye, she quickly looked away and removed her hand from Sol's arm.

"Now," the King continued, "I have ordered for two rooms to be prepared for both of you on the seventh floor of this tower, and I am certain that you shall find everything there that you shall need to make yourselves feel at home."

When the three had reached the seventh floor and exited the elevator, they found themselves in a long hallway with many doors on each side of the passage. The walls were decorated with marvelous patterns and designs of floral life. The floor was made of a cream-colored marble that shimmered in the light of the arched ceiling's beautiful glass chandeliers, whose candles flared with the same mysterious and fireless light of all the Sanctuary candles. A pair of tall, bronze statues of soldiers stood beside each door, and an array of expensive vases of all sizes and colors were arranged about the hall. Upon noticing their King, a couple of Wingel servants, who had been walking through the hallway, knelt to the floor and bowed their heads until Sol had passed them before they rose to their feet and continued down the hall.

After a while, Sol came upon two doors that stood side-by-side. He produced two silver keys from His pocket, and opened the doors. "Here you are," He said to His friends. "Your rooms are adjoining so that you can speak to each other privately whenever you wish. I hope that you find everything prepared to your liking and comfort."

With that, Grandma Arliana choose the room on her left, and Laurel took the room on her right, and the King watched Laurel from the doorway as she gawked and gasped at the room that was to be her own. She was astonished to find that the bedroom was larger than that of her one-roomed cabin and that it was furnished with the most elegant furniture she had ever seen. The polished wood flooring shined brightly in the light of the small chandelier that hung from the ceiling, which was surfaced with blue patterned tiles. The walls were decorated with a silvery design of diamond patterns, and a couple pictures depicting floral sceneries hung along them. There was only one other door in the room, besides the entrance and the adjoining doorway, which led to a bathroom fully furnished with any and all commodities of comfort.

By one wall, there stood a dark-wood table in front of a cream-colored couch, where a tray of freshly brewed tea rested. Along another wall a velvet cushioned chair stood beside a magnificent oak writing desk, where an ink quill and a few sheets of parchment were laid upon. Across from the writing desk, an elegantly carved wardrobe caught Laurel's eye as she viewed from the open closet many beautiful dresses and delightful shoes. But, the very best part of the whole room to Laurel was the large bed that stood across from the entrance. The covers were royal purple in color and of the finest quality and comfort. Three large feather pillows rested against the carved, wooden banister of the bed, and a baldachin hanging above had a beautiful white veil that flowed down to the floor.

"Laurel!" Grandma Arliana exclaimed coming through the adjoining door, "Are these not the most beautiful rooms you have ever seen?" Then, she quickly returned to her room, gazing around at its many furnishings.

"Is this really *my* room? I mean, may I really stay here?" the blissful child asked Sol in disbelief.

"Yes, of course, Laurel! Is everything to your liking?" He smiled amusingly.

"O, yes! It is all so wonderful! It is like a dream!" Suddenly, Laurel's gaze beheld the room discouragingly as a feeling of uncertainty surged within her spirit.

Sol had all of this prepared just for me, she thought to herself, *but I am still unsure about staying here and being a part of this War. For some reason, I just do not feel right about all of this…and Him… He is the King…*

"Is there something wrong?" Sol inquired coming from behind the maiden as He saw her changing expression.

"Oh! Well, I…" Laurel started quickly, not yet willing to speak her mind about her uncertain thoughts. "I—I… I believe—here is Your cloak...back," and she swiftly unwrapped the long shroud from her shoulders and handed it to Sol. "Oh...and thank You for everything that You have done for me and Grandma Arliana. We are both very grateful and—"

Unexpectedly, Sol took Laurel's hand and, bowing over it, placed a tender kiss on her knuckles. "You are welcome," He smiled, rising from His bow. "I shall be going now, but I wish you both a good night."

"Oh... G—good night..." Laurel replied in a surprised daze.

With that, Sol departed from the room, leaving the keys to both bedrooms hanging from a small hook by the door. Laurel beamed with sweetness as she thought of the kiss that Sol had placed on her hand, and she turned back to her splendorous room.

"Aw, how sweet!" she heard Grandma Arliana's voice come from the adjoining doorway, and the bashful girl caught the old woman's unforgettable smile as she leaned against the wall.

"Uh... Well, I—" the maiden began embarrassingly, when Grandma Arliana suddenly rushed to her and embraced her with excited laughter.

"Ha ha!" the old woman giggled jollily as she twirled around with Laurel joyfully. "I told you everything would be all right, Laurel!"

"Granny!" Laurel cried as she teasingly pulled away from the old woman.

"But it is true! O, just look at where we are now! And to think we were so flustered about those riders back in the valley! Ha! The devilish liars were working against the King and Queen and were not to be trusted. See, Laurel, I told you everything would be all right, once we got some answers!"

"Yes, yes, well," Laurel sighed tiredly, when she looked down and noticed her soot-black feet. "I think it is time that I cleaned myself up, and we get ready for bed!"

"Whatever you say, Laurel," Grandma Arliana chuckled in a cheerful stupor as she returned to her room.

Left alone to herself, Laurel sat in a small chair by her bed to examine her feet. *Wait, that is peculiar,* she mused in bewilderment as she stroked her soft-skinned toes. *Were they not...? Back in the forest...? I could have sworn that they were burned...*

Despite the comforts of an elegant, warm bed and the luxuries of her beautifully soft nightgown, Laurel could not fall sleep on that first night. To her dismay, her nightmares had returned. Since she had met Sol, Laurel's nightmares had seemed to be a thing of the past, as they had occurred less frequently, and she soon forgot all about them. But now, every time she closed her eyes to finally drift into dreamland, her mind's eye would be filled with horrible scenes of the Tempters chasing and slashing after her in the burning woods of Serenity Forest. Panting and sweating, Laurel would sit up quickly in bed when she awakened, just after the Tempters had surrounded her in the nightmares.

It is because of these horrible creatures that I cannot join this War! The trembling maiden thought, lying back on her bed after realizing where she was. *I just cannot face them again… I just cannot! And, I know that if I stay here…surely I shall have to face them.* Laurel rolled on her side, trying to find a comfortable position in her bed, for her body ached with all the stress that she felt in her being as she thought of the Tempters.

There is something else bothering me, too, she began again in her thoughts. *What the Queen said about the Curse… Is there really some kind of darkness inside me? Is there really something wrong with me?* She put a hand to her heart and felt its rapid beating. Somehow, the words of the Queen's story made sense to Laurel. If there really was a dark curse that was inside of her, then that would explain her anxiety, fears, and overall weakness, despite her daily yearnings for complete goodness.

That would explain my reoccurring nightmares, too… But, O! I just cannot stand this! And, Laurel sat up in bed, wiping away the many tears that began falling down her cheeks.

Why does this have to happen to me? Why should I have to be a part of this War? I did not start this nonsense! I did not want this Curse on the human race! Why should I join? Suddenly, her thoughts turned to Sol and of everything she had learned of Him that day. *And Him! Why? Why did He not tell me of all this before? How can He be the King of Terra? O, it is too much! Too much to know, too much to think about! Why did He not tell me?*

Frustratingly, Laurel sat back again on the soft pillow and stared up at the veil of the bed's baldachin. *I wish everything was back to the way it was…when Momma and Poppa were still with me. They would know what to do…but now I am just alone…without them… Where did they go? O, where did they go…?*

Laurel finally fell asleep once more, but it was not long before her nightmares began haunting her for the remainder of the night.

After a bountiful breakfast feast in the morning, Sol decided to give Laurel and Grandma Arliana a tour of the entire Sanctuary, since it was their first day dwelling within the enchanted tower. The Sanctuary held many rooms on its ten floors, including a library filled with books on many different subjects, a dining hall where breakfast had been served, a war room where the King and Queen discussed war strategies and tactics for Their Army, and a sparing room filled with different equipment for physical fitness. Grandma Arliana and Laurel were amazed and astounded by the magnificent paintings, sculptures, expensive vases and statues, gold trinkets and jewel-encrusted tokens that were found throughout the tower.

"Wow, Laurel! Just look at these works of art!" Grandma Arliana gasped in amazement, as the three were strolling down a long hallway decorated with different portraits and stone figures. "I mean, you could spend a whole week exploring this one hallway, and there would still be something to surprise you!"

The threesome even visited the tower stables, where to the amazement and joy of both Grandma Arliana and Laurel, the animals that they had for so long cared for in the Valley Fioré were found resting contentedly in the stalls' warm grass. They both ran to their dear creatures and thanked Sol ardently for having saved them from the Tempters' fires, as He told them the tale of how the Wingel found these beloved animals. Happy to see this joy in His friends, Sol insisted that the two should come to see the animals often, especially Gudrun the mischievous goat, Mable the pushy hen, and Ginger the motherly sheep.

The tour about the tower lasted for almost the entire day, for Grandma Arliana was enthusiastic about visiting practically every room in the Sanctuary. Laurel kept up with the jolly nature of her friend throughout the tour, especially after her joy in the stables, but every time she looked at all the beauty that was the enchanted Sanctuary, she felt a pang of despair in her heart as she remembered last night's restlessness and frustration. Once in a while, she would notice Sol watching her questionably as if He could sense her conflicting thoughts, but Laurel would quickly return a smile to her face and look away, trying to amuse herself with the grand décor of the tower.

Once the late afternoon of that first day had drawn near, the three friends decided to retire from the grand tour and take to their own doings. Sol left for the Queen's companionship, while Laurel and Grandma Arliana continued to stroll about the tower, for the old woman, in her opinion, was not quite finished admiring all of its grandeur.

"So, Laurel, where should we continue from? The library we saw on the fourth floor looked pretty interesting!" the old woman mused, slowly pacing down one hallway.

"Um... Actually, Granny, I am just going to return to my room for now. I am a little tired." Laurel said this as cheerfully as she could without revealing to her friend the great struggle that she carried in her heart.

"All right! That is fine with me. Do as you please!" Grandma Arliana replied ecstatically, continuing her walk.

Laurel turned away and began down the hallway, when she suddenly stopped in her tracks, pondering a question deep in her thoughts. "Granny?" she asked, turning back to her aged friend.

"Yes?" she called, not looking back.

"Yesterday, when we had that talk with the Queen... Did you really mean what you said about staying at the Sanctuary?"

Grandma Arliana smiled sweetly as she crooked her head to Laurel, "Yes, I did. I want to stay and help Them."

"Even after everything that you said you have been through...with the War?"

There was a pause as Grandma Arliana recollected her past. "Yes," she sighed finally. "Despite everything, I am going to stay!"

"Why?" Laurel's voice crackled as she posed this last question.

"Because... I realized that...I was wrong to run away. I was wrong to think that I could run away from this War, and now...I regret having left my family to whatever trials and tribulations that they had to face without me. Now, I know that I cannot run away, not again. I may be just some old biddy, but maybe there is something for me in this War... I do not know... I do not know if I can describe what I feel in my heart, but I know that I must stay here and help in any way that I can. Does this make sense?"

"A little...maybe..." Laurel looked down at her shoes, thinking over everything Grandma Arliana said.

The old woman chuckled lightly, "Do not worry. I am sure that we will all make sense of all this...soon." Then, she turned away and continued on through the tower.

"Granny?" Laurel spoke up again.

"Yes, Laurel?" The old woman replied, her eyes gazing wonderingly at her friend.

"Well... I...just remembered... You mentioned something else during our discussion with the Queen. When I asked you why you never told me about the War, you said that you had *two* reasons, but you only mentioned one of them. So, what was the other reason?"

An anxious expression appeared on the face of Grandma Arliana as if she was considering whether to respond to the maiden's questioning. However, with a sigh, the old woman relented and answered, "Sol told me not to speak to you about the War."

"What do you mean?"

"Well, as I said before, because I did not want to remember the War, I did not speak to you about it. However, after we met Sol, I felt that sooner or later you should come to understand the War, since He was from outside our little sphere of isolation, so I spoke with Him, once when you were away. We talked a little about many of the things that you have heard from the Queen, and then He told me not to reveal anything to you just yet. And now that I see that He is the King...I feel that maybe He was right to say this."

After these words, Laurel turned away, unsure of what to think. "But, why would He not want me to know... And even though you did not know that He was the King of Terra, why did you listen to Him?"

"I am sorry, Laurel," Grandma Arliana said, coming closer to the troubled girl. "I was sure that He had good reason to say this, since He had just come from out beyond the Valley Fioré! You just have to believe me, I would have told you —"

"I know, Granny," Laurel interrupted swiftly, "I know... Look, I — I am tired, so I think that I should go rest for awhile."

"All right, Laurel... I shall see you later...then."

The two friends parted from each other's company then, thinking about all that had happened between them and of what they may come to face in the future.

Despite what she told Grandma Arliana, Laurel did not return to her room after taking leave from her cherished friend. Instead, she found herself continuing through the halls of the tower and eventually outside to the balcony. She felt that she needed to find a secluded place to reflect on all that her friend had discussed with her. She also felt a deep aching of despair within her being, for she could not believe that Sol would keep her from knowing about this evil time of War.

It is just... I wonder why He did not tell me about all of this sooner, Laurel thought to herself as she walked along the wooden balcony around the tower. *I mean, so much has happened in so little time, and...I cannot make sense of any of it!*

She walked to the end of the balcony and leaned her hands against the railing, her head bent over in despair. Her long dress flowed in the breeze of the northerly winds that blew from across Serenity Forest, and Laurel did not lift her head, as was her custom, to breathe the winds sweet fragrance. Instead, she continued to sink ever lower into her despondent thoughts.

There is no way that I can do this, she thought to herself. *Staying here... I would be no help to Him. I am just too weak for this, and...I could never face those Tempters again!* Suddenly, tears welled up in Laurel's eyes, and they dripped down her face as her mind recalled the terrible scenes from her nightmares. A terrible aching seized Laurel's heart as her spirit fell weakly to the fear and darkness of these memories. *I just cannot stay here. I just...cannot —*

"Laurel?"

The tearful girl turned quickly to find her King, who had also been walking along the balcony when He saw her by the railings lost in thought. "Oh, hi, Sol," she replied, trying in vain to hide her despondent face and wipe away her streaming tears. "Is there something wrong?"

"I believe that I should be the one asking you," He said approaching her, and without warning, He gently wiped the tears from Laurel's face. "Why are you crying?" He asked, concernedly, meeting her eyes sweetly.

In surprise and timidity, Laurel swiftly looked down saying, "It…is nothing really. I — " Sol then lifted Laurel's chin so that her eyes would lock with His.

"It is about your decision to stay, true?" He asked solemnly.

Laurel was surprised by such a question from Sol, and in her diffidence, she could not find the words to answer Him. Seeing this, Sol removed His hand from the maiden's chin, so that she could be free to turn her face from Him, as she did again. He then leaned against the balcony railing, looking out over the treetops of Serenity Forest.

"Laurel…I know that you are going through a difficult time trying to understand all that you have just learned about the War and the old tale of Malum's Curse and of…Myself. Believe Me, I never wished for such wickedness to arise in My Kingdom, and I especially never wanted My people, like you, to be caught up in this evil time."

"Is that why You never told me about any of this before?" Laurel asked suddenly, and she was a little astonished to find the tone of her voice straining impatiently as she spoke to Sol.

In spite of this, Sol turned to her with an expression of understanding, shaking His head in response. "No, Laurel. I never wanted to keep the truth from you. Since the first day that I met you, you were not yet ready to know the truth about Terra nor about My Kingship, and so I waited until it was the right time."

"What do you mean?"

Sol gave a heavy sigh, but one that exuded kindness and patience. "Well… Tell Me, Laurel, would you have believed Me about the War and about My Kingship if I had revealed these things to you earlier?"

At that moment, Laurel felt a pain in her heart as the answer to the King's question rang true within her thoughts. *No*, she told herself. *No, I would not have…because…because…* Laurel looked away then as it was hard to meet the King's eyes under the pressure of the truth. *I would not have believed Him…about everything…if I had not seen those Tempters with my own eyes, if I had not seen the Wingel and Peterel who saved me from them, if I had not met with the Queen to learn about the old tale of Malum and his fallen Wingel.* As her thoughts drifted back to the Tempters, the young maiden's heart sank ever deeper into despair and fear.

As if sensing this, Sol placed a hand onto her shoulder asking, "Laurel, tell Me, what is troubling you?"

Suddenly, Laurel drew back from Sol as she declared forlornly, "Sol, I have decided to leave!" Without looking at His face, Laurel saw His hand fall to His side as she continued, "I — I cannot stay here any longer. I cannot stand anymore of this talk of war and darkness and curses. I mean, this is not the Terra that I know! This is not the Terra that I remember, back when I lived in the Valley Fioré! I...I think that it would be for the best if I just went away...went away and forget this War and forget the Curse and — "

" — And will you forget Me, too?" Sol interrupted, and Laurel looked up to see her King, carrying on His face an expression of solemnity. Still, His eyes were filled with distress. "Laurel, I know how difficult it must be for you to accept all that has happened and all that you have learned of My Kingdom, but you cannot run away! You must not. This War...is not just about saving Terra from an evil tyrant. This War is about saving yourself from becoming enslaved to the evil that has entered Our Kingdom."

"But, Sol! I...I just cannot..." Laurel began again, and her throat ached with sorrow as she tried to speak.

Her hands, clenched together as she listened to Sol's words, suddenly fell upon the golden ring that the King had given to her on the night of the Tempters' attack in the woods. Just thinking of that awful night brought Laurel's heart further into misery. "I...I want to leave," she continued distressingly, "and...I want to return this to You." Laurel then began removing Sol's ring from her finger, but He swiftly stopped her by placing a hand onto hers.

"No, Laurel," He said severely. "I gave you this ring, and I want you to keep it, no matter if you stay here or leave forever."

This surprised Laurel, and she watched her King intently as He promptly turned and began walking away from her down the balcony. Abruptly, He stopped and for a long moment paused before turning back to Laurel.

The young maiden watched His eyes, filled with hurt, as He said, "Laurel, if your decision to leave is final and true, then I want you to know that I shall continue to fight, even to the end of days, until the evil of this Kingdom is defeated and My people, like you, are safe from Malum's tyranny. However, you must know that, if you choose to leave and become indifferent with the War, I have tolerance for only two kinds of hearts in My people, and by that I mean: you are either with Me or against Me."

With that, King Sol left Laurel to consider all that He had said.

Chapter 11
Laurel's Decision

"Please! I am sorry! I did not mean — Wait!"

Laurel sat up in bed as she quickly awakened from her nightmare. A cold sweat ran down her back, dampening her long and elegant nightgown. The frightened girl looked around to find herself in her beautiful bedroom in the Sanctuary. An exhausted sigh escaped from her trembling lips, as the young maiden was relieved to know that her previous terror was nothing more than a nightmare. For a moment, Laurel was afraid that her cries had awakened Grandma Arliana next door. Hearing the sound of the old woman's blissful snoring, however, she laid back against the soft pillows of her bed. Laurel gazed up at the elegant veil of the baldachin, thinking of the terrible nightmare she had suffered.

That must have been the worst nightmare of all! I dreamt that I was back on the balcony telling Sol how I wanted to leave just as I did this afternoon, only after I did, a whole swarm of Tempters emerged from the shadows and began attacking me! The last thing that I remember was what I cried before waking up… I was calling out to Sol, trying to take back what I said…but when I searched from Him, He was gone…

When droplets of tears began forming in her eyes, Laurel reprimanded herself for troubling her spirit. *Stop it, Laurel! Thinking about your nightmares will only make you feel worse…* However, the tears would not obey her will, and they began pouring down her cheeks.

Eventually, Laurel kicked off the bed covers and blankets and sat up to wipe away her tears. In doing so, Laurel felt the mild scraping of her gold ring against her cheek, and she stopped to look at it in the pale moonlight that glowed from a nearby window. The ring's small diamond glittered and glowed in the soft light and a rainbow of colors formed into tiny, thin rays around Laurel's finger. The gold also sparked in this light, making the two hearts carved on the ring dazzle with great beauty. Laurel's thoughts suddenly drifted to the rings mystical abilities as she remembered its powerful protection of her during the Tempter's attack in Serenity Forest.

What an amazing ring! She marveled as she watched the sparkles in the moonlight. *It should not even belong to me! Sol should be in possession of such a ring… Why, I wonder, did He not want it back?* As her thoughts returned to her conversation with Sol, Laurel's heart grew heavy, and she sighed with despondency. *O, why did I not wait to tell Him of my decision to leave? I know that I have to leave the Sanctuary. I must, but still… O!*

Laurel's heart seemed trapped in a storm of confusion and anguish as she struggled with her conscience. Despite her fears on joining the War, she could not bear the thought of Sol's sorrow at seeing her leave and of His last words to her before parting on the balcony. *Why am I crying?* Laurel asked herself as fresh tears streamed down her face. *Why do I feel this way…?*

Soon, the mournful child could not bear to stay in her beautiful bedroom any longer, for it all reminded her too much of Sol's tender kindness towards her. She at once got up from the bed and silently tiptoed out of her room, hoping not to disturb Grandma Arliana or anyone else in the hall outside. Closing the door behind her, Laurel looked down the long corridor of the seventh floor and wondered where she could find a quiet place to think. She remembered the Sanctuary's balcony and decided to make her way there quietly. Once she was outside, she caught a fresh breeze from the northern winds and inhaled a deep breath to calm herself.

Coming upon the balcony railings, Laurel leaned forward and looked over the lofty, treetops of Serenity Forest that stood below her and out beyond the dark horizon. She saw the moon glistening and shining above her with many stars twinkling in different constellations, some of which she remembered learning of in her childhood. She heard the chirping of the tree frogs and hooting of the owls in flight and the rustling of leaves as the wind blew around the trees and small shrubs of the forest. Regardless of the beauty she heard and saw before her, Laurel still felt an uneasiness drifting in her spirit.

"What is wrong with me?" she sighed distressingly. "I know I must leave this place, but…I…just cannot bear the thought of doing so…"

"Then why leave at all?" came a soft voice behind the maiden, and turning Laurel found herself face to face with Queen Mariah. The beautiful Queen was dressed in an elegant blue nightdress. A long, white robe and veil surrounded Her and shimmered in the light of the full moon. A pair of pink slippers adorned Her feet. "Please, I did not mean to startle you," She said kindly, noting the surprised expression on Laurel's face.

"Oh, no, It—It is not that!" Laurel replied quickly, "I just did not expect anyone to be awake at this hour."

"Likewise," the Queen rejoined. "Now, tell me what is troubling you?"

"Oh right, you heard…" Laurel murmured uneasily, remembering the Queen's greeting. "It is nothing really," she turned away then, pretending to look over the balcony, for she felt her heart's fragility giving way to sorrow again.

"It does not seem like nothing," Queen Mariah began coming up to the maiden and standing beside her as She leaned onto the railing.

The Queen was silent for a long moment, as if waiting for Laurel to respond, but when the girl remained silent as well, the only thing heard was the many sounds of the forest creatures that sang into the night. Finally, the Queen put a gentle hand onto Laurel's, which laid across the balcony railing, and turning, Laurel looked up into the warm eyes of the beautiful Woman.

"Laurel, I was wondering if you would like to join Me for tea."

"Tea? At this hour?"

"Why, yes! I think it is the most perfect hour for tea," She replied sweetly. "Please, will you come with Me?" And She motioned Her head towards the door, welcomingly.

"Well..." Laurel began shyly, wondering why the Queen had asked her to tea. "Do You really mean it?" When Queen Mariah nodded in agreement, a small smile appeared on Laurel's face, and she agreed with a nod of her head.

The Queen's tea room on the sixth floor was a spacious and luxurious room. An open window stood at the southern wall, decorated with silky, light-blue drapery. The walls were silvery in color with a pattern of various sized golden diamonds painted on each of them. The floor was made of a light-silver tile, and a dark blue carpet of beautiful design was laid under a dark oak table. A large cream-colored settee sat facing the table, and two cream-colored chairs sat facing each other on the other sides of the oak table. Other furniture in the room included a magnificent bookcase filled with all sorts of literature, a golden-framed mirror on the western wall, a couple paintings of flowery valleys and meadows, a grand glass chandelier, and a marvelous crystal vase, which sat atop a roaring fireplace, holding roses of all colors.

When Laurel entered the Queen's tearoom, she was so caught up in marveling at the great beauty of the room that she almost did not hear Queen Mariah when She invited her to sit on the couch, which faced the warm fire of the hearth. Across the dark oak table sat a china set filled with a scrumptious milk and honey tea and a delightful aroma of a plate of freshly backed chocolate chip cookies, which permeated the room.

"This is a lovely room, and everything looks so delicious!" Laurel gaped, admiring all the splendor before her.

"I thank you," Queen Mariah said graciously as She began serving the tea.

"Oh, You need not *serve me* tea! I mean, You are the Queen after all," Laurel spoke up at the Queen's humble gesture.

"It is quite all right," Queen Mariah chuckled sweetly. "You see, My dear, one of the many things I have learned as a Monarch of Terra is that, as Queen, My duty to My people is to *serve*. As a ruler, I must show love and mercy to My people if I want to rule Terra rightly. Besides, being blessed with a royal life does not make one entitled to think of themselves as superior to others. This is especially true when thinking that one should be excluded from the labors and sorrows of daily life or that one should expect to be pampered and fawned over by others. That is not at all what it means to be and live as a royal. In other words, a princess should never act like a princess around others, for it is not princess-like."

Laurel giggled at this last comment as she accepted the tea from the Queen's hands. After the Queen was seated, the two peacefully sipped the warm tea, and when Laurel was offered one, she politely nibbled on a small cookie with child-like delight.

"Laurel..." Queen Mariah began as she gracefully replaced Her teacup onto its saucer. "I am hoping that you shall now tell me what has troubled you in such a way that you would go out to the balcony at this late hour."

Laurel shifted embarrassingly in her seat, startled that the Queen was still concerned with her troubles. "Umm..." she sighed uneasily not knowing what to say, for she really did not wish to speak of the matter at hand. "Well...why were You out on the balcony at this hour, if You do not mind my asking?" Laurel asked courteously, hoping this question would deter the Queen from her misery.

Queen Mariah smiled at this so amiably and so beautifully, that Laurel was in awe of the great Queen's loveliness, once again. "I do not mind at all," She replied kindly. Sighing lovingly, She continued, "I was wakened from My sleep with thoughts of My people. As you now know, Our Kingdom is besieged in a most distressing time, and My heart breaks at knowing this. And so, every night, My heart is filled with deep sorrow for My people, and I sometimes go out to the balcony, for I have found it to be a peaceful place to contemplate. There, I think of the words that Sol's Father, the Emperor, said to Me long ago. 'Be strong, My Dove,' He said, 'for through You, the people will know the King, and in Him, they will find their rest from this world's troubles.'"

At the name of Her Son, the Queen bowed Her head in respect, causing in Laurel a great admiration for the love of this beauteous Mother for Her Son. As the maiden listened intently to the Queen's words, she found that they soothed her troubled mind.

Suddenly, she found herself speaking up, "I came to the balcony to think, too."

Queen Mariah smiled at the simple child, as if content to hear something out of her. "War," She continued somberly, "is a dastardly thing...especially, when one is troubled by its many trials, true?"

Laurel looked down slowly. She was not sure how to reply to this, but she knew what the Queen was getting at. "Sometimes...things are just...complicated," she finally answered.

"How so?"

"Well, like...if one is...afraid..."

There was silence for a long moment, and Laurel wondered what the Queen thought of her statement. Finally, Laurel looked up and found Queen Mariah, with Her eyes closed and Her face lifted up, feeling a gentle breeze that had mysteriously blown in from an open window. Then, She looked at Laurel, and Her face seemed to glow with a mystifying inner light.

"Laurel, do you remember, in the story that I told you, why the fallen Wingel, Malum, revolted against the Emperor?"

"You said that he was looking for power," Laurel replied, as she set her teacup onto the table.

"Yes, because his pride led him to lust for power and the Emperor's right to the throne of Terra. Now what caused such pride in him?" When Laurel shrugged her shoulders, the Queen continued, "Well, because of his powers as a Wingel, he thought he could become better than his Master by attaining more power. However, there is another reason...a reason that involves Me."

When Laurel's face exhibited a concerned expression, Queen Mariah gave a small smile as She resumed with a sigh, "In My early beginnings, I came from a nobleman's family that had been reduced to a humble, nevertheless joyful, lifestyle. Despite this, the Emperor saw My great faith and love towards Him, and asked Me to be His Queen. This, I joyfully accepted. However, to this day, I feel as though I am but a worm in worth to such a state of life as the Queen of Terra. Anyway, when Malum became aware of the Emperor's intentions, he was greatly indignant to the fact that I, a person whose existence he considers is lower in state to that of the Wingel, would rule as his Sovereign and that the future King would also be of My lineage. Thus, in the course of Malum's attempted coup d'état, I became the dastardly Tempter's Archenemy, and forever, since then, he has sought the end of My existence and that of My Son. We, as the Monarchs of Terra, are the only ones of the Emperor's people who escaped the sickness of Malum's dark Curse, as was the blessing of Emperor Abba."

"So...what are You saying?" Laurel asked all of a sudden, but deeply considerate of what the Queen had related.

Queen Mariah then placed a gentle hand upon Laurel's arm, still gazing lovingly into the windows of her soul. "I just want you to know that there is nothing that you have to be afraid of in this War. You can even become just like me, a great Enemy of Malum, but no matter what, I promise you, Emperor Abba and My Son will stay by your side always, never to abandon you. As proof of this, I have related the cause of My trials in this War, and here I am today, alive and well, still fighting for My beloved Family. So...do you understand what I mean in telling you all of this?"

"I...I think so..."

"Well then, Laurel... What is it that you are afraid of?"

Here, Laurel learned a valuable lesson in facing her fears: the longer one dwells on one's fears and keeps them bottled up inside, the more unconquerable they appear and the more they take possession of one's will. She discovered that the best remedy was to give them up to charity and wisdom, as she at last, though a little reluctantly, related to the Queen of her nightmares. From beginning to end, she told of their occurrences in her childhood and up to the present night. She related how, once she realized that these awful creatures were none other than the Tempters, she fell into greater terror towards them and even into despair over them. All the while, the Queen listened attentively to the troubled maiden, whose eyes were now brimming with tears as she choked out her remaining woes. "I—I guess I should have said something sooner, but…my nightmares seem to grow more and more horrid since I connected them to the Tempters. I was just…too afraid to tell You or even Sol…"

"Here, My dear," Queen Mariah said, handing Laurel a white-laced handkerchief from her dress pocket, and the young maiden gratefully whipped her tears with the gentle cloth. "He told Me about what happened the other evening," She continued, and Laurel looked up timidly at the Queen, "as He has told me many things about you and your circumstances. Your nightmares then, My dear, are your reason for wanting to leave the Sanctuary, true?"

"Yes," Laurel nodded pathetically, "it is true. I… I thought it was for the best if I just left and…"

"Best for whom? My Son and I certainly do not want you to leave."

"Then, for myself, I guess…" the maiden sighed sorrowfully.

Queen Mariah grasped Laurel's hands tenderly in Her own. "Despite your fears, do you truly wish to leave?"

With her eyes streaming with tears again, Laurel murmured, "No… No, not at all. I mean, I really have no other place to go, and…Grandma Arliana said that she wanted to stay here, so…"

"Are those your only reasons?"

"Well…no," Laurel replied, her head turning downcast. "Truly, I *do* want to stay. I mean, I may not understand very much about everything that I have learned about You and Sol, especially of His Kingship and of this War. Still… I want to help. It is just…I just feel like…I would only be weighing You down with my fears. O, I know that it sounds insincere for me to want to stay without facing my fears, but…"

Suddenly, Queen Mariah began wiping a tear from Laurel's face as She related, "My dear child, I have told you that there is nothing for you to be afraid of, and I meant every word! Believe Me, My Son would give His very own life in order to keep you safe from all harm, and the ring that He gave you is proof of this." The Queen then touched the mystical ring on Laurel's hand.

"You know about the ring?" Laurel sniffled, eyeing the golden band considerately.

Queen Mariah chuckled warmly, "Yes, I know of all the ways and doings of My Son. Now, this ring is of very powerful and mysterious origins, for it was made by our Great Emperor, and whosoever wears this noble ring shall be emboldened with newfound courage in every battle and protection from all darkness. Now, this is not to be superstitious in saying that you shall never be afflicted with any earthly or physical pains, but that when it comes to the matters of the heart, you shall truly be safeguard from the Tempters' evil. However, this is only if you believe in the ring's power that comes from My Son and His Father, the Emperor. Do you understand?"

"Yes," Laurel answered, fingering the ring delicately. "You know... There was a time in the forest when I was escaping the fire...the ring did protect me from the Tempters..."

"Ah, yes. The attacks of the Tempters, though they can be seen in the physical, greatly target the hearts of their prey. Therefore, if the ring's power ever seems to flicker or fade for a moment, be cautious! Though the Tempters' attacks may not hinder you physically at the moment, your heart may be in danger all the while."

"I see..." Laurel mused, as she remembered how the light of the ring's protective aura flickered once during her encounter with the Tempters. *During that time, I did sense a weakness within my heart,* she reflected, *and the ring's power faded a little, just as the Queen said it would.* Pondering all that she had spoken of with the Queen, Laurel thought again of her true, hidden desire to remain at the Sanctuary.

"Well, My dear," Queen Mariah spoke up once more, rising from Her chair, "I believe that it is time for us to retire to our chambers for the night, if there is nothing more to speak of for the present moment."

Laurel nodded in agreement, as she realized how somnolent her body felt. Swiftly, she got up from the elegant couch and gave a low bow to the Queen. "I just...wanted to thank You for listening to me and for everything that You have told me...my Queen."

Queen Mariah beamed lovingly with joy as She took the young maiden's hand when she straightened. "You are welcome, My dear, and remember that whenever you need someone to talk to, you can always come to Me, *and* My Son as well."

Laurel smiled shyly, "Yes... I think that I shall go see Him tomorrow, too."

"Very good," Queen Mariah's smile seemed as though it could melt the coldest heart, at that moment. "Good night, My dear."

Laurel returned the gentle parting as she released her hand from the Queen's grasp and made her way towards the tearoom's door.

"Oh, and Laurel?" the Queen called unexpectedly.

"Yes?" the young maiden replied, turning back as she began opening the door.

"Sweet dreams!" came Queen Mariah's soft voice as if bestowing a numinous blessing.

"Hmm, yes, my Queen!" Laurel answered, before leaving for her warm, baldachin bed, and mysteriously, a restful, soporific sleep.

The next day was filled with apprehension and trepidation for Laurel. Though she felt more ready than ever before to relate to Sol all that she had told the Queen, He could hardly be found alone, for He was continuously being needed to attend to war matters with the Wingel, especially with General Mikhail. At other times, however, Laurel's chances of speaking with the King slipped away by her own consent, as she could not find the courage to approach Sol whenever she did find Him alone. Seeing that her own weakness was keeping her from the task at hand, she finally gathered the strength that evening to approach Sol. Therefore, when evening befell upon Serenity Forest and the winged inhabitants of the Sanctuary hastened to finish their daily duties before they would return to their chambers to rest, Laurel was ecstatic to find the King alone on the balcony of the seventh floor, just as He had found the young maiden on the last evening.

All right, Laurel, this is it! The determined girl counseled herself, *Just tell Sol everything you told the Queen, and everything between you and Him will be all right. Right?*

The truth was that Laurel's heart ached with the tragic thought that her weakness would only sound disgustingly pathetic to Sol and that He would reject her feeble whim to help Him in the War. *Goodness, Laurel! Sol would not think such a thing! That is impossible!* she tried to tell herself, despite her continuing fears. *This...this must be from the Curse's power...*

Nonetheless, Laurel took in a deep breath and advanced towards Sol from across the balcony. As she drew closer, at first distracted by her nagging thoughts, she stopped in her tracks when she noticed what it was that Sol was doing as He stood silently alone. Sol stood leaning against the railings with His hands gripping the bright, iron railing bars. His face, composed and motionless, was upturned to the bright twilight sky, though His eyes were closed. Abruptly, a soothing breeze blew across the forest canopies of the trees below the Sanctuary and up the tower walls towards Sol. When He breathed in the refreshing wind, a smile lightened across Sol's face as He mysteriously chuckled to Himself.

"Yes…" He suddenly said aloud, though in a voice almost as hushed as a whisper. "Thank You…"

Perplexed by what she observed, Laurel finally spoke up, "Um…Sol?"

Unruffled by Laurel's sudden presence, Sol glanced up at the young maiden, and beaming cheerfully, greeted her warmly. "Good evening, Laurel. Is there something that I can help you with?"

"Oh, yes…" Laurel started nervously as she suddenly remembered her purpose for talking to Sol. "Uh…but first I am curious to know, if You do not mind, what You were doing just now."

Sol sighed distantly as He looked towards the horizon of Terra. "I was…conversing," He finally replied.

"Conversing?" the maiden inquired, stepping closer to her King. "With whom? No one else was here but You and I."

"With My Father." Sol replied unambiguously, and perceiving the puzzled look on Laurel's face, He went on to explain Himself, "My Father and I are able to communicate with each other by means of the Wind[8]." When Sol noted again Laurel's befuddlement, He bid her to stand with Him at the balcony railing, which she obeyed. "By now," Sol continued, "I am sure that you are aware of the mystical ways of Myself and the inhabitants of this Sanctuary." When Laurel nodded, He went on, "Well, in adding to the list of such transcendence, My Father, in His way, sends out His Spirit across the land of Terra, which is carried by the northern Wind of the Blissful Mountains, where My Father resides. In receiving His Spirit, I am able to understand His thoughts and desires, and I too send out My Spirit in reply."

"How does something like this work, exactly?" Laurel asked, curious of her King's mysterious ways.

"As I said, with the Wind as your messenger, just surrender your spirit across the land to Him," and in saying this, another gust of Wind blew up the Sanctuary and wisped into Sol's face as He breathed in the fragrant breezes. "And if you do receive a reply, the words do not come in a dialogue, per se, but in a discourse only understandable to the heart. This may be complicated to comprehend at first, but the truth is, this is the way I commune with My Father, being away at War as I am."

The King's words were true, for Laurel was not quite sure if she could ever wrap her mind around such a mysterious power no matter how often she considered Sol's explanation. Despite this, she could not help the curiosity and amazement that bubbled within her being. "So is this why You would turn Your face to a breeze when we were in the Valley Fioré?" the young

---

[8] When referring to the mystical communication of the King and others (such as Emperor Abba), this term will be capitalized.

maiden asked, persisting with interest as the memories of the valley returning to her.

Sol laughed at this replying, "So you did notice! Yes, that is the reason, and I do believe that you also had the same mannerism, true?"

Laurel blushed, feeling a little bashful that Sol would remember their days in the Valley Fioré as she did. "Oh, yes... Well, I have always enjoyed the wind's breeze, especially since the valley was so blustery all the time. I never really thought about why I enjoy the wind so much, but I suppose my little dreams of discovering what life was like beyond the valley were a result of this. I mean, the wind can always come and go as it pleases, while I never set foot from the valley, except so far as my own home... I always told myself that one day I would leave the Valley Fioré, but when I befriended Granny, I knew that I would feel terrible if I left her all alone."

"This is why you never went away to search for your parents," Sol stated, His hands clung the railings tightly as He listened to the young maiden's story.

"Mm-hmm," she mused in reply. "As well as the fact that I did not know where they were, so I could never think of where to start searching for them."

"I am certain that you shall find them one day, Laurel," Sol said, turning His head to look upon the young maiden.

"Hmm..." Laurel murmured, her eyes watching Sol for a long moment before fixing out onto the horizon.

I may not understand Him and His ways, Laurel thought, *especially with learning of His Kingship as I have and of this War, but in Sol... I still see Him as my friend, just as we were in the valley, before...all of this happened. Because in Sol, I found someone to talk to about my parents.* Her mind was suddenly drifting from the conversation, thinking again of her parents and of where they might be. For the moment, there was silence between the two, except for the singing noises of the forest critters below as they hummed at the bright, evening sunset in the West.

"Laurel," Sol spoke up suddenly, "was there not something that you had come to see Me about?"

Laurel's eyes widened with astonishment as she remembered why she had approached Sol that evening. With the coming of this jolt of memory, her courage and readiness to speak with Sol died out like a candle soaked with water. "Uh...well..." she began uneasily. *O goodness!* She thought to herself in worry, *How could I have forgotten...! Come, Laurel! Do not be so weak!*

"Laurel, what is the matter?" Sol asked concernedly, suddenly taking her hand in His own.

This sent a shockwave through Laurel's heart, as her fears of Sol's repulsion of her suddenly arose again. *What if what I have to say sounds wretchedly contemptible to Him? What if...* Laurel stopped herself mentally before these hateful thoughts took hold of her, and she prepared herself to relay her woes to Sol.

"Sol...?" she murmured anxiously.

"Yes? Is something wrong?"

The trembling maiden gave a small nod as she looked down, not wishing to meet the King's eyes through her ordeal. "There is something that I have been meaning to tell you...about my...decision to leave the Sanctuary...or stay."

"Yes?" Sol asked again, and Laurel could feel a slight tremor in His hand as He continued to hold onto her own.

"Well...for a long time—" as Laurel started to speak, her voice suddenly began to choke and quake within her throat. *Do not do this, Laurel! Just bear with this for now!* Then, she began again, "F-for a long time now...I have been...having these nightmares...about the Tempters, and..." When Sol began gently tightening His grasp of Laurel's hand, the young maiden hurriedly began to relate her afflictions in one long, tearful statement.

"You see, they have been bothering me for so long that I did not think of them as anything more than just nightmares, for I have had them since as long as I can remember, but after what happened in Serenity Forest with the Tempter's attack, I suddenly realized that those monsters were the ones from my nightmare, and I guess that I should have said something, but I was too afraid because I know now that those monsters are real, and I thought that if I stayed here then I would have to face them again, so on the last evening we spoke, I just thought that it was best if I left because I knew that if I ever saw those beasts again then I would just crumble with fear, and I did not want to burden You with that, so leaving seemed like a good idea, especially since my nightmares have gotten horribly worse since I have been here, but when I told the Queen about my nightmares, She told me that You would be understanding about all of this and...and...I..."

That was when Laurel broke down with an abundance of tears, for she could not relate any more of her heart's afflictions. She cried because she was relieved that she had finally told Sol the truth about her nightmares, but also because she was not sure what her King was thinking, and this caused her evermore heartache until He would speak up. However, Sol never spoke up. Instead, Laurel felt His hand releasing from her own, which compelled her heart to sink quickly into deep despair. Suddenly and to Laurel's astonishment, Sol drew the young maiden into His arms and firmly held her there for a long moment. Laurel found her hands clinging lightly against the King's shirt as her head rested motionlessly under His chin. Laurel's tears had stopped streaming, for the astonishment of this moment had prevailed against all of the past despair-filled emotions of her heart.

"Laurel?" the King finally voiced, His tone mellifluous and amorous. "Thank you... Thank you for coming to Me..."

"I am sorry," the maiden sniffled whisperingly. "I should have told You sooner."

"You came to Me now, and that is all that matters," the King replied, tilting Himself backwards to see into Laurel's face, as He wiped her tear-stained face. "Now, I want you to know that I shall always be here to protect you and that you have nothing and no one to fear. Do you understand?"

The teary-eyed maiden nodded, "Yes. Queen Mariah...She told me that You would say that, but... I was worried that it was not completely true."

"Why would you think that?" Sol asked with a troubled look appearing on His face, and Laurel looked down awkwardly.

"Well...like I said...I thought that I would only be a burden to You if You knew how fearful my nightmares made me. I mean, I know that I am not very strong or fast or brave anyway, so if I had to face the Tempters again..."

"But *you shall* not have to face them again," Sol interjected emphatically. "*We* will, together, just as we did in the forest. And no matter what, the Wingel will always be there to help you, as well." Then, He lifted Laurel's chin, and the shy maiden met the King's sweet and tender eyes. "I promise," Sol concluded, smiling down at her, and Laurel returned the caring expression in agreement.

"You know," she began suddenly, "I was kind of troubled at first when I realized all of these things about the War and Terra, especially about Your Kingship. But, I want You to know that...You were right. If you had told me earlier about...well, everything...then I would never have believed You."

"Laurel, I may not have revealed to you at first about this War, but I did reveal to you about My Kingship."

"You...You did?" the girl questioned with perplexity as the two released each other from their embrace.

"Yes, remember when you asked Me if I was a prince?" When Laurel nodded in remembrance, Sol continued, "Well, I told you that I was the King of the ants, and that was the truth, for I am the King of the ants, the flowers, the trees, the birds, and all of Terra."

Laurel stood in bewilderment for a moment as she realized this, but then smiled unwittingly. "And do not forget the King of the boars, too!"

Sol laughed merrily. "Yes, that too!"

"Sol...I am sorry that what I said is true," Laurel's smile faded. "I am sorry that I would not have believed You without seeing everything for myself."

"Laurel," Sol smiled as He clasped the young maiden's hands at her sides, "remember what I told you about believing?"

"Hmm...? Oh! Back at the valley, You said that to believe in the absolute truth, we do so without anything getting in the way...like fears or uncertainty."

"Yes, that is faith, my dear. Faith is having confidence in the truth."

"Faith," Laurel murmured. "Well, if You still want me to stay here and help in this War, then I am going to be in need of a lot of faith...especially with *my* fears and uncertainty."

"Laurel," Sol began suddenly as He took up the young maiden's hands close to His heart, "at this time, I wish to bestow a blessing on you."

"A blessing?"

"Yes, one that will be your safeguard against the Tempters and give you strength of heart, especially when faith is found wanting."

"You mean like the power of the ring?" Laurel asked, holding up her hand to look upon the mystical band as she remembered the Queen's words on the subject.

"Yes..." Sol continued, gently enfolding Laurel's hands benevolently with His own, while His other rested chastely on her cheek. "Something very much like that..." His voice came mysteriously and softly as He drew forward and kissed Laurel's forehead compassionately.

Laurel's heart seemed to stop beating all at once as she comprehended the blessing that Sol had given her. A new emotion stirred itself within the heart of this simple child, and she wondered unsurely how she was to cope with this strange grace. As her face began blushing bright red, Sol withdrew His kiss and Himself from the young maiden as He smiled blissfully at His dear friend. Laurel stared up at the King in astonishment, not knowing what to say.

Suddenly, before the two could ever begin to speak on the matter, a door to the tower's interior swiftly swung open, and Peterel appeared in the doorway.

"Peterel?" Laurel called curiously.

Then, seeing his Master and Laurel by the balcony railings, Peterel speedily hovered towards them, with a manner of great importance airing about him.

"Master, Master!" he exclaimed hastily, stopping in front of his King and giving a courteous bow to Him. "I have important news from the Queen. The Knights[9] have arrived!"

---

[9] When referring to the group of the King's warriors, the Knights of Terra, this term and all related terms (such as the King's Company, and the Knights) will be capitalized.

Chapter 12
The Knights of Terra

The Knights of Terra were King Sol's personal band of twelve warriors, whose recruitment He had solicited during His many travels across the land of Terra. The Knights were an impressive-looking crew of combatants, as they sported long brown and green tunics, embroidered with the symbol of the Royal Family across the front. Each man had his own weapon of choice, and attached to their stiff belts around their waists, they holstered small hand axes and daggers and trusty pouches for security. The dozen each had a pair of metal plates protecting their shoulders and a flowing cloak that hugged around their arms. Their thick, dark pants were covered with meshes of chain mail, and their large, brown boots made quaking thumps and thuds across the ground whenever these tall, well-built men walked about.

At first glance, these gallant men, with their menacing weapons and strong statures, gave the impression of belonging to the family of those who were skilled warriors from birth, bred to fight from a noble class. However, some time ago, these twelve warriors would have laughed at the thought of fighting in grueling battles and journeying across the land of Terra beyond their homes. Their backgrounds were of humble origins as these men were mostly tradesmen and anglers, with even a tax collector being among them. Nevertheless, they had learned under the watchful eye of their Master, King Sol, and had become the finest group of fighters in all the land of Terra. They knew this too, though too well sometimes, for their pride usually provoked tension in their midst.

At any rate, once Sol and Laurel were made aware of the arrival of the Knights, the King hastened to greet His friends and introduce them to the young maiden that evening. Coming into the entrance hall, Laurel beheld the twelve burly men standing in a row below the staircase. She could not see their faces at first, for they genuflected as they saw Sol approaching them. However, noting their war-like clothes and appearances, Laurel was curious to learn more of their identities.

"My friends!" Sol exclaimed joyfully, nearing the end of the marble stairs. "I am glad to see that you have all returned to the Sanctuary safely!"

The twelve saluted their King with the proper, respectful greetings that should be imparted to their Sovereign. After, they congregated around Sol, offering virile embraces and humorous remarks of their recent adventures in their rough but vigorous accents.

"Two by two, we departed, Master, just as you requested, and with no difficulties whatsoever," informed one combatant.

"I beg to differ," said another, "though not because of any complications in the campaign, but because of a certain *soldier* who was determined to have things done *his* way!"

"Oh, you are one to talk!" replied his companion, huffily but rather humored. "I never heard of a person complain over such nonsense in my entire life as a soldier!"

Then a fourth and fifth spoke up, "I think you are all full of nonsense! We had no trouble at all...though there was a time when we did almost lose our way. Say, Master, why was it that You said not to take a map with us? It would have been very useful at the time of *our* tribulations, and we probably could have arrived at the Sanctuary a lot sooner than this lot of half-wits."

"As if a map would do you two knuckleheads any good," muttered one of the first, showing no real attempt of concealing his words. "Besides, anyone can see that the Master wanted us to learn our own way around Terra, as a proper lesson of achieving true cognition and awareness!

"Men! Men!" exclaimed the King sternly, as if He had spoken thus bleakly towards His Knights' foolish bickering before. "Come now, enough with such talk! I have a right mind of sending you all to a nightly toil in the stables for such disagreeable remarks, but fortunately for yourselves, I have a very lovely visitor who I would like to introduce to you." Then turning to Laurel, who had stood quietly at the end of the staircase as she listened jovially to the entertaining group of warriors, Sol announced, "I present to you My dear friend, Laurel of Serenity Forest."

The men all straightened swiftly and gave a warm bow towards the young maiden saying cordially in unison, "Welcome!"

Laurel also gave a polite curtsey towards the brawny gentlemen, though rather timidly, as was her nature. "Thank you very much!" she replied back with a simple smile on her countenance.

"We are very pleased to meet you!" began one Knight, who carried a long, double-edged sword against his belt, as he stepped forward to introduce himself to the young maiden. "I am Feoras of the Southern Sea, the Rock of the King's Knighthood," the Knight brazenly declared, giving another bow. He was a man of massive features, from his large, calloused hands to his immensely, crackled-split feet. His physique was broad-shouldered with a tempered, yet determined, air about him. He had a short and scruffy darkened beard that covered his stone-like face. His earthen eyes showed brightly and boldly amid his short, dark-curled head. True to his title, Feoras' looks and nature exhibited the characteristics of a mighty and forceful rock.

"I am second in command of the Knights of Terra behind our King," he continued, his confident air never faltering as he spoke. "Yes, for many laborious days, I have led my men on the most perilous journeys all across Terra. Despite my hardships, not for one moment have I missed my past life, heaving and pulling at the lines and nets of my father's fishing boat during my days as a common fisherman. For you see, my dear girl, the life of a Knight has — "

Suddenly, two of the Knights, each carrying a crossbow and a quiver of fresh arrows against their backs, broke into Feoras' introduction as they rushed up behind him and forcefully pulled him back from Laurel's presence. "Come now, Feoras, you rock-head!" the two chided comically.

"Enough of your fulsome introductions!" continued one, "We too, and some others here, were fishers of the high seas, as you know, but you do not hear any of us hurrying to brag about our own past lives."

"Indeed! So give the other eleven of us some room for exchange with the King's young friend!" finished the other.

Laughing in spite of herself, Laurel found it odd that the two Knights spoke in such unison together until she realized that they were twins. The twins were light-hearted brothers, who took pleasure in causing an uproar of laughter, but also in instigating their own ideas of wholesome mischief. Both had brown jaw-length hair with ecstatic, glowing dark eyes filling their youthful faces. Despite their slender physique, they were muscularly strong men, who were the swiftest runners of the group.

"Don't mind, Feoras," the twins continued, turning to Laurel. "He means well and is a great leader, but we think that square head of his is a little too thick sometimes, if you know what we mean!"

"Why you thunderous troublemakers!" Feoras exclaimed irately, recovering himself from the twin's dynamic entry.

The brothers only laughed this off and resumed their conversation with Laurel, "Speaking of thunderous, allow us to introduce ourselves as the Brothers Thunder, according to our King's initial naming of us. This is Taran," continued one twin as he acknowledged his brother, while the other relayed, "and this is Radi, the younger of the two of us. We are pleased to have your acquaintance!" Taran and Radi finished with a graceful bow to Laurel, who smiled and giggled.

Feoras, who stood watching with the others, had a stern look of discomfiture, as if sulking in the termination of his fine, introductive speech. Then, another Knight with a battle-ax strapped to his back came beside him. He patted the forlorn Knight firmly against his back, greatly shocking Feoras from his thoughts.

"Now, now, my brother!" he started in a booming voice, "Do not let the joking nature of the Brothers Thunder bring about your sulking temper!" Then, when Laurel took notice of the strapping Knight, he too acknowledged her with a bow. "How do you do, my dear? I am Andres the Mighty, older brother of our dear leader, the Rock."

Andres looked very much like his brother in every way, though he was thinner than Feoras and much more cheery in initial encounter. Turning back to his brother, who stood evermore morosely at his side, Andres exclaimed tauntingly, "Though, remember, my dear *younger* brother and faithful leader, that it was *I* who was knighted in the King's noble Order first! So, remember there are other things, besides the twins' merriment, that you can huff about later!" And a shout of laughter broke out among the Knights at this jeering and jollity.

"Are you all brothers?" Laurel spoke up suddenly, seeing a pattern in the relations of each Knight that presented himself so far.

"Oh, no, my dear! Not all of us!" Radi replied in amusement. "Then again, we all regard ourselves as brothers of the King's Order. Anyway, there are three pairs of brothers in our assembly of twelve, and the last, but of course not least, of the pairs are Yaakov the Humble and Zimran, Singer of the Emperor's Praise."

Then, two of the Knights, one with a hand-mace strapped to his belt and the other wielding a spear as a staff, stepped forward out of the cluster of the remaining, unnamed Knights. Yaakov, the older and taller of the two brothers, had short, thin dark hair with a trim beard. His eyes were like two small black marbles against his lighter skin, but as his name suggested, they showed with true sincerity and modesty. Zimran, the wielder of the spear, was the more youthful of the two, as his jaw-length, fair locks gave him a more refreshing impression. As for his title, Zimran was known for his melodious voice in singing songs of majesty and merriment during the Knights journeys for their entertainment and for the praising of the Emperor.

"You shall find that we do not chatter much, unlike are boisterous companions, for we feel that they say all that there needs to be said," Yaakov related and Zimran meekly nodded in agreement.

"Come, come," the twins jeered to the rest of the Knights, "and introduce yourselves!"

Donato the Generous, whose weapon of choice was a spike ball, approached next. He was the former tax collector that had joined the ranks of the King's Order. He was an older man with a balding head and a bright, white trimmed beard. His light eyes showed brightly with aging wisdom and a thoughtful countenance. His former occupation and given "surname" seemed oddly paired together, for not many tax collectors in the land of Terra abided by the Emperor's commands of mercy and forgiveness when debts were due from the commoners. However, Donato the Generous was the grand exception as he worked his misrepresented occupation with patience and kindliness, before he was called to the Knighthood.

"You know, it was actually quite interesting how I first followed our King to be His Knight!" Donato related when revealing his past occupation. "I mean, all of a sudden, I find the King of Terra standing in front of my tax-collecting desk, and without a warning He asks me to follow Him. Well, what else could I do, but follow the King and leave the lines of debtors to the tax collector beside me!"

Another Knight, Maso of Many Questions, was, as his name suggested, a very skeptical young man, whose hazel eyes seemed to always be calculating and discerning everything that was laid before him. He had short, light hair that curled around his wary ears, and his tall stature towered over all of the other Knights. Maso had fastened to his left and right sides a pair of twin boomerangs with sharp, piercing edges. "'Two *are* better than one', as the old saying goes," Maso related, patting the sides of his weapons.

Caius, Taam, and Saimen were three other Knights known for their great passion and ardor towards the Monarchy. Therefore, they were together dubbed the Knights of Zeal. The three were energetic youths. Caius had short, wavy brown hair, a moustache, and ecstatic, dark eyes. Taam sported short, curly brown hair with bright, chestnut eyes. Saimen, on the other hand, bore short black hair and a dark, flowing beard. Their weapons of choice were respectively a jagged club, a large battle hammer, and a simple but potent slingshot. They greeted Laurel with humble introductions and, as always, gave praise to the Emperor of Terra.

The last Knight to be named was a man named Sadu, who wielded a long, piercing saber. He was shorter than most of the Knights, but still quite an intimidating fellow. He had a balding head, and what was left of his short, dark hair was scruffily laid around his head. His face was wrinkled with fatigue as if he was tired from the long journey that he had just finished, but his eyes were anxious and distrustful, though not in similarity to Maso who was a simple skeptic. He did not say much to Laurel, other than the common greeting that was due to a new acquaintance, and he stood in thought, fingering his saber's hilt, while he waited for the other eleven to desire retirement from their merry introductions.

"Well, there you have it, my dear!" came Andres' booming voice as he turned to Laurel. "We are twelve, the Knights of Terra!" And all of the Knights gave the young maiden one final bow in acquaintance as they ended their presentation.

"Oh, yes! I am very happy to have met you all this night!" she replied cheerfully.

"Very good!" came the Queen's melodious voice from above the stairs, and all looked up the marble steps to find Queen Mariah, who had been watching all the while, waiting above. Instantly, the Knights were on their knees in reverent greeting of their sovereign Queen.

"I had hoped that you would all return to the Sanctuary soon," She continued gracefully, "and now I am glad to see all twelve of you here before Me!" Then, looking to Her Son, who stood amid the Knights, She announced,

"My Son, I have been informed by the Wingel servants that a grand feast has been prepared for Our Knights."

"Food!" the Knights shouted jollily, unable to contain their excitement over the thought of a well-cooked meal.

Sol laughed heartily at this, saying, "Well, then, My brothers! Come, let us have our feast!"

The dining hall of the Sanctuary was a large room of the most elegant design and majesty, for it was renowned for the great and glorious feasts that had been held there in the days of yesteryear. The ceiling was decorated in an array of golden-leafed colors and silver-molded, floral designs. A brilliant crystal chandelier was hung in the ceiling's center, which brightened the room with its flameless light. The floor made of a white marble, and a long purple carpet stretched from one end of the dining hall to the other. A roaring fire had been made in the stone fireplace that stood on the eastern wall, while a large circular window displayed the glowing sunset from the western wall. A long, dark dining table of the finest wood in all of Terra stood in the center of the room and held seven seats on each side. Six Knights sat on each side of the table, while Laurel and Grandma Arliana, who had come to join the feast, both took the remaining seats at the ends. The King and the Queen both sat at opposite ends of the table. Being courteous Hosts of the feast, the two Monarchs waited for Their friends to be served their meals before They began to enjoy the delicious food that was set before Them.

The feast that night was a most magnificent and grand indulgence of delicious meats, fruits, vegetables, grains, and scrumptious desserts, and there were many Wingel servants in beautiful robes and other attire about the room serving these delightful foods. As always, Laurel found great delight in all the wonderful victuals that she had to choose from, and the Knights of Terra likewise displayed the young maiden's festal enjoyment. While the diners enjoyed their meal, the Knights relayed to the King of all their findings on their journeys around Terra.

"There is much trouble in the Kingdom," related Saimen. "The people's loyalty to the Crown is growing continually weaker."

"We found some towns under the security of faithful followers," replied one of the twins, "but it seems that they cannot hold out any longer, for the tide of betrayers seems to be growing stronger."

"It is because of those horrid Tempters!" Feoras began disgustedly, giving a light thump on the table with his brawny fist. "Every day, they are flooding the hearts of the people with deception! It is like they never rest, those awful creatures, and I cannot believe that any right-minded person would listen to their hateful trickery!"

"Come now, my brother!" Andres now spoke up. "You know, as well as I, that it is because of Malum's Curse that the people have become so weak to such evil."

Zimran concurred, "The evil demon has a hold on the hearts of every citizen of Terra by his Curse, including our own. There is not one Knight among us who has not had his own undertaking with temptations."

Hearing this, all of the Knights gave their honest, yet reluctant, agreement, and all fell silent, pondering Zimran's words. Laurel herself felt a new sense of determination to help Sol, for she realized then that she could find understanding and support from the Knights, though they knew nothing yet about her own encounters with the Tempters. Because of this, Laurel began to regard the Knights as her new friends.

They understand a lot more of this War than I do, she consider to herself. *With them, maybe I can come to understand more about myself as well, and help Sol in the process.*

Peering down from one end of the long table to the other, Laurel noticed that Sol and the Queen both eyed each other, as if they were disclosing a private conversation mysteriously by their gazing. Then, Sol finally spoke up, "Do not despair, My brothers! In time, we *will* see the end of this War."

"Yes, but with which side as the victor?" Sadu mumbled gloomily under his breath.

"Say that again!" Feoras exclaimed vexingly, his hand clenching his butter-knife. "You should not dare to speak so, especially to our King!"

"Stay, Feoras!" Queen Mariah spoke up, eyeing the Knight disapprovingly. "That will be enough of such tension."

As Feoras calmed himself, Maso turned to the Queen saying, "If You shall permit me, my Lady, I would have to agree somewhat with Sadu's statement. I mean, as we all know, the people are not holding out very well in this War, and Malum's power has practically reached every corner of Terra and back again. I daresay that our victory does look bleakly uncertain at the moment."

"All I am saying," Sadu began again, quite irritated by Feoras' anger, "is that after all our journeys, after traveling from one end of Terra to the other, we have still found ourselves in the same position that we started with: the Realm in division and at war."

"I suppose that you are right," Donato considered hesitantly. "All we have ever done on our missions is visit the citizens and try to rally their spirits for the Emperor and not much else."

"And do you truly believe what you are saying?" Sol asked, and the Knights, grudgingly, proclaimed their agreement with these despondent considerations. "So you all believe that every mission that I have sent you on, every journey and every traverse was meaningless, with no purpose in helping the people of Terra?" The Knights were silent at this moment as they felt the empathetic glare of their King weighing down on them. "Well, if you agree with such a thought," Sol continued, "then I tell you that you are wrong. Now, can you think of any reason as to why I would send you out to My people?"

As Sol gazed from Knight to Knight, waiting for His answer, the twelve thought long and hard about the King's questioning, not certain if they knew the answer. "To learn?" Caius finally inquired.

"And what did you learn?" Sol asked again.

"Well... Now, we know more than ever before that the people are in great peril," Radi stated frankly.

"And that if we do not do something soon, then Malum might just take over the land of Terra and rule with his evil plot to destroy us all," continued his brother.

"Precisely!" Sol agreed ardently. "However, in knowing this, you also know that there is one thing that stands in that vile creature's way of completely taking over the hearts of the people: virtue! Through virtue, Malum's evil Curse will be destroyed all together, and the land of Terra will be saved."

"That sounds easier said than done, my Liege," Sadu spoke up again. His expression was melancholy with tension. "Malum's Curse has already done a fine job of subduing control over many of the citizens."

"That is why, My dear brother, we must instill within the people's heart the three King Virtues[10], which are essential for conquering Malum's evil."

"The King Virtues, my Lord?" Donato inquired, leaning forward to peer down the long table at Sol.

"Yes, the King Virtues. Do you not remember the story of old that tells the tale of the fallen Wingel's attack on My Father's Kingdom? When the Great Wingel War broke out and Malum was banished from the Eternal Palace, he then undertook his plan to destroy virtue in the people's hearts in order for them to turn away from My Father. However, in an effort to preserve the three greatest virtues, the King Virtues, My Father hid them away across the land of Terra, so that they may not be abolished by the fallen Wingel's Curse. Now, tell Me, My brothers, what are these three virtues of which I speak?" Sol then looked again about the table, awaiting His answer.

"Faith," said Yaakov, who had been silent for some time, "for in order to follow their Monarchs, the people must believe in them."

---

[10] When referring to the three great virtues, this term and the names of the virtues themselves will be capitalize.

"And…Hope," Andres voiced, "for throughout the hardships of this war, they need to know that they can trust their Monarchs and that a better future lies ahead."

"Yes, yes, very good!" Sol beamed delightedly. "And the last?"

Surprisingly, the Knights had to think long and hard before any answer could come to them. Every time their answers were good, but not quite the one that the King had hoped for. Courage was said to be the last, but then again Faith gave the means for such a virtue. Confidence? No, Hope would surely be the answer to any self-doubt. Could obedience be the answer? No, a very good virtue, though, but one grows in obedience by the Faith that they have in the goodness of their Master. A host of other well-beloved virtues were named, but there was still one that the Knights could not recollect at that moment.

"Come now, Knights of Terra!" Sol encouraged them. "There is still one virtue that rules as the greatest of all the other virtues!"

"Love?" squeaked a small, almost inaudible voice, and all turned down the long row of Knights at the young maiden Laurel. She had been quietly sipping her warm soup, at the time, listening to the dinner conversation. Suddenly, she was reminded of her own conversations with Peterel on the *mysterious coat of arms*, which she had seen on Philippe's blanket, which was the time when her dear little friend had made known to her the greatest virtue. Sitting now at the end of the table and watching as all eyes stared at her with surprise, Laurel realized how she had unconsciously voiced an answer to Sol's question. Her face reddened embarrassingly.

"Very good, Laurel," the King said satisfactorily. "Love is the answer."

Despite this, the shy maiden turned away from the onlookers, self-conscious that she had even spoken up at all. She looked up only once afterwards to see Grandma Arliana, who had been and would remain silent for the whole diner, being content with listening, as she gave the girl a gleeful and pleased wink.

"Yes," Sol continued anyhow, "Love is the answer, for no Kingdom can rule without compassion for the people who are ruled! Therefore, in knowing that these King Virtues of Faith, Hope, and Love were of great importance to the salvation of the Kingdom, My Father ordered that they be hidden away, so that Malum's Curse could not destroy them. Now, the time has come that these great virtues should be restored to the people, which shall be our present mission."

"Permit me, just a moment, my Liege," Feoras broke in suddenly. "I have to wonder, how is it that we are to restore these virtues to the Kingdom? I mean, are not virtues intangible and abstract qualities? So, how is it that the Emperor 'hid them away' and how must we find them?"

"What you say is true, My friend. However, herein lies the answer: you see, Malum so hatefully wanted to destroy the relationship of My Family with the people, that he used his evil might to form his own hate into a real and true presence, that is, his Curse. My Father, on the other hand, used His power to form the King Virtues, which were being lost by the people and in danger of being destroyed by Malum's Curse, into real and true presences, and, like all royal treasures, the virtues of Faith, Hope, and Love were formed into three precious stones. With these virtuous stones in His possession, My Father was able to send them far out of Malum's reach. Up until this present moment, they have all but been forgotten, for it has come to My attention that the whereabouts of the King Virtues are being discerned by Malum as we speak. Therefore, it is pertinent that now be the time that we seek them."

Hearing all of this, the Knights sat in wonderment for a long moment, bearing in mind the King's new and courageous plan to save the people. They talked amongst themselves silently of all that this plan might entail.

"Can this really be?" Maso's skepticism arose. "Virtues in the form of precious stones?"

"Well, if the King said it, than surely it must be!" Saimen interjected.

"Yes, but can we really do it?" Andres asked in amazement. "There is no doubt that there will be more journeying across this land, once again!"

"And we were just beginning to hope that we could take a break!" The twins sighed wearily.

"Come now! Show some respect!" Zimran reproved. "You know we must do as our King commands, no matter what the circumstances may be. This is what we swore to at our Knighting!"

"Here, here!" exclaimed his brother, Yaakov. "For the King!"

"Yes, for the King! Long live Our King!" Feoras shouted, too, holding up his glass as a toast, and all of the Knights drank to this salutation.

As Laurel sat as witness to all of this, she felt a persistence in her heart to join the Knights' journey. *What am I thinking?* She thought to herself, *Come along on the journey! Even if they agreed for me to come, which they surely would not, how could I ever be of service or of any help to them, especially to Sol! Then again…if I truly want to prove myself to Sol, and make up for my weakness…to truly make myself useful for Him…*

Suddenly, a tender hand fell across Laurel's own, and the young maiden looked up to see Queen Mariah's loving gaze, as She sat next to Laurel at the opposite head of the table. Her sweet, affectionate eyes seemed to give Laurel a sense of encouragement, as if they could see right into the maiden's very soul and into her own thoughts. Timidly, Laurel nodded her head in agreement at the Queen's persistence, and turning to the clamoring Knights, who now talked of all the preparations for their journey, she told herself that now or never was the time to ask to join the mission.

"I... I want to follow, too!" she said, in her trembling voice, as loud as she could, or rather dared. To her astonishment, all of the Knights once again turned to face the small girl at the sound of her very small voice. "I... I want to follow, too...please..."

"You?" Sol asked, not willing to hide the pleasure He derived from Laurel's words. "You wish to join us on our mission?"

"You cannot join us!" Feoras cried aloud before Laurel could reaffirm her resolution. "Andres was right before when he said that there will be, no doubt, much more journeying on this mission than we ourselves have experienced thus far. You, only a young and inexperienced maiden, could not possibly bare the pressures of such excursions!"

"'Only a young and inexperienced maiden' is she!" Queen Mariah spoke up suddenly, Her expression disapproving of Feoras' hasty rebuff of Laurel's intention. "Unable to 'bare the pressures of such excursions'! Well, there is no need, Sir Feoras, to jump to such hasty rejections, if those are all your reasons that trouble you of the young maiden. Surely, such hindrances can be mended in due time."

Seeing the folly haste of his outspokenness, Feoras bowed his head embarrassingly. "I am sorry, my Lieges."

"Good Feoras," began King Sol, "I can see the concern of your heart clearly, but do not be so rash as to think that I would allow our dear Laurel to join us without experience or preparedness! Therefore, I tell you all, Knights of Terra, that from this moment on we shall work together to ensure that our newest member of the Sanctuary, Laurel of Serenity Forest, is thoroughly capable of journeying with us to acquire the three King Virtues. That is," Sol continued, turning His eyes to Laurel, "if you are truly determined to join us."

Timorously, but without hesitation Laurel nodded in agreement, wanting still to join Sol and the Knights of Terra.

"There you have it, My brothers! Now, let us not speak another word of this War, for dessert is now upon us!" And as Sol said this, the first course of dessert was brought out to the sixteen diners.

All of the Knights gave there congratulations to Laurel, except for Feoras, who still brooded over his headstrong words, and Sadu, whose morose nature caused him to disregard the King's words and continue his thoughts of the War. Laurel in turn gave everyone, including Grandma Arliana and the Queen, who both beamed with delight for her, a tentative smile. The child's heart was madly racing within her, and her mind was already swirling with second thoughts of her decision.

What have I just agreed to? She wondered, sinking into her chair and taking a first bite at her chocolate cake. *Hmm, yummy!*

True to Sol's words, Laurel spent the next few days training and preparing for the mission under the watchful eyes of the Knights of Terra. Since the maiden was going to be a part of this War, she was going to have to learn how to defend herself in the face of danger. In the sparring room, a wide and spacious chamber of the Sanctuary with an assortment of tools and equipment, which the Knights used for training, Laurel was taught many basic techniques for defense, stealth, and secrecy. Each Knight also tried to teach the young maiden how to use their own weapons of choice. However, no matter how hard she practiced, Laurel could never find a weapon that suited her well. Many of the weapons were either too large or heavy for Laurel to use, being unfitting for the young maiden to carry for defense. Once when Laurel took a chance at using one of the twins' crossbows, she instantly fell onto her back as she released the trigger. The arrow shot right through the distant wall, obviously missing its target.

"Maybe I should just go without a weapon," Laurel stated despondently as Andres helped her to her feet.

"I know that it is difficult," Andres replied, "but if you are going to join us, then you really must have a weapon to defend yourself with. Though, we hope that you shall not need it for any fighting on your part, but it is still necessary for precautions."

"Say, maybe she can use a sword!" exclaimed the Brothers Thunder enthusiastically. "Feoras, come over and —"

"I would rather not!" Feoras replied emphatically. He sat in one corner of the room, sharpening his blade.

"Come now, Feoras," Zimran spoke up. "You heard what the King said! We must all help Laurel to choose a suitable weapon, and the only one left for her to learn of is a sword."

"Then get Sadu to teach her! He has a sword, too!"

"Yes, but today Sadu has gone out again," said Saimen. "You know how fond he is of riding that dark stallion of his."

Then, Andres approached his brother, hoping to change his stubborn-minded ways. "Come now, brother, and teach the young maiden how to use a sword."

"No!" came the Rock's indignant reply, looking up into the pleading eyes of his brother.

"Please, Sir Feoras!" Laurel now spoke up for herself. "I very much want to learn, and I am sure it would be a great honor to learn from you!"

"I, too, am certain of this, but my answer is final: No!"

"As you wish, but if you shall not teach her, then I shall!"

All of the Knights and Laurel turned then to see Queen Mariah at the doorway, and Laurel was thoroughly amazed, as well as mystified, that the Queen would volunteer to teach her sword fighting.

"You know how to use a sword?" Laurel inquired.

"Why did you not know?" Taran and Radi asked, each placing a brotherly hand on the maiden's shoulders. "Queen Mariah is the most well-known swordswoman in all the land of Terra. Many call her the legendary Woman of the Seven Swords!"

"*Seven* swords!" Laurel gasped, turning back to Queen Mariah with wide eyes.

"Yes, my dear, seven swords, and each I have acquired in facing many hardships in my life," the Queen replied mysteriously, stepping forward. "Now, as for your defense, I want you to take this."

Saying this, Queen Mariah removed from her dress pocket a long gold chain of a series of bright, crystal beads that shined in a spectral of colors when exposed to the light. The chain had two sets of beads and two gold pendants with one of the pendants in the shape of the Emperor's Seal and the other a round portrait of the King and of the Queen on each side. For a moment, Laurel felt a strange sense of familiarity as she received the beauteous chain from the Queen's hands. However, she could not seem to remember exactly where she had seen such a mystifying token.

"This is very beautiful!" Laurel marveled, "but how am I to use it for my defense?"

Without a word, Queen Mariah placed a hand onto the bright beads of Her gold chain. Suddenly, a dazzling light shined forth from the beads, and in an instant, the gold chain had transformed into a golden, sheathed dagger.

"This is called the Oracion," said the Queen. "Whenever you are in need of anything, anything at all and as long as your request is unselfish and noble, all you must do is plead your request in My name and it shall be granted to you."

All Laurel could do was stare and marvel, for she was greatly bewildered by the mystical gift that the Queen had given her. Queen Mariah then took the royal dagger from Laurel's hands to examine it. The sheath was decorated with spectacular floral designs, the hilt was encrusted with shining diamonds, and the pommel was engraved with the Emperor's Seal. Drawing the dagger, She revealed the magnificent blade, whose point was sharp to the touch. Then, She pointed out to Laurel an engraving of words that had been etched into the dagger's edge: *With zeal am I zealous for the Lord and Emperor of Terra.*

"With this dagger, I shall teach you not only to defend yourself against the evil of the Tempters but also to have courage in all that you do for the Emperor. Now...will you let Me teach you My ways?"

Looking up at the Queen in wonder and with a new sense of determination, Laurel replied, "Yes, my Queen!"

Chapter 13
Journey to the Sea

Laurel was an avid and quick learner as she studied under the tutelage of Queen Mariah, learning to defend herself with her new weapon. Soon after, the time for departure had drawn near, and everyone who would embark on the King's search for the three Virtues had prepared extensively for this mission. Those who made up King Sol's band of followers on this mission, besides the Knights of Terra and Laurel, also included Queen Mariah and a small group of Wingel warriors who were under the command of General Mikhail. Peterel was also ordered by the King to accompany Laurel on the journey as her personal guard, to which the maiden was immensely grateful, as well as pleased. Despite this companionship, the young girl's heart would continually be troubled on this journey. She had discovered to her dismay that Grandma Arliana would not be following at her side.

"Why, my dear? Did you think that an old woman like myself would be coming along on such an excursion? Nonsense!" Grandma Arliana related, when confronted by the lass. "Now, now, do not shed such soggy tears! We shall see each other again, and it is not the end of the world if we are parted!"

"Bu—but, Granny," Laurel blubbered sadly, "where will you go if you are not coming? And who is going to take care of you?"

"O, Laurel," Grandma Arliana began, wiping tenderly at her friend's falling tears. "I have decided to go back to my home in the East with my animals. There, I wish to search for my family and reunite with them as I should have done long ago. Besides, the Queen told me that we could always use some rallying witnesses anywhere to gather the people under the Emperor, and during my stay there, that is what I intend to do. Now, I know you want me to come along with you, but your battle is at the King's side and mine is with His citizens who need encouragement. That is all I am capable of doing at this moment, so you must leave it at that! All right, enough about me—but look at you all dressed up and ready to conquer the world!"

Grandma Arliana then motioned for Laurel to turn around in her new outfit, for, since today was the day of departure, the Queen had commanded that proper travelling attire should be made for Laurel. The girl wore a long brown dress, whose skirt stretched down to her ankles. She also wore simple brown sandals on her feet and a short cream-colored veil to cover her head. The Emperor's Seal adorned an elegant, purple cloak that hung around Laurel's shoulders, as well as the pendant that was used as a clasp for the cape. A long golden rope was fastened around Laurel's waist like a cincture with its cords hanging from her right side, while the Queen's treasure, the Oracion, hung on her left side.

"But, dear, why are you wearing that, um, what did you call it again?" Grandma Arliana asked pointing to the girl's mystical chain.

"Oracion."

"Oracion. Why are you wearing the Oracion at your waist?"

"Well, it is my weapon, and like all weapons, one keeps them at one's side."

"Hmm, well, you look exceptionally geared for your long journey, my dear."

Just then, before Laurel could again relate how sorrowful she was for having to leave Grandma Arliana, Peterel came into the parlor room, where the two had been conversing. "Laurel, the King is ready to depart, so we should hasten along now."

Laurel's heart felt a little devastated at hearing this, for the only words she could impart to the old woman were, "Good bye..." before falling into her arms for one last embrace.

"There, now, my dear. Remember *why* you are going on this mission! To help Sol in all the ways that you can, and, knowing you for as long as I have, I know that you shall be a great help to Him!"

"You really think so?" Laurel asked, squeezing her friend all the more.

"Yes, my dear, I truly do."

With that, the two parted, and Laurel started for the door where Peterel awaited her. "What will you do until you depart for *your* journey?" Laurel asked turning back to Grandma Arliana.

"Well, first I shall have to wait a while for the next Wingel general to arrive; his squadron will escort me into the East, and from there I shall begin the search for my family. Until then, I suppose that I shall see what sort of mischief I can stir up within this enchanted tower!" And an impish grin appeared across the old woman's face as she looked about the room with hearty jest.

"Somehow, I am not surprised!" Laurel remarked, half lightheartedly and half heartbreakingly, as she gave the old woman a final farewell before following Peterel out of the parlor.

The King's Company left the Sanctuary in the early hours of one breezy morning, for this beginning journey to their first destination would take about three days' time to complete. Trekking through the dense, green shrubs and woods of Serenity Forest on horseback, King Sol and Queen Mariah led the expedition followed by the Wingel soldiers headed by General Mikhail. Riding close behind were the Knights of Terra, where Laurel and Peterel also traversed in the courageous group. The young maiden, who rode a strawberry-blond horse named Sorina, who was a serene and docile mare, was more apprehensive than ever as she cautiously followed the Knights throughout the journey in Serenity Forest. Many uncertain and restless thoughts whirled in her head, as she thought of how important the mission that she now embarked on was.

"Where exactly are we headed again?" Laurel asked Andres solicitously.

"To the sea," replied the Knight, "the Southern Sea. We will journey to Madeira Harbor since that is the closest village between us and the Southern Sea, and from there we shall sail to the southern pole of Terra."

"To the South Pole?" Laurel gaped in astonishment. "We are going all the way down *there*?"

"Well, that is what the King wishes," Caius spoke up, "and the King's wish is our command."

"Ah! The Southern Sea!" Radi mused aloud in a dreamy sort of voice. "Just the name brings back old memories, does it not, Taran?"

"Indeed, my brother! Ah, to hear the rising and falling of the tides as those crisp, rolling waves clash against the warm, sandy beaches! Ah, the ocean!"

"O, my brother, just think! In a matter of days, we, born fishermen, will be home in our native land once again!" Radi continued blissfully, and the twins sighed ecstatically in their reveries.

"Do not rest your hearts too hastily, Brothers Thunder," Feoras interjected. "Our first priority on this mission is to obtain the three stones of Virtue. Once this is completed, then you two may reminisce of your past, youthful adventures at sea."

"Aw, come now, Feoras!" cried the twins eagerly, riding up to the Knight. "Are you not a least somewhat keen to see the sea again, with its salty breezes and whirling waves and chattering gulls and sun-warmed beaches?"

Feoras' face seemed to glow for a moment at these illustrative thoughts, but he quickly nudged his horse forward and away from the twin. However, the twins had already witnessed the brightening of their leader's face, and they laughed heartily in triumph. Then, some of the other Knights joined their gleeful laughter, and Feoras grew annoyed at such jest.

"All right, that is enough out of you two dreamers! Can we not go through one journey without hearing your trivial recollections? Besides, you both should have learned long ago to forget your past, for when we took the oath of our Knighthood, we swore to abandon our bygone days."

"We know that," the twins replied, somewhat hurt at hearing this. "We were only just saying how wonderful it will be to see all of those things again."

"Feoras, you must not be so hard on our youngest Knights," spoke up Andres. "You take such youthful discretions too seriously."

"May I remind you, my brother, that *I* am the leader of this Knighthood? I am only trying to be practical by keeping our objective on focus."

"And may I remind you that it was *I* who was called by the King to join the Knighthood of Terra *first!*" Andres replied, riding past his brother with a triumphant sense of glee. "And if it were not for *me*, you might never have become a Knight of Terra, for I was the one who appealed for you to follow our King."

"Oh, you shall just never let me forget, now will you?" Feoras gritted his teeth.

"Settle down, you two!" Saimen interrupted. "I have heard quite enough of such silly nonsense!"

"Saimen is right," Taam agreed. "If the King and Queen were to hear your talk, then they would greatly disapprove!"

Then, Sadu interposed, "I do not see how that would matter anyway, considering that Feoras' stubbornness usually leads to this at least once or twice an hour."

"Say that again!" Feoras replied, almost threateningly, as he turned in his saddle.

"You know, Feoras did have a point!" Maso ruminated, having considered the past conversation. "We really should be focusing on the King's objective at hand and not our immature whims."

"Who are you calling immature?" asked Radi and Taran irritatingly.

"Who else would he be calling immature, you nitwits," Feoras muttered crossly under his breath.

"Oh really, you malt-worm!" they cried back at the Rock.

"Moldy-warted miscreants!" he shouted in return.

"Vain fat-kidneyed hedge-pig!"

"Loggerheaded measle-lumps!"

"Sheep-biting boar-face!"

"Spongy fly-bitten maggot-pies!"

Laurel could hardly believe the scene that she now witnessed and was unsure of how long it would last. However, the ridiculous bantering of the Knights soon ended, for the King had at that moment drawn down from the head of the Company to inspect the welfare of His Knights. He was not at all surprised by what He was witnessing.

"Silence, the three of you!" He shouted disapprovingly at Feoras and the twins. "We have been journeying for only a couple of hours, and yet this is how I find you? Already squabbling over misplaced pride and meaningless obstinacy?"

"We tried to tell them," said the Knights of Zeal.

"That will be all!" replied Sol, not wishing for their involvement in the rebuking.

"Sorry, my Lord," Feoras mumbled ashamedly.

"Yes, sorry, my Lord," the twins also spoke up. "We will try to have custody of our tongues, next time."

"I shall take your word for it, then," Sol replied sternly. Once the reprimand was over, Sol quickly dropped down the ranks again until Philippe strolled at Laurel's side.

"And how are you faring so far, Laurel?" He asked cheerfully, as if the past nonsense of the Knights had never happened.

"Oh! Um, good so far, I guess!" she replied indefinitely, for all the excitement previously provoked had caused her past feelings of anxiety to almost completely fade away. "I really like riding Sorina!" Laurel said patting her mare's neck gently. "She has not given me any trouble at all, considering this is my first time riding a horse by myself."

"You seem a natural!" Sol laughed warmly. "And Peterel, how are you managing as Laurel's attendant?"

"Very well, Sire!" the Wingel said smilingly, flying a little above the ground, as was the travelling style of the Wingel. "And, I am sure that You shall be pleased to know that Laurel has not given me any trouble either!"

Laurel and Sol laughed warmly at this, and the young maiden felt a return of the happy memories from her days in the Valley Fioré within her heart. Looking up towards the rest of the Company, Laurel noticed a silent air between the Knights as they continued advancing forward towards the South.

"Do you think that they are going to be all right?" she asked concernedly.

"Oh, yes," Sol replied. "They just need time to diminish their hurt pride, but soon they will be chatting away and, most likely, vexing each other again. They are truly good men at heart, and as they mentioned before, they see each other as dear brothers in arms. However, sometimes they can lean more towards brothers *at* arms. On the other hand, that is the way of a family sometimes, for 'familiarity breeds contempt' as the old saying goes."

"Hmm..." Laurel mused for a moment on the King's words. Then suddenly, she burst out with laughter, holding onto her side with utter hilarity.

"Tell Me what amuses you?" Sol asked smilingly.

"Oh, I was just wondering," Laurel began, still giggling with glee, "what in the world is a 'spongy fly-bitten maggot-pie'?"

Laurel laughed heartily again in hilarious wonderment and was pleased to find the King and Peterel laughing with her as they continued south on their journey to the sea.

That first day's journey had continued into the late evening, for the Company wished to arrive at the sea as soon as possible. And so, when the sky began to darken and the twinkling of stars began to appear overhead, the Company halted in a fertile clearing where a runoff of The Great River ended. Here, a marvelous waterfall was found, whose rushing water sounded like the roar of a lion, giving it the name of Lion's Roar Falls. The crystal-clear water of Lion's Roar Falls fell into a large pool just below the sloping mounds in the depths of Serenity Forest, around which the Company set up camp. While Queen Mariah and Laurel camped on one side of the pool of Lion's Roar Falls, King Sol and His band of Knights rolled out their sleeping sacks and covers on the other. The Wingel, who were ever on guard for the Company, encamped themselves high in the trees, watching the looming, darkening sky intently as the evening star loomed overhead. The horses were housed between the two camps where they could be cautiously protected.

"Laurel," whispered the Queen as She stood outside Her tent. "I shall be retiring for the night now, seeing how late it is. How about you?"

"Oh...no. Not yet," replied the maiden looking out past the pool, where she could make out the campfire in the King's camp. "I am not very tired, so I am going to walk around, for a while."

"All right, my dear, but be sure to have Peterel with you, if you desire to walk beyond the camp."

"Yes, I shall," Laurel nodded, bidding the Queen goodnight and marching off towards the pool.

Lion's Roar Falls of Serenity Forest was a spectacular sight in the twilight as the moonlight and starlight glittered and twinkled in the crystal blue waters that roared down the mounds into the shining pool below. Laurel paused a moment to look at her reflection in the clear pool and watch the fish swimming here and there around the water grasses. Looking up at the sound of laughter over the roaring of the falls, Laurel could perceive the King and His Knights far across the pool merrily talking amongst themselves as they sat in a large circle around a campfire in the still and quiet night air. Curious of their merrymaking, the young maiden slowly walked around the pool towards their camp. At first, not wanting to disturb the pleasant conversing of the King and His Knights, the shy girl was content to observe them from far beside a nearby tree, but soon she unthinkingly drew nearer to hear the laughing voices of the Knights of Terra.

"Ha, ha! Yes, what an awesome sight that was, was it not brother?" Laurel heard Taran laugh jollily.

"Yes, brother," replied Radi. "I just could not believe the sight myself, and we were all so scared!"

"Especially Feoras!" laughed Andres heartily, elbowing his perturbed brother.

"Ah, now!" cried Feoras huffily, "we can forget the rest of the tale, and just skip to the end where our King saves us again."

"Ah, yes, because you do not like the part where you get into trouble, do you?" Sadu taunted eagerly.

"All right, all right!" Feoras huffed resignedly. "I shall admit my share of fear in that adventure, but do not forget *all* of yours as well!"

"That is right! We have all had our share of fright and turmoil, and if it was not for the help of our King, then we surly would never have grown in courage," Zimran spoke up, and all turned to Sol, who had been listening contently to the Knights' reminiscing.

He nodded thoughtfully. "Despite your trials, you all have done your very best to work together and to keep the Emperor's will always before you, and I am very proud of you all for that." All of the Knights beamed with pleasure at the satisfaction of their King, and they fell silent, quietly pondering His words.

"So, Laurel, would you care to join us?" Sol spoke up suddenly as He looked towards Laurel, who stood only a couple yards behind the Knights' camp.

As the twelve Knights turned towards her in surprise, Laurel blushed with embarrassment, startled that the King had noticed her. "Oh, no," she started shyly. "I do not mean to disturb you all. I only meant to see how you all were doing."

"Nonsense!" cried Andres. "Come over and sit with us. We were just in the middle of telling stories, anyway."

"Yes, you can sit with us!" the twins agreed happily.

Joyful towards this acceptance, Laurel made her way towards the circle around the campfire and sat between the young twins who each gave her a hot cup of tea, though she only took one to sip at.

"Now, before we continue," began the King as He looked around the circle of Knights and Laurel, "I believe there is an important matter that we must discuss with our maiden friend." And as Sol looked to Feoras, the Knight nodded his head and cleared his throat as he addressed Laurel.

"Ah, yes, there is a matter to be discussed about the King. You see, once we are underway with our campaign in the South, you cannot, under *any* circumstances, address Sol as the King of Terra in public."

"But why?" Laurel asked as she shifted in her seat curiously.

"It is My rule," Sol spoke up, His eyes watching the firelight considerately.

"The King," Feoras continued, nodding to Sol, "has asked all of us not to reveal Himself as the King of Terra to any of His citizens, no matter the circumstance."

"I do not understand," the young maiden replied, turning to Sol. "Do not Your people know that You are the King?"

"No, they do not," the young King said, looking up at the maiden. "They do not know that there is such a person as the King of Terra, for they only know of My Father, the Emperor. As for Myself, I have revealed to them of My plan to assist them and teach them the ways of the Emperor against the evil of Malum, and so they only know me as a Teacher, Confidant, and Friend in battle."

"But...we all know who You are," Laurel continued, addressing the circle of Knights, "so why cannot the other citizens, Your people, know about You as the King of Terra?"

"It is because of Malum's Curse that I have yet to tell My people of who I am, for their hearts are not yet ready to understand. To know what you all know will only bring great trouble for My people, if My Kingship was revealed at this present time. And know this, Laurel, Malum does not know of Me as the King of Terra either, and that is how I wish to keep things. If he came to realize these things and if the people were to know of Me before the proper time... Well, just know that it is important that all know as little as possible about who I am as I lead this campaign."

"What would really happen," started one of the twins, "if Your Kingship were made known?"

"That...I cannot tell you," replied Sol secretively. Then, He addressed the circle, as He looked into the eyes of each Knight. "Now, as for all of you, I revealed My Kingship to you because I choose you out of the multitude to follow Me and fulfill the plans of My Father for the people of Terra. And, I know that you all have faced your own share of doubts, despair, and frustration in answering My call, but I tell you that in the end, together, we will bring back Virtue to the people and bring an end to this ancient Curse." Finally, Sol looked at Laurel as she felt as though these words were meant for her, too.

"Now, My friends, where will we continue with our storytelling?" King Sol suddenly asked as the mood of the circle merrily changed from their serious discussion.

"Oh... Well, the twins told the last story, and Saimen, Taam, and Caius told all the others so far..." Donato puzzled through the names.

"Um..." Laurel began timidly as all turned to her attention, "I was wondering...could you all tell me how the Knighthood was formed? I mean, how did you all meet?"

"Ah, that is a great story to tell," Sol said eagerly, "and everyone will have a share in the tale, as well!"

"O, yes, what a wonderful story to tell, Laurel!" giggled the twins joyfully. "So, who should go first?"

"Well, I suppose that I should start," Feoras began, "seeing as I am second in command of the Knight—"

"Ah-ah, Feoras!" Andres interrupted. "But it was I whom the King called first, if you remember correctly."

"Why do not I begin the story, dear Knights?" said the King, before the prideful tension of the Knights boiled over.

Then, Sol turned to Laurel, whose ears had waited patiently for the tale. "I began My mission, to reunite the people of Terra under the reign of My Father, sometime after many years of living in the village of My Mother's family. I knew that I needed to form the Knighthood because I was looking for men whom I could call friends and who would loyally serve Me in defending Terra from Malum's forces. First, I journeyed to the South, to the sea, and there I met Feoras and Andres."

As Sol nodded to the two brothers to continue the story, Feoras brazenly began to speak, when Andres swiftly, and much to his brother's consternation, took up the tale. "My brother and I are from a fishing town called Magnolia Town, which is far eastward of Madeira Harbor, where we are headed."

"We come from a long line of fishermen," continued Feoras quickly. "We spent almost all of our lives at sea and catching fish."

"At times, we even smelled like fish!" Andres said, and Feoras could not help chuckling at this truth.

"And, one day, as we were fishing close to shore with our father, we noticed a young Man," and Feoras nodded to Sol revealingly, "sitting on the pier with a small net at His side. We asked Him what He was doing, since, if He was trying to fish, He was going about it the wrong way, for the fish never swim out so close to the boardwalks, except the minnows and other small fry. Besides, He did not even have a boat or a fishing rod."

"And when He said that He was indeed fishing, and though we tried to enlighten Him about the fish, the Man would not listen. In the end, we returned to our own fishing."

"'Poor man' we had thought," continued Feoras sadly, as if he was reliving this past memory. "We had never seen Him in town before, so we figured that He was a vagabond looking for a meal, but we never stopped to help Him."

"Anyway, after a long day, we had not caught a single fish, not one! And our father was steamed, since he had no idea why the fish were not biting. So, with heavy, frustrated, hearts, we started to return to the shore, when we saw the Man, still sitting at the pier. When we saw that His net was still empty, we were actually relieved, for we realized that we were not the only ones with fishing problems that day."

"So," Feoras smiled thoughtfully, "we asked the Man, 'Terrible fishing day, huh?'

"The man shrugged, 'I found it enjoyable, sitting here watching the boats and the sea.'

"'What?' we cried, 'But you have not caught a single fish, and the day is almost ended.'

"And the Man replied, 'O, you are right!' He said, 'Well, I better get started then.'"

"At that moment," Andres continued, "the Man stood up and held out His net over the water saying, 'Come into My net, fish!' And we could not believe our eyes at the sight! Hundreds of thousands of fish, it seemed, swam to the Man and jumped right into His net!"

"Then, we oared our boat over to the Man to see if we could help Him, but we were so amazed that we just stood there staring, especially when we realized that His net did not tear, not one thread!"

"Then," Andres said, his voice sounding with wonderment, "the Man handed me the net, which was light as a feather, saying, 'Here, I have no need for them.'

"He started to walk away at that moment, and — and I just knew that I could not let Him leave, at least without finding out who He was, so I called to Him, 'Wait, who are you?'"

A smiled appeared on the gentle Knight's face as he continued, "He turned to me and smiled saying, 'Come and see.'"

"So, I left my father in the boat and followed the Man. *That* is when *I* turned to Feoras and said, 'Come, Feoras!' The Man also called, 'You, too, come and see!'"

"*Anyway*," continued Feoras evasively, "to our joy, the Man made known to us of His true identity. He was Sol, the King of Terra, and He spoke to us of all that was His mission. There was…nothing we could do really after that…for our hearts were opened to the truth about our world, and we knew where it was that we belonged."

"Ooh, ooh! Now it is our turn! Our turn!" exclaimed the twins joyfully, and they both gave a gentle nudged to Laurel saying, "This is the part where we come in!"

"A small part," continued Taran, "but nonetheless a good part!"

"You see, Laurel, we are also from Magnolia Town," said Radi, "and fishermen, as we mentioned to you before. And it just so happened that Taran and I and our father were also out fishing the day that the King met Andres and Feoras."

"But we were *so bored*!" exclaimed Taran. "There were no fish biting *all day*, and we had already considered giving up on the fishing business sometime before."

"But our father, would not have it, since he thought that it was important that we 'conduct ourselves civilly' by taking up the traditions of our town's fishing industry."

"Then, we noticed Feoras and Andres, for we had all known each other as neighbors before, walking with a Man from the pier and down the beach. We called to them saying, 'Hey, Andres! Feoras! Where are you going?'"

"But, before the two could answer, the Man cupped His hands and shouted back, 'Come and see!'" Radi laughed, "That was all we needed to here! It did not matter to use what they were doing or where they were going!"

"All we knew was that we were going with them! So we dived into the water and swam to shore, much to our father's wrath as he called out, 'Taran! Radi! Come back here! Where are you going?' As we swam away, we called back, 'We do not know! But anywhere is better than in a smelly fishing boat!'"

"It seemed though," Radi considered, "that father was not too angry at our leaving, for if he wanted us to return home then he would have tracked us down, with dogs most likely!"

"We were wondering what was to become of us, after we left," Taran continued, "but as it turned out, we were greeted by the King of Terra Himself, who told us of His mission as He had done with Feoras and Andres."

"And we have never regretted our decision since!" the twins ended proudly.

Then, Taam brought up the story, "I was the next Knight to join the Knighthood, and I remember that day so vividly... I was walking about my hometown with a strange sense that something new was going to happen that day, but as the day wore on and the sun began to set, I almost questioned my sanity, when I found myself still strolling the streets in search of...something—though I did not know what that something was! And just as I was about to turn in for the evening, a hand came across my shoulder and I jumped—I was so startled, being deep in thought!

"Sol was standing before me then, though I did not know Him, and before I could ask anything of Him, He smiled and said, 'Follow me!' And like all of the others, I did, and I, too, learned of the Emperor's will. Then, though late in the evening it was, I ran to find Caius, for we have been good friends for a long time as we talked and studied all that was available to us about Emperor Abba. We both knew, as many still hoped would be true, of the rumors that the Emperor would send help to His people."

"I was a little skeptical at first," Caius joined, "but, in truth, I only wanted to be certain that this Man was the help that we had been seeking. When Taam brought me, then, to Sol, and before I could question Him, He said, 'Ah, here, I see now a man after the heart of the Emperor, seeking always to please Him and to know His will!' I was stunned because Taam told me that he had not mentioned anything of my ardent studies, so I surrendered my doubt at that moment, and afterwards became a Knight."

"You think that you had doubts!" exclaimed Maso laughingly. "Do you not remember when the King came upon me? I was like you, minding my own business, when He appeared, and when I heard all that He had to say of His mission, I barraged Him with every question that came to my mind. 'Where are you from?' 'How was it that you came to be chosen for this mission?' 'I do not understand — this and this and so on.' But then I came to realize, 'Yes, He must be the King of Terra, He must!'"

All the Knights then finished their tales of how they met the King: Zimran and Yaakov related similar tales of how Sol enlightened and embolden them with His words of truth, urging them to follow Him, Donato again related his experience at his tax collecting table, and Sadu's story was less complex all together, for it was his initial curiosity and the authoritative words of the King that slowly pressed him into joining this growing group. And as the Knights related their tales, Laurel enjoyed learning how mysteriously the King had appeared into their lives and how willingly the Knights had responded to His calling. The young maiden listened with amazement, and though the stories soon came to an end, she would forever after remember them within her heart.

"O, that was wonderful!" she applauded at the conclusion.

"It was!" sighed the twins contentedly.

"But, there is one thing that I do not understand," related Radi. "Master, why *did* You choose us?" Then, all of the Knights turned to King Sol questioningly. "I mean, we are men of little fortune and even smaller status, but why did You choose us to form Your Knighthood?"

Sol smiled in the glow of the fire light. "I did not choose you because of your fortunes or status, for I care for none of these things. I chose you because I could see potential in your hearts — the potential to do only good and to remain loyal to My cause and to My Family. Though you all are simple and think of yourselves as the very least of mankind, I see great men, who deep within their hearts care about what happens at the end of this War, who want to see an end to the darkness."

"And me," began Feoras concernedly, "why did You choose me to be the leader of the Knights?"

"Do you not remember, dear Feoras?" Sol smiled. "On that day, when I asked you all to official form My Knighthood, I told you of what might happen if you all choose to stand with Me: 'you shall be persecuted by the people, your names will be slandered, and at times, many will drive you out of their cities, for I came to establish the reign of My Father again in Terra, and, to those who will not concede, they will be separated from those who are truly My people, and war, to their contempt, will be waged against them.'

"And you, Feoras, upon hearing these words, were the first to speak up as you replied to Me, 'As You wish, Master! To the end, we will stand by You.' And it was then that the others followed you, for you have the spirit of a leader within you, and so, upon you, I wanted to establish My Kingdom."

As silence fell upon the circle of friends, all looked from Feoras to Sol, whose eyes studied each other. Then, the Rock chuckled under his breath as he turned towards the fire. "Yes…" he said. "Yes…I remember."

"Well then," Sol started after a moment as He rose to His feet, "I believe that it is time for us to retire."

"What? No, Sire, not now!" cried some of the Knights.

"What is this? You are all not even tired?"

"Please, Sire, just one more story!" the twins pleaded like little children, much to Laurel's humor as she giggled at this sight.

"Oh, dear!" Sol groaned with amusement. Rubbing His eyes, He sat back down upon the log beside Him. "All right, I concede. One more story, and *then* we must withdraw to dreamland! So, who will tell the tale, then."

"Hmm… Why not you, my Liege?" Yaakov interjected considerately after a moment's reflection.

"Yes, Sire! Tell us one of Your stories!" Taran and Radi exclaimed with childlike delight.

"So, you all want to hear one of My stories again?" Sol smiled as He looked into the eyes of each Knight.

"Oh, right! Laurel has not heard any of Your stories before, has she?" Maso began looking towards the young maiden.

"All right, then," Sol began again, His eyes brightening joyfully. "I shall tell a story, for Laurel."

The Knights cheered happily at this as they all leaned forward eagerly to listen to their King. Smiling at each of them, the King fondly began His story:

"Once upon a time, there was a miner
Whose son he hoped would be even finer.
But his young son did not want to pursue
His father's life work as a miner, too.

He wanted to be like the fancy man
Who had come to town with his caravan.
The boy watched the caravan as it drove
Out to the desert from the seaside cove.

In the desert, the fancy man halted,
As the poor camels fainted and faltered.
As the fancy man helped his caravan,
The sun burned brightly, scorching the poor man.

He sweated and burned and blistered bright red,
For nowhere could he find shade for his head.
Seeing the bright sun, the boy said aloud,
'I want to be like the sun, bright and proud!'

And so the boy left the man for the sun,
Enjoying the sun's rays and having fun.
Then, a dark cloud drew over the blue sky,
And the sun was hid, unable to fly.

The cloud was strong. The cloud could not be beat.
Now, the boy could not feel the sun's great heat.
'I want to be like the cloud,' he said then.
'For the cloud is stronger than sun and men.'

And the boy followed the cloud where it went,
Across the land and town, his day was spent.
Soon, the cloud came upon a tall mountain
That stood like a lofty, princely fountain.

When the cloud tried to pass over its peak,
It found that it could not make its sly sneak.
The great mountain was too tall and too strong,
For the cloud was dispelled, after so long.

'I want to be like the mountain,' the boy,
With such immense passion, said lacking coy.
Then, the boy sat and watched his new teacher,
Memorizing its shape and large features.

Suddenly, the boy saw his father come,
For he heard his whistle and jolly hum.
His father, the miner, had work today
At the mountain his boy had found this day.

With his chisel and hammer, he would work
To chip at the mountain, though his back hurt.
Watching all the while, the young boy then saw

The chipping mountain and was in great awe,

For his dear father had worked by and by
To tame the mountain, working up so high.
The boy came to his father then to talk,
So they decided to go for a walk.

'Father,' said his son, looking up with care,
'I want to grow up like you! This I swear!'
The father only gave him a shrewd smile.
For he knew this day would come, all the while."

At the conclusion of this tale, all of the Knights sighed peacefully as they sat back on the long logs around the campfire.

"I like that story, Sire," Taam spoke up. "It was beautiful, especially the ending."

"But what does it mean?" asked Maso, looking inquisitively at the King.

"The King's stories always have a moral to be learned," the twins whispered to Laurel as Sol began to speak.

"It means exactly as it says," replied Sol. "True love is not forceful. In the story, the father wanted his son to grow up and become like him, but instead of forcing his desires upon the boy, he allowed his son to have the freedom to choose. This is the same as My Father, for He desires that all of His people become good as He is good and to want and desire the things that He longs for. However, instead of forcing His wishes onto His people, My Father gives all of His citizens the free will to choose, and He believe in His people that, in the end and after their long roaming from His sight, they will see His goodness and want to follow Him."

Laurel smiled considerately as she pondered Sol's words, for deep within her heart, she felt a stirring of tenderness towards her mysterious King. All at once, however, the young maiden and the Knights felt the forthcoming of fatigue as a contagious yawn spread around the campfire.

"Well, then," began the King as He rose from His seat. "You all had your *last* story, so now it is time for us all to go to bed."

"Aw! Do we have to?" voiced Taran and Radi. "Laurel might want to hear more!"

"Oh, no, that is all right," replied the tired girl humorously as she rose from her seat. "I really had a wonderful time, but I think that the King is right. Anyway, I should return to my tent now."

"Oh, all right! Maybe you shall hear more next time!" the two yawned as they followed the others from their seats.

The twelve stretched their arms high into the air and yawned with all their might before bidding goodnight to all, especially Laurel. Swiftly, the maiden made her way from the campfire, but she had not walked far until she heard Sol coming up from behind to join her.

"I just thought that it would be best for Me to escort you back," He explained as He fell in step at her side.

"Oh, thank you," Laurel replied happily. "Actually, I wanted to tell You how wonderful I thought all of the stories were, especially Yours."

"So, you really enjoyed it?"

"Of course! I never knew that You were so good at them! And, I wanted to know...when You explained the story, is that really how Your Father is?"

Sol smiled fondly, "Yes, though words cannot truly describe His goodness. Still, to help the Knights understand these things, I have always found it helpful to relay My Father's ways in stories."

"Well, I really hope to hear more of Your stories," the maiden smiled as she rubbed her hands in the crisp air of the forest. "I remember my father always telling me stories at night. I especially enjoyed them when he would sing his tales to me." Laurel sighed considerately at this memory. "That was my favorite..."

"Well, I shall be sure to tell more then," Sol said, taking the girls' cool hand at His side, "just for you." Laurel looked down for a moment at her hand resting in Sol's, as the two rounded the large pool of Lion's Roar Falls.

"Sol?" the young maiden asked, after a moment.

"Yes?"

"About...about what You said at the campfire, about not revealing Your Kingship to the citizens...did You ever mention this to Grandma Arliana before we left her?"

The King nodded as He replied, "Yes, I made sure to warn her as I have warned you this night, but You must know that I do want so much to tell My people who I am. However, the time is still not right."

"I see..." Laurel murmured. She suddenly felt a pang of resentment at the thought of having been revealed to such an important matter so later than her friend, as if she was always having to wait before learning such needed information.

What? Why am I feeling this way? Sol was right all of the times that He held back from revealing such things to me...

"Laurel?" Sol spoke up again.

"Uh, yes?" the girl looked up quickly.

"I wanted to know, after Peterel and I left the Valley Fioré, there were some black riders who met up with you and Grandma Arliana, right?"

"Yes, I remember."

"Did they...give you any trouble at the time?"

"Oh...no, but Peterel said something once about them...being the Tempters, right? In disguise?"

When Sol nodded, Laurel abruptly continued, "Well, I remember that they did not seem to care much about us at the time, but they were unsure about who we were, I think. When they left, Grandma Arliana and I were really confused by them because of the things they said about You and who You were, and—O, no!" The maiden suddenly halted her steps and held her head in despair, her eyes looking downcast.

"What is it, Laurel?"

"O, no!" Laurel repeated again despondently, for she remembered all too well her great uncertainty and frustration after the departure of the black riders and of the things she now wished she had never said nor did. "O, I completely forgot—O, dear!"

"Laurel, what is it?" Sol asked again, placing a hand concernedly on her shoulder.

Laurel looked up at the King uneasily as she sighed, "You are not going to like hearing this, but... O, I am sorry to say this, but I lost the rose that You gave me before You left the valley."

"Oh, is that all this is about?" Sol asked composedly.

"'Is that all'?" Laurel cried anxiously. "But, Sol, You do not understand! You were so kind to me in giving me that beautiful rose, and I went and... You see, after You left and when Grandma Arliana and I were confronted by the riders, like I said, we fell into great confusion about You and...well... I did not know what to believe, and I said some things that, now that I have realized so much about who You are, I am sorry to have said! And with Your rose...I was so confused that I went and...threw it away in the river—but I never would have done such a thing if I had not known about You and...Your Kingship." Laurel looked down disheartened with a dreary sigh.

Seeing this, the young King smiled sweetly as He replied, "Laurel, I understand you perfectly, but My dear, there is nothing to be so discouraged about. Look!" And saying this, the King lifted the maiden's chin to look up at Him as He held out in His other hand a bright, beautiful yellow rose. Laurel's eyes brightened with amazement and wonder as she realized that she had seen this beauteous flower before.

"Is that—?" she began, taking the yellow rose into her hands, and Sol nodded smilingly. "But how, if it really is —?"

"I found it floating in The Great River. You may have thrown it away in despair, but in the end, it found its way to Me. The moment I saw it, I knew that there must be trouble for you and Grandma Arliana, and I kept it until a time when I could give it to you again."

"But why did You not give it to me before?" Laurel asked. "At the Sanctuary?"

"I would have," Sol began, "but you were very much troubled with other matters at the time, with your fears."

"Oh…" replied the regretful girl as she hid her face in the rose's sweet petals.

"And then, the Knights came, and you were preparing for our present journey. No, I decided that I would give it to you whenever you remembered," Sol smiled good-humoredly as He took up Laurel's hand again and led her back to the Queen's camp.

As the two came upon the site of Laurel's tent, which stood next to the Queen's, Laurel's heart had been contemplating all of the goodness and kindness Sol had shown her since they had met, despite her many instances of difficulty.

"You know, Sol," the considerate child started as Sol began to part from her, "I wanted to thank You for everything You have done for me, and I know that I have not been as grateful as I should have been and sometimes I have been very inconsiderate and trying of patience, but I really will do everything I can to help You and the Queen and the Knights on this mission, I promise!"

"And I believe you, My dear," Sol replied, placing a gentle hand onto her head. "Now, I want *you* to know that there is nothing in the past, whether it be about the Tempters or Myself, that you should dwell on. I mean, whatever mistakes or inconveniences you think you may have caused are not to be thought of any longer, for there is nothing of you, My dear, that needs to be forgiven. Do you understand?"

"I…I think so," Laurel replied quietly, looking up into the eyes of her King, which seemed to glow in the glistening moonlight.

"Very good. Well, then, My dear, good night," and with that the King went off down the path back to His camp.

Laurel followed Him with her eyes for a moment before starting into her tent, when suddenly, she turned back uneasily. She made a motion to call Sol back, but He was already gone down towards the pool.

Oh, well! Laurel thought resignedly. *I really did want to ask Him, though, about that one matter… After I arrived at the Sanctuary, I wonder what happened to my feet that were burned… Oh, maybe I am not remembering everything quite clearly, but then again it was strange how I thought that they had been burned – had they not been? – then why did I find them healed? Is that what happened? O! I am not so certain what to think, but maybe next time, I shall bring it up.* Tired as she was, the young maiden returned to her tent and received a good night's rest.

Chapter 14
Madeira Harbor and the Southern Sea

Madeira Harbor was a small seaside town of about five hundred and twenty four men and a combined population of about four hundred or so women and children. Half of the town was constructed over a board walk, as one neared the shore, while the other half consisted of dirt roads and very few grasses. The homes, which were closely concentrated together, were constructed of fine wood from Serenity Forest and could sustain violent winds and flooding waves. The small marina only housed a few privately-owned fishing boats as Madeira Harbor sustained itself on fish of all species found along the coastline of the Southern Sea.

Three days after their departure from the Sanctuary, King Sol's Company traversed down the long main street of Madeira Harbor towards the town square, which lied just before the port. The company of Wingel led by Mikhail was not among them at this time, for the King had sent them ahead to prepare the vessels for the journey to the South Pole, as was the next destination of the King's plan. As the Company navigated down the roads of Madeira Harbor, many of the port's citizens came out from their homes to view and, in some cases, inspect the travelers. The children stopped playing their games in the streets, and the woman put down their laundry baskets and halted their daily duties to look upon the King and Queen and the Knights of Terra in awe and amazement. Most of the men were not as emotional and seemed to only look on with criticizing gazes.

After a while, the King's Company came upon a large building, which looked similar to a court house but more regal in structure, at the center of the town square. There, standing on the top of the steps that lead up to the building, a tall man with a thick gray beard and short graying hair waited, and he was dressed in fine robes of different noble colors. He also carried a large metal staff with him, on the top of which was a silver ornament of the Emperor's Seal. The man looked down from where he stood, noble and dignified, as Sol led His Company towards him. Three attendants stood around the man and followed him as he approached Sol. By now, a crowd, practically the entire town, of the harbor's citizens had followed the mysterious travelers to the building, and the people murmured amongst themselves with wondering anticipation.

"Greetings, travelers!" cried the man from the steps. "I am the Duke of Madeira Harbor, and I welcome you all from your travels."

"I am Sol," replied the King in a loud, authoritative voice, "and I come this day seeking the able men of this town!"

The crowd gasped in bafflement at hearing this, for they had not known that the Company belonged to Sol, whom they had only heard of as the Great Teacher. News of the mystifying Teacher had spread from outside of their small village where the King and His Company had been seen many times. Despite the crowds bewilderment, there was not an air of joy or gladness among the people as Laurel would have thought, for she sat in Sorina's saddle studying their uncertain faces.

"Ah-ha, yes, the good *teacher*[11]!" replied the Duke critically, though somewhat timidly. "Yes, we have heard of a certain delusional man roaming around the Kingdom proclaiming nonsense here and there, and I was certain that these rumors were true the moment I saw your little group enter my town."

The King held His ground at this statement, as His face was calm and determined. However, the Knights of Terra could not hide their expressions of repugnance and antipathy as the Duke spoke so disdainfully to their King.

"Why is he saying those things to Sol?" Laurel whispered to one of the Knights, unsure if she had heard the Duke correctly. Her white veil flowed in the breeze of a gentle wind.

"It has happened again," replied Caius, filled with anger. "Another Duke, who is an appointed representative of the Emperor to govern His villages and towns, has fallen for Malum's trickery."

"What do you mean?"

"Through his evil power, Malum has created the lie that Sol's claim as the Teacher of the Emperor is only a mask to hide intentions of leading the people astray, and many of the dukes have fallen for this falsehood."

"So, even though He is not revealing Himself as…you know…then there is still confusion as to who He is?"

"I am afraid so, Laurel. The dukes are under Malum's wicked Curse just like the rest of us, and in this case, this Duke has fallen for the lie that Sol is not from the Emperor but is a fraud. It looks as though we will have some trouble finding people who will join our cause in this town. The people's hearts are weak and no doubt they have given into Malum's lies just like their leader."

"I am Sol, a Teacher here to proclaim the ways of the Emperor," the King spoke up again, "and I am in need of this town's support."

"You dare to come to the Emperor's Embassy claiming such falsehoods!" cried the Duke indignantly. "Be gone, before you suffer our town under the wickedness of Malum, whom you follow!"

At this, the crowd went wild with horror, fearing the influence of Malum's evil in their town, and they began shouting at Sol for Him to leave Madeira Harbor at once. Sol paid no mind to this, and instead, jumped down from Philippe and resolutely climbed the steps towards the Duke, who cried

---

[11] When referring to the King or Queen of Terra, those who do not believe Sol and Queen Mariah as coming from the Emperor will not have their dialogue reflecting the capitalized nouns and pronouns of these Sovereigns. However, those who believe in Their origins, even if they do not know Them as the Monarchs of Terra, will have their dialogue reflecting capitalized nouns and pronouns.

to his attendants to keep Sol away from him. However, the attendants, feeble-minded and cowardly men, dropped away from their Duke and ran up the steps towards the doors of the Embassy. As Sol came upon the Duke, the gutless man backed away fearfully, regretting his rash statements when Sol met him eye-for-eye. Instead of saying anything to the Duke, Sol turned to the people, who watched Him with waiting, doubtful eyes, and cried out in a loud voice:

"Citizens of Madeira Harbor! Believe not what you here from this lying traitor's mouth, nor from the false rumors of My identity. I come to you now with no deceit, with no trickery, as a Follower of the Emperor! Truly, I am here today to call on you all to bear arms mightily and follow Me into battle *against* Malum." He stopped for a moment, as the people talked amongst themselves in fearful astonishment at what Sol asked of them.

"I know that this War," Sol continued, "has span generations of lifetimes and lifetimes of generations, and with every passing day Faith seems destroyed, Hope seems lost, and Love seems forgotten as Malum's forces draw upon us. However, I tell you this day that the future of mankind will not succumb to the destruction of its tragic fall from the past, for I, sent here by the Emperor, pledge My life to assist you in the redemption of Terra. Dear people, have you forgotten the ancient and disastrous treachery of Malum and his traitorous followers, who seek your ruin and wish your death?

"Dear people of Terra, let us unite as one this day: as one family, and like a true family, let us stand together against the evil of Malum, the ancient traitor of old. Let us unite Terra by bearing arms against that which seeks to destroy! I ask you this day to follow Me, for I, with My Company of warriors, am journeying now into battle against Malum's forces. I ask you for your support, for your redemption cannot occur without your consent! Therefore, take up the burdens that this dark Curse has forced onto your life and follow Me into the great battle, and let us together, as one nation, one family, defeat the evil that seeks our death. Be true in choice this day, My friends, for this is our quest for Faith!"

Both the Duke and the crowd were speechless for a long moment. Suddenly, about one third of the men and their women and children stirred from the crowd and came forward to Sol and His Company.

They looked past the King towards the Duke and said, "My lord, we will not follow this man, for what he speaks of is nothing but falsehoods. Nothing good can come from a liar such as this man, so we shall make haste back to our daily lives!" Then, they departed from the scene, throwing hateful glances and rude remarks as they left.

After a while, another third of the original population of men, along with their women and children, stirred from their silent places among the other townspeople, and they came forward to the King and His Company.

"O great Teacher!" they said to Sol. "We hear Your plea and understand the importance of what You ask of us. Nevertheless, we are a tired people, tired of this War and its burdens. We cannot bear of such grievous and demanding tasks as helping You and Yours fight in this battle. 'No' is our reply as we return to our daily lives." Then, the second third of the crowd of Madeira Harbor left the King for their homes and places of business, not even turning back once to look at Him as they departed.

Once the second group of men with their women and children had disappeared into the town, the final third of the population of Madeira Harbor's men and their families looked up at the King of Terra. They turned their gaze swiftly on the Duke, who smiled wickedly with the belief that they too would turn from Sol and leave for their daily lives as their other fellow citizens had done.

Finally, when the citizens spoke, they said, "Duke of Madeira Harbor, from this day onward, our allegiance to you, which we declared to be true and faithful as we always have been, is forgotten in our minds now and forever! At this moment, we are in utter shock and dismay that you would deceive us with the falsehoods and lies that belong to none other than Malum the traitor!" The people looked to their King, and with reverent devotion, they knelt to the ground and lowered their heads. "To you, O great Teacher, loyal to the Emperor, we seek guidance and servitude!" came their bold cries.

"There you have it!" Sol said, turning back to the Duke. "From henceforth, bear for these brave people to no longer be subject to you. To those who have chosen to remain under your misleading authority, I allow their choice, for their demise is of no one's fault by yours and their own."

"Who—who are you to speak with such authority?" the Duke cried feebly and in bewilderment.

Sol paid no heed to the man as He turned to the new followers crying, "Come My brothers and sisters! We shall leave now for battle!"

Without further delay, the newcomers prepared for their journey with the King of Terra across the sea to the South Pole. The women and children, who would not be accompanying the men on this dangerous and unexpected journey, helped prepare the foodstuffs, clothing, weapons, and other necessary supplies for their brave warriors. Once arrangements were complete, Sol and Queen Mariah led their warriors followed by Laurel to the seaports of Madeira Harbor where their three ships, the HMS Navi, HMS Cura, and HMS Rey, awaited them. Each ship was about one hundred and seventy-five feet long and about forty feet tall with long, white unfurled sails flowing in the breeze of the seaside winds. They were made of a sturdy wood for enduring the harshest weather at sea and were of the noblest and finest artistry in all the land of Terra.

Having prepared the three ships as the King had ordered, the Wingel awaited the arrival of the Company from the ships decks. Knowing that their naturally extraordinary forms as Wingel, whom were rarely seen by most commoners, would give rise to suspicion of Sol's identity, as well as induce a fearful amazement in the hearts of the citizens of Madeira Harbor, they had disguised themselves as brawny, vigorous sailors. Their wings, which never disappeared with their changing forms, were completely concealed under the cloaks of their new uniforms, giving the Wingel the appearance of human sailors. Because of this clever transformation, the newcomers only surmised that these robust sailors were other men that the great Teacher had commanded to journey with Him to the South Pole.

Once it was agreed that the horses were to stay with the faithful women of Madeira Harbor, the time had come for the Company to leave for the sea, and the men were given time to bid farewell to their wives and sisters and mothers and children. However, all were devotedly eager for the sailing away of the three ships, for these loyal people wanted to fulfill their duty to the Emperor in fighting for His cause, with the men surrendering their lives for Him and the women and children supporting the decision of their men at home. The men were then divided into three groups, and they took stations in their respective ships dutifully. The Knights were also divided into three groups of four in order to lead each ship's convoy of soldiers. The chain of command divided into a skipper, a quartermaster, and a second and third mate on each ship, which followed respectively with Andres, Saimen, Yaakov, and Radi on the *Navi*, Donato, Maso, Caius, and Taam on the *Cura*, and Feoras, Sadu, Taran, and Zimran on the *Rey*. The King, Queen Mariah, Laurel, and her guardian, Peterel, would reside on the *HMS Rey* with King Sol reigning as Commander of all three ships and as the Captain of the *Rey*.

"Onward, My men! Across the sea, we set sail!" Sol hailed His men of the three ships.

"Aye, aye, Captain!" came the thunderous roar of His warriors.

Within the first strokes of the Embassy's clock tower, the three ships sailed off into the Southern Sea at noon. The men had taken their positions on the decks and sails and riggings as they hastened to launch the ships at sea. The faithful women and children of Madeira Harbor could be seen waving and cheering and calling near the shores of the seaport, full of joy and pride that their men had answered the Teacher's calling. From the stern of the *HMS Rey*, Laurel stood watching the beachside as the land began to shrink and grew distant from her. Looking up at the magnificent sails of the King's ship and spotting a flag bearing the Emperor's Seal flapping triumphantly from the mainmast, a fervent smile developed across her joyfully beaming face.

Here we go, Laurel! She thought to herself, *We sail now to the South Pole where the climax of this adventure awaits, it seems. To think that once I was walking through the simple, carefree grasses of the Valley Fioré, and now I am sailing away from the world I once knew on such as grand sailing ship. What else could be in store for me?*

The King's three ships had been at sea for three or four days since their departure from Madeira Harbor, when the weather had become bitterly blustery and arctic for the tropical-native sailors. The Knights of Terra did the best that they could at rallying the sailors' spirits and relaying the King's commands, which He communicated to the other ships by way of secret Wingel messengers. However, the chilly winds and somewhat frequent frosty rains were enough to freeze the enthusiasm of the sailors as thoughts of their warm beds at home began to haunt them.

"Well, they will just have to suffer it out," Sadu said as he and the other Knights conferred on the mission's progress in the Captain's cabin. "They chose to join us, so they will have to deal with the consequences of their choice, just like the rest of us."

"Now, I think you are thinking too harshly of them," Zimran spoke up considerately.

"Yes," confirmed Taran. "We need to show these men that we will support them to the end."

"My warriors are doing all that they can to strengthen the will of these faithful men," said General Mikhail, who also attended the conference. "However, like the rest of the human race, their hearts are weak from Malum's Curse."

"Andres and Donato have related the same from their perspectives," replied Feoras. "Maybe we were hasty in our decision to begin this journey so soon."

"That is just what Malum would want you all to think!" Sol spoke up, having listened to His companions who sat around the room with Him. "My Father and I have discussed this matter at length, and we decided that the time for locating the King Virtues is upon us." Suddenly, there was an unexpected knock at the entrance, and when Taran rose to open the door, the King smiled to see Laurel walk into the room.

"Oh…uh, sorry! I did not mean to interrupt Your meeting, but um…" the maiden began uneasily, brushing a stray bang under her veil. Then, reaching within her dress pocket for a slip of paper, she relayed her message. "Queen Mariah wanted me to tell You that we are still on schedule to the South Pole and that our position lies about 2,000 leagues from where we had set off at the shores of Madeira Harbor, and She believes that it is only a matter of time before we arrive at our destination. So, um…that was all I had to say, and I guess that I will be going now—"

"No, no," Sol began, holding up His hand. "I am glad you have come, for we were just about to discuss something of great importance that you too must hear." King Sol then motioned for Laurel to claim an empty seat opposite of Him.

Something else to hear...about the mission? I wonder what it could be... the maiden contemplated as she took her seat curiously.

"There are one or two matters more that you must know of before we arrive at our destination. You know that our mission now is to obtain the three King Virtues."

"Yes," replied the girl, interested to know of her King's important thoughts.

"At the South Pole, there is a small island where we shall find a tall tower, like a lighthouse, and this is where one of the King Virtues resides: the virtue of Faith. As I told you before, the Virtue of Faith, no longer ethereal but a tangible form, has been shaped into that of a stone or jewel. We know that Faith is located at the very top of the tower in a large room accessed by a long flight of stairs that circulate up the lighthouse. As of now, we are in need of someone to volunteer to retrieve the jewel of Faith. However, after careful planning, I have decided that *you* shall be that someone!"

"Me?" Laurel gasped astonishingly.

"Her?" huffed Feoras. "I mean no disrespect on Your decision, my Lord, but are You certain that the girl is ready for such a responsibility?"

"Oh, Feoras!" Taran cried. "Of course, she is ready! I mean, the Queen has been training her, right? Besides, all that is required of her is to run up that tower and retrieve the stone! How hard can it be? Right, Sadu?"

"Leave me out of this," Sadu muttered under his breath. "I would have to agree with Feoras, for once."

"I would not have decided this if I did not think that Laurel was ideal for the task, Feoras," Sol replied to the Knight. "I have full confidence in you, Laurel," Sol continued, turning to Laurel, "that is if you agree to this."

"Well...I..." At first, Laurel did not know what to say. *Surely, if this is what Sol wants, then I should accept.* She thought, *Then again, I am not entirely certain about all of this still. In fact, it might be a lie to say that I understand even half of this mission and everything I have learned thus far in general! Still...* "Well...if this is how I can be of assistance...then, yes. I accept." Sol smiled satisfactorily at this, and Taran gave the young maiden a congratulatory pat on the back.

"Sire," General Mikhail spoke up, then. "There is the *other* matter, which I believe necessary to disclose to Laurel at this moment."

"Yes, of course, I have not forgotten," Sol returned to the Wingel, before gazing back at Laurel. "In accepting this responsibility, you must know, Laurel, that from this point forward there are great dangers that lie ahead for you, as well as for all of us. As you know, once we arrive at the

South Pole, we shall also head into battle against Malum's forces. You also know of the ruthlessness of his forces as seen during the Tempters' attack in Serenity Forest. However, this battle will be much worse, for both Tempters *and* men will be fighting on Malum's side."

"You mean, there are other citizens of Terra who will fight *against* us?" Laurel asked gravely.

Here, Feoras interjected to respond, "It is just as you saw in Madeira Harbor. There are people who have a deep hate for Sol, who reject Him and hold not respect for Him and disbelieve His words, as a result of their choice, they listen to Malum's lies and allow their weakened hearts to control them. These merciless men will stop at nothing to appease their evil master, and they will *kill* in cold blood, this you must understand."

"And these traitorous men," Zimran carried on the relation, "these vile forces of Malum are led under the command of a scoundrel known as Lues."

"My great enemy," Sol murmured as He clenched His fists against the arms of His chair. "He is not human, though he takes that form, and he will seem understanding and sensitive at times, but he holds no emotion within his being. Everything he is, everything he seems to be, is a lie. Laurel, what you need to know and understand is that you must not ever, not even for a moment, trust this villain, no matter what he says and no matter what he does. His only purpose, the reason he exists, is to destroy any loyalty you have for My Father and for Me. Lues will do everything he can to deceive you, to crush you, to destroy you. Laurel, if you give him the opportunity, even the slightest chance, he *will* kill you! Do you understand?"

"Y-Yes," Laurel's voice quivered at her response.

Because of her ignorance, Sol's countenance frightened her more than His words, for He spoke with great concern about the subject at hand. However, her response satisfied the King, for He sighed with reassurance at her answer.

"So…who is this…person, if he is not human?"

"Lues," Mikhail began again, "was created by Malum from the same essence of his Curse. In fact, they are the same, and you could say that Lues is like a tangible form of the Curse. Because of this, Malum uses him as a way to control the hearts of man."

"What do you mean by 'control'?" Laurel asked, on the edge of her seat.

"He means that Lues has the power to will your heart's desires," Feoras said, with an air of passionate distaste about him. "Lues can make you think things that you never would have in your entire life. He will tempt your heart to go against the King in every way possible. His power over you…is an awful, horrible feeling that we Knights…have felt before." And he sighed with sorrow as if he was relating some distressing memories in his thoughts. "Forgive me, Laurel," Feoras finally continued. "*This* is why I am so concerned about your presence in this battle. This is why…"

Feoras sighed again with great passion before quickly rising from his seat. "Forgive me, my Liege, but I feel needed elsewhere," said the Knight, as he strode away hastily and escaped from the room.

"Forgive him as he says," Sol spoke up, looking towards the door. "He has seen many dear friends lost to that vile Lues…as we all have…"

As the room filled with a mournful silence from this scene, for once, Laurel began to realize just how distressing this War really was.

Later that evening, when the sun had almost set and the twinkling of stars could be seen through the distant clouds, some of the soldiers and the Knights on the *HMS Rey* had gathered along the decks, talking amongst themselves about their lives and their families. Laurel stood along the ships railings as well, thinking of all that the King had told her about her new responsibility.

I wonder how this will all turn out, she thought, looking out at the sea. *Sol must really believe in me or else why would He have asked me to be the one to retrieve the jewel of Faith! I am still not sure… When have I ever been sure about anything? I have never known this kind of life, War against ancient evils and battles against brethren and fighting for one's freedom! It all sounds like some kind of fairytale that I have read, but I know it is real and that I am a part of it. I wish Grandma Arliana was here…we never really talked much about such grand adventures, but I wish that I had something familiar to hold onto.*

Laurel looked around, then, at all of the soldiers who stood reminiscing about their families and dreaming of what their wives and children were doing at this time. *They are all like me. They unexpectedly found themselves in the middle of this War. Still, they resolved to join for the Emperor, led by Sol, whom they see as their great Teacher. However, unlike me, they joined so quickly, and despite their commonplace complaints about the journey, they seem ready to fight for Sol. It took me a couple days before I even resolved to join this War, and even now, I still feel anxious because of my disbelief… Is all of this real? There is just so much for me to comprehend and know. I wonder if my confidence will ever be certain…*

"Zimran, come along now!" cried Taran suddenly, who was among the other soldiers. "Singer of the Emperor's praise, let us here that musical voice of yours with a song!"

At this, all of the soldiers heartily agreed as they turned to Zimran, who was standing against the railings of the ship. He smiled meekly at the encouragement of his fellow soldiers. For a moment, he seemed to search his memory for something to sing before his face lit up with enthusiasm at an internal discovery. Then, he sang in a melodious baritone:

"The Lord of our fathers, our Kingdom's Head
Has called us to a destined path.
We leave our great homes and our lives and bed,
To fight a great evil of fiery wrath.

O, keep guard Terra's stars so far away
The love that is true, that glows so bright,
And be still the trembling of my heart this day
That fills me with terror this night.

As fear inside me calls thoughts of home,
I wonder if I have chosen a right.
So, dear Emperor, hear our plea and moan,
And lead us not into evil plight.

Through faith, hope, and love I shall go
To wherever You need me now,
For I trust the Lord of my fathers from long ago,
Just tell me what to do and how.

Remember, the ancient hymn. O, men!
'Redemption is still at hand,
For the Curse that shackled you then,
Will feel the heat of Sun throughout the land'

Keep true to the words of our Lord. O, men!
His House shall see victory in time.
And soon we shall see our freedom again,
As the love that once was is finally mine."

Throughout this devoted song and while the soldiers hummed along dreamily, Laurel had closed her eyes, listening to Zimran's words and feeling the cool breeze of the sea against her face. As the song ended, Zimran's voice seemed to drift away into the wind and far out past the horizon, and Laurel's mind seemed to whirl and flow with the song's inspiration. She thought then of turning to Zimran and asking him to sing more, but when she opened her eyes, she gave a start as she found herself lying in the bed of her cabin. Laurel sat up quickly and looked about the room to be sure of where she was. Then, seeing the wooden room, her yellow rose which stood in a vase on the nightstand beside her bed, and the picturesque furniture of her cabin before her, Laurel sighed with understanding.

I must have been dreaming about this evening, she told herself, reassuringly. *I really admired Zimran's song...* As she began to reposition herself in bed, Laurel noticed that one of the portholes of her cabin was open, letting a gentle breeze into the room.

Oh, no wonder I was dreaming of the wind! She realized as she got up to secure the window.

However, when Laurel began to close the porthole, she stopped suddenly as she heard a faint humming from outside the ship. The humming sounded in a tenor range and was a sweet, affectionate tune. For some reason, Laurel stood for the longest time, listening to the humming melody as it drifted through the wind.

Whoever could that be? She wondered as she opened the porthole wider to listen. *It sounds so beautiful yet strangely mysterious. There is something about this tune that intrigues me. Maybe...* and Laurel looked to the cabin door questionably, *Maybe, I should investigate this mystifying humming? Ah-ha, an adventure!*

Without considering the sensibility of endeavoring nightly explorations, Laurel pulled a long robe over her nightgown, shuffled into her brown sandals, and gracefully veiled her head before lighting a candle to lead her way out of the cabin. Her door creaked open squeakily, but thankfully, it was not loud enough to wake anyone up. Laurel looked down both ends of the long hallway and tiptoed away when she found no one around.

Peterel went away with the Wingel to the other side of the ship, so I better not get into any mischief, since he is not here to help me. Laurel reminded herself as she found the stairs to the outside of the ship.

Coming to the top of the stairs, Laurel opened the door leading to the ship's decks and searched again for anyone awake. The twelve soldiers, who were on watch that night, were posted on the ship's three masts, and Laurel began to fear that her nightly excursion would come to an end if they spotted her. However, their attention was towards the seas, and some of them were nodding off at that moment from the long night's watch. Still, Laurel was careful not to remain long in the moonlight as she crept along the deck.

Now, where did that humming come from? The young maiden wondered as she searched the main deck.

That was when the mysterious humming started up again, and with strained ears, Laurel heard the enchanting melody originating from the bow of the ship. Stealthily, Laurel continued along in the shadows towards the forecastle deck, where she scaled a ladder in order to reach where the foremast stood. By now, the humming was louder and clearly distinct, so Laurel looked around the foremast near the deck's railing, where she heard again the humming melody. To Laurel's astonishment, she discovered the King leaning against the bow railings, His face lifted up to the starry sky as

He continued to hum His tune. Fascinated by this, Laurel stepped forward to disclose her presence, when Sol began to sing in tenor:

O, Wind of Terra, speak to My people,
Whose sleep calls them sweetly tonight.
Speak to them softly. Speak to them lightly.
Speak to them as the loves of My life.

Whisper My wanting. Whisper My dreaming,
As I dream of a world bright and true.
I wish for My people to be free of evil,
And to sleep peacefully in the light of truth.

I shall stay awake, now. I shall keep the watch, now.
To see that they are cared for this night.
Dear Wind of Terra, keep My people sleeping.
Keep them from all lies and deceit.

Even though they sleep tonight,
Even though they hear Me not,
Keep them safe from evil tonight,
And lead their hearts to freedom's sleep.

Despite all their struggling
Despite their uncertain strife
Keep them close to love's great light,
And let them know of My love tonight.

For love is My wanting. Love is my dreaming.
I seek to be loved as I do love.
O, Wind of Terra, speak to My people,
And ask them to love Me this night.

When Sol had finished His song, He gave a long sigh as He silently lowered His head. Laurel stood by the foremast for a moment before endeavoring to approach Sol.

"Sol?" she asked stepping into the moonlight, which glowed brightly from behind the gray clouds above.

There came a small chuckle from the King before He turned towards the maiden, revealing a knowing smile as He began, "So, you heard My song."

"Oh...yes," Laurel replied quietly. "I heard humming from my cabin porthole, and I was so intrigued that I just had to see where it was coming from. It...it was very beautiful."

"Thank you, My dear," Sol replied considerately. "I made up this song a long time ago for My people, and I like to sing it whenever I find Myself alone. However, I am glad that you have heard it this night." And Laurel could not help blushing at this as a small smile developed across her face.

"Come!" Sol said, motioning for the maiden to stand beside Him at the railing. "There is something I wish to show you." When Laurel drew to the railings, Sol pointed up to the sky, where a large cloud was slowly sailing amongst the stars. "Look there for a moment, and you shall see an amazing sight."

Laurel watched curiously as the cloud floated past, revealing the dark sky and a host of glorious constellations twinkling about. Suddenly, two flashes of light shot across the sky as two gliding comets appeared.

"Wow!" Laurel exclaimed in wonder. "Shooting stars!"

To this, Sol laughed gaily, "Yes, they usually are common around this time of night, and I have already seen a couple more before you arrived."

"Wow, that is truly amazing!" Laurel continued her wonderment. "In Serenity Forest, with the leafy canopies of the trees all about, I can never see the sky at night very clearly from my cabin, and I usually never stayed out past sunset because I did not want to get lost in the dark. So, seeing the sky now is a real marvel for me!"

"Do you know anything about the constellations, Laurel?" asked the King.

"No, not really. I mean, my father tried to teach me them once when I was young, but that was too long ago for me to remember correctly."

"Well, here! I shall show you," Sol said, placing an arm around Laurel's shoulder and pointing up at the patterns of stars. "Off to the left there is the Blue Rose, for the stars in this pattern have a bluish tint in color. Above that, we have the Set of Keys, which are a gold key and a silver key. To the right of that is the Shepherd's Crook. Then, there is the Lion King who sits above the Ivory Throne. And on the right here, you can see the Crystal Wine Glass. And behind us," Sol continued looking northward in the sky, "is the Royal Star, the brightest star in the entire sky, which always points North to the Eternal Palace." Then, He took Laurel's hand, which rested at her side.

At this, Laurel looked down at her hand resting in Sol's and at the twinkling of the mystical ring that Sol had given her. *He is holding my hand… Why does that make my heart beat a little faster and with more joy?*

"Laurel?" Sol asked, looking down at the girl.

"Oh, I am sorry!" she replied looking up again. "I was just lost in thought, I guess…"

Sol smiled sweetly at this and continued, "There are some other constellations that we can see from here, too. There is the Burning Heart, the Footprints, and the Lily, the Mother Hen, the Fig Tree, and the Warrior —"

"Do You think I am ready for this mission...?" Laurel asked aloud, though she had meant it as a silent thought. When she realized her interruption, she began to apologize to the King, but He stopped her with the greatest assurance.

"It is fine, My dear. Besides, I do not mind telling you that, yes, I do believe so, for that is why I consented for you to join us."

"O, thank You for that. I do not know why I asked, anyway. It was just a slip of the mind, maybe."

"And what do you think, Laurel? Are you having second thoughts about being here?" At this, Laurel found herself hesitant of declaring an answer, and Sol caught sight of this. "How are you with the idea of our coming battle?"

Laurel hesitated still, uncertain of herself and her feelings. Finally, she released her hand from Sol's in order to turn back to the sea as she said, shivering in the breeze of the sea winds, "O, I am not sure! I feel very anxious about the whole thing, especially after You asked me to be the one to retrieve the jewel of Faith. To tell You the truth, I have never had very much confidence in myself. I am always a clumsy fool, doing and saying things without thinking, though I really mean well! O, and I am not sure that I am ready for any responsibility at all! I am still having feelings of disbelief, even though everything You have told me rings true in my heart... There is just so much that I did not know before and...I just do not want to let You down..."

The uneasy girl stopped suddenly as Sol placed His arm around her again, but this time placing His cloak around her as well, for He noticed her shaking in the cold. "Laurel, you are anxious and worried over nothing," He assured her, looking into her face. "You are also too scrupulous with yourself, which I believe we talked of once long ago, did we not?"

Laurel nodded sadly as she realized this memory. "I am sorry..." was her quiet reply.

"Laurel, I promise you that I *never* once found you to be anything like a 'clumsy fool', as you put it. Forever since I have known you, I have always seen you as a charming and cheerful friend."

"I—I know You do," Laurel replied timidly. "It is just... I never really saw myself as anything special or great, so why should I think that I can achieve anything impressive now?"

"But you *are* special, My dear," the King stressed, turning the young maiden's face towards Him. "You are *Laurel*, like the small tree, or the small shrub as you prefer."

"Yes, but...what is a laurel, anyway? Just some silly, old shrub and nothing special at all!"

Sol smiled sweetly saying, "Did you know that laurel leaves are a sign of victory and royalty?"

"Hmm? What do you mean?" Laurel perked up at this information.

"It is true! During tournaments of strength and ability, the victors are awarded branches of laurel leaves as wreathed crowns, and look!" Sol pointed to the Oracion at Laurel's side, which she always kept with her as instructed by the Queen. "Even on the Emperor's Seal, there are laurel branches to symbolize the authority of the Monarchs of Terra."

Seeing this, Laurel retrieved from her nightgown the Oracion and looked at the golden sun at the end of the beaded chain, where she found the image of the royal seal's red heart wreathed with laurel leaves.

"That is right..." she whispered astonishingly. "I remember...Peterel mentioning the wreath one day when I asked him about the seal on Philippe's blanket...and it was the Royal Seal..." Then, the two looked into each other's eyes as the maiden remembered their carefree moments so long ago, it seemed, in the Valley Fioré.

I never realized it, Laurel thought, blushingly turning her eyes back to the Oracion, *but it was at that moment when I was introduced to everything I am learning of now...*

"That is right!" an epiphany flashed within the simple child's mind.

"What is it, Laurel?"

"The Oracion!" she looked up into Sol's eyes determinedly. "I — I think that I have seen it before — before the Queen presented it to me."

"Ah, truly?" the King eyed the maiden questioningly.

"Yes...though it has taken me a while to remember exactly, but... That night, when the Tempters attacked Serenity Forest, I — I had a dream, and in that dream, there was the Oracion." Then, the considerate maiden related in full all that she remembered of the dream, including the experience of seeing her parents and of how she had come to see the Queen's beauteous treasure.

"Hm, that is interesting," replied Sol as He took the Queen's treasure into His hands.

"So...do You think that there is a reason that I saw this in my dream?" Laurel asked, leaning towards the King with curiosity.

"Well, when it comes to dreams, they often relay series of completely unrelated events that can make no sense when we try to think them through. At times, people we know or places we have seen may be involved, but overall dreams have little to do with reality. Still, in general, they can tell us something about our hearts, especially when people or places we know are involved. You said that your parents were in your dream, correct?"

"Yes. And it is strange that they were because it was the first time that I ever dreamt of them. I was thinking about them a lot at the time of the dream, more so than I have ever before."

"Hm, that would explain why your parents were in your dream," Sol said, "since your heart was so concentrated on them at the time. But as for why the Oracion was in your dream, as you say, the answer is similar to the reason why you had dreamt of the Tempters before."

"You mean the Tempters made me dream of it?" Laurel gasped concernedly.

"No, no. I mean that you dreamt of the Tempters because they have the power to disturb the hearts of the people of Terra, no matter whether they are asleep or awake. This is a corrupt form of the power bestowed on them as Wingel when My Father created them. You see, My Father has also been known at times to relay messages, to those He has chosen, in the form of dreams. As I said, the Tempters as Wingel were given this same power, but for the use of good, though since their fall, they use it to attack the hearts of others."

"So then...the Emperor...could have been giving me a message?" Laurel gazed at the Oracion in amazement.

"As I have said, He has been known to do this before," Sol replied mysteriously.

"But, wait," Laurel began confusedly, "how could the Emperor do all these things to me if we have never met before?"

Sol chuckled. "You are forgetting, Laurel, that He is the Emperor of Terra; it lies within His duty and powers to know all of His citizens, for His sight encompasses that of the whole land and His mind knows all the deeds of the Men of Terra. Besides this, do you not think that I, His only Son, would not talk to Him of you?"

"You...you talk to Him about me?" Laurel was astonished, and when Sol nodded smilingly, the young maiden looked down shyly, for her heart would never have dreamed that her life would be the concern of someone so eminent as the Emperor of Terra, or even His Son.

That...is so strange... All along, the Emperor...thinks of me, Laurel's heart brimmed with fascination as she considered all that the King had said.

Without a word, the gentle King placed a hand onto the glittering Oracion, which instantly transformed into its noble dagger. "My dear Laurel," Sol began softly as He patted her head tenderly, "The most important thing that My Father and I want you to know is that things will seem much harder from here on out. However, you must trust in this blade, the blade of My Mother, and you shall be safeguarded in every battle. I promise."

Looking down admiringly at the Oracion, which Sol now placed within her grasp, Laurel felt deep within her heart as though she were holding a precious treasure of great majesty. "I remember..." she began after a moment, "how You fought the Tempters in the forest, and... You are a strong fighter, Sol. I just hope that...I can be as brave as You..."

"But, do you not remember? That is what we are here for; we are on a quest for Faith, and when we have finally claimed Faith for the people, you too will see the power of the King Virtue in your own heart. But always remember, Laurel," Sol continued as He lifted her chin, "as I told you that evening on the balcony of the Sanctuary, I shall always be here for you, no matter what. Right?"

Looking up again at the King's contented smile, the young maiden found her heart unable to cease from flowing with serenity, and she gave a nod to her King in agreement. This satisfied the King, for He concluded, "Now, it is very late, My dear, and I believe it would do both of us good to be well rested for our continuing journey ahead."

When Laurel agreed to this, for she felt the fatigue of interrupted sleep drawing upon her, Sol stated His decision to walk Laurel back to her cabin, and He took her hand back into His own as He guided her tired steps. Once they had arrived below deck, Laurel remembered Sol's cloak and began removing it to return to her King. However, He stopped her shortly in the process.

"No, please," Laurel insisted, "it is very chilly this night, and You might be in need of —"

"Which is why I want you to have it for tonight," Sol quickly interposed, refastening His cloak around the maiden.

"But—" And Laurel's insistence was again prevented, but this time by a kiss from Sol, which He planted lovingly on her forehead as He had done once before.

"Good blessings, My dear," He said afterwards before departing from Laurel before she could think of what to say.

Happy though the childlike girl was of having discussed with Sol about all the things that had welled within her heart that night, Laurel still knew, deep within her heart, that there was much more for her to understand and reason about her mysterious and loving King.

Chapter 15
The Stronghold

Near the end of the three ships' journey to the South Pole, there came a very blustery and violent storm across the Southern Sea, which from dawn to dusk thrashed and crashed the dark blue waves and darkened the sky with fearsome, ominous clouds. The soldiers grew very frightened with the increasing forcefulness of this grave storm, and many did not dare to resurface above deck, unless by obligation to their work in operating the vessels. Laurel, too, did not venture away from her cabin as she perceived the dangers at hand. Because of this, she sat in her cabin with nothing much to do other than to enjoy her frequent conversations with Peterel, who accompanied her more and more as the end of their sea travelling drew near. She also enjoyed listening to the conferences of the Knights and Sol, who increased His encouragement of Laurel's decision to participate in the forthcoming battle.

"Through careful discernment, I have planned that we should arrive within an ample amount of time before Malum's forces have even begun to depart halfway towards the South," the King said during one of His conferences. "Thus, we should be in no danger of battle until we have retrieved the jewel of Faith and have begun our departure back to the mainland, for I plan to foil our enemy's pride with a surprise attack from the front. I believe that the only threat to our current strategy would be if Malum's forces were aided with knowledge of the location of the jewel of Faith."

"Ha! Then, we are assured of victory!" cried Feoras confidently. "No one among our ranks could be so base as to disclose Your careful planning and harbor treachery among us, my Liege."

Sol's poise gave no external sense of His thoughts on this. "Still, our foe is devious, so stay on your guard. All of you!" He commanded.

That evening the storm was at its worst as a dangerously thick fog covered both the sea and the sky, clouding the view ahead for the three ships. As the wind and waves, thrashed and crashed at the King's ships, the men hurried among the riggings and sails to secure their vessels from the storm's crushing blows. With the howling winds and raging waves pounding the energy and mirth from the seamen, all were greatly disheveled at heart as doom seemed inevitable for the courageous sailing ships. And as the sailing men were swamped by the waves of this tempest, a strange happening occurred. As the fog thickened, the *HMS Rey* lost sight of the other two ships, and the men found themselves alone in the tumultuous sea. Though the soldiers searched and called franticly for their lost men, the *HMS Navi* and *Cura* were lost!

After a few hours, in the midst of the fog, shouts of warning and cries of urgency were heard eerily from all sides of the HMS *Rey* and even up towards the veiled sky. The ghostly voices sounded like the other Knights and sailors of the two lost ships as they pleaded despairingly with the men of the HMS *Rey* to abandon their own ship and hurry aboard the others. The soldiers of the HMS *Rey* became frightened to the core, and they urged Feoras, as first mate of the ship, to adhere to these ominous warnings.

"We should listen to the men," began Sadu, coming up behind Feoras on the lower deck. "It is suicide to continue on with the mission under these present circumstances. We must turn around or abandon ship."

"We will do no such thing," Feoras shrugged the persistent Knight away, "until we have consulted with the Master."

The Master and Great Teacher of Terra, as He was known to His people, stood at the ship's helm where Taran endeavored to navigate the determined vessel on its course to the South Pole through the ghastly tumult of the waves. At the King's side, there stood the Queen, Laurel, and her faithful guardian Peterel, whom had surfaced from the lower cabins at the Queen's bidding. Together the foursome listened at the railings of the helm to the vile voices of the sea.

"These are not the tongues of Our followers, My Son," said Queen Mariah as she looked out into the fog.

"I know. I can sense *them*."

"What is it?" Laurel asked, coming closer to the railings. The ill-tempered air wisped through her hair and veil.

"Something evil is here," replied the Queen. "In the air and sea and storm..."

"Master!" shouted Feoras, followed by Sadu as they came upon the helm.

"The soldiers are growing restless," began Sadu quickly. "We must discontinue our mission presently or all will be doomed."

"Master," Feoras said, looking intently at his King, "what will You have us do?"

Turning His gaze away from the storming sea, Sol replied, "We must continue the mission, as the will of My Father has decreed."

"But, Master!" Sadu started, filled with uncertainty as he advanced towards the King.

Feoras pulled him back at his elbow, ordering, "That is enough, Sadu! The Master has spoken; now, return to your post."

"Can you not see the fear in these men?" Sadu pulled away from the Knight. "They are too weak of heart to continue—" and suddenly, a forceful wave made a crushing blow to one side of the ship, sending almost everyone to their knees until it subsided. "We shall all die here if we continue as we have!" Sadu cried defiantly, rising to his feet, and saying this, the men who were within hearing range to the Knight's ominous shouting grew evermore afraid.

"It is you who bring fear into the men's hearts with your distress!" cried Feoras adamantly. "Now do as our Master has ordered and as I, the leader of the Knights, command!"

Then, Feoras made to leave the helm for the lower decks, when Sadu viciously cried, "Leader of the Knights! Ha! You are willing to lead these men to their death! In everything you have done, nothing has ever gone aright save when the Master was assisting. Leader of the Knights! How could the King be so unwise as to appoint you as my leader; why, you are nothing but a horse's—!" And before anymore of Sadu's cruel words could slip from his spiteful tongue, Feoras' enormous fist furiously swung into Sadu's jaw, and the staggered Knight fell onto his face.

"Say whatever you like about me, but you should not dare to slander our Master! You are very quick to say a lot about the shortcomings of others, but you are slow to point out your own jealous and vain appetites!"

With a howl of rage, Sadu quickly flew to his feet and drew his sword, as did Feoras, and the two Knights, quick as lightning charged at the one another. However, just before the two blades came within inches of clashing, a strong, powerful hand forced the tips of the two swords to a halt. General Mikhail, in his disguise as a rugged sailor, swiftly appeared in time to prevent bloodshed.

"Hold your senses, Men of Terra[12]!" the great Wingel forcefully decreed as he pushed back the swords of the Knights.

"Enough of this!" Sol cried in aggravation. "Sadu, Feoras, return to your post and do as I command. Now, go!"

With that, the Knights reluctantly sheathed their swords and parted in separate ways. Laurel, looking on beneath the arm of the Queen, as she was frightened by the spectacle. She gazed at her King, Whose eyes returned to the sky and the storming sea.

"What is to become of them..." the King began, though saying so as a statement rather than a question.

After a moment, Sol's attention returned to the task at hand with the return of the ghostly voices. "Taran, we shall continue on course through the fog!"

"But, Master, the voices, and the storm—!" the Knight began hesitantly.

"—*will* end, Taran, and pay no mind to what you hear!" Sol interposed determinedly as the Knight obeyed. "I sense it now; we are close

---

[12] This phrase is capitalized as an honorable reference for the people of Terra as the Emperor's subjects.

to our destination." Then, in a low voice that only the Queen and Laurel seemed to hear, the King said, "Quiet yourself, storm of the sea, and remember your King!"

And suddenly, as if in answer to Sol's command, the raging storm was quieted and the sea became calm. Then, the thick fog of the air diminished into a hazy mist until the view was clear and the white stars of the night could been seen shining overhead. Not a sound was heard on the still sea, for even the ghostly voices had ceased in the quieted storm, and as all the tumult of the squall had subsided, all were in awe as the HMS Rey neared the final stage of its journey: the southern pole of Terra. For, close at hand in the distance, alone in the silent sea, there stood a great tower in the center of a rocky isle. It acted as a lighthouse, for a small light could be seen flickering at its highest point. The stronghold reached high into the starry sky, much like the Sanctuary of Serenity Forest only taller and more ominous in appearance.

In the moment of this amazement, there came several shouts from behind the King's ship. Out from the diminishing haze of the sea, the HMS Navi and Cura were seen sailing safely forward. One of the disguised Wingel sailors lit a flare in the dim starlight and shouted in response to the newfound ships. And as suddenly as the calm of the storm came, the water between the three ships began to bubble and swirl in a raging torment, but by no wind or force of tormented sky was the sea disturbed. All the soldiers watched in terror and fear as from the bubbling, foaming sea erupted a dark fortress. As the ominous figure rose from the dark waters, the soldiers were even more frightened to behold a powerful, dark sailing ship, almost double the size of the King's ships, push past them all, forcing a host of crashing waves into their wake.

"Wha—what is that?" Laurel asked fearfully from the Queen's side.

Before the frightened maiden could receive an answer, the dark ship, having positioned itself parallel to the others, opened its side hatches of cannons and fired a malicious force of flame and iron straight for Sol's Army.

"Brace yourselves!" Sol shouted to His men as the ship was bombarded with heavy cannon fire.

Almost all were either catapulted from their posts to their feet or pushed back against one another, but the ship itself, strongly built and blessed with the power of the Emperor, held fast against the attack of the villainous, dark ship. Laurel was once again protected under the mantle of the dear Queen Mariah, who stood firm and unafraid against this evil force.

"The Tempters, My Lord!" She called to Her Son. "Malum's forces have anticipated our arrival."

"But how can that be?" cried Taran, retrieving his balance from the helm. "How could they have known—?"

"There is no time to question these things!" interrupted the King. "We must be swift—Men, prepare the cannons!"

The sailors and soldiers rushed to help one another and obey the commands of the Great Teacher, and as the King's ship readied their cannons, the sound of bombardments echoed again but this time from the *HMS Navi* and *Cura*, whom with all of their might pushed back the ship of Malum's forces.

"Now for our strike! Ready, men?" Sol charged the sailors. "Fire!"

Laurel held her ears and cringed as the loud booming of the artillery crashed in the air with the explosion and striking of the Tempter's ship. However, Malum's forces carried an evil power within them, and they were not known to give up so easily, no matter how intense the pressure, no matter how high the stakes were.

Knowing this, the King called for the aid of His three Knights and the Wingel Mikhail, "Time is of the essence, My friends, and we need to make a break for the Stronghold while the Tempters' ship is occupied with their defense. Therefore, I leave General Mikhail in charge of My ships after the Queen, while the Knights and I go after the precious jewel of Faith."

"Yes, Sire!" the Wingel answered obediently.

"Feoras," Sol said to the Knight, "have the other ships signaled for the rest of the Knights to follow us."

And as Feoras and Sadu left to complete the King's commands and while Taran was replaced at the helm by a Wingel sailor, the King turned to Laurel and her guardian saying, "Come, Laurel, Peterel! Our time has come!"

And parting with the Queen, who took over command of the ships, Laurel received a special blessing in the form of a kiss on her forehead by the gentle Woman. "Go, My dear, and remember the Oracion!"

With that, the King, His Knights, and Laurel with her guardian Peterel left for the rowboats, while the Queen and the King's Army fought on the high seas against Malum's evil cohorts. When, the boats were lowered into the foaming waves, for the Tempters used their ill powers to stir up another storm across the sea, Sol's group set out for the Stronghold of Faith. The Knights of the other ships soon met them in their own boats, and they all wrestled with the turbulent waves that struggled to obstruct their way.

"We shall never make it to the isle at this rate!" shouted Maso over the swirling wind.

"No, we shall not," began the King, "but I am not one to give up!"

Then, as Sol touched His hand against the foaming waves, the sea surged with the command of a new power, and the waves grew behind the three rowboats. Coming to their aid, the mighty waters sent the boats off across the waters towards the isle. At such speed, there was no need for the oars as all held tightly onto the sides of the boats.

When Sol said He was the King of Terra, Laurel thought at the sight of this great power, *He really meant that He was* the King of Terra!

The great power of the waves charged the boats straight for the isle of the Stronghold, and once they arrived at the rocky terrain of the shores, the Knights forced iron stakes into the crevices of the rocks where they tied their ships, as there was no other way to dock their boats. Then, the group scaled the slippery rocks on the edge of the isle, and they helped each other along the rough, wet rocks, climbing until they reached the topmost point where the entrance to the Stronghold of Faith lied. Two great stone doors with two large, brass handles stood as the entrance into the ominous tower, which seemed to moan in the rising wind of the new storm.

"Hasten, My friends!" Sol called as the Knights followed Him towards the doors.

There, finding the heavy doors unwilling to budge, the twelve Knights pulled on each handle together with all of their strength. Laurel, with Peterel at her side, stood in awe as the enormous doors were forced open and the group slowly entered the Stronghold.

The round tower floor was formed of a bright white tile, likened to the color of sea foam, while the walls were made of a light blue brick, with chipping paint from long years of abandonment. Circling endlessly, it seemed, up the tower was a long staircase of bright, white stone that led to the top of the Stronghold, where a solitary room of great mystery awaited for the King's Company. Except for the soft groaning of the Stronghold as the winds blew against it from outside, all was quiet in the ancient tower, almost *too* quiet it seemed.

"So..." thought Andres aloud as he looked up the long flight of steps, "all we need to do is get up there to retrieve the jewel of Faith...right?"

"Yes..." replied Sol distantly as His eyes followed the path of the stairs leading up to the top of the Stronghold.

Without warning, however, the young King unsheathed His sword and threw it swiftly across the room, where it squarely pierced into the light blue stone. As suddenly as the sword had pierced the wall, it let out a glowing shockwave of power all around, and ugly cries of hate and pain sounded from the shadows of the wall and floor around the sword's aura. Then, to Laurel and the Knights' surprise, a host of Tempters revealed themselves from their lurking hideaways in the shadows of the tower.

"But first, we fight!" Sol continued, as each Knights readied their weapons for battle.

Before any movement was made for attack on either side, the Tempters, prodigious in number, lifted their cloaks from their sides, and from the dark aura that emitted from their grotesque bodies, another host of evil creatures came forth for battle. However, it was only after a moment's study before all recognized these grievous monsters to be Men of Terra, only their true nature had now shown forth on their faces and in their eyes as they were full of death and cravings for power.

"O, Men of Terra!" the King cried, His heart beating with agony at the sight of these evil men with their attire and expressions of filth and evil pleasure and their hands wielding weapons sharp and deadly with hate. "What has become of you?"

"We are no longer Men of Terra!" the villainous men interrupted. "Hate has grown in our hearts, hate for you and your words! Our allegiance is to Malum, for we are men of Malum forever!"

"Vipers, the lot of them!" growled Taran and Radi filled with rage. "Sire, at Your command, shall we defeat these men of evil?"

"It has come to this then, My brothers?" Sol began, looking into the eye of each wicked man, which angered their foul hearts. "Then, reap the justice you have won!"

And with a blink of an eye, the young King charged at the beast-like men and Tempters, flying over them in a single bound as He landed behind them to retrieve His sword. The Knights, with ready weapons, followed suit and braced themselves for the impact of war.

Before landing a single blow, however, Sol turned His gaze to Laurel and Peterel, "Go, My friends! Fly quickly to Faith!"

Taking the young maiden's hand, Peterel urged his friend forward with determined eyes, and Laurel quickly came to her senses, having momentarily lapsed in disgusted astonishment of the horrid power and vice of Malum's forces.

That is right! Laurel thought as she began her ascent of the stairs. *I have my own mission to complete – for Sol!*

Two Tempters, seeing this break in the group, rushed ahead of the young maiden, blocking her path, but Peterel pushed through them and tore away his sailor disguise, revealing his true Wingel form. From the mystical quiver on his back, the Wingel readied his golden bow with silver arrows and shot down the first Tempter on his left.

"Come, you evil one!" Peterel shouted as he dodged the second Tempter's slashing claws, and the beast flew after the Wingel, flaming with fury.

As Peterel flew away with the Tempter, Laurel caught sight of the King within the crowd of slashing and furious battle below. The soft yet determined expression of His eyes seemed to fill Laurel's heart with strength as she returned her attention to the task at hand and forged ahead up the long stone staircase. All the while down below, the Knights and the King valiantly fought both man and Tempter. Feoras with his slashing sword, Taran and

Radi with their swift crossbows, Andres and his mighty ax, Saimen's faithful slingshot, Caius with his jagged club, Taam with his powerful battle hammer, Maso and his twin boomerangs, Donato's sharply spiked ball, Yaakov and his intimidating hand-mace, Zimran with his trusty spear, and Sadu with his deadly saber—all defended, with every blow they made and with every wound they sustained, the truth of their King, their Emperor, and their Queen.

The battle was long fought with both sides determined to see an end, but the King's side was stronger and pure in heart, and victory appeared inevitable for their side, no matter the hot flames, the furious clawing, and ruthless strikes of their foes. Throughout the battle, Laurel determined to reach the top of the stairs, and she strived with all of her heart and might with every step she made.

"Ah, goodness!" Laurel panted as she stopped in her tracks to rest, looking up at the many hundreds of steps that she still needed to pursue. "The jewel of Faith… Oh, why does it have to be so far away?"

Then, out of the corner of her eye, Laurel caught sight of a dark shadow as it slithered from behind and stopped before her. As the dark figure of a Tempter drew forth from the shadow, Laurel's hand frightfully flew to the Oracion at her side. With a malicious grin, the Tempter's claws sprang out from under its cloak, rushing towards the young maiden before she had time to draw her mystical dagger. However, the Tempter was forced backwards as the yellow aura of Sol's ring surround Laurel protectively.

"The ring…" Laurel gasped in realization, and just before the evil creature could rise for a second attack two arrows shot straight through the evil Tempter's chest.

Turing around, Laurel beheld Taran and Radi running up the stairs with the other Knights following close behind. It seemed that, as Laurel ventured further up the winding stairs, the battle below had followed close behind, for the Tempters and evil men had not forgotten the young maiden's breaking form the group of fighters.

"Go on, Laurel!" the twins called to the young maiden as their attention was drawn back down the steps with the other Knights. "We have you covered!"

Laurel smiled thankfully as she parted from them, and she showed an extra quickness in her step as she continued to the top of the Stronghold.

Chapter 16
The Jewel of Faith

The entrance to the high chamber of the Stronghold was reached from a small room at the end of the winding stairs, where Laurel pushed open two heavy, oak doors with all of her strength. Once inside, the young maiden climbed a rickety ladder to a dimly lit opening above. Cautiously, she peered her head out from the opening, and beheld the chamber of the jewel of Faith. The chamber was a large round room with alternating rows of white and orange tiles adorning the floor. Large, oval windows were stationed across the gray-blue walls, which showed the darkening sky outside with its thunderous clouds and ominous rain. Tall stone pillars were positioned around the room, where small torches hung to light the room. Laurel was surprised to notice that the light of these torches was the same as the mysterious lights of the chandeliers of the Sanctuary in Serenity Forest, which glowed with no flame. In addition, the ceiling of the tower was painted with the symbol of the Royal Family.

"Wow..." Laurel whispered to herself in wonder at the strange chamber.

Then, as her eyes traveled the room curiously, Laurel noticed a mystifying stone structure in the center of the chamber. The structure was round and stood almost as tall as Laurel's shoulders. Sitting atop the structure was a rounded alcove, and coming closer with curiosity in her wake, Laurel noted a slab, which sealed the alcove, bearing an image of the Royal Family Seal painted across it.

I wonder... Laurel thought, placing her hand against the stone slab. *Is this where I find the jewel of Faith?* Unexpectedly, the maiden's hand perceived what seemed to be as keyhole carved into the stone slab, and she stood amazed at the sight.

Wait a moment...if the jewel of Faith is in here, then...how am I supposed to get it out? Sol did not give me a key — Oh no, have I forgotten something! For a moment, Laurel felt swelled in a wave of panic as she did not know what to do. However, that was when the words of Queen Mariah sounded in her heart: "Remember the Oracion!"

"The Oracion!" Laurel cried aloud with understanding, but when she did retrieve the beautiful item from her side, she looked down at the Queen's gift with skepticism.

Well, it has worked before to call forth a weapon of defense, so it should work for anything. But, then again... I guess that I shall just have to try as the Queen instructed me.

And with determination in her heart, the desperate girl made her request in the Queen's name, though uncertainty swirled in her troubled mind. To her amazement, however, the beaded crystals of the Oracion glowed with brilliance, and suddenly a bright, golden key displaying the Emperor's Seal appeared in her hand. Laurel eyed the key in wonder before carefully fitting it into the keyhole of the slab.

Please work! Laurel's heart pleaded as she turned the key, and as she did so, the keyhole glowed with an intense radiance.

After removing the key, the stone slab disappeared as if into thin air, and behold, in the alcove of the stone structure, Laurel saw with her own eyes the great and mysterious jewel that all of the Kingdom had longed for: the jewel of Faith. A luminous stone glowing with the light of the sun in rays of golden orange, the jewel of Faith shined forth from the alcove, lighting the maiden's face and eyes. In awe of the spectacular radiance of the stone, Laurel could not help losing herself in the light and warmth of the jewel's beauty. Slowly in awe and after dazedly replacing the Oracian at her side, Laurel stretched forth her hand towards the light of Faith, ready to take hold of this beauteous treasure for the Kingdom of Terra.

"I would not do that if I were you," a strange voice gravely spoke up.

Startled, and uneasy that she had let her guard down, Laurel stepped back from the jewel of Faith. "Wh—why do you say that?" she answered timidly, trying to sound brave in the wake of this hidden observer.

Laurel quickly scanned the room all around her, searching for the face of the voice that had spoken. Suddenly, she perceived to her right, hiding far in the shadows beyond her observance upon first entering the chamber, the form of a man, dark and portentous. Upon her noticing him, the man stepped forth into the light of the torches, his large, dark boots thumping with each stride he made. The man was tall and handsome with large, sinister hands. On each of his pale arms, he bore a black dragon tattoo. He wore a dark-gray tunic with black pants and had a silver skull with red-jeweled eyes as a clasp for the long, tattered shadowy cloak that he wore around himself. Then, Laurel observed the man's shady eyes, as mysterious as the ominous darkness of the shadows, and his wide, deceitful-looking grin, which eerily flashed as he watched the young maiden.

"I insist that you refrain from retrieving that stone, my dear," the man said calmly, coming to the answer of Laurel's previous question, "because, if you do not, then I shall have to kill you." And the threatening man's hand drew slowly to the dark blade that he carried on his back.

Fearful of the man's intentions, Laurel quickly withdrew the Oracion from her side, which instantly transformed into her mystical blade of defense, and the trembling girl, though filled with fear, readied herself for battle.

Seeing this, the man laughed mockingly. "Now, now, my dear! There is no need to be so taut! Hmm, I see you have one of those nasty little trinkets. Well, that is interesting, my dear, *very* interesting!" And the man seemed to study Laurel's blade pensively.

"Look," Laurel's voice quavered uneasily, "I—I do not want any trouble here. I just—"

Before the wary child could finish, the evil man swiftly unsheathed his dark blade and rushed towards Laurel, his sword ready to lacerate the girl to pieces. However, the ring on Laurel's hand gleamed abruptly and the barrier of protective aura surround her just as the man's sword made impact. Laurel had only time to flinch before she realized what had happened. Seeing that his blade could not penetrate the power that surrounded Laurel, the man withdrew away from the stone structure where the maiden stood.

"I see…" began the man as he relaxed his sword to his side. "You are also in possession of that abominable ring! Well then, if my surmising is correct, you must be one of Sol's little friends." And, Laurel looked up at the man at the sound of her King's name as he continued, "Though, I believe we have never met before."

"Who…who are you?" Laurel stammered, still quiet in shock at her attacker.

"I am called many things," the man replied, "but you may call me Lues, my dear!"

Lues! Laurel thought frightfully, *So, he is the one Sol warned me about!*

"It seems you have heard about me," Lues said, having studied Laurel's expression carefully. He slowly stepped towards the young maiden, who kept her guard up as well as her dagger close at hand. "Tell me, my dear, what do you know about the great Lues?" And, he raised his sword menacingly as he watched the fear appear on Laurel's face.

"Lues! Get away from her, you viper!" Turning to the entrance of the chamber, all beheld Sol, who had appeared wielding His mighty blade. An expression of just fury showed brightly in His eyes.

"Ah, Sol, my old friend!" Lues began mockingly. "I was beginning to wonder when you were going to show up!"

"Silence, you treacherous snake!" Sol cried angrily.

"You know, Sol," Lues continued, ignoring this command, "I am a little disappointed that you never introduced me to your little friend here." And, he motioned his sharp blade towards Laurel. "We were only just getting acquainted before you arrived, anyway!"

"Pay no mind to the girl!" Sol shouted heatedly. "Remember, your fight is with Me!"

"Ah, yes, as seems to be our eternal doings. But, this little girl intrigues me; she has both the sword of your mother and that despicable little ring of yours! Hmm, she must be of some importance to you, is she not?" Saying this, Lues pointed his wicked blade towards Laurel with a malicious grin drawing across his face.

"Point your cowardly blade this way, Lues, or feel the sting of mine!"

"The blade of Death is not to be ridiculed!" the evil man said, turning heatedly towards the King. "You of all people should know that!"

"Neither is Justice, My blade of truth!" Sol scorned him. "Or have you forgotten the power I have?"

"Power!" Lues laughed abominably. "And what power do you have, little *master*? I have terrible power beyond even this girl's imagination! But, yes, let us discuss power!" And as Lues spoke, Sol began to slowly circle around towards Laurel, and Lues followed Him, drawing away from the young maiden.

"So tell me, little master, what have you told our dear friend here? That I am 'not human' and 'hold no emotion within my being'? That everything I am and everything I say is 'a lie' and 'not to be trusted'? That my only purpose is to 'deceive, crush, and destroy'? Now, all these things I have heard you tell many of your followers before, but have you really told *her* everything? Sol, have you revealed what power *I* have over her!"

And having said this, Lues raised his hand, quickly drawing it into a fist, and in doing, so a mysterious, dark aura, like a black fire, glowed around his fist. Suddenly, Laurel found herself crying out in pain as she fell to her knees, for her heart began aching terrible by some strange, dark force.

"Laurel!" Sol cried, rushing to His young maiden, but Lues rushed ahead of the King and met his dark blade with Sol's sword of Justice.

"Ah, so that is her name!" Lues said jeeringly as he pushed heavily against Sol's blade. "Laurel! It certainly has a ring to it!"

"Laurel!" Sol shouted earnestly as He kept Lues' blade at bay.

What was happening to the maiden not even she could discern at the time, but deep within her heart there arose a sickening, torturous pain that seemed to suffocate her very being into utter darkness. For that is what she felt within her heart: darkness, fighting her reason with hate and shadows. The pain in her heart was so great that the girl could barely move, let alone speak except for a few gasps of agony, which she moaned from her deepest being as she held her hand close to her aching heart.

What...is...happening to me? Laurel struggled to think as the wave of painful darkness that filled her struggled to control her thoughts. *What...is...happening?*

"Now, you know my power, little maid," Lues said sinisterly. "For this is the power that *I* have, that *I* can control! I, Lues, was created by Malum from the same essence of his brilliant Curse on the hearts of man. I am one and the same with his power, for I have control over the hearts of man; I have control over your innermost desires!"

"Release her!" Sol cried enraged as He pushed hard against Lues' sword, and the evil man jumped back from the King's force.

Lues only laughed with spite in his throat. "You know I cannot! Once the temptations of the Curse have begun, it is up to the tormented to choose for themselves who they wish to serve, and I highly doubt that your little friend will remain on your side any longer!"

Filled with righteous anger at these words, Sol flew at the hateful man, slashing His sword left and right with all the strength of His heart. Lues kept up the pace with these attacks, blocking as best he could the speed and force of the King's blade. All the while, Laurel fought with the dark torments within her heart. They spoke of hate, shadows, and all the evil vice of the world for her taking, if only she would. The young maiden was restless with uncertainty, not knowing how to break free from her agony.

What am I to do? All of these shadows…in my mind, my heart, before my very eyes! It is too much! Too much!

"Do not be afraid, Laurel. Listen to Me!" Sol called, seeing her weak condition. "You must get up and fight! Do not heed the temptations of Malums' Curse! Please, stand up and fight!"

Hearing the gravity in Sol's voice, Laurel made an effort to stand, though her knees wobbled with weakness and her breathing was slow and heavy. Throwing in a counterattack with his blade of Death, Lues, having noticed the young maiden's exertion, clenched his fist again as a flare of dark flames rose up around his hand. Laurel felt the darkness within her heart grow stronger, only this time flames of dark, shadowy fire flared up at her shoulders and heart, and she sank back to her feet in deeper pain. The shadowy flames, though they burned her very spirit and being, had the touch of cold ice and darkness, as they rose around her powerfully.

"Hmm, such an easy prey!" Lues laughed victoriously, but then was cripplingly pushed back by Sol's slashing sword of Justice.

"Laurel! Please, get up! Laurel!" Sol pleaded earnestly as He continued His battle with Lues. As He fought the evil man, Sol occupied his dark force with His overpowering attacks, giving Laurel time to find her reason.

I…I cannot do this, she thought to herself. *I am too weak to endure this! My heart wants to give up, now… I cannot! But, I cannot endure this any longer! No, it is too much! I cannot…*

Tears rolled down the struggling girl's eyes with despair as her head rested uneasily against the stone structure beside her. Then, she looked up wearily at the alcove, where the jewel of Faith resided.

But the jewel of Faith…I have to – Laurel thought as she tried to rise from her feet. However, she sank down again as the pain of her heart continued to increase. *It is no use…no use…*

After jumping back from the King's attacks, Lues observed the weakness of the fainting child and laughed again in scorn. "You see, little master! No matter how hard you try, you can never win against the power of Malum. Even now, your dear little Laurel is drawing ever closer under the full control of my power!"

Having lowered his guard at this gloating, Lues was thoroughly forced back by the might of Sol's sword of Justice. "*Your* power? You and your master have no power over the Kingdom of the Emperor of Terra, and you have no power over Me and Mine!"

"And just who are you, little *master*, to speak with such authority?" Lues questioned with a sense of uneasiness at Sol's fortitude.

"It is just as you have said!" Sol replied crushing His blade down against Lues' sword of Death. "I am the Master!" Then, He released a series of attacks on the hateful villain, which cut at Lues' blade and staggered him on his feet. "And I am not alone in My endeavors!"

Enraged by these attacks, the ruthless Lues found his balance and continued his fight with the King of Terra, for he was not to be beaten so easily. "Or, have you forgotten, Lues," the King continued mysteriously, "Whom it is that I fight for?"

"And, just *what*," began Lues irritably as his blade of Death locked with the sword of Justice, "are you going on about?" Suddenly, the vile man noticed again the ring on Laurel's hand as his eyes were drawn to it by a twinkling gleam that began to shine forth. "No, that is impossible!"

"You are too quick in your pride, Lues!" Sol retorted, "Too soon do you and your master forget the true power of this world!"

And as they spoke, the weakened maiden too noticed the gleaming of her ring as she continued her internal struggle with the darkness of her heart. Before her clouded mind could make sense of this light, the world around Laurel suddenly seemed to disappear from her, and a strange sight emerged in her mind's eye. Standing arrayed in the white brilliance of pure light, there was a Man, aged in appearance but youthful in the expression of His eyes. His long white hair flowed down His shoulders, and His white beard glowed with the same light that surrounded His hair. He white robe and purple cloak gave Him the appearance of a royal monarch, and as Laurel stared in awe at the Man, her heart recognized Him as Emperor Abba of Terra, though she had never seen Him before. The Emperor smiled lovingly at the troubled child, like a father to his daughter, and though He said not a word, this beauteous vision and affectionate glance of the Emperor warmed the icing heart of the darkened maiden. In that instant, Laurel felt a strange peace within her whole being.

Just as suddenly as the vision had appeared, it quickly vanished, and Laurel found herself kneeling against the stone structure of the jewel of Faith. Then, the pain within her heart swiftly returned with full force, and Laurel cried aloud in agony. However, she felt a new courage within her, and with increased determination she found herself rising to her feet. Seeing this, Lues prepared himself for another attack on the heart of the strengthened girl, but Sol quickly unleased quelling strikes against the hateful man, pushing him back, cutting at his blade of Death, and knocking him squarely against the columns of the chamber. Meanwhile, with dagger in hand, Laurel dug her weapon into the aged crevices of the stone structure as a means of supporting her weakened body, struggling to reach the alcove where Faith awaited. Desperately, Lues inflicted his attacks on the King and whatever he could manage on the heart of the maiden, but neither would concede to the evil man's desire of defeat, neither would give up their fight so easily.

And at the very end of this battle, as the blade of Death strained, but inevitably failed, to pierce the heart of the King of Terra and as the dark Curse of Malum determined to capture the heart of the fair maiden, an incredible, wonderfully brilliant happening occurred before Laurel's very eyes. With hand outstretched, with all the fortitude her heart could muster, the young maiden's fingertips came upon the beauteous jewel of Faith, which glowed with bright golden-orange rays as her hand drew closer. Finally, with the final effort her weakened being could manage, Laurel enclosed the stone within her grasp.

"No! No!" Lues cried in defeat as Sol's final attack with His powerful sword thrust the evil man into another chamber column.

Standing upright before the alcove, as she felt numb to her subsiding pain, Laurel then admired the precious treasure that she now possessed, which glowed like a fiery, warm flame, in the palm of her hand.

"Faith," she murmured, as she felt her heart receiving the power of this most precious stone.

Suddenly, the jewel shined incredibly, even brighter than the sun, and the light glowed all around the maiden and throughout the chamber. Then, this great light shined out through the Stronghold and beyond its walls, out into the sea where the King's ships were in battle, out across the waters and the lands of Terra, out to the hearts of all the people, and every citizen of Terra at that moment felt the grace of Faith within them. With its light poured out into the Kingdom, the jewel of Faith subsided its brilliance and returned as a bright, shining treasure in the hand of the innocent child. For a long moment, Laurel stared down at the jewel, when she suddenly felt a gentle hand on her shoulder. Turning, she beheld the loving smile of her King, who held Justice at His side.

"My King!" were Laurel's first words at the sight of Sol, and happily the two embraced with warmth and friendship.

"My dear," the King began, releasing the girl from His arms, "you have found it, the jewel of Faith!"

Before Laurel could relate her joy to her dear King, there came a shout from among the columns, "No! No! I shall not have this!"

Lues, beaten and defeated to a lowly existence from his battle, was found on his knees, a piteous sight, filled with grief at his lost, for Faith had return to Terra. "You!" he cried, looking up at Laurel, his eyes red with hate and evil desire. "You, despicable wench, will *pay* for your crimes against the true ruler of Terra!" Suddenly, dark shadows and icy flames of hate poured forth around the grieving Lues and they reached around him into all the corners of the chamber.

"Come, Laurel, quickly!" Sol cried, pulling the young maiden along to the chamber's exit. Lues cried out in anger, and his dark forces of evil grew furiously across the chamber.

Then, the benevolent King, quick thinking in His deeds, took up the cherished girl within His arms and swiftly jumped down through the hole of the chamber, just as Lues' darkness drew nearer.

"We have to get out of here," Sol said, landing nimbly on His feet and starting off again for the door to the stairs. "Lues is going to try to consume the Stronghold with his darkness in an effort to seize the jewel of Faith, for he knows that he still has a chance to destroy it, if he can get to it."

At the door to the stairs, Sol commanded the heavy doors to open, and they swiftly allowed the King of Terra to pass between them. Running out upon the stairs that winded down to the Stronghold's entrance, Sol quickly looked over the stone rails for His Knights, who were still fighting off the last members of Tempters and men from the previous battle. Peterel was also seen in midflight, his hands full with the entangling attacks of the Tempters.

"All right," the King smiled to Laurel, "hold on!"

"Wait, what are You — ?" Laurel tried to ask, but Sol swiftly ran down the stairs and jumped onto the stone rails, letting Himself slide His way down the many and numerous stairs of the Stronghold.

Once Sol reached the Knights, He called out to them, "Come, My brothers! We must leave for the ships." Hearing His voice, Peterel too, along with the Knights, swiftly came to their Master's side.

"Yes, Sire, and it seems we will not be having very much trouble getting there," replied Feoras, after finishing off a cowardly Tempter.

"All of Malum's forces have started to retreat, Master, since You arrived," Caius spoke up at the Knight's side.

"Yes, because we have released one of their greatest fears into the world: Faith! Now, come, My brothers, and let us make haste to the ships!"

With that, the Knights were all gathered as the group made their way swiftly down the winding steps to the entrance of the Stronghold, just as the darkness released by Lues drew to their very feet! Once outside, the King ordered His men to return to their boats and to sail away to the ships, being sure to protect the jewel of Faith in Laurel's possession from any Tempters or men of Malum that may seek its destruction.

"But what about You?" Laurel asked, realizing that Sol meant to stay on the island. "Are You not coming with us?"

"In time, My dear," Sol said, placing a considerate hand on the maiden's shoulder. "As of now, Lues has not yet given up his fight, and I want to be sure that the ships can safely pass through the Southern Sea without his following. But, do not fear, for I shall return to you all shortly."

"But, how will You return if we are taking the boats with us?" the maiden called to the King desperately as He began to leave for the Stronghold once more.

"I have My ways," the King replied mysteriously, and He vanished into the ominous, darkening tower.

"Come, Laurel," Peterel said, pulling at her hand. "We must bring Faith safely to the ships."

Laurel complied with this, and followed as the King's Company hurried along down the steep, slippery rocks to their boats, where they hastened to sail away to the three ships that were in the midst of battle on the sea. For it happened that, as the King and His companions set off to retrieve the jewel of Faith, the Queen and Her Wingel warriors led the Madeira sailors against the terrible, dark ship of Tempters in the raging and tormenting storm, newly crafted from their evil claws. There was much cannon fire, explosions, and struggling as the Tempters flew the evil men of Malum onto the three noble ships in an effort to defeat their enemies in hand-to-hand combat.

However, they were no match for the trained Wingel warriors and the Queen of Terra, the legendary Woman of the Seven Swords. Calling forth Her mystical blades one by one to Her hands, the valiant Queen protected the Men of Terra from the fiery, malicious attacks of the Tempters, for She slew the beasts with each sword that came to Her hand. Finally, after calling forth six of Her powerful weapons, there appeared clasped against the Queen's back a magnificently formidable sword of great splendor and strength. With it, She conquered Her enemies and drove them in terror from the Men of Terra, whom they had wished to torment and kill. In the end, when the jewel of Faith had released its power into the hearts of all throughout the world, the Tempters grew fearfully aware of their impending defeat and doom in this battle, and they began to retreat as best they could, though none around the great General Mikhail or Queen Mariah could escape a vanquishing fate. With the return of the Knights and Laurel to their respective ships, the Queen was overjoyed at the reclaiming of the jewel of Faith.

"Now, there is no time to waste, My dear," started the Queen solemnly afterwards. "Though the Tempters and their forces are retreating, we must sail away to safety, lest these evil creatures fulfill their current planning to steal away the jewel of Faith for destruction." Swiftly, the Queen called to General Mikhail and ordered the ships to sail away with their precious treasure. Laurel stayed protected within the Queen's mantle.

"But—what about Sol?" Laurel inquired after the Wingel had left to attend to his orders.

"I know My Son, Laurel. He will be all right," and the Queen placed a kindly hand on the young maiden's head. "Now, My dear, if you are to carry the jewel of Faith for us, I want you to stay hidden in this last battle as best you can. Peterel, be certain that no Tempter lays a hand on Laurel!" Queen Mariah finished, charging the Wingel at Laurel's side earnestly.

Peterel nodded determinedly in reply, as he took the young maiden's hand and led her off the decks. Suddenly, a great force shook the *HMS Rey* as a bombardment of cannon fire shot from the Tempter's dark ship.

"Quickly, Laurel, we must—" Peterel began, when a second force attacked the ship, this time a raging tidal wave, almost half the size of the *HMS Rey*.

"What is going on?" Laurel asked, falling to her knees at the second attack.

Looking out from the railings, Peterel saw how the great dark ship circled around the *HMS Rey*, pushing away the *HMS Navi* and *Cura* from its aid.

"They know that the jewel of Faith is on this ship," Peterel said, after a moment. "They are pulling all of their forces together for attack now, and this time it will be almost too much for us to bear. Come, Laurel, quickly!"

The two raced as best they could from the decks to safety. However, the attacks of Malum's forces swamped and rattled the ships so that Laurel could not keep from falling to her knees repeatedly. Then, the Tempters came aboard the King's ship once again, as last effort to find and capture Faith. The Queen and Her soldiers, especially those from Madeira Harbor who had now found their confidence to fight for the Emperor's cause, were determined to keep their ship free and safe from these evil creatures' attacks. As these vile beasts waged their fiery claws against the formidable weapons of the Queen's soldiers, Peterel found himself in the midst of battle as well, for the Tempters found Laurel in her escape and, seeking the destruction of Faith, attacked her Wingel guardian with all the rage and darkness of their beings.

"Run, Laurel!" Peterel cried, holding off the Tempters from the young maiden. "Hide away, quickly!"

Keeping the jewel of Faith close to her heart, the young maiden hid from the fury of this last battle, though not finding a clear access to the lower decks to the cabins. She ran from her attackers towards the very back of the ship. Suddenly, an enormous tidal wave appeared from the Tempter's power, and as all braced themselves for impact, the treacherous wall of water plowed into the side of the *HMS Rey*. As the dark waters swept onto the decks of the ship, forcing into anyone within its path, Laurel was caught up in the icy waters and cascaded over the ship's railings. Not knowing her predicament but keeping the jewel of Faith securely against her heart, Laurel saw the whole, dark world turned upside down before her as she was plunged into the black, frigid waters of the Southern Sea. The sea was filled with shadows and sweeping currents, and the cold water stabbed the young maiden painfully like fiery needles. Swimming quickly to the surface, Laurel gasped for air, struggling to keep her head above the storming waves. She searched hurriedly for the *HMS Rey* and found it sailing quickly away in the midst of battle against the great, dark ship of the Tempters.

"Wait!" her little voice cried softly in the churning waves. "Wait!"

It was no use, for even if she could reach the ship that sailed from her, the Tempters' ship would certainly run her down as it circled formidably around the King's ship. Still, Laurel would not give up as she swam with all of her might forward. Though she was an excellent swimmer from her days in The Great River in the Valley Fioré, Laurel had never experienced the ocean's terrible currents and was thrown to and fro in the swirling waves. As if this was not enough trouble for the miserable maiden, the dark ship of the Tempters launched another attack of cannon fire at the *HMS Rey*, and some of the overshooting cannonballs came right into Laurel's path. There was nothing the frightened girl could do as the cannon fire exploded around her, and she was catapulted under the dark waves.

Coming to her senses, however, Laurel determined ahead as she resurfaced from the freezing water. Turning around, though, at the sound of loud roaring, Laurel beheld the awesome, horrific sight of an enormous wall of water rushing towards her, and in her fearful amazement, Laurel was swept up in this terrible current and forced down into the belly of the sea in a torment and fury of swirling, churning waves. After a while, in the midst of these terrible currents, she opened her eyes and found herself in the deep shadows of the Southern Sea. To her horror, out of the corner of her eye, Laurel noticed the bright gleam of the jewel of Faith, which had slipped from her delicate fingers and was now floating slowly down into the abyss of the Southern Sea.

Swiftly, Laurel swam mightily downwards towards the precious treasure of Terra, fighting the evil currents that tried to suppress her. Her hand reached out towards Faith, and the stone shined like a star in the night sky, as if sensing her heart moving towards it. Laurel had to hurry now, for her lungs were aching with a need for fresh air. Her heart beat painfully with fatigue as her little fingers came within reach of the jewel of Faith. Seeing that precious jewel within her hands, Laurel gave up all efforts to continue onward. Drawing Faith close to her heart, she could perceive a bright hand reaching out for her as her mind succumbed to the surrounding darkness.

Chapter 17
Faithful Repercussions

When Laurel awoke, at first, she did not know where she was. Her vision was blurry, and it took a while before her eyes adjusted to the light that surrounded her. After a moment, the young maiden realized that she was lying in the elegant bed of her chamber at the Sanctuary. She heard the gentle roar of a fire burning contentedly in the hearth to the far right of her bed, and she stared up at the graceful baldachin of her bed, as she tried to reason how she had come to be in the Sanctuary.

"I see you are awake," came the sweet voice of the Queen, and turning her head to the right, Laurel beheld the beauteous Queen Mariah sitting quietly in a chair beside her bed.

"Queen Mariah!" Laurel started in delight at seeing the loving Woman, and she began to sit up. Suddenly, the stiff girl's head swam with uneasiness and fatigue.

"Careful, My dear!" the beloved Queen said, helping Laurel to sit up comfortably. "You must not rush yourself, after everything you have been through. Please, rest a little while longer."

"Queen Mariah," Laurel started again, "what happened? I mean, how did I get to the Sanctuary, and what about the battle at sea and the Tempters and —?"

"Now, now, My dear!" the Queen smiled at the young maiden's returning strength. "All is well. The Tempters were defeated, and the Army of the Emperor was victorious in battle. As for how you came to be here, dear Laurel, you shall have to thank the King."

"Sol? What do You mean?"

"Why, He was the one who found you lost in the sea. He told Me that, after He had left to return to us, He found Peterel, who had been searching everywhere for you, and in the midst of their search, the King discovered you and brought you back to the ship before we sailed away back to Madeira Harbor. All this time, Laurel, you have been asleep, unconscious for almost a week."

"A week?" Laurel moaned in astonishment, having not realized how much time had gone by. Then, she sat for a moment thinking over her last few memories of the battle at sea. "I remember...falling into water, when this huge wave struck the ship, and...when I fell in..."

Suddenly, the maiden looked about in fear as a terrible thought came to her attention. "O, Queen Mariah! The jewel of Faith! I—I had it with me when I fell in, and I remember losing it in the current and—!"

"Peace, dear one!" the Queen said, withdrawing a small item from Her cloak. "Do not fear; here is the jewel of Faith, which you have saved."

Then, She handed to Laurel the precious treasure of the Emperor, the King Virtue of Faith, and Laurel's heart felt a wave of relief and splendor overcome it, as she took up Faith within her little hands.

"Why did You not give this to Sol?"

"We both agreed that We want you to present it to Him but in your own time, My dearest, for I wish for you to rest a little while long, and when you can, a Wingel will come to bring you something to eat."

Just as the Queen rose to leave the young maiden, Laurel quickly took up Her delicate hand. "Please...wait. There is...something that I must know."

"Yes?" She said, sitting down before the young maiden.

Laurel looked down presently, unsure of how or where to begin. "Queen Mariah, there...there is something that I do not understand...about when I went to retrieve the jewel of Faith. You see, at the Stronghold, I met Lues."

"Yes, Sol made Me aware of this."

Laurel nodded, as she continued, "There was something that he did to me, though I do not know how to explain it, but in my heart...I—I just do not know what happened."

Placing Her hand lovingly atop Laurel's, the Queen replied, "Laurel, do you remember everything that My Son spoke to you about Lues?" When Laurel nodded, Queen Mariah continued, "You see, Lues has the power to control the Curse of Malum in your heart, and through this power, he uses the darkness and evil of that traitor to tempt your being into serving him. This comes as a terrible, horrible pain to the heart, unlike any other pain, for you are experiencing the fullness of the War between good and evil in your very being. The temptations of the Curse come at the beginning as a great pain because if you accept the evil of Malum, the pain will seem to diminish easily. This will lead you to desire surrendering to these wiles of the world, the flesh, and to Malum himself, if only to release yourself of the terrible pain. However, this is only a mask, for in surrendering to Malum, your whole life and heart becomes enslaved to the lacerations of his evil Curse."

Feeling understanding towards these words within her heart, Laurel asked, "But how is it then that the pain disappeared from me?"

Then, the Queen smiled saying, "Because you received Faith into your heart and did not give in to the ways of Malum. Now, the power of Faith has been released to the whole world of Terra. The first step of the Emperor's plan for His Kingdom has been completed." With that, the Queen allowed for Laurel to rest comfortably in her charming chamber, with peace and Faith growing within her little heart.

Once she had been well-fed by a Wingel servant, Laurel went in search around the Sanctuary walls for her King. All was quiet in the many rooms and halls of the enchanted tower, for all of the inhabitants were still resting from their long return journey from the Southern Sea. In this great silence, Laurel tiptoed from floor to floor, determined to find and greet her dear friend Sol; however, after countless efforts, she almost gave up her search entirely, when a familiar voice called to her from down the hall:

"Laurel! Laurel!"

As she was turning to greet the cheerful voice, Laurel found herself in the midst of a strong, loving hug, and looking down she found the wise young boy she had once known from her days in the Valley Fioré.

"Peterel?"

"Hi, Laurel!" the boy smiled, "You recognize me!" Then, he turned around for the maiden, showing his bright, white wings, which fluttered behind him.

"O, it is you!" Laurel cried astonishingly. "Oh, Peterel, you shall have to be patient with me with all of the shape-shifting you do!"

The Wingel laughed with his childlike voice. "Do not worry; you shall get used to it! So, the Queen told me that you woke up, and I am so happy to see you. Are you feeling better?"

"Oh, yes, and you know, the Queen told me that you and the King were the ones who saved my life during the battle."

"Oh, well," Peterel began modestly, "it was really all the King's doing. I was just trying my best as your guardian."

"Thank you, Peterel! I really mean it," Laurel replied, smiling down at the Wingel joyfully.

"So, where are you headed to now? Some of the Knights are in the dining hall, and they would be overjoyed to see you again, Laurel."

"Well, that is something I am meaning to do, but for now, I really want to see the King. Though, He does not seem to be anywhere that I have looked."

"That is because He is not around here, but I know where you can find Him," Peterel said, taking the young maiden's hand. "Come along, and I shall take you to Him."

Then, the faithful Wingel led Laurel up to the top of the Sanctuary, and coming to the ninth floor, the two found a mysterious, winding staircase that led up to the highest room in the tower.

"He likes to go up there to think sometimes," Peterel said, after directing Laurel up the stairs. "I think it reminds Him of His Home high up in the Blissful Mountains."

"Really…" Laurel mused as she curiously climbed the winding stairs.

"Oh, and Laurel?"

"Yes, Peterel?" the maiden turned back to her dear friend.

"Do not give the jewel of Faith to the King just yet. Wait for my signal when the time is right!"

With that, the little Wingel turned to leave, and Laurel had not the slightest chance to inquire of this mysterious request. Her better judgment, however, persuaded her to believe in the Wingel's good intentions, and she resolved to hold off in giving up the precious jewel to the King.

Finally, coming through the opening in the floor, Laurel looked around at the small empty room. The walls were made of a gray brick, and the floor was an old, dark wood. There was nothing much in the room, save for a few votive candles glowing with the mysterious, fireless light of the Sanctuary. Just as Laurel was considering the peculiarity of the silent room, she heard her name being called from behind her. Turning, she saw Sol standing by the only window in the room, which showed the diming brightness of the late afternoon sun.

A sudden shyness overcame Laurel, then, as she saw the eyes of her King lighting at the sight of her. "Oh — uh, Sol. I — I was just looking for You, now, and — but I could come back, um, later if — "

"O, no — not at all, Laurel! Please, come up," Sol replied, coming towards the railings of the staircase, as Laurel agreed to His pleading.

Then, the King joyfully embraced the shy girl, holding her warmly in His arms, and Laurel was surprised by such a jubilant greeting. "I am so happy to see you, Laurel!" Sol related smilingly, as He released the maiden from His embrace.

"I, uh," Laurel stammered, "I just came to thank You for saving me in the battle — um, the Queen told me about it."

"You are welcome, My dear, and I would do it again a thousand times over..." Here, the King smiled so benevolently that Laurel could not keep from blushing. "Now, come, there is something that I wish to show you."

Sol led Laurel to the open window, which He had been looking out from before she had appeared. There, Laurel beheld the great beauty of the northern sky, in colors of orange, yellow, red, and pink, overlooking the green sea of Serenity Forest, just as a wave of northerly winds passed over the land.

"It is beautiful, is it not? The air is very peaceful here, and I enjoy looking out at the world from up here in this still silence."

"Yes," Laurel mused enjoyably, "I feel as though I could stand here for hours!"

Sol chuckled amusingly at this. "Well, no one besides Myself ever really comes up here, so if you ever need a quiet place to think, you may come here as often as you please."

Content with these words, the young maiden and her King enjoyed the beauteous scene before them in soundless companionship. It was then that Laurel felt the uneasy weakness of her head returning, and she tried to hide her discomfort but her wincing expressions soon exposed her.

"What is it?" Sol asked concernedly, noticing Laurel's distress.

"It is nothing, just...my head. I have been feeling very dizzy since I woke up, but I am sure it will pass — " As Laurel spoke, Sol suddenly placed a gentle hand onto her head, and instantly the pain and uneasy feelings vanished from the her consciousness.

"There," He said smilingly, as He drew away His hand. "You should be feeling better, now."

"Wait, did You...do that?" Laurel asked astounded, feeling her head in bafflement.

"Yes, but you knew that I could, did you not? Or did you forget how I did the same for your feet during the Tempter attack?"

"So, it was You!" the maiden cried accusingly, as her distant concern finally resurfaced. "I mean, at first I was not sure — but then I thought — I mean — !"

Sol laughed richly in good humor at Laurel's astonishment. "I was wondering when you would figure it out! But yes, I have the power to heal whenever I choose," He said, leaning serenely against the windowsill as He looked out into the dim evening. "My power comes to Me from My Father, and it is through Him that I do these things and more."

"Well...I guess there is a lot that I do not know about You," Laurel said, looking down after a moment's reflection. "You...are very mysterious...the most mysterious person that I have ever met."

"That may be, Laurel, but you may find yourself just as mysterious, in everything that you have learned thus far and still what you may learn in the future. You are only just beginning to find that there is still much for you to understand."

"About that," Laurel began again, "Queen Mariah told me about what happened in the Stronghold with Lues... It was a lot to take in — I mean, I do not know what to think about myself now, let alone everything that I have learned about this whole world. I never knew that all of these things — like this war — were happening all around me...and in me. It seems so strange at times, when I think about everything that I have experienced so far." Then, Laurel looked up into the eyes of her King as she continued, "But, I believe. I believe in You and the Queen and the Knights and the Emperor! I know...before, I said that I believed but that was only because I began to see the war with my own eyes. But now...now... It must have been Faith, for now, I know that I may not understand everything about this War, but I want to see it to the end. Though, I do not know what *will* happen..."

"Laurel," the young King interposed, placing a benevolent hand on the faith-filled maiden's head. "You do not know how happy I am to know that you are with Me in this War, for I have known many people who have turned from Me in the face of danger and uncertainty. However, you, My dear friend, have made Me a joyful King, even this day!" And saying this, Sol's hand fell sweetly onto the Laurel's cheek, which He caressed compassionately.

In the midst of their conversation, the faces of the two friends were suddenly alit from the flare of a loud explosion that sounded in the darkening sky. Looking up, the two beheld a second and third flare bursting beneath the shrouding clouds above.

"What is it?" Laurel asked watching Sol's scanning eyes.

"Signal flares. Look there, just below the last flame!"

Searching through the shadowy, evening sky, the young maiden perceived a winged figure flying towards the Sanctuary. Though she could not see the creature's face, Laurel believed the soaring shape to be that of a Wingel, and she questioned Sol on this discernment.

"Yes, it seems one of the generals has come bearing news for us. Hasten with Me then to the throne room, Laurel, for there are the trumpet blasts of the Wingels' assembly horns!" Sol answered as blaring trumpets called all of the King's Company to the Hall of His Majesty's Throne.

Hastening in His decent of the enchanted tower, Sol proceeded to the throne room, where the Queen and the Knights of Terra awaited the King. The golden throne room was arrayed with large red curtains that draped against three rounded windows, which overlooked the forestry evening. The marble floors shined in the beauteous light of the chandeliers, and the flowering plants stationed about the room complemented the gold-tinted walls and ivory paneling. Standing at the end of the glorious hall above three large steps were two golden thrones, one upon which the Queen of Terra sat. Adorned elegantly above was a magnificent embroidered drapery of the Emperor's Seal, which proudly declared the authority of the Sanctuary's royal Dwellers.

Laurel had been following the King all the while, but upon His entrance into the throne room, a gentle hand quickly pulled Laurel from the door. Peterel, in his most noble Wingel form, stood in the hall adorned in a princely attire. In his arms, he held a royal purple robe and a kingly red pillow, with embroidered designs which awed the young maiden.

"Swiftly, now, for there is no time to lose!" began the Wingel as he helped Laurel into the robe.

"Wha-what are you — ?"

"The time has come, Laurel, for you to present before the whole host of Wingel, before the Knights of Terra, and Their Majesties, the precious jewel of Faith."

"*Me?*" whispered the maiden in astonishment.

"Indeed! For you were the one chosen to retrieve it, and now, aglow with royal pomp, you shall deliver it to the King."

The words of the Wingel rang with truth, for in that instant, Laurel looked as though a princess bearing in her hands a ruby red pillow, upon which was laid the precious jewel of Faith.

"It is time, my dear," smiled Peterel. "Wait for my signal!"

In the throne room, the Knights and the host of Wingel stood before the King who sat upon His central throne. At His right hand, dressed in a golden gown with adornment intricately wrought, sat the Queen of Terra upon Her throne. At the King's left, there stood another throne, though it remained empty, and Laurel, peeking into the chamber, pondered the identity of the mysterious figure who must have once sat at the King's left side.

Suddenly, Peterel spoke up: "Your Majesties!"

"Speak, loyal Wingel!" the King granted from upon His throne.

"Sire, may I present to You the jewel of Faith!"

At the wave of Peterel's hand, Laurel unhesitatingly stepped into the chamber and found herself in the wake of the whole inhabitants of the Sanctuary. They all stared in wonder at the bright, glowing jewel that laid in the pillow upon the maiden's hands, as she walked with measured steps towards the Monarchs' thrones. Laurel was initially surprised at the ease of her manners, despite the anxiety that welled within her heart. Then again, she always kept her eyes on the King, whose gaze seemed to give her the strength to walk down that long, red carpet in the presence of all.

Finally, the girl came to the very steps before the throne, and when Sol rose from His golden chair, Laurel immediately knelt to the ground. Her heart was beating rapidly with excitement now, but Sol never took His encouraging gaze from the maiden. Then, Sol took up the precious treasure, the jewel of Faith, in His hand and held it up for all to see. In a booming, magnificent voice, Sol proclaimed:

"Behold, Friends of the Emperor, Servants of the Monarchy, and noble Soldiers of the Royal Court of Terra! See here, at last — *the jewel of Faith!*"

In an instant, an uproar of joyful shouts and cheers and clapping and clamoring sounded from the crowd of Wingel and Knights, as the precious jewel became aflame with a bright golden-orange light. For finally, the jewel of Faith was within the rightful grasps of the King of Terra. Now, the power of Faith, already released to the hearts of the Men of Terra, was secured from the destruction of Malum. Now, Faith was safe from the darkness that had sought its ruin. Now, the Monarchy of Terra once again held the splendidness of Faith for all ages to come.

"The Monarchy of Terra," Sol continued, "from the halls of My Father in the Eternal Palace to the very ends of the world, is pleased with your faithfulness, O noble Wingel and glorious Knights of Terra! For by your will to take up arms in the darkest of battles, you have helped to secure Faith for the world."

Then, still holding the beauteous jewel in His hand, Sol looked down upon the young maiden, whose eyes were aglow from the light of Faith. "And, We are pleased of your efforts, dear maiden, for taking upon the task to retrieve, from the highest tower of the end of the world, the most precious jewel of Faith!"

At this, shouts of "Hurrah! Hail to the Emperor! Hail to the King! Hail to the Queen! Hurrah!" echoed throughout the throne room. Laurel blushingly bowed her head in joy to the King and Queen, Whose faces were radiant with gratification towards the young maiden. The jewel of Faith was then laid back upon its royal red pillow and placed for all to see on a marble pillar that stood on the Queen's right side.

When the King departed to His throne, Laurel, with Peterel at her side, took her place among the Knights of Terra within the crowd. The Knights rejoiced heartily at the sight of their dear friend, congratulating her on her glorious presentation, and were overjoyed to ascertain the knowledge of her recovery from her ordeal in the Southern Sea. As the happy maiden and the Knights enjoyed this reunion, King Sol greeted General Mikhail, who drew from the crowd with another noble-looking Wingel. Before he reverently knelt before his King, Laurel noted the tall, noble stature of the Wingel and his bright golden eyes, which shined from his princely countenance. His snow-white wings and light golden robe gave the lovely Wingel the appearance of pure light. He was the Wingel whose arrival had initiated this meeting, and Laurel marveled at the splendid creature as Sol spoke to him.

"What news do you bring, General Riel?"

Indeed, General Riel was his name but another title he possessed: "The Emperor's Breath", for General Riel was the chief messenger of the Great Sovereign of Terra.

"My King," General Riel began, "I bring You good tidings from His Majesty and a formal declaration of His new plans."

Then, the general handed a golden sealed parchment to the King, who opened it delicately and read its contents. All watched the silent expression of Sol's face, earnestly hoping and searching for any sign that might reveal the matters of the mysterious message.

"What does it say, My Liege?" Donato asked anxiously, as the other Knights seemed battling a storm of angst feelings within their concerned hearts.

The King only smiled as He looked over the message again. "It is just as We have planned," He finally said, looking up into the faces of His men.

"You shall all prepare for your leave of the Sanctuary and your journey to the villages in the North."

"Our leave? Journey to the villages?" Andres murmured in wonder.

"You mean, we are not continuing the search for the King Virtues?" his brother Feoras spoke up.

"No," Sol replied seating Himself in His throne beside the Queen, "not presently, anyway. Yes, we have just begun the search for the King Virtues and have been victorious in the redeeming of the jewel of Faith, but there are things at present that greatly concern My Father, which must be attended to first. Do not fear, however, for in time all will be accomplished."

"Then…when do You wish for us to depart?" Yaakov asked.

"Why, tomorrow of course!" the King smiled innocently.

"Tomorrow!" the Knights gasped in surprise, for they never knew a journey when they were needed away on such short notice.

"And Laurel will accompany you all, as well."

"Me?" the astonished girl questioned aloud. "I am going, too?"

"Well, it only makes sense!" replied the twins eagerly. "You have been through many trials with us, thus far, anyway."

"You are one of us, now," Peterel agreed, taking the maiden's hand caringly.

"And I shall accompany you, as well," Queen Mariah spoke up tenderly, "to be a guide for our maiden and all of you, Knights of Terra."

Sol agreed joyfully at the noble leadership of His Queen. "And you, My dear generals," He said, turning to the Wingel, "shall lead My Company to their destination for Me."

Once the Wingel agreed obedient with their King's wishes, Laurel beseeched questioningly, "Then, You shall not journey with us?"

King Sol met the gaze of the young maiden with His endearing eyes. "No, I shall stay here at the Sanctuary. There is much that I must reflect on and consider with My Father before My next move. Still, have patience, My friends, for I shall return to you sooner than you think."

With the arrangements accomplished, all retreated into the still night, preparing and contemplating for the next journey that awaited them in the splendor and glory of tomorrow's early morning sun.

Epilogue
A New Journey Begins

The next day, the hearts of all were filled with new energy and readiness for the adventure that laid ahead but also with sorrow for having to part with the King of Terra, even if it was only for a short time as He had implied. Still, the Knights especially had great difficulty rising from their last, peaceful slumber in the enchanted tower, but they did so with obedience to their King. When it came time for Laurel, accompanied by her guardian Peterel and the devoted Queen Mariah, to part with Sol, the maiden related her innermost desire to speak with Him more on the Kingdom of Terra and on their previous journeys and travels in the near future. The King in turn related His wish to see her soon, stressing importantly that He awaited the celebration of her birth, which Laurel had once again forgotten.

"On that day," He told her sweetly, "watch for My coming."

With these words, Laurel parted from Him in tender friendship, her heart beating with increased Faith in her King. Everyone to leave then united outside the Sanctuary, and around midmorning, they set off on their noble steeds northward. Laurel, however, turned in her saddle to look up at the beauteous Sanctuary, which she had come to know as her new home. Then, she perceived the King watching from one of the balconies, and He smiled down benevolently at the sweet child who had won His friendship.

"Come, Laurel," Queen Mariah began, and Laurel turned to see the Queen gazing lovingly at Her beloved Son. Then, She turned her eyes onto Laurel saying, "the quest for Faith has ended; now the journey of Hope begins."

Smiling in pure Faith, Laurel followed the Queen with her guardian Peterel flying beside her. The King's Company then trekked from the clearing of the Sanctuary as the vines and shrubbery opened up before Them at General Mikhail's command. With one last glance, Laurel contemplated at that moment all that had been accomplished at the Sanctuary and all that she had experienced since the day she met Sol, as the greenery and vines formed again along the path to the enchanted tower, hiding it away from all, except from those whose hearts truly believe!

TO BE CONTINUED